MEN

MA

*the*

# DOCTOR

# MEN IN UNIFORM:
## COLLECTION

January 2017

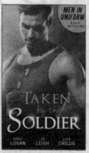

January 2017

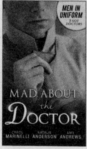

January 2017

February 2017

# MEN IN UNIFORM:
# MAD ABOUT
## *the*
# DOCTOR

CAROL
**MARINELLI**

NATALIE
**ANDERSON**

AMY
**ANDREWS**

MILLS & BOON

First Published in Great Britain 2017
By Mills & Boon, an imprint of HarperCollins*Publishers*
1 London Bridge Street, London, SE1 9GF

MEN IN UNIFORM: MAD ABOUT THE DOCTOR © 2017
Harlequin Books S.A.

*Her Little Secret* © 2011 Carol Marinelli
*First Time Lucky?* © 2012 Natalie Anderson
*How to Mend A Broken Heart* © 2012 Amy Andrews

ISBN: 978-0-263-92758-0

09-0117

# HER LITTLE SECRET

**CAROL MARINELLI**

**Carol Marinelli** recently filled in a form where she was asked for her job title and was thrilled, after all these years, to be able to put down her answer as 'writer'. Then it asked what Carol did for relaxation. After chewing her pen for a moment Carol put down the truth – 'writing'. The third question asked – 'What are your hobbies?' Well, not wanting to look obsessed or, worse still, boring, she crossed the fingers on her free hand and answered 'swimming and tennis'. But, given that the chlorine in the pool does terrible things to her highlights, and the closest she's got to a tennis racket in the last couple of years is watching the Australian Open, I'm sure you can guess the real answer!

# CHAPTER ONE

'AFTER you.'

Alison Carter gave brief thanks as someone stepped aside and she shuffled onto the bus, coffee in hand, and took a seat in her usual spot, halfway down, to the left of the bus and next to the window.

Morning was just peeking in and the sky was full of purples and oranges as the doors hissed closed and the bus made its slow way up the hill. Even though she'd bought a newspaper, till the bus turned the corner Alison did as she always did and stared out at the glorious view—to the energetic joggers on the foreshore, the walkers on the beach, the swimmers in the ocean and out beyond, to where the patient surfers bobbed quietly, waiting for the next good wave.

It was a slice of heaven.

A view that reminded Alison, because sometimes she needed reminding, that she lived in surely the most beautiful part of the world, that she had absolutely nothing to complain about. It was an internal pep talk that she delivered to herself quite often when the travel bug stung—yes, there were other beaches, other worlds to explore, but here was where she belonged and, if you had to be stuck somewhere, then Coogee was a very nice place to be...

Stuck.

Alison closed her eyes for just a second, leant her temple against the window and told herself to stop using that word.

Having recently read an article on positive thinking and the harm of negative self-talk and thoughts, she was resolutely reframing and rephrasing, but she was finding it to be an almost full-time job.

It was a very nice place to *be*, Alison told herself.

To just be!

As the bus took on its next load of passengers, then commenced its slow turn into the hilly street that would take them from Coogee to Eastern Beaches Hospital where she worked, Alison turned away to concentrate on her newspaper.

Then she saw him.

Craning his neck for a final glimpse of the beach too, it was, Alison was sure, the man who had let her on the bus before himself. The flash of blond hair and pale shirt that she'd glimpsed as she'd turned and briefly thanked him actually belonged to a man more beautiful than any she had ever seen and only then did she recall his English accent, and she was sure, quite sure, that the man she was looking at was *the* Nick Roberts.

Despite having been on days off from her job as an accident and emergency nurse, Alison had heard all about him from her friends and colleagues. Ellie had told her all about the gorgeous, *completely* gorgeous new locum registrar, who was filling in in Emergency while the senior registrar, Cort Mason, took some long overdue extended leave. Even Moira had sent her two texts worth of information about the nice surprise she'd found on her late shift one afternoon, warning her that he had to be seen to be believed.

Presuming that it was him, thanks to the hospital grapevine, and because nurses loved to gossip, Alison knew rather a lot about the handsome stranger on her bus. He had been travelling for six months and was doing a two-month stint in Sydney, getting some money together to spend on his prolonged journey home, first to New Zealand and then home to the UK via Asia, and, Ellie had said droolingly, while he was in Sydney, he was staying in Coogee.

It probably wasn't him, Alison told herself. Coogee was hardly the outback, there were loads of gorgeous men, loads of travellers, yet she was quite sure that it was him, because this man *had* to be seen to be believed.

Taller than most, he was sitting on a side seat, doing the crossword in the newspaper, and he kept forgetting to tuck his legs in, having to move them every time someone got on or got off. He had on dark grey, linen trousers and a paler grey shirt. And, yes, there were loads of Englishmen staying in Coogee—he could be anyone, but holidaymakers and travellers weren't usually on the two-minutes-past-six bus. It was, Alison knew, after nearly three years of taking this very route, a fairly regular lot she joined on the bus each morning.

Of course he caught her looking and he gave her a very nice smile, an open, possibly even flirting smile, and all it served to do was annoy Alison as she pulled her eyes away and back to her newspaper. In fact, she wanted to tell him that she'd been looking, not because he was drop dead gorgeous but because she thought she knew who he was.

And if she was right, then he'd be the last person she'd be interested in.

She'd heard all about him from her friends—the string of broken hearts he had left behind on his travels and daredevil attitude in his quest for adventure.

So, instead of thinking about him, Alison, as always, read her horoscope, which was too cryptic for such an early hour, so she turned, as she always did on a Friday, to the travel section, only the sting she so regularly felt became just a touch more inflamed as she read that airfares had come down dramatically. Even if it was too early for cryptic horoscopes the arithmetic was easy— her meticulous savings, combined with the money her father had left her, were enough for a tiny deposit on an even tinier flat or a round-the-world trip and a year or two spent following her heart.

Alison knew what her father would have chosen.

But she knew too what it would do to her mother.

She glanced up again to the man she thought was Nick Roberts. He had given up on his crossword and sat dozing now, and Alison stared, annoyed with a stranger who had been nothing but polite, jealous of a man she had never even met—because if this was Nick Roberts, then he was living her dream.

Maybe he felt her watching, because green eyes suddenly opened and met hers. He had caught her looking again and smiled. Embarrassed, Alison stood as her bus stop approached, and it was either be extremely rude or return his smile as she walked past.

'Morning,' Alison said, and then to show him she said morning and smiled at *everyone*, she said it to someone else who caught her eye as she moved down the bus.

And it *had* to be him because he was standing up too and this was the hospital bus stop and there certainly couldn't be two people as lovely as him working there.

They probably weren't, but Alison felt as if his eyes were on her as she walked through the car park and towards Emergency, and she was rather relieved when her friend and colleague Ellie caught up with her.

'Nice days off?' Ellie asked. 'Any luck with the flat-hunt?'

'None,' Alison admitted. 'Well, there was one flat that I could just about afford but it needs a kitchen.'

'You could live without a nice kitchen for a while,' Ellie pointed out.

'There's a hole in the side wall where the kitchen burnt down.' Alison managed a wry laugh as she recalled the viewing, the initial optimism as she'd walked through the small but liveable lounge, and then the sheer frustration as the renovator's delight that she'd thought she had found had turned out to be uninhabitable. 'It's impossible...' Alison carried on, but she'd lost her audience because Dr Long Legs had caught up, and Ellie, who never missed an opportunity to flirt, called over to him and he fell in step beside them.

'This is Alison. Alison, this is Nick,' Ellie said, and none-too-discreetly gave her friend a nudge that said he was *the* Nick. 'He's with us for a couple of months.'

'Hi, Nick,' Alison said, and then to salvage herself, she gave him a smile. 'We met on the bus.'

'We did.'

'Anyone new tends to stand out—it's a pretty regular lot on the six a.m.,' Alison added, just to make it clear why she'd noticed him!

'Alison's flat-hunting,' Ellie said.

'Shoebox-hunting,' Alison corrected.

At twenty-four it was high past the time when she should have left home. Yes, most of her friends still lived at home and had no intention of leaving in a rush, but her friends didn't have Rose as a mother, who insisted on a text if she was going to be ten minutes late, and as for staying out for the night—well, for the stress it caused her mother it was easier just to go home.

Alison had moved out at eighteen to share a house with some other nursing students but at the end of her training, just as she'd been about to set off for a year of travel that her mother had pleaded she didn't take, her brother and father had died in an accident. Of course, she had moved straight back home, but though it had seemed right and necessary at the time, three years on Alison was beginning to wonder if her being there was actually hindering her mother from moving on. House-sharing no longer appealed and so the rather fruitless search for her own place had commenced.

'There are a couple of places I've seen that are nice and in my price range,' Alison sighed, 'but they're miles from the beach.'

'You're a nurse...' Ellie laughed. 'You can't afford bay views.'

'I don't need a view,' Alison grumbled, 'but walking distance to the beach at least...' She was being ridiculous, she knew, but she was so used to having the beach a five-minute walk away that it was going to be harder to give up than coffee.

'I'm on Alison's side.' Nick joined right in with the conversation. 'I'm flat-sitting for a couple I know while they're back in the UK.' He told her the location and Alison let out a low whistle because anything in that street was stunning. 'It's pretty spectacular. I've never been a beach person, but I'm walking there every morning or evening—and sitting on the balcony at night...'

'It's not just the view, though,' Alison said. They were walking through Emergency now. 'It's just...' She didn't really know how to explain it. It wasn't just the beach either—it was her walks on the cliffs, her coffee from the same kiosk in the morning, her cherry and ricotta strudel at her favourite café. She didn't want to leave it, her mother certainly didn't want her to leave either, but, unless she was going to live at home for ever, unless she was going to be home by midnight every night or constantly account for her movements, she wanted somewhere close enough to home but far enough to live her own life.

'I'm going to get a drink before...' He gave her a smile as they reached the female change rooms. 'I look forward to working with you.'

'Told you!' Ellie breathed as they closed the doors. 'I told you, didn't I?'

'You did,' Alison agreed, tying up her long brown hair and pulling on her lanyard. 'Have you got my stethoscope?'

'That's all that you've got to say?'

'Ellie, yes, you did tell me and, yes, for once you haven't exaggerated. He's completely stunning, but right now I need my stethoscope back.' She certainly didn't need to be dwelling on the gorgeous Nick Roberts who was there for just a few weeks and already had every woman completely under his spell.

'Here.' Ellie handed back the stethoscope she had yet again borrowed. 'Have a look at him on Facebook—there's one of him bungee-jumping and he's upside down and his T-shirt's round his neck...' Ellie grinned as Alison rolled her eyes. 'There's no harm in looking.'

Ellie raced off to the staffroom, ready to catch up on all the gossip, and for a moment Alison paused, catching sight of her reflection—brown hair, serious brown eyes, neat figure, smart navy pants and white top. Her image just screamed sensible. Too sensible by far for the likes of Nick. Yes, he was a fine specimen and all that, but he also knew it and Alison was determined not to give him the satisfaction of joining his rather large throng of admirers.

He was sitting in the staffroom as he had on the bus, with his long legs sprawled out, drinking a large mug of tea and leading the conversation as if he'd been there for years instead of one week, regaling them all with his exploits—the highlight a motorbike ride through the outback—which did nothing to impress Alison. In fact, the very thought made her shudder and prompted a question.

'How is that guy from last week?' Alison turned to Ellie. 'Did you follow him up?'

'What one?'

'Just as I went off last Sunday—the young guy on the motorbike?' And then she stopped, realising it sounded rude, perhaps a touch inappropriate given Nick's subject matter, though she hadn't meant it to. Nick had just reminded her to ask.

'We didn't have any ICU beds,' one of the other staff answered, 'so he was transferred.'

'Thanks,' Alison said, looking up at the clock, and so did everyone else, all heading out for handover.

She really didn't want to like him.

He unsettled her for reasons she didn't want to examine and she hoped he was horrible to work with—arrogant, or dismissive with the patients. Unfortunately, he was lovely.

'I'm here for a good time, not a long time,' she heard him say to some young surfer who had cut his arm on the rocks. Nick was stitching as Alison came in to give the young man his tetanus shot. 'I want to cram in as much as I can while I'm here.'

'Come down in the morning,' surfer boy said. 'I'll give you some tips.'

'Didn't I just tell you to keep the wound clean and dry?' Nick admonished, and then grinned. 'I guess salt water's good for it, though. I'll look forward to it.'

'You're going surfing with him?' Alison blinked.

'He lives near me and who better to teach me than a local?' Nick said. 'Do you?'

'Do I what?'

'Surf.'

Alison rolled her eyes. 'Because I'm Australian?'

'No,' he said slowly, those green eyes meeting hers. 'Because you want to.' And she stood there for a moment, felt her cheeks darken, felt for just a moment as if he was looking at her, not staid, sensible Alison but the woman she had once been, or rather the woman she had almost become, the woman who was in there, hiding.

'If I wanted to, I would,' Alison replied, and somehow, despite the wobble in her soul, her voice was even. 'I've got a beach on my doorstep after all.'

'I guess,' Nick said, but she could almost hear his tongue in his cheek. 'I'll let you know what it's like.'

His assumption irritated her, perhaps more than it should have, but she wasn't going to dwell on it. She'd save a suitable come-back for later—perhaps this time tomorrow morning when she was stitching his forehead after his board hit him, Alison thought, taking the next patient card from the pile.

'Louise Haversham?' Alison called out to the waiting room, and when there was no answer she called the name again.

'Two minutes!' came the answer, a pretty blonde holding up her hand at Alison's interruption and carrying on her conversation on her phone, but perhaps realising that Alison was about to call the next name on the list she concluded her call and walked with Alison to a cubicle.

'How long have you had toothache for?' Alison asked, checking Louise's temperature and noting it on her card.

'Well, it's been niggling for a couple of weeks but it woke me up at four and I couldn't get back to sleep.'

'Have you seen your dentist?' Alison asked, and Louise shook her head.

'I've been too busy—I'm working two jobs.' She glanced up at the clock. 'How long will the doctor be? I'm supposed to be at work at nine.'

Then Alison had better hurry the doctor along!

'Who's next?' Nick asked cheerfully. 'A nice motorbike crash, perhaps?' He winked, just to show her he'd heard her in the staffroom.

'I'm saving the good stuff for later,' Alison said. 'I've got a toothache.'

'I'm sorry to hear it.'

She rolled her eyes at the very old joke, but it did make her smile just a little bit and he *was* so easy to talk to, because somewhere between the work station and Cubicle Five she'd told him that she was going to the dentist herself next week. He opened the curtain where the very pretty blonde with a sore tooth that couldn't possibly wait till nine a.m. for a dentist was no longer chatting on her phone but cupping her jaw in her hand and looking an absolute picture of misery.

'Good morning.' He introduced himself and Louise introduced herself and managed, Alison noted, despite her agony, to perk up just a touch and give him a very brave smile.

'I'm so sorry.' She was far nicer to Nick than she had been to Alison. 'I just couldn't stand it any longer. I haven't slept all night…'

'Not at all. Dental pain's awful,' Nick said. Warning her he wasn't a dentist, he first had a feel of her jaw before he looked in her mouth, then long brown fingers examined her jaw again and felt around her neck. 'What was her temperature?' Nick asked, and Alison told him it was normal. 'There's no swelling. Still, I think we should give you something for the pain and a poultice for the tooth, but you really do need to see your dentist.' He turned round. 'Alison, do we have any oil of cloves?'

Right at the back of the treatment cupboard.

'Busy?' her friend Moira asked minutes later as she watched Alison curiously.

'Frantic!' She rolled her eyes to show that she wasn't in the least. 'I'm making an oil-of-cloves poultice,' Alison said, her own teeth slightly gritted.

'A what?' Moira frowned. 'What's that?'

'Some old English treatment. Actually, I remember my mum giving this to me once. I've never been asked for it.'

'Nick?' Moira checked and gave a little sigh. 'He asked me for some gentian violet yesterday.' She held up her palms to show the evidence. 'He dishes out the TLC, wish he'd dish some out in my direction!' Moira was Irish, just passing through Coogee too as she nursed and travelled her way around the world. She was fun and flirty and just…fun!

'Is he always so nice to everyone? It's like a social club in Section B.'

'Always,' Moira said cheerfully.

Returning to Cubicle Five, Alison wondered if he'd still be so nice when the place *was* frantic, but for now he was taking his time with his patient.

'Okay, Louise, I've given you a note for the dentist— you need to get that seen to this morning.'

Louise, once she'd bitten down on her cotton bud soaked in oil of cloves, managed to rally enough to tell him the name of the bar she worked at in the city, and that she was on at the weekend if he wanted to stop by for a drink on the house.

'I'm working…' Nick grinned '…but that's terribly kind of you.'

'He's worth getting toothache for,' Louise commented as he swept out and only the fresh scent of him lingered. They shared a little smile. 'If I suddenly come over all dizzy, will you call him back for me?'

'I'll get Amy, the other registrar.' Alison winked. 'She's good with dizzy females.'

'Shame.'

Nick changed the atmosphere of the place—he seemed delighted to be there, nothing was too trivial and nothing major unnerved him, as Alison found out when the husband of a swollen-ankle case suddenly complained of chest pain and started to pass out. Still Nick remained unruffled, breaking the gentleman's fall as Alison quickly wheeled out his wife, pressing the emergency bell and collecting the crash trolley.

By the time she returned, about twenty seconds later, the man had gone into full arrest and between them they had him clipped to the portable monitor, with Alison commencing cardiac massage even before help had arrived.

'Let's get him down to Resus.' Amy, the emergency registrar, called for a trolley, but Nick thought otherwise.

'Let's just keep going here.' It was a tiny override, or just a difference of opinion—nothing really—but when Amy, who easily took offence, simply nodded and they all just carried on working on the man on the cubicle floor, Alison realised the respect he had garnered in the short while he had been here.

Pads on, Nick shocked him, and before the crash team had arrived, the poor man was back in sinus rhythm and starting to come round.

'It's okay, sir…' Nick's was absolutely the voice you wanted to come round to. He didn't talk down to the man and he didn't scare him as he lay there groaning. 'You're doing fine—your heart went into an irregular rhythm but it's beating normally now.' He smiled up to Amy. 'Okay, let's get him on a trolley and down to you guys. I'll go and speak with his wife.'

'What was he in for?' Amy asked.

'He's here with his wife, Doreen,' Nick explained. 'She's got an ankle injury.'

Having seen what was going on, Libby, the reception-ist, had taken Doreen to an interview room and taken the husband's details from the shaken woman. After quickly writing his notes and checking the new patient's name, Nick walked down to the interview room with Alison.

He was very thorough, first checking her husband's details and assuming nothing—that Ernest was, in fact, her husband and finding out if she had contacted anyone. Then Nick got to the point, explaining that it would appear Ernest had had a heart attack.

'It probably doesn't feel it now, but your husband is an extremely lucky man—he could not have been in a better place when this happened.'

'Will he be okay?'

'We certainly hope so. He's conscious, the cardiolo-gists will be running some tests now, but certainly the next twenty-four hours will be critical. I'm going to go and speak with my colleagues now and find out some more for you. I suggest you ring your son and get some family here to support you.' He stood and shook her hand. 'And I'll be back soon to take a good look at your ankle.'

He was a complete and utter pleasure to work with, to be around, so much so that when Alison ducked into the staffroom for a ten-minute break later that morning, she wanted to turn tail and run, because it was just him in there and to be alone in his rather dazzling company rather terrified her.

'What about this…?'

She frowned as he handed her the local newspaper with an advertisement circled—a one-bedroom flat, two streets from the beach, and it wasn't that expensive. 'I've already seen it,' Alison admitted. 'It's above a pub that has live music six nights a week.' She sat down next to him. 'I did seriously think about it, though. Thanks,' she added. 'You didn't have to do that.'

'Can't help myself,' Nick admitted. 'I love looking at real estate—I've chosen the one I want…' And he showed her the stunning apartment he'd circled, with bay views and a balcony as big as the staffroom they were sitting in. 'Nice to dream.'

And it was, because Alison had circled the very same one in her own local newspaper, had looked it up on the net and taken a virtual tour of the place.

'You can't have it because it's already mine.'

'It's a great spot,' Nick said. 'I can absolutely see why you don't want to move away.'

And they got to talking, about she was on late shift tomorrow and she had to squeeze in two flat inspections beforehand, and there was a mixture of both relief and disappointment when he told her he was off for the weekend. Relief that he'd told a little white lie to

Louise and the stab of disappointment Alison did her very best to ignore. Instead she told him how she loved to walk on the cliffs on her days off and, strange as it sounded, there was the most beautiful cemetery that he just had to explore, then about the coffee bar that did the ricotta cheese and cherry strudel which she rewarded herself with now and then. Then the intercom buzzed— someone searching for Nick—and Alison realised that her fifteen-minute break had turned into twenty-five.

'Told you.' Ellie smirked when she came round that evening on her way out for the night.

'Told me what?' Alison said, letting her in. There was no way she'd give Ellie so much as a hint that he'd won her over too, but Ellie was having none of it. Once she'd said hi to Rose, and chatted for a few minutes about an engagement present for a friend's party the following week, she asked to go on the computer.

'There!' Ellie was already a friend of his on Facebook—along with four hundred and thirty-seven others—and, yes, hanging upside down on a rope, his stomach looked lovely with his T-shirt around his neck. Alison did note that his status was single, and held her breath as she read about his crazy adventures—whitewater rafting, rock-climbing, swimming in waterholes. And she didn't care if there were only freshwater crocodiles there, he was dangerous and reckless and everything she didn't want.

*Great day at work—I love this place,* Nick suddenly updated his status, and Alison blinked.

She thought of the toothaches and grumbles and

moans down in section B and the drama with Ernest, which was pretty much routine in Emergency—it had been an okay day, even a good day perhaps, but hardly great.

Except, somehow he'd made it so.

*Out to sample local delights,* he added, and Alison rather hoped it wasn't Louise.

Ellie happily scrolled through what was just loads of chatter and comments from friends, and about a thousand photos.

'He broke off his engagement before he came here,' Ellie said knowledgeably.

'How do you know?'

'You can find out anything on this. Well, I'm not sure he broke it off, but I think so, and look…' Ellie was a machine and in no time at all had located photos of the once happy couple, but Alison had better things to do than fill her head with Nick.

'Come out with us,' Ellie pushed. 'Get some dinner… listen to a band.'

And Alison was about to again say no, she had to be up early for flat inspections and then work a late shift tomorrow, as Rose pointed out.

'There are a few of us meeting up.' Ellie smiled. 'You never know who'll be there.'

Which was a very good reason to decline, a very good reason to stay away, but instead of declining Alison gave her mum a smile.

'I'll be fine for tomorrow.' She tried not to notice her mother's pursed lips as she left Ellie on the computer and headed to her room, straightening her already straight hair till it looked a little more *done* and pulling through some hair gloss, then putting on make-up as she changed from her shorts and T-shirt into something a little more dressy, but not too much. She checked her reflection in the mirror and tried to tone down the blusher on her cheeks before realising it was her own complexion.

'If you're going to be out late...' Rose came to her door.

'I'm not going to be late,' Alison said and then, unusually, she qualified a touch. 'But if I am, I'll give you a call.'

'You can't really stay out too long...' Rose didn't add the unspoken *You've got work...*

Alison didn't want to argue, she didn't want to point out again that she was twenty-four, that Ellie was on an early shift tomorrow and was still going out—that she had a life, that she wanted to live it...

Instead she crammed her ATM card, her mobile, some cash and her keys into a tiny bag and only when she had bitten back a smart retort did she look up.

'I'll let you know if I'm going to be late.' She gave her mum a kiss on the cheek and said goodnight then headed out to the cool, dark street and along to the bar, trying to join in with Ellie's easy chatter, but it was hard to be light-hearted when her mother made it such an effort to just go out. As she stepped into the bar, however, it wasn't her mother's veiled warning or an excess of blusher that had her cheeks pinking up again.

There was Moira and a few others, even Amy the

registrar was sitting at the heavy wooden table. Making room for Ellie and Alison to join them, they ordered pizza. It wasn't at all unusual for the emergency crew to go out on a Friday night and, yes, Coogee was lovely and this bar was one hospital staff often frequented. It was just a rather good turnout from Emergency and Alison knew why—because coming back from the bar, balancing a jug of beer and some glasses with a bottle of water tucked under his arm, was the reason.

'Hey!' Nick gave her a smile and gave Ellie one too. This was her local, Alison told herself as she took a seat and glanced through the menu. She didn't just work nearby, she lived here, so more than anyone she had good reason to be there.

Except, Alison silently admitted, he was the real one.

# CHAPTER TWO

EMERGENCY staff the world over knew how to have a good time when they were out, as Nick pointed out. Even the rather aloof Amy was letting her hair down and had had a dance, when she wasn't monopolising Nick.

'It's like a home from home!' Nick said to Alison as the table got louder and louder. 'Not that I regularly joined the Friday night out.'

'Too senior?' Alison asked.

'Too sombre,' Nick said, at least that was what she thought he said, because the music was really loud. 'Do you come here often?'

Alison grinned as, tongue in cheek, he delivered the cheesy line with a smile. 'I live five minutes away, but, no, not that often,' she admitted, because, well, it was true. 'I like the cafés and restaurants.' She didn't get to finish as Moira tottered over, a little the worse for wear, and tugged at Nick to go and dance. Alison didn't await his response, instead she disappeared through the beer garden and to the loo, where she stood for an inordinately long time, fiddling with her hair. Not that it made any difference but, ridiculously, she felt safer in there.

She could hear the thud-thud-thud of the band through the wall and it matched the thud-thud-thud of her heart, because she'd never, not once, found someone so instantly attractive. Oh, she knew she wasn't the only one, yet he was the only one—the only one who just on sight triggered something, just on voice confirmed it, just on scent…

'Moira…' Nick peeled the nurse's arm from around his neck with a smile. He was actually very good at letting a girl down gently, he'd had plenty of practice and though he'd enjoyed his holiday to date, the fun stopped when he started work—that sort of fun anyway. He took his work seriously, commanded respect and that was rather hard to come by the morning after a reckless night before. 'I don't dance.'

He didn't flee to the toilets like Alison had, but he made his way there, a little annoyed that he had come, but Amy had suggested it and it had seemed a bit rude to say no. He had sensed things were getting a little out of hand and had been about to head off, but had got talking to Alison and somehow forgotten that he was supposed to be heading for home.

And there she was, walking toward him right now, and here too was the very reason he hadn't headed for home when he should have.

'Hey.' He smiled down at her and she stopped walking. They stood in the beer garden amidst the noise and the chatter.

'I thought you were dancing.'

'Not for me.' He gave her a smile, but it was a wry

one, a lying one, a strained one, because as the music tipped into something a little slower, he would at that very moment have danced, would have loved to do just that, because somehow she exceeded his limits, somehow he knew she could break his self-imposed rule, because all of a sudden work didn't matter.

'I'm just about to head off,' Alison admitted, because even if her stilettos seemed glued to the floor her heart was telling her to run.

'Do you want to go somewhere?' Nick's mouth said the words, though his brain insisted he shouldn't. 'Just us.' And Alison's eyes jerked down instead of up. Down to his forearm, to the blond hairs on it, to long-fingered hands that she wanted to wrap around hers. And maybe it was the overhead gas heaters in the beer garden, but the air was hot and her mind wasn't clear because with the pulse of the music and the laughter from beyond, it would, at that moment, have been so very easy to just be twenty-four.

To just be.

And, of course, just a moment later she recalled why she couldn't just be.

Alison looked up then to green eyes that awaited her response, that could never guess the inner turmoil inside her, who assumed, that for Alison, it was as easy as making a decision and grabbing her bag.

She shook her head and with good reason. Coogee was teeming with holidaymakers, with good-looking, testosterone-laden, 'here for a good time not a long time' males, and even if he was gorgeous, Nick could never be any different.

'No, thanks.'

'Hey, Nick!' Moira's radar located them and rather unsteadily she teetered towards them. 'We're heading into town...'

Alison didn't wait to see if Nick was joining them. Instead she said goodnight, gathered her bag and walked, not along the street but along a beach that was dotted with small groups and some couples, and it was a relief to be out of there and a relief to be alone.

He *was* dangerous.

At least, he was to someone like her.

He had been flirting—oh, not anything major, but his glorious attention had homed in on her, more than a touch. She was quite sure that Nick did want to get to know her a little better—which, to Alison, just seemed pointless. He'd be gone in a few weeks, he was just there for some fun, which Alison didn't readily do.

Why, she asked herself as she walked along the beach she knew and loved, couldn't she be like Ellie, or Moira—just out there having fun, without worrying about tomorrow?

Her phone buzzed in her bag and she didn't need to check it to know it was from her mother. It was fifteen minutes after midnight after all.

'I just texted you!' Rose said as she walked in the door. 'I just wanted to know if you were going to be late.'

'I said I'd call if I was.'

'Well, it is after midnight.'

*'Well, it is after midnight.'* For a shadow of a second, she could almost hear Tim's voice, could almost picture her brother standing right where she was in the kitchen, good-naturedly teasing Rose when he came in late at night and Rose complained.

Except there had been Dad then to argue his case for him and, anyway, Tim had a way to him that always won their mum around.

God, but she missed him.

And her father too.

Missed, not just the people but the family they had been then, the security the others had provided, unnoticed at the time, the certainty they were there for each other, which had all been ripped away. So instead of a smart retort Alison looked instead at the fear in her mother's eyes and apologised for not texting and had a cup of tea and a chat with her mum, till Rose headed off for bed.

Then later, alone, when surely all her friends were still out, she went on the computer and checked her social network profile. She had one friend request and, yes, it was from Nick. He must befriend everyone, Alison decided, but she did click on his name, hoping for another little peek at his profile, except that, apart from his photo, all the rest of the photos and information were private.

She went to accept his friend request and for a moment her finger hovered, then she chose to ignore it.

*Very* deliberately she ignored it, even if they did have eighteen mutual friends between them.

It was one a.m. on a Saturday after all.

A girl had some pride.

# CHAPTER THREE

'ARE you okay?'

They were waiting for a multi-trauma at eight a.m. on Monday morning. The sky was black with a storm and the roads like ice after a long dry spell. Alison was in Resus this morning and so too was Nick. She'd said good morning at the bus stop, then moved to her regular seat. Ignored him in the staffroom that morning, her head buried in the crossword, but now they stood on opposite sides of the trauma bed, all set up and gowned up, waiting for the patients to arrive, though they were taking longer to get there than anticipated and Alison was quiet.

'I'm fine.'

'Look, about the other night...'

'What about the other night?' She frowned over her mask to him.

'I got waylaid by Moira and then you'd gone.'

'I'm not even thinking about that—I just hate getting kids in.'

Yes, it happened day in and day out, but some days you just hated it so and Nick, cool, confident Nick, actually coloured up a little bit, because for once, with a woman, it wasn't about him. He'd awoken slightly disconcerted on Saturday, and had spent the rest of the day trying ignore a niggle. He'd swum, walked for a while, but had ended up at a cemetery that was, strange as it might sound, both fascinating and beautiful, and then back to the flat, where that niggle had developed a name as he'd checked his social network profile and, no, she hadn't responded to that request either.

'ETA five minutes!' Sheila called, and he watched as Alison blinked twice.

'They're taking ages.'

'Rush-hour.'

'It's still ages.'

'It might not be that bad,' Nick said. 'We're set up for everything; we'll worry, if we need to, when they get here.'

It was actually very good advice and Alison gave a thin smile. 'Is that what you do?'

'I try to,' Nick replied. 'Right now I'm trying to work out seven down—begins with L, ends in E, recurring.'

'Life,' Alison said, and he grinned. 'I'm stuck on it too.'

'How's the flat-hunting?' he asked. 'Any luck?'

And she was about to shrug, to get back to worrying about the family that was coming in, but Nick was right. Until they arrived there was no point, so instead she followed his lead.

'Actually, yes!' She'd sworn not to get her hopes up, not to say a word, but she was so delighted she couldn't help herself. 'I got a phone call from a real estate agent about a flat, and though it's not officially on the market yet, he's arranging an inspection. It's within my price range and they want a quick sale... It all sounds a bit too good to be true.'

'It might be your time for some good luck.'

'How was the rest of your weekend?' Alison asked, because, well, she was interested and she wanted to get back to normal with him and he *was* so easy to talk to. 'Any surfing?'

'Well, I wouldn't quite call it surfing, but I did manage to get up and stay up for about half a second. It was great...' He stopped in mid-sentence as a siren blared the first ambulance's arrival. 'Okay,' Nick said, 'now we can get back to worrying.'

Her name was Polly and she was seven and petrified and on a trauma board, her head strapped down. She was so scared that she wasn't even crying.

'Hi, there, Polly.' Nick smiled down at her. 'I'm Nick, I'm a doctor. You're having a rotten morning, aren't you?' He spoke reassuringly to her as he rapidly examined her while Alison transferred the oxygen tubes. The paramedics had started an IV and were feeding information as they worked on. Alison was cutting off Polly's school uniform, attaching her to monitors and getting her observations.

'Where's my mum?' Her little teeth were chattering, just one thing on her mind, and Alison glanced over at

Todd, the paramedic, who nodded his head towards the door and Alison went over.

'She's being cut out of the car,' Todd explained. 'She's conscious, but she's got some nasty cuts and is really agitated. She should be in soon. The police are trying to get hold of Dad.'

'Thanks,' Alison said, but nothing else, and headed back to Polly. 'Mum will be coming in soon, and we're getting hold of Dad, but right now we need to make sure you're okay.'

Amazingly she appeared to be.

There were some minor cuts and bruises, but she was neurologically sound and her abdomen was soft and non-tender. After a thorough examination and some cervical spine films, they peeled off the board and beneath it was a little girl who was a bit calmer, but still shaky, asking after her mum and very worried about her dad.

'He's got an interview.' Now Polly did start crying.

'Hey,' Nick said, 'don't worry about that. Your dad will be so relieved that you're okay.' Except the little girl could not be consoled.

'Can I move her over to a cubicle?' Alison checked with Nick, and then spoke away from Polly. 'Mum's about to arrive…'

'Sure, just…' He didn't finish, and Alison didn't wait to find out or to be told—yes, she would keep a very close eye on Polly.

She could see Todd hanging around, taking ages to sort out the blankets, and she deliberately ignored him. Alison didn't like him. He was good at his job and everything but he had asked her out a few times and didn't know how to take no for an answer. He'd also been out with half the department, and expected Alison to follow suit.

'Hey, Alison.' Todd came over. 'How is she?'

'Fine,' Alison answered. 'We're just about to move her out of Resus.'

'How are you?'

'Fine,' came her reply, but she didn't elaborate, actually refusing to speak to him about anything other than work.

She was glad she had moved Polly out, though her mum's sobs still reached the cubicle and after rechecking the little girl's obs, Alison didn't try to placate her. 'I'll go and find out how she is.'

The police were outside in the corridor and they brought Alison up to speed on things before she went in. Ellie and Sheila, the unit manager, were helping Nick and Alison observed for a moment before asking how she was doing.

'She's got a nasty arm laceration that needs to go straight to Theatre,' Ellie said. 'She's hysterical. Nick's told her that her little girl's okay.'

'This is the nurse looking after Polly,' Nick told his patient, and Alison went over to the distraught woman. 'Rebecca,' he added, and Alison nodded.

'I'm looking after Polly,' Alison said. 'She's doing really well. As soon as you're more settled you can see her.'

'David?'

'Your husband?' Alison checked. 'I've just spoken to the police and he's on his way in.'

'He'll be so worried.'

'I'll look out for him,' Alison promised. 'I'll speak to him the second he arrives and I'll bring him in to Polly and to you just as soon as I can.'

'He'll be—'

'I'll look after him,' Alison said gently. 'Try not to worry.'


'Where are they?' The man, who was chalk-white and looked as if he might pass out any second, needed no introduction. Alison knew this must be the father. A security man was running in behind him, about to tell him to move his car, but Alison dealt with practicalities, got the keys from him and asked for permission for Security to move it. David was really in no state to drive.

'They're going to be okay,' Alison said, and guided him straight to a side room. 'Let me just talk to you for a moment and then I'll take you in to see Polly.' She knew he needed to see his daughter, but in the state he was in, he would just upset Polly more.

'Polly's escaped lightly,' Alison explained. 'She's got some cuts and a few bruises across her chest and to her shoulder from the seat belt, but she's talking and she's fine.'

'Rebecca?'

'She's got a nasty arm laceration and they're talking about taking her straight to Theatre. There might be some concussion and they're going to arrange for a head

CT. She's very distressed, they had to cut her out of the car, but she knows where she is and what's happened, and she's very worried about Polly and about you.'

'Oh, God.' He bunched his hands by his head and took in some deep breaths. 'I thought the worst...'

'Of course you did,' Alison said gently. 'We were prepared for the worst too, but they do seem to be relatively okay. I'll get the doctor to speak to you just as soon as he can.'

'I don't think I even said goodbye this morning. I've got a job interview today...' Alison frowned, because she'd heard Polly going on about it. 'I was so worked up about it, I can't even remember if I said goodbye...' And he broke down then and Alison listened and found out that he had lost his job nine months ago, that he had, in fact, had a nervous breakdown and was still struggling to deal with things, but was slowly picking up. And because she listened she heard too that today was a vital day, so much hope had been pinned on it, that this job had meant everything, right up till this point. She could understand now how upset Rebecca would be, not about the job but about her husband's reaction.

'Let me take you in to Polly,' Alison said when he had calmed down. 'And I'll let your wife know that you're here.'

He did really well, he smiled and said all the right things to Polly—that the interview didn't matter a scrap, just as long as she and her mother were okay, that they would be fine, that they were all going to be fine. Rarely for Alison, she felt a sting of tears at the backs of her eyes and left them to it to go and speak with the wife.

'Hi, Rebecca.' Alison came in as Nick and the trauma surgeons looked at the patient's arm, and though Nick was concentrating, he still heard her speak. 'Polly's fine, her dad's with her—and he's fine. He really is okay.' Rebecca started crying and bizarrely for a second it sounded to Nick as if it was the husband who was hurt. 'I've told him that when the surgeons have finished looking at your arm I'll bring him in to see you. Rebecca, he's holding up really well.' And the arm Nick was holding down for the surgeons to assess relaxed just a little bit beneath his fingers.

'David's told me all that's been going on,' Alison continued, 'and, honestly, now that he knows you two are going to be okay, he really is fine.'

'He can't cope with things,' Rebecca said, and it was the first proper conversation she'd managed since her arrival.

'Not the little things perhaps,' Alison said, and stroked the poor woman's cheek. 'But he's dealing well with this. Maybe he's finding out he's stronger than he thinks.'

'So much hinges on today...'

'I know.' She glanced up at Nick. 'David had an important job interview today,' Alison explained, then looked back at the patient. 'When things are more settled we could ring the company and explain what's happened.' She paused and hoped, not wanting to presume but grateful when he stepped in.

'I'm happy to do that,' Nick said.

'That's good,' Alison said to Rebecca. 'It will sound better coming from a doctor.' And Nick looked down at his patient and saw her close her eyes in relief, felt her body relax and he realised that head CT wasn't quite so urgent.

'There's a lot of stress going on for them,' Alison murmured to Nick. 'They really didn't need this.'

'Thanks,' Nick said. He realised he'd learned something, and whatever it was he decided he would process it later.

As Ellie prepared Rebecca for Theatre, knowing what would put his patient's mind at rest more than any medication, Nick made the phone call Alison had suggested, then returned to tell the couple how it had gone. 'They were really grateful for you letting them know,' Nick told David. 'Especially with all that's going on. They've asked you to ring later in the day or tomorrow if you get a chance to arrange another time. They sound pretty keen,' he added, then glanced up as Alison came in with a nervous Polly.

'Here's Mum,' Alison said, and Rebecca and Polly had a kiss and a cuddle before Rebecca was taken to Theatre, because only seeing her mum would truly reassure the anxious child.

'I'm going to take her up to the children's ward soon,' Alison told Rebecca. 'Just for observation. They'll make a fuss of her. You can ring her this evening when you're back from Theatre and feeling better—or one of the staff might bring her up for a little visit.'

'She's nice...' Rebecca said when Alison had left. Nick agreed, saying that Polly was being well looked after by her, then told his patient to put her oxygen mask back on because he didn't want to think about how nice Alison was—there was more to Alison than there was time to know, more to her than there was scope to explore. No, he really didn't need this.

Heading into the staffroom for a quick lunch break later, when Ellie asked if he was going to the social club that night, it would have been far more sensible to answer that gleam in her eye with a smile and a 'Yes', or take Moira up on that offer to go to that Irish pub, because instinct told him that they knew the rules—that he was on holiday and not here for a long time, just a good one, but instead all he *really* noticed was that Alison had glasses on today while doing the crossword and didn't look up to hear his response, though her cheeks burnt red and her ears were pink as she pretended to concentrate on the puzzle in front of her. Because the seat next to her was the only one left, he chose it, peered over her shoulder and, yes, she was stuck on the same word as he'd been. He was about to nudge her, to tease her, because 'leitmotif' was a word it had taken him a full morning to get, but he deliberately stopped himself.

'Leitmotif!' He heard the triumph in her voice and ignored it, felt the haste of her pen beside him, and it took every bit of effort not to turn round and join her in that moment.

No, *this* Nick really didn't need.

# CHAPTER FOUR

'ALISON doesn't want to be my friend.'

He lasted two days.

Two days trying not to notice how her neck went a little bit pink when he spoke to her. Two days ignoring the fragrance of her hair when their heads occasionally met over a patient, or that now and then she'd rub her forehead and on would come her glasses. Two days of just talking, just keeping it as it was, then, as happened at times, but had to happen on this day, Alison came off the worse for wear with an inebriated patient. Showered and changed into the most threadbare, faded scrubs, Nick got the most astonishing view of what appeared to be a purple bra and panties, before Sheila pointed the problem out and Alison put on a theatre gown. Like a dressing gown over pyjamas, Nick thought, and then tried not to think, and then just stopped thinking for a dangerous moment as she sat next to him writing up his notes, her ponytail wet and heavy, and he forgot, just simply forgot not to flirt.

'Why don't you want to be my friend, Alison?' He nudged her as if they were sitting in a classroom and

Alison, who wasn't having the greatest day, annoyed with herself for not replacing her spare uniform, found herself trying not to smile, yet she did carry on the joke and put her arm over the notes she was writing as if he was trying to copy her.

'I am your friend, Nick.'

'Not on Facebook...'

'I haven't got time to *play* online...' Alison said. 'Some of us live and work in the real world—I'm studying to get on this trauma course.'

'You're friends with Ellie.' He grinned and then stopped, and so too did Alison. There was this charge in the air; it would be far safer to carry on writing, or just get up and go, but she didn't, she just sat. 'Are you going to have to get the bus wearing that? Only I can—'

'I washed my uniform and begged them on the rehab ward to use their tumbledryer...' She didn't get to finish because screams filled the department and Nick jumped up as a man was stretchered in, sucking on the gas, in sheer agony at the prospect of being moved from the stretcher to the gurney.

'Can I have a quick look before you move him?'

His jeans had already been cut off and it was a rather horrible sight, his dislocated patella causing the whole leg to look deformed. It was an excruciating injury and Alison blinked as, without X-ray, without delay, Nick told the man to suck on the gas and with one flick popped it back.

A shriek filled the department and then a sob and then the sound of relieved silence.

'Let's get him on the gurney and then we'll need X-rays.' He chatted for a moment to his extremely grateful patient, then chatted a bit more to the rather impressed paramedics, then he walked over to where Alison was now on the computer, checking some blood results, and she could feel the heat whoosh up her neck as he came over.

'God, I'm good.' He grinned and, yes, it was arrogant, but it was funny too, and Alison couldn't help but smile as she rolled her eyes.

'Yeah, but you know it.'

He looked at her and he wanted to look away, to walk away, to remember he was there for reasons other than this, except there was something about Alison that was hard to resist. Something about her that meant stern warnings could so easily be ignored.

'Hey...' Moira dashed past '...are you coming to the beach later, Alison?' She gave a hopeful glance at Nick. 'There are a few of us going—Amy...'

'Not for me,' Alison said.

'Or me!' Nick said. Moira shrugged and moved on. It was like sugar to artificial sweetener, Nick decided, because sugar was something he was trying to give up too. Yes, sweeteners tasted okay, once you got used to them, and for a while there they sufficed, but sooner rather than later you went back for the real thing.... And maybe he should just go to the beach, or a bar, or just home and have that takeaway that Amy had offered. Instead he found himself asking Alison if she wanted to go for a coffee.

'I've got a dentist appointment.'

'Ouch.' He pulled a sympathetic face. 'Hope it's not too painful.'

'Oh, it's just my six-monthly check-up.' And she smiled, but it sort of faded as she turned back to the computer, because it just about summed her up.

She *had* six-monthly check-ups, and when this one was done, no doubt, she'd do as she always did and while she was there make an appointment for the next one and write it in her diary, and she'd be there—she never missed.

Same as her eight-weekly trim at the hairdresser's.

Same as she booked in the dog to be shampooed and clipped.

She bet Nick hadn't spent ages on the computer, researching dentists to ensure he didn't miss his six-monthly check-up.

The most gorgeous, sexy man was asking her for coffee and she'd turned him down for a dental appointment!

'We could meet up afterwards, but not for long, I've got to look at that flat.' She could hear her own words and inwardly reeled at them, and even as she mistyped the patient's UR number she sounded almost blasé as she dipped in her toe and felt only warmth. 'So long as I don't end up getting a filling or something.'

'Let's just hope you've been flossing.'

She had been.

\* \* \*

Alison lay in the chair with her mouth open as the dentist tapped each tooth in turn.

Not a single filling.

Again.

He cleaned them, polished them and they felt like glass as she ran her tongue over them. As she paid and headed out, she didn't get why she was so nervous.

Why she wanted to just not show up.

Because it might just be coffee and strudel and then she'd be disappointed, Alison thought as she stepped out onto the street with her sparkly clean teeth. Or, worse, it might be more than coffee and strudel...

Maybe that was what he did—pick someone wherever he went, dazzle her with the full glare of his spotlight.

And he really could dazzle.

Since two minutes past six on Friday morning, he'd been on her mind.

She rang her mum, told her she was having coffee with friends before she went to look at the flat, and as she turned the corner he was there already and looked up and smiled as she made her way over and took her seat at the pavement café.

'How was the dentist?'

'Fine,' Alison said, 'I've earned my strudel.'

He ordered, and her nerves disappeared because, absolutely, he was still easy to talk to and easy to listen to, too. Not working for a few months, Nick said, was the single best thing he had ever done. 'Because,' he continued, spooning *four* sugars into his coffee as Alison tapped in a sweetener, 'I actually missed it.'

'Well, you love your job,' Alison said. 'That's obvious.'

'But I didn't,' Nick said, and Alison blinked at his admission. 'That's one of the reasons I took a year off. I wasn't even sure if I wanted to do medicine any more, let alone work in Emergency.'

'But you seem to enjoy it.'

'I'm starting to.' He was in no rush, just sat and drank his coffee as if he'd be happy to sit there all evening and told her a little about himself. 'There was never any question that I'd be a doctor—preferably a surgeon. My dad's one, my grandfather was one, my elder brother is, as is my sister...' He rolled his eyes. 'Can you imagine what we talk about over dinner?'

'What about your mum?'

'Homework monitor,' Nick said, and Alison laughed. 'There was no question and, really, I accepted that, right up till the last year of medical school—which I enjoyed, but...' He shrugged. 'I don't know, I wanted to take a year off to travel, but I ended up taking an internship.'

'I was the same,' Alison interrupted, which was rare for her. Normally she sat quietly and listened. 'I wanted a year off when I finished school, but Mum and Dad said I should finish my studies.'

'I had the same conversation with mine.' Nick groaned. 'So I did my internship, decided I liked emergency work, met Gillian and it was all...'

'Nice,' Alison offered.

And they could hardly hear the other's story for telling their own, or hardly tell their own for hearing the other person's.

'Work was okay about it—they gave me a year's unpaid leave, but they made it pretty clear that there'd be no extension. I've no idea how bad divorce must be,' Nick said, 'because breaking up after four years was hard enough. I mean, there was no real reason—it was just the talk of mortgages and babies and if we'd hyphenate our names...' He called the waiter and ordered another coffee and Alison ordered a hot chocolate. 'I was having a midlife crisis apparently!' Nick said. 'At thirty!'

'I had one too,' Alison said, 'and I'm only twenty-four.' And she laughed, for the first time she laughed about the sorry situation she had found herself in a year ago. She told him a little about Paul, her one serious relationship—how well he'd got on with her mother, how hard it had been to end it—but there was something she wanted to know about him. 'So...' Alison was cautious, but terribly, terribly curious. 'Are you two having a break...?'

'No,' Nick said. 'I ended it and it wasn't nice, but it was necessary. I just hope one day she can see that— four weeks later I'd got a round-the-world ticket and was flying to New York.'

And she sat outside a pavement café with a man who came from the other side of the world, but who felt somehow the same, and there was a fizz in her veins she'd never felt before, a glow inside as they chatted on, and she could have stayed and spoken to him for hours, except she had her real estate appointment at seven.

'Do you want me to come?' Nick asked. 'I love looking at houses.'

'It's an apartment.'

'It's someone else's!' Nick grinned. 'I love being
nosy.'

And Alison smiled back because, even if flat-hunting
was hell, yes, she liked that aspect of it too, loved that
peek into others' lives, the solace that wardrobes the
length and breadth of Coogee were filled fit to bursting,
that some people didn't even make their beds when they
had people coming round to view. And she told him so
and told him some more. 'One couple were rowing on
Saturday,' Alison said.

'The owners?' Nick asked, and she loved how his
eyes widened in glee.

'I think they were breaking up.' Alison nodded. 'They
stood on the balcony and had this screaming match
during the open inspection.'

'God, I wish I'd been there,' Nick said, and she kind
of wished he'd been there too—liked that he liked the
same things as her, that odd little things pleased.

'Come on, then.' She went to fish out her purse, but
Nick waved her away and it would have been embarrassing really to protest—and even there he was different.
Paul had decided on their first date that equality meant
you split the bill—and she told him so as they walked
down the hill and turned at the chemist's.

'He lived in constant terror that he might end up
paying for a round of garlic bread when he hadn't eaten
a slice,' Alison said, and then wondered if she should

have said that, if it was bitchy to talk about your ex like that. 'He was a great guy, just toward the end...' She trailed off and Nick got it, he just completely got it.

'Gillian and I ended up the same,' he said as they walked up the hill to meet the real estate agent. 'At first I used to love it that she did my crossword, but near the end I was setting my alarm early and nearly breaking my neck to get down the stairs and to the newspaper first.' He glanced over to check that she got it too and Alison smiled. 'It's not the crossword, or the garlic bread, is it?'

'He was great,' Alison said. 'It was more...' And she told him a bit about herself, not enough to have him running in the opposite direction, just a little. 'It was too nice,' Alison said. 'Too easy, almost. Mum's a bit over-protective and he didn't seem to mind... In fact, Paul suggested he move in.' She still burnt at the memory. 'Mum was delighted, it felt like they had it all worked out.'

'They just forgot to ask you,' Nick said, and for the first time in her life, she felt as if someone got her.

# CHAPTER FIVE

ALISON had very few expectations as the real estate agent opened the front door and she stepped inside. There had been so many disappointments, so many let-downs, that, in the name of self-preservation, she kept her hopes determinedly down.

Even as they looked at the surprisingly spacious lounge, even that this apartment actually had a kitchen, though even the real estate agent managed a wry smile at the supposed glimpse of the bay. Nick could see it because he was a full foot taller, but apparently, there at the top right hand side of the kitchen window was her beloved beach.

'There is a second bedroom.' Alison peered into a cupboard. 'Well,' the real estate agent attempted, 'it would make a nice nursery.'

'Or study,' Nick offered when Alison laughed, and then they moved along the hall.

'This is the main bedroom.'

It was larger than expected too, and, really, all Alison's wishes had been answered. The owners were off to London, the husband leaving the next day apparently, and the wife following in a month's time. 'Really, he'd like to know it was all taken care of before he leaves,' the real estate agent explained. 'They want a thirty-day settlement…'

And she listened to the wah-wah white noise as the agent did his spiel, but it wasn't the large airy bedroom Alison could see but the suitcase beside the bed, and it truly dawned that if she bought this flat, she was, without doubt, saying goodbye to her dream of travelling, and even though she'd thought it through, even though she'd gone over it a hundred million times, when it came to it, she stalled at the final hurdle.

'Can I have till the morning?' Alison saw the agent's eyebrows rise in surprise. For weeks he had seen her at open inspections at places far less nice than this and now he was almost handing her this opportunity on a plate and at the last minute the *genuine buyer* he'd ensured the vendors he had was faltering.

'The vendors want to save on advertising, that's why I agreed to bring you through, but the photographer is booked for midday and it will go on the market then, unless I hear otherwise.'

'Sure,' Alison said. 'I'll ring tomorrow.'

'I'm impressed,' Nick said as they walked down the street.

'Why?'

'I thought you'd snatch his hand off to get it—you certainly know how to play it cool.'

'It's not that,' Alison started, and then halted herself.

She was hardly going to tell a virtual stranger, albeit a very nice virtual stranger, her dilemma—and then, in that moment she realised the stark truth, it wasn't even a dilemma. She really had no choice in the matter. 'I just want to speak to Mum first.'

'It's a big decision,' Nick said, and Alison stopped walking.

'I turn off here.' She gave him a nice smile. 'Thanks for the coffee.'

'Thanks for the company.'

It was a strange moment. The light-heartedness of earlier had gone—Alison heavy with indecision and Nick no doubt not understanding why.

'I'll see you at work tomorrow.'

She turned up the street and bizarrely felt like crying. She knew, was positive in fact, that he was watching her and that made her walk faster. She wanted to turn, wanted to run back to him, to go to a club or a bar, to ask him about his adventures, she wanted to sit and listen to music, to be late, to not go home. Instead she turned the key in the door.

'Hi, Mum.'

'I was just starting to get worried.'

'It's not even eight!' Alison pointed out.

'You said you were out for coffee,' Rose said. 'A quick phone call would have been nice…'

There was a retort on Alison's tongue, an urge to yet again point out her age, another beginning to a row that had never taken place but one they were steadily building towards. Then Alison caught sight of her father and brother's photo on the shrine that used to be a mantel-piece, and swallowed down her bitter response, knew this was the small price she paid for living, knew she would do her best to avoid arguing and knew for certain that she had to move out.

'I went to look at that flat.' She saw her mother's rapid blink. 'I think I've finally found one.' She spoke quickly into the ensuing silence. 'It's a ten-minute walk away, it's got everything—two bedrooms, even a little balcony…' And she waited for her mother to fill in the gap, to point out that she could live here for nothing, that it was stupid, pointless, but for once Rose didn't speak, and not for the first time Alison tried to be honest. 'I don't know if I should take it. I mean, I'll have a mortgage, there's no way I'd be able…' She glanced up and saw Rose swallow. 'You know I always wanted to travel…'

And Rose in that moment had a choice between the lesser of two evils. She must have, because for once she didn't jump in with all the reasons Alison would be stupid to leave home; for the first time ever she bordered on enthusiastic about her daughter moving out.

'It sounds a nice flat.' There was a wobble to Rose's voice. 'Two bedrooms, you say?'

'Well, only one that's actually big enough for a bed, but the other could be a nice study.'

'You'll need a study if you do your trauma course.'

'The thing is, Mum—'

'I know you want to travel…' Rose broke in. 'I've been thinking. I've given it a lot of thought, actually. We deserve a treat.' As Alison opened her mouth to protest,

Rose overrode her. 'I know you've always wanted to go to Bali. I wouldn't mind seeing it too… My treat,' she said loudly as Alison tried to interrupt.

And as she lay in her single bed later on, Alison tried not to cry. She felt horribly selfish actually, because in the space of a few hours she'd found a flat and been offered a fortnight's trip to Bali. It was just…

The first year after the accident she'd taken her mum for weekends away, she and Paul had taken her for a holiday once too, with Alison sharing a room with her mum. Then last year they'd been to Queensland for a week—her mum saying all the time how much her father and brother would have liked it.

She ripped back the sheet, and almost ran to the window.

There were no bay views from her bedroom but there was the distant roar of the ocean as she pushed the window open and gulped in the cool night air. And there were the sounds of the bars and the backpackers and youth and fun, and she was tempted to run down in her nightdress, tempted to find what ever bar Nick was in, to rush up to him and kiss his face off, to take him by the hand and dance and dance, to come back at dawn *without* sending her mother a text.

To be free.

# CHAPTER SIX

'YAY!' The whole staffroom cheered when a beaming Alison revealed her news as she walked into her late shift.

She'd soon got over herself—a brisk walk on the beach at the crack of dawn and a stern talk with herself had turned things round in her head. Then, at nine a.m. she'd rung the real estate agent, at nine-forty she'd been at the bank, at nine fifty-five she'd handed the deposit over and signed a mountain of forms, and now, at midday, she almost had a mortgage.

'Congratulations.' Nick pulled her aside the first chance he got. It had been a busy afternoon and Alison had been working the paediatric cots while Nick had been in Resus, but as she came back from her coffee break, he was just heading off for his.

'Thanks!' Alison said. 'It's pretty exciting.'

'How about dinner,' Nick offered, 'to celebrate?' And when she paused, when she didn't just jump in and say yes, Nick upped the offer. 'With lots of garlic bread.'

'Why?' He didn't understand the hurt in her eyes, he

didn't really understand the question. 'Why would we go out for dinner?'

'Because you want to?' Nick said, because he was sure that she did. 'Because I want to?'

'I don't…' Her voice trailed off, and her words hung in the air, the wrong words because she did want to, very much. She had been about to say that she didn't see the point in pursuing this, except when he was around she did see the point—he was nice and funny and whatever attraction was, it was there, for both of them.

'I'm not sure.' She changed tack, headed for safer ground, used a method far safer than exposing her heart. 'What with work and everything.'

Nick could have pointed out that it was just dinner, that, given they'd been out on Friday, clearly work colleagues did meet up outside the walls of Emergency. Except it wasn't just dinner and it wasn't the emergency crew he wanted to see more of out of hours—it was her. And, yes, he was bending his own rules, but it was, after all, just for a short while and even if it was work, it was still a holiday. He wasn't asking for for ever, he wasn't threatening to run away with her heart, he just wanted more of the smile that sometimes brightened her serious face, wanted more of the woman he was getting to know.

'We could keep it quiet.' He ran a hand through his hair as he renegotiated his own boundaries.

'Sounds good.'

And those words were the bravest she'd uttered.

'About ten?' Nick said, and her smile disappeared

when she realised he meant tonight, that his impulsive world was invading hers. 'Ten-thirty?' he said, and named a nice bar. 'I'll pick you up.' And she thought of her mother and shook her head at the image.

'Ten-thirty's great.' She forced a smile. 'I'll meet you there.'

Thankfully, she was kept almost busy enough not to be nervous. It wasn't a date, she kept telling herself, it was just friends going out for a couple hours. She managed not to think about it, especially when dealing with a very restless baby and an extremely anxious mum.

'She's putting on weight.' Lucia, the paediatric intern, was thorough and nice and doing her best to reassure Shelly, the mother of an eight-week-old. 'I know reflux babies are hard, but you are doing everything right.' And she went through all the medications and thickeners that little Casey was on, and checked that she was being positioned properly.

'She won't settle, though,' Shelly said. 'She hardly goes two hours.'

'That's why my registrar suggested you look at the mother and baby day clinic,' Lucia said. 'She's well, though.' Despite everything, the baby was well. There were no signs of dehydration, her nappies were wet, her obs were normal—she was just a very fussy baby. 'You've got an appointment coming up with the paediatrician...' Her pager was going off, her registrar had already looked over the baby and deemed little Casey well enough to go home, and there was only one paediatric bed left to last the night. Lucia was only checking her over again because the mother was still concerned, and despite Lucia's reassurances, as she said goodbye Alison knew Shelly wasn't reassured. Neither was she, though her concern wasn't just for the baby. She could see Shelly's shaking hands as she did up the poppers on her baby's little outfit, saw that despite the baby screaming, Shelly said nothing to soothe her, just wrapped her up and put her in her little car seat, without a word, without a cuddle. There was no malice in her actions. She was just a mother very close to the edge.

'Amy saw this baby and handed her over to Paeds.' She handed Nick the notes. 'Amy's gone home and Paeds have seen the baby and they're happy to discharge. I'm just concerned…' She waited as he read through the notes, waited for him to roll his eyes, or sigh, or say 'I'll get to it,' but instead he listened as Alison voiced her concerns and he read easily between the lines. 'Lucia did suggest the day clinic to sort out her sleeping pattern.'

'What did Mum say to that?'

'She agreed to it, but there's normally a two-week wait.'

'Do you think she's depressed?'

'I'm sure she is,' Alison said, 'just not enough for an urgent admission. And frankly I'd be feeling depressed. I tried feeding her and it was hard work.'

'Okay.' He slid off his stool and went over and introduced himself. He chatted to Shelly about her babe, taking her out of her little seat and examining the infant himself. 'When is she due for a feed?'

'She's constantly due!' Shelly said through gritted

teeth. 'She never finishes a bottle, she screams as if I'm pouring acid down her throat instead of milk...' The young mother bit back angry tears as her baby lay on the mattress, screaming. 'I know she's got reflux, I know it will get better...'

'Okay,' Nick said, and when Shelly didn't, Alison started to dress the baby again. She waited for him to suggest she get a bottle, that he observe the babe feed, or a little bit more of what had taken place on and off for the last four hours, but he did none of that. He gave a brief smile and nodded and said he'd be back in a moment as Shelly blew out a long breath.

'What's happening?'

'I'm not sure,' Alison said, as the baby's screams quadrupled. 'Here,' she said, when Shelly sat down beside the cot and put her head in her hands, 'would you like me to take Casey for a little walk? I'll see if I can find out what's happening.'

Casey did stop crying, the motion, the bright lights, the activity all distracting her enough as Alison walked through the department and found Nick perched back on his stool.

'What's happening?'

'She'll be admitted,' Nice said. 'I've just paged the paed reg.'

'He's happy for her to go home and be seen in Outpatients...'

'Well, I'm not,' Nick said. 'Which means that she's going to be admitted.'

And he told the paediatric reg the same when he

picked up the phone. Yes, he was friendly and perfectly reasonable at first, and then Alison got her first glimpse of a different Nick, an extremely assertive Nick who, despite the smile and the easygoing banter, took his job very seriously and would not be argued with.

A Nick who was going to go far.

'It's not even an option,' Nick said, turning his pen over and over between the desk and his fingers, clearly in no rush. 'She can be transferred to another hospital if there are no beds here, but I'm not happy to send her home, so either ring your intern and tell her to come and do the paperwork, or I can ring your consultant to discuss it further. But whatever comes of it, this baby isn't going home.'

'That told them,' Alison said.

'I don't see why everything has to be an argument— it's the same everywhere,' Nick added. 'I know there are hardly any beds, I know she's not acute, but...' He glanced down towards the bay. 'I'm going to have a word with Mum.'

He was nice and practical and explained that Casey should be monitored and was upfront about Shelly's tension. 'We need to be really sure we haven't overlooked anything and if everything checks out, we need to make sure you get the support you need with Casey.'

He just dealt with things, without fuss or drama, and he didn't moan as he did so.

'He's nice, that doctor,' Shelly commented as Alison took her up to the ward, the porter wheeling the mother and baby in a chair.

'He is,' Alison agreed, and then she remembered.

She was having dinner with that nice doctor tonight.

Taking the bus simply wasn't an option. By the time she had taken Shelly up to the ward *and* dashed back, it was already well after nine and she'd missed her bus, and as much as Nick might be expecting her to change quickly and dash back out, and as much as Alison wanted to look as if she'd changed quickly and dashed back out, there was no girl facing such a prospect who would. Which was why, despite now being a responsible, soon-to-be homeowner, Alison splurged on a taxi, though she made sure that it dropped her off at the end of the street to avoid even more questions from her mum.

'Out?' Rose frowned as Alison flew in the door.

'For dinner,' Alison said. 'To celebrate getting the flat.'

'Who with?'

'Friends from work,' Alison said, and it wasn't a lie, she consoled herself as she dashed up the stairs. It was just a slight exaggeration, or rather playing the situation down, because friends from work was safe, a friend from work a bit different.

A male friend from work.

A gorgeous, blond, funny, sexy, 'here for a good time, not a long time' male friend from work.

Getting ready for Nick was rather like getting a patient quickly prepared for Theatre. Alison went through a rapid mental checklist, cleaning her teeth, shaving her legs, even cleaning her ears, body lotion, perfume, subtle make-up, hair gloss, nice underwear, really, really nice underwear—not that he'd be seeing it, but just because, because, because…

She was simply meeting a friend from work, Alison told herself over and over as she trawled through her wardrobe till the contents lay on a heap on her bed, wondering how she could have nothing to wear when her entire bed was covered. She settled for a pale grey tube skirt that she'd had for ever and a cheap but cheerful top she'd bought the previous week, pulled on some bracelets as she dashed downstairs, wished her mum goodnight and flew down the street, rather surprised to find Nick waiting for her at the end.

'Don't want you walking on your own.'

'I do it all the time,' Alison said.

'You look nice.' His eyes told her that he meant it.

'Oh.' She gave a casual shrug, one that said it had been no effort at all! 'Thanks.'

He was just a friend, Alison told herself as he went to kiss her on the cheek.

Or maybe not, because very deliberately he avoided her cheek and met her mouth, and it was slow and deliberate and its meaning was clear, crystal clear, that this was more than just friendship.

And for Nick it was confirmation too.

He felt first her hesitancy, her guardedness and then he felt what he knew, or rather had guessed at. Felt this gathering of passion on full lips and despite self-issued warnings he wanted to unleash it.

'Just so we don't spend the whole night wondering,' Nick said, and pulled back, even though he wanted more. And she smiled because now, instead of wondering, she knew.

So she kissed him, just to confirm it, and despite Nick's best-laid plans, now they would spend the whole night not just wondering but wanting too, because one taste of his tongue and Pandora's box opened and it was passion that slithered out. Alison could feel the press of brick wall on her back, feel the silk of his hair on her fingers, and ten doors from prison he turned the key and she flew, her body just flew to his, met his, wanted his, and she'd never kissed or been kissed like this, his hands on her hips and his mouth drinking hers. And it was absolutely right that he stop, that he look into her eyes, pupils so dilated he might have put in atropine drops, and she watched him taste his own lips, taste her again and try to get his breath.

'Let's eat,' Nick said.

Let's not, Alison wanted to reply as his forehead met hers as they rested just a moment to regroup, because, as Alison had just found out, kisses changed things.

Good ones especially.

Their restaurant was chosen by the delicious herby scent that wafted onto the street, and it was Italian. Alison chose giant ravioli in a creamy mushroom sauce and Nick didn't skimp on the garlic bread either.

It was different from any other date she'd been on because there was neither awkwardness nor ease, or rather there was, just not in the usual rhythm.

There was ease to the conversation, it was the table between them that made things awkward—just watching each other's mouths as they ate, that made them tense.

'Is everything okay?' The waiter checked when, plates quickly cleared, Nick asked for the bill.

'I'll get dinner next time,' Alison said when he paid, and it was as assured as that, for both of them, that there would be a next time.

'Your wine.' The waiter handed them their half-bottle and Nick smiled at the little differences around the world, because till a few minutes ago they could have been anywhere. Walking out of the restaurant with wine in hand, they saw the show of the ocean endlessly unfolding, the night warm, the sky thick with stars. Yes, it was late, but too early to end their evening, and a walk on the beach was cleansing after the noise in the restaurant. 'Do you want to come back for coffee?' Nick said, and then he winced a bit. 'I do mean coffee.'

Alison would have loved to because she wanted more of him and a coffee would be nice too, except she couldn't.

'I really have to get back soon.' She hadn't dared check her phone. 'I've got loads on tomorrow.'

So instead they sat and Nick had a mouthful from the bottle and so too did Alison and, yes, she was home, but it felt like paradise.

She stared out at the stars and there were millions of them. The more she looked the more she could see, and she wished she could read them, wished she could point to a constellation, and she told him that. 'I'm going to do an astronomy course one day.'

'Never interested me,' Nick admitted, 'till I came to Australia. I've never seen stars like it.'

And they lay back on the sand and just stared, and she could have lain there for ever, but she really did have to get back and she told him, well, not quite the truth but a little bit more than she had previously—that her mum would be starting to worry.

'Why don't you ring her if she'll be worrying?' came Nick's practical suggestion, because for most twenty-four-year-olds a phone call would suffice.

'And tell her what?' Alison dodged the issue. 'That I'm lying on a beach and I'm worried that he's going to kiss me, because I really don't think I'll be able to stop?'

'I'm worried this time too,' Nick said, and her heart twisted as they spoke their own shorthand, that he remembered her words as she remembered his.

'I have visions,' Alison admitted, turning from the stars to his lovely, lovely face, and for some reason she felt free to be just a little more honest. 'Of me at forty, or fifty, and I'm a lot larger than I am now, I've got a big shiny red face and I'm a virgin, and it's Tuesday and Mum's serving me dinner at the table—beef stroganoff...'

And he didn't leap from the beach and run. He just smiled and rolled over on his side and his hand moved and toyed without thinking with the bottom of her skirt, because her admission brought only one question.

'And are you a virgin?'

'No,' Alison said, 'but in this vision I've lied for so long, I think I've turned into one.'

That unthinking hand was at the side of her knee. She could taste his breath and they were still talking and not going anywhere.

'Why would you lie?'

'It's just easier to with my mum.' And it was impossible to explain, so she didn't try to—impossible to tell this gorgeous, free man about the tentacles that were tightening ever more firmly around her, impossible to admit what he could never understand.

'Do you get them?' She broke the silence.

'What?'

'Visions of a possible future.'

'No.' His mouth found her cheek and then slid to her ear and she was terribly glad she'd cleaned them.

'Never?' Alison checked, trying to talk, trying to breathe, trying very hard not to kiss him. 'Don't you see scenarios, like if you don't do this, then that might happen?'

He nibbled at her neck while he thought about it. 'At work.' Nick stopped in mid-nibble with his answer. 'Sometimes when I'm looking at an injury I know if we don't do that or prescribe that, then this might happen.'

He got it.

'And in your life?' Alison asked, rolling into him, feeling his jean-clad sandy legs in between her bare ones, feeling his long, tanned fingers circling her nipples through her T-shirt, and she wanted to rest her breast in his palm, just kissing and lying and talking, and her body was the most alive it had ever been.

'No.' But Nick did think about it as he played with her breasts and what she loved the most was that he *did* think about it. 'Actually, I did have one.' His hands moved from her breasts and made lovely strokes through the cotton on her skirt down her stomach as he spoke. 'When I was having my supposed premature midlife crisis.' He could see her teeth as she smiled. 'I was on call and the baby was screaming, the nanny had the night off and we were rowing because Gillian was working the next day…' He blinked at his own admission. 'I get it.'

'What was the nanny's name, then?' Alison asked.

'My visions aren't that detailed,' Nick said. 'Helga?' he offered, but she shook her head. 'Svetlana?'

'Better,' Alison said.

And he got it and that came with reward—her lips, unworried, met his and he kissed her mouth and pressed her into the sand. She felt the damp salt of the ocean on his shirt and she tasted it on his mouth.

She felt the press of his leg and the roam of his hands, the sand in her hair and the slide of his tongue, and the dangerous beckoning of his loaned flat, and the pull of her home, all tightening in her stomach as his mouth pursued.

It was a kiss that struck at midnight, and she turned, but only in his arms, a kiss that had her hips rise into his groin, and it could never be enough.

A kiss that had her breast slip out of her bra and though encased in fabric still fall into his palm.

A kiss where you didn't have to go further to enjoy it, but for Alison it was already too late to stay, though it was Nick who pulled away, because if he kissed her for a moment longer, he would forget they were on a beach!

'I ought to go,' Alison said.

'Yes, you ought to,' Nick said, and she let him help her up, and then he did the nicest of things—he dusted her down.

It was *the* nicest thing.

The stroke of his hand on her body, the attention to detail, the warmth of his palm stroking her bottom and then dusting damp sand from her calves. It was so seemingly innocent but it was like sex with clothes on—actually far better than any sex Alison had ever had—and she stood, compliant, but she wanted to run with him, back to his flat, and never mind the coffee. And she nearly said 'Your turn', nearly put her hands out to deal with his sandy jeans, but he took her hand instead because it would have been far too dangerous, and they walked up the beach, tossed the bottle in the bin and then headed for her street. They walked in silence to her turn-off and this time when she went to say goodbye, Nick insisted on walking her to her door.

With their kiss she was a little more his, even if just for a little while, which meant he walked with her. She just wished he wouldn't, but couldn't say so.

'We're both off at the weekend.' Nick knew because

he'd looked. 'I was thinking of getting a bike, going for a ride in the mountains…' He sensed her reluctance and misinterpreted it. 'I'll book two rooms.'

'I don't know, Nick.' So badly she wanted to go, but it wasn't just the weekend and sleeping arrangements that had her in knots, but getting on a bike, the recklessness of it—all of it. 'Actually, I've got some things I need to do and then I've got a week of nights…' And the evening ended there, and she gave him just a little kiss on the cheek, because she knew her mother was watching, and she knew too that he was watching her as she walked to her door.

He was.

And he must be getting good at her vision game, because as Nick walked home he was having one of his own and there wasn't a crying baby or Svetlana in sight, more an Alison uncut vision.

Alison let loose, Nick thought with a smile, pulling up in surprise at just how much he wanted to share his vision with her…

'Oh, you're back.' Rose stood by the kettle, as if she hadn't been at the window. 'I was just making a cup of tea to take back to bed. Do you want one?'

'No, thanks, Mum.'

'Nice night.'

'Really nice.'

'How was your friend?'

'Great,' Alison said, hearing the singular, and she

turned to go to bed, but then relented. 'We just had some pasta, and then walked.'

'You're covered in sand.'

'We walked on the beach.'

Rose humphed, and no doubt there was half the beach in her hair and why did she feel guilty? Why was her mother sulking when she had done absolutely nothing wrong? 'Am I allowed to ask his name?'

Alison hesitated. It was all too new and too soon to be naming him, she wanted to pull apart her own thoughts and feelings without sharing things first, but her mum wanted conversation, inclusion, and at every turn Alison did try.

'Nick,' Alison said, and her mum just waited. 'He's a friend from work. So what did you do tonight?'

'Not much—I looked through some photos.' She gave a wan smile. 'I'll have to find something to do once you're gone.'

'I'll be ten minutes away, Mum.'

'Oh.' Rose suddenly changed the subject. 'Your uncle Ken rang. They're having a barbecue at the weekend, so don't go making any plans—they're looking forward to seeing you.'

'What day?' Alison asked, sure, quite sure what was coming next.

'I'm not sure…' Rose's forehead crinkled as she tried to recall. 'Memory like a sieve—I'll ring tomorrow.'

To arrange a sudden barbecue, Alison thought, but didn't say. ''Night, Mum.' She kissed her mother on the cheek and went upstairs, headed for her room and wished, wished, wished she'd met Nick in a couple of months' time, when she had her own flat.

But as Alison climbed into bed, she knew it wasn't that simple.

In thirty days' time, twenty-eight, in fact, she'd have been in more of a position to let him into her life.

To climb on a bike and head into the hills and, yes, maybe not tonight, but the way her body had thrummed to his kiss, soon, very soon, the night would have had a very different conclusion. Her own reaction tonight, though so natural at the time, startled her now as she lay there. She wanted to ring him, right now this minute, to explain that this was out of character for her. That wine and kisses on the beach… She burnt at the memory, but it was in embarrassment now. She wasn't like that—well, she was, but only with him.

He'd hardly appreciate the admission, Alison realised. Nick had wanted fun, so too had she.

Maybe it was better this way, Alison decided, turning to the wall and willing sleep to come.

Maybe caution was merited here, even if she resisted it, because, as a little voice in her head grew louder, Nick would be around for a couple of months only and two weeks of that had already gone.

Yes, if she had the flat, if she had some freedom, she could let him more into her life.

But how much harder would it be then to have him leave?

# CHAPTER SEVEN

'ALISON, could I have a word?' Nick caught her right at
the end of her shift on Friday when all week she'd done
her absolute best to avoid him.

Of course they'd talked, but about patients and things,
and Alison had been very careful to take her break
only when Nick was busy with a patient, but just as she
thought she'd got through the working week he caught
her at three-twenty p.m. as she and Ellie headed for the
bus stop.

'I'm rushing for the bus.'

'We've already missed it, the next one isn't due for
twenty minutes.' Ellie, dear Ellie, beamed. 'I'll wait for
you at the stop.'

'Sorry,' he started, 'I haven't been avoiding you, and
there just hasn't been a chance to talk to you.'

'I know.' Alison smiled, even though she'd engineered
it that way. 'It's been a crazy week.'

'Look, about this weekend,' Nick said. 'I thought we
could go out.'

'You're going away.'

'I'd rather…' There was a rare awkwardness to him.

'I'm happy to give it a miss. I'd rather spend some time with you.'

'I've got a family thing tonight…' Alison said, which was now true. 'My dad's brother's having a barbecue, it's always a bit awkward…' She saw him frown. 'My dad's dead, we get together and it always ends up a bit of a reminisce…'

'What about the rest of the weekend?' Nick was direct. It was a barbecue she was going to after all, so she struggled for an answer, one that let her off the hook.

'I really have to go to the home furnishings store.' It was the most pathetic of excuses. 'I need some stuff for the flat.'

Somehow, and she really didn't know how and certainly not why, but for reasons of his own, a shopping trip and dinner at his place afterwards was more appealing to Nick than a bike ride in the mountains and somehow, and she did know why, he was still so very easy to talk to, still so very hard not to want to like. 'I need to give the car a run,' Nick explained when he offered to pick her up, 'or the battery will go flat.'

'I'll see.' She gave him a thin smile. 'I just need to…' She didn't bother to explain, in fact she didn't have to explain, Alison realised, didn't have to tell him about every beat of her heart. 'I'll let you know.'

She caught up with Ellie at the bus stop. 'Thanks a lot.' Alison gave her friend a wry smile. 'I was actually trying to get away back there!'

'Then you're mad!' Ellie said. 'He's gorgeous, he's

nice and from the way he's always looking at you or, oh, so casually asks "Who's on a late today?" or "Who's on in the morning?" and loses interest after it gets to your name, I think we can all safely assume he likes you. Lucky thing.'

'Hardly—he's only here for a few weeks.'

'So?' Ellie gave her an odd look.

'There's just no point.'

'Well, I suppose there's no point if you're looking for a husband.' Ellie let out a laugh. 'I don't get you, Alison. He's gorgeous. You were saying the other week you wanted some fun and adventure, and now it's handed to you on a plate...'

She wished, how she wished she could be more like Ellie, could see only the positives, but all Alison could see was a sure-fire recipe for hurt and she told Ellie so.

'I like him,' she admitted. 'I could see myself *really* liking him.'

'So go for it.'

'You know what Mum's like,' Alison said. 'Once I've got my own place...'

Ellie just laughed. 'How did you survive your teens? I mean, before...' Yes, Ellie laughed at most things, but her voice did trail off then. She genuinely liked Rose and knew all Alison had been through.

'Tim was the one who was always in trouble.' Alison could smile at the memory now. 'I used to just say I was staying at a friend's if I wanted to go out.'

'Do that, then.' Ellie shrugged. 'Till you get your own

place, say you're staying at mine. Anyway, by then you might find out that he's the most crushing bore, or walk in to find him dressed in your underwear and stilettos. Go out and have some fun, for God's sake…he doesn't have to be "the one" to enjoy him.'

Ellie was right.

Alison stepped off the bus and instead of heading for home she walked on the beach, sensible shoes in hand. She felt the sand between her toes, and the sun warming her back, tasted the salt on her lips and felt the wind in her hair, and for the first time in years she tasted adventure, for the first time in so long Alison felt just a little bit free.

She'd yearned for adventure, escape, and Nick was just that.

Nick didn't need to know all of her—Nick didn't need to know that the nights out and kisses on the beach were rarities.

She could do this, Alison told herself, walking past the very spot where they had lain. She could throw caution to the wind, could be the woman her body was begging her to be, could close her mind to the pitfalls and problems and for once just enjoy.

But how? the sensible part of her mind asked. When even staying out after midnight required the stealth and ability to lie like a teenager to her mum. Surely the last thing Nick needed from a holiday romance was the crush of her problems landing in his lap.

Why should she put herself through it?

*Because you want to.*

Nick's voice seemed to carry on the wind, echoing her own thoughts, and she *did* want to.

And surely she could handle it?

She was far too serious about things, Alison conceded. It didn't have to be for ever to be worthwhile.

*Around 10:30 if you can still make it.*

She held her breath and sent the text and then held it again till he replied: *Great.*

And Ellie was right again.

She didn't want to lie to her mum, she didn't want to *have* to lie to her mum, but she did enjoy having him in her life.

And he could never be boring. As for Ellie's other suggestion, well, the thought made her laugh.

Right there at the barbecue that evening, as she cut herself a slice of pavlova, she let out a little laugh so, yes, she did enjoy having him in her life, even when he wasn't there.

As she stood, chatting to her uncles and aunts, there was an inner glow in knowing that she would see him tomorrow, just this extra smile as she described the flat to her uncle Ken, because she'd seen it with Nick.

'I'm going to look at furniture tomorrow,' Alison said as her mum came over. 'I want to look at desks.'

'I might come along,' Rose replied. 'I was thinking of getting some bar stools for the kitchen bench. Are you taking Tim's car?'

It was one of the reasons she rarely drove; the car would always be Tim's. Her mother wouldn't part with it, insisted Alison use it, then got teary when she did.

'Actually, Nick's taking me.'

'Nick?' Ken smiled, pleased to see his favourite niece not just with a sparkle in her eyes but gently standing up to his sister-in-law.

'A friend from work,' Alison said, smiling back at her uncle.

And friends dropped around and friends were asked in.

'Mum, this is Nick.'

Alison tried very hard to treat him as if it were Ellie or Moira or just any friend coming in on Saturday morning before they headed out for a shopping expedition. Rose did the same as Alison finished getting ready, offering him a cup of tea, which Nick accepted, and chatting to him about the hospital and about England and how she and her late husband had wanted to take a trip around Europe when they retired.

'So you're just here for a couple of months, then?' Alison heard her mum saying as she walked into the kitchen.

'That's the plan.' Nick nodded. 'I've got a cousin in New Zealand who's getting married.' Nick was pleasant and polite, and from the way he chatted he was in no rush to head out—in fact, he even accepted Rose's offer of some toast and ginger marmalade.

'Alison can't stand it,' Rose said as Alison rolled her eyes. 'It was Tim's favourite.'

'Tim?' Nick said as the air in Alison's chest stopped moving.

'My son,' Rose said, and thankfully Nick didn't push. But his eyes swept past her a couple of times to the endless photos on the mantelpiece and when Alison went to her bedroom to find a missing shoe, it came as no surprise when Rose followed her.

'What time will you be back from the shops?'

'Actually…' Alison swallowed. 'There's a party on tonight. Vicky, one of the A and E nurses, is getting engaged.' She saw her mother's rapid blink. 'I told you last week.' Which she had, and it was true, except Vicky was actually Ellie's friend and Alison's was more a casual invitation than an expected guest, and she could have sworn she felt her nose grow a touch as she continued. 'She's down the road from Ellie—Ellie said I could stay at hers.' She gave her mum a hurried kiss on the cheek. 'I'll text and let you know what's happening.'

And then finally, *finally*, they were in the car and heading off, and following blue lines to a parking spot.

'You'd rather this than a bike ride in the mountains?' Alison commented as she grabbed a pencil and tape measure.

'We can do that another time,' Nick replied, and Alison walked on in silence. 'I've missed this.' He nudged her as they walked through. 'I'm not joking. I want to do something *normal*.'

He was actually very helpful. The fact he had seen the flat, combined with a male brain, meant he could remember strange details like there was a window where she wanted *that* large bookshelf, and that there was no way on earth that desk was going to fit where Alison intended.

'It's the same the world over.' Nick grinned as they sat in the canteen with their meatballs and chips and red berry jam amidst frazzled couples, yet maybe because they weren't a couple and it wasn't *their* bed or their sofa they were buying, they could just sit there and enjoy. Nick even bought her a little bottle of wine with a glass that screwed to the bottle.

'I'm going to keep this.' Alison was delighted.

'Emergency supplies for your bedroom!' Nick said, and went up to get one for himself too. It was just a tiny reference that he'd picked up on the tension at home, though he said nothing else about it.

Not until later, much later when they were sitting on the balcony, having eaten a mountain of prawns. Nick had cooked and Alison had tossed a salad—a ten-minute meal that would stay in her memory for ever. They were looking out at the ocean and the view was somehow nicer than the one from the bus and from the one walking on the beach. The sun was setting behind them, the colours reflecting on the water, and the waves were very active that evening. She had pinched one of his jumpers and it was worrying how nice his company was, how thrilling it felt to just be with him—for normal things to be so invigorating. He made no suggestion that they go out, or head off to Vicky's party, gave no indication the day had been less exciting than what he was used to.

In fact, for Nick, silence, mutual silence, was lovely.

For months now he'd been a guest—in another country, or at a friend's, or a hotel or hostel, or a hospital—with strangers who were about to become friends. Yes, it was fun and exhilarating, but it was also exhausting—perpetual new faces at breakfast, having to dress for bed in case you needed to get up in the night to go to the loo. It had been a welcome relief to have, after all this time, a flat to himself and a glimmer of a routine, but he shared that precious space with surprising ease now.

And looking over at Alison, who was staring out to the ocean she loved, there was no need to regale, just a deeper need to know, to go that bit further, to find out a little more, and so he asked her.

'What happened to Tim?'

She'd sort of known that the question would come all day, and in some way she'd been waiting for it.

'He was with my dad,' Alison said. 'They were fishing.' He didn't say anything and she was glad of that. 'The weather wasn't that bad, probably a day like this. They got into trouble, ended up too close to the rocks...'

'When?'

'Two, nearly three years ago. I'd finished my training—I was doing some shifts in emergency before I headed off overseas.'

'They weren't, I mean, you weren't there when they...?' She could hear the dread in his voice and immediately she shook her head.

'No. I wasn't at work or anything. I was sharing a

flat with friends. I got a call from Mum to come straight home and the police were at the house when I got there. It was all over by then.'

'Doesn't it kill you,' Nick said, after a very long silence, 'working in Emergency?'

Again Alison shook her head.

'I like it. Dad and Tim never even got to Emergency— at least the people who get there have some chance. It's nice to see that there are some happy endings, despite the most terrible odds.'

'It's not just the kids that upset you, is it?' He remembered that morning how he had learnt something, he just wasn't sure what.

'It's the family.' Alison nodded. 'All that's taken away, and the chaos that they're thrown into...not just the ones who are killed. Like with David. That interview was so important to him—and it all just fell apart. I know in the greater scheme of things his wife and daughter were far more important, but I can remember when Tim and Dad had their accident—I was supposed to be flying out at the weekend and I knew it didn't matter, but it did.' She closed her eyes as she tried to explain it. 'I felt selfish even thinking about me, but I did and I wanted someone to step in, to cancel the tickets, to deal with the airline, to deal with the details, to help look after Mum.'

'How's your mum now?'

Alison shrugged. 'Stuck in a time warp, really. I moved home when it happened, but...' She looked over into his kind green eyes and even though she'd sworn not to land it on him, somehow, under his gaze, she could. 'She's petrified of anything happening to me. I'm petrified of it too,' Alison admitted. 'Not for me, though, but for her. I mean, how would she cope if something happened to me?'

'You can't live like that.'

'I know,' Alison said. 'Which is why in a few weeks' time I'll have my own place, and won't have to account for my every move.' She gave him a smile, tried to move the conversation away, because he didn't belong in that space. 'It's complicated.' She gave a small shrug. 'It doesn't matter.'

Except it did.

It did matter, because when they were lying on his sofa and revisiting that kiss on the beach, only this time without Alison having her top on, when she should be able to close her eyes and just sink into him, she was all too aware that she was five minutes away from a call that needed to be made—a lie that she was willing to tell.

His back was against the sofa, his long legs holding her from falling, and there was a film coming to end of which they'd only seen the opening credits, and there was the bliss of privacy for them both. His mouth was on her ear and his hand was stroking her breast. Her hands, which had traced his chest, were stealing downwards now. They had left the balcony door open but neither the roar of the ocean nor his kiss in her ear could dull the call of duty. She wriggled back just a little, breathless and moist from his kiss. Yes, hell yes, she would lie for him.

'I've just got to make a phone call.' His mouth was in her neck and her body was in his arms and it was almost torture to pull just a little further away. She didn't know whether to pull on her top and hamper an easy return to his arms, but neither did she want to shiver half-naked in his bathroom.

'And tell her what?' His question came as a surprise, not to Alison but to Nick. He shouldn't ask, he told himself, because it was no business of his, and he shouldn't really care.

He just did.

'Nick?' She shook her head, would not elaborate—was a little cross even as he thwarted her attempts to stop reality invading. 'I won't be a moment.'

'Alison.' He caught her wrist and even though she'd been half-naked in his arms, she felt stupid standing there with her top half exposed, could feel the blush creeping down over her chest as he asked questions a man like Nick shouldn't have to. 'You don't have to lie for me.'

'Who said I'm lying?'

'They did.' He pointed to her rosy breasts and somehow she almost managed a smile.

'My mum's…' Alison swallowed, she truly didn't want to land him with all of it; even Ellie, who had seen it all, struggled to fathom how rigid her mother could be. 'She's difficult.'

'They often are,' Nick said, and he handed her her top. 'And with all she's been through.'

'She was the same before,' Alison admitted, 'though

when Dad and Tim were there...' She couldn't really explain, but without further explanation Nick seemed to understand.

'You weren't in the full spotlight?' When she nodded he continued, 'So where are you tonight?'

'Don't worry about it.' She tried blasé, tried casual, but Nick could tell otherwise and she knew it. 'You really picked the wrong girl to have your torrid Sydney fling with.'

And he looked up at her and was silent for a moment because, yes, he had. He could see stains of hurt in her serious brown eyes and he didn't want to add to them, except inevitably he already had. Already this was turning into something else, something bigger, something he hadn't come to Australia for.

'It doesn't feel like a fling,' Nick admitted.

'It's all it can be.' Alison was practical, even if she was shaking inside.

'Come on.' He stood and looked around for his keys. 'I'll walk you home.'

'It's five minutes away.'

And he should say goodnight here, Nick knew.

End it here.

But Nick never went for the easy option, so he reached for his keys.

'You're not walking on your own.'

They walked back to Alison's home in pensive silence, and he didn't kiss her on the doorstep, because he knew she didn't want him to, but as she let herself in her mouth still tingled from his and her body held the scent and memory of him. Her eyes must have glittered with stirred passion because Rose's face screamed of martyrdom as she offered Alison a cup of tea. Even though she didn't want tea, even though she wanted to go to bed and think of Nick and read the text he'd just sent because she could feel the vibration of her phone in her bag, that this time made her feel giddy with wanting to read it, she said, 'That would be nice,' and curled up on the sofa and took the mug from her mum.

'I thought you were at a party.'

And instead of saying she had been, or offering the usual half-truth, Alison was honest.

'We gave it a miss,' she admitted. 'We went back to Nick's for dinner.'

'He seems nice,' Rose said, because after all he'd brought her baby home.

'He is nice.'

'How long did he say he was here for?' Skilfully, so skilfully, Rose took the pin and deflated the bubble Alison was floating on. Carefully, lovingly, perhaps, she warned her daughter that this could never, ever be. 'Nice-looking man,' Rose said. 'He must have broken a few hearts on his travels,' she added, just to make sure her daughter got it.

'I'm going to bed.' Alison tried to keep her voice light.

She peeled off her clothes and read her text, which was hardly torrid, hardly from a man hell bent on getting in her knickers and promptly breaking her heart. It just thanked her for a nice day and a really nice night, that he'd enjoyed it.

She should stop this now, common sense said.

Just turn her back on his charm, because there really was no point.

She swam between the flags, certainly wasn't into casual relationships, and that was really all it could be with Nick. In a few weeks he'd be off and she'd be left, and if she wasn't extremely careful, Alison knew she'd be nursing a broken heart.

Actually, she already knew she would be.

He'd arrived in her life as blonde and as dazzling as summer. He just lit everything up and enhanced it all some more.

She didn't get him, but she wanted to.

She wanted the little bit of him that was possible, because there was something about Nick that got her, something that was…just a little bit like the single word she sent back to him.

*Same. x*

# CHAPTER EIGHT

'I'M NOT stalking you!'

She grinned as she walked across the foyer to Emergency on Monday night and Nick joined her. 'Amy asked yesterday if I could cover her week of nights.'

'Oh.'

'I got called in yesterday,' Nick explained.

'I didn't see you on the bus.'

'I drove. It was a last-minute thing. I didn't know whether to ring and offer a lift...' He admitted only a quarter of it—if the truth were told, he hadn't known what to do, full stop.

Despite her kisses, despite the thrum between them, there was more to Alison, of that he was sure. He didn't want to hurt anyone, didn't want to get involved.

Or that was what he had told himself.

Sunday had been spent turning down offers to go out, and not just from colleagues. He'd been called in for a multi-trauma late afternoon and had found a rather blatant card from a Louise H., reminding him where she worked and that she'd love to see him there.

It would actually have been the safer option.

Instead he'd accepted Amy's suggestion they ring out for takeaways, which they'd eaten in her office. The conversation had been easy and before he'd known it, the clock had been edging towards midnight and he'd agreed to take over her week of nights.

But Alison was on nights too.

He headed straight for the staffroom, Alison to her locker, and if she hurried there was time for a drink before she started.

'God!' Moira was tying back her hair. 'I'm tired before we've even started. Try sharing a house with eight travellers and doing a week of night shift!' She gave her dazzling smile. 'All worth it, though.' They walked through to the staffroom and Moira gave a delighted whoop as she saw Nick. 'Are you on nights too?'

''Fraid so.'

'Now, that *does* cheer me up,' Moira said, and she was just so light and uninhibited with her banter, Alison would have killed for a little of the same. 'There's not a spare room at that fancy house of yours, is there?' Moira rattled on. 'For a fellow travelling night worker?'

'It's a one-bedroomed flat.' Nick grinned.

'Move over in the bed, then!' Moira winked. Of course, she had no idea about Alison and Nick, she was just having fun...

Sort of.

'Alison.' Sheila popped her head around the staffroom door. 'We've had a lot of staff ring in sick tonight. Mary will be in charge, but apart from that it's agency.' She gave a brief smile to Moira and a couple of the others. 'Luckily it's been quiet. The wards all have beds, so you shouldn't have too many problems. Can you make sure the restocking and drug orders get done, and make sure the trolleys are all wiped down. Oh, and there's a list up on the notice-board—you need to do a refresher lifting course. Make sure you tick off what session you're attending.'

So Alison did, and tried not listen to Moira's chatter and Nick's easy replies—tried not to feel as if he was surely thinking he'd set his sights on the wrong girl. After all, he and Moira were both here on holiday.

This was her life.

It showed in so many little ways through out the night, perhaps because it was a particularly quiet one.

Moira and the other nurses sat chatting when it was quiet.

Alison did the stock ordering. Working around them, she climbed up on footstools to count packets of gauze, and to everyone else Nick appeared not to notice her. He did notice, she knew, because she could feel his lingering eyes at times, or a smile that was there waiting every now and then when she looked up and turned round.

He was brilliant with each and every patient that came through the doors, but during the many, many lulls that filled this quiet night Nick scrolled through his social networking site—there was no registrar's office bulging with a backlog of work for him...probably because there was no backlog when you were just passing through.

'Moira,' Alison asked, 'can you put these boxes away?'

'Sure.' Moira jumped off her stool. 'Where do they go?'

'In the second storage room.'

And she *was* willing, but by the time Alison had shown her where it was, and when for the third time she had to borrow Alison's ID to gain access, it was just far easier to do it herself. There was just a touch of a martyred air to Alison as an hour later she took a gulp of cold tea in the nurses' station and found out all the biscuits she'd brought in were gone.

'I've bought earplugs,' Moira chatted on happily, 'but hopefully everyone will be so hungover, no one will be up before midday and I can get some peace and quiet. I'm a shocking sleeper on nights. What about you, Nick?'

'Sorry?'

'How do you sleep on nights?'

'Like a log,' Nick said, without looking up from the computer, and Alison realised that despite being pleasant, despite the good-natured bantering, there was no flirting from Nick, that he gave nothing back to Moira, as he hadn't to Louise. It was aimed all at her, Alison realised as now he did look up from the computer and gave her a very nice smile, those green eyes turning her pink as she gave a small smile back.

'Is there anything you need me to do?'

'Nothing,' Alison said. It was five a.m., the board was clear and as Nick checked an X-ray with the resident he stretched and yawned. 'I'm going to lie down—call if you need me.'

'Lucky,' Alison grumbled, hauling out the trolleys to be cleaned, and for just a moment their eyes met and Nick felt as if he was back in far North Queensland, standing on a platform with a piece of elastic around his ankle, wanting to jump, knowing it was reckless, ridiculous, that there was no rhyme nor reason to it, yet wanting to all the same.

'What time do you finish?'

'By the time we've given handover—about seven-thirty.'

'I'm here till eight, if you want to hang around—I'll be quicker than the bus.'

He would be, there wasn't one till ten minutes to.

'Thanks,' Alison said.

She cleaned and polished the trolleys, and tried not to think about it as she dealt with the occasional patient, who was seen by the resident and didn't require Nick.

In the morning, when Moira was still teasing for a loan of his bed and he was skilfully deflecting her thinly disguised offer, the rest of the night team, apart from Mary, sped off on the dot of seven-thirty. Alison hung around for a quick chat with Ellie, put her name on the list for the lifting refresher course and then, when Sheila asked if she had five more minutes to go over some annual leave requests, she nodded. When there was nothing else to linger for, except Nick, he walked down the corridor, blonde, tired, offering a lift. Alison smiled and said thanks.

When with him, when it was just them, the doubts that plagued her when they were apart were silenced as always.

'Better than the bus?' Nick asked as she sank back into the passenger seat.

'This morning—yes,' Alison admitted.

'Do you drive?' He glanced over.

'Sometimes—I just prefer the bus for work. The traffic getting in and the staff car-park is impossible sometimes so it's nice just to sit and read the paper.'

'It's been nice *not* driving,' Nick admitted, 'but I can't stand the thought of a bus ride after being on all night—I'd fall asleep.'

'It's always happening to me,' Alison said. 'I end up being woken by the driver.'

He was so easy to talk to—about the complicated, about the mundane—but even though they chatted easily, there was a definite charge in the air, which had a sleepy Alison on the alert. He must have shaved yesterday morning, rather than before coming to work, because he was clearly unshaven now, she noticed. Just as she noticed when he pulled on dark glasses against the glare of the morning sun. Just as she noticed his long tanned fingers tapping on the steering-wheel as they sat in heavy traffic.

'Do you sleep well?' Nick asked, because he had heard about the whole nursing crew's habits and he wanted to find out about hers.

'Depends,' Alison said. 'Mum's at work so the house is quiet...' And her voice trailed off, because somehow that charge in the air intensified, and there was this pause, this silent pondering, a false night that stretched ahead and a shining window of opportunity.

'Do you want to go somewhere for breakfast?' Nick asked as the bay came into view.

'No, thanks,' Alison said, because she wasn't thinking about breakfast.

Just bed.

Bed.

And though they were both tired and sleepy and longing for bed, as he pulled up outside her door, there was no denying it—they were longing for each other too— and as naturally as breathing she turned to him. There was no awkwardness, no will he, won't he, just the bliss of a night spent looking and thinking and pretending you didn't want to, all melting away now that no one else was around. It was a really nice kiss, a slow, morning kiss that could tip easily to more, but there was no way she was asking him in because Alison knew where his kiss could lead and probably there was no chance of her mum coming home, but she just couldn't put herself or her mother in that situation.

'Have a good sleep.' She pulled her mouth away, but she wanted to dive back in.

'I doubt it,' Nick said, and Alison doubted she would either.

She was a kiss away from his bed, Nick knew that, and for the first time in his quest for freedom Nick felt as if he needed to spell out the rules, needed to be very sure that she knew, and so he said it.

He made himself say it.

'I can't stay...'

And she smiled and was very brave, even managed a little joke. 'I didn't ask you in.'

But he wasn't talking about that—she knew he wasn't talking about that as she climbed out of his car.

He watched her walk up the garden path and for the first time in a long time, at least where women were concerned, Nick was confused—Nick the one almost willing her not to turn round—because of how much he wanted her, and for the foreseeable future, this wasn't how it was supposed to be.

Except this was how it was.

She was exhausted, utterly and completely exhausted, but though her body ached for bed as she walked up her garden path, she ached for him too. It was just criminal that a few streets apart he'd be in bed and she'd be in bed and they had a whole day, a whole wonderful day, if only she would take it. She had her key in the front door, and she opened it, turned round to give him a wave, and he just sat there, looking at her, and she stood there, looking at him, and wished he'd drive off, would just go, except he didn't.

Then she panicked that he would drive off, that he'd pull off the handbrake and she'd miss her chance.

Her one lovely chance to be wild and brave and sexy and impulsive.

Alison slammed the door closed again and turned round. She could see his smile even from the garden, see the want in his eyes as she made the one reckless decision of her life and sped down the garden path. He had the passenger door open before Alison got there. She jumped in like an eager puppy, and he was an equally eager master because he was pulling her in and kissing her, this smothering kiss that sighed and groaned with mutual consent of what was to come. There was just a flicker of sanity, of what would the neighbours think because it was eight a.m. and they were necking like teenagers. Then he pulled back and gave her the most fantastic smile and Alison, who had craved wild, craved passion and adventure, took a breath, took the plunge, and what she said was from her wildest dreams, because she said what Alison Carter would never have—looked into eyes that looked into hers, and in the mirror of them she saw herself, found herself, was finally herself. 'I want breakfast in bed.'

# CHAPTER NINE

HE KISSED her even as the front door closed and for a moment, just a moment, she did wonder what the hell she was doing and tried not to worry that she'd been working all night and must smell of hospitals, consoling herself, that so too must he, but then his kiss did its magic, produced an Alison that only he could.

'You taste fantastic.' She said her thoughts out loud, because with him she could, and his hands roamed her body, as they had been longing to all night, and she leant against the hall wall and he kissed her some more.

It was a relief to get to the bedroom.

Yes, it had the most stunning view from the bedroom, except they didn't want to see it. It was an exercise in frustration as they tried to quickly close the blinds and for the first time she heard him swear as it stuck halfway down, but then, yippee, they were closed and he was kissing her again.

'God, Alison…' He made light work of the buttons on her blouse because he'd been undoing them in his head all night. He stripped her—it was such a brilliant word, Alison thought. He stripped her blouse, her navy three-quarter-length Capri pants, he stripped her mind of doubt because his hands and mouth adored her, he stripped her of care and worry till all that was left was her bra and panties and a mind that was free. Now it was her turn and she would, Alison decided as she took off the grey shirt he had been wearing that first day, remember this for ever and ever, because she'd been guessing and peeking and driving herself insane with imagination. Now the big day was here and, unlike Nick, she didn't tear open the wrappers on her parcels. No, she had a nice feel of his chest through the material, tried one more image of what might be inside and slowly, very slowly, tongue on her bottom lip, she peeled one button open, and then another, and he was telling her to hurry but she refused to be rushed.

One more button and she could see a flat brown nipple. She ran her hand over it then bent her head and kissed it, and she could feel his hands undoing her bra, feel the drop of aching breasts as he freed her. Yet still she would not be rushed. She had his shirt open a little more now, down to that lovely flat stomach, and all his online pictures combined couldn't capture how nice it was in real life, taut and smooth. She ran her hands over him and he was pulling off her bra and she slid down his shirt and then she went back for another taste of his nipple, heard him moan, felt his hands in her hair and then he moved them, because Nick wanted his pants down.

'Don't spoil my fun.' She pushed his hands away and she was cruel and she wasn't kind. She fiddled with the button and refused to let him help her. He was breathing so hard, his hands toying with her bottom, laid-back Nick, just brimming now with urgency, but she was in no rush.

Well, maybe a little bit, because beneath linen pants that he almost fell over to step out of were the sexiest hipsters and she felt him again, gave her present a little squeeze to gauge it and she couldn't tease any more, because she wanted to see, she wanted to feel, wanted what was hers. And he was completely spectacular, and hers for now and she held it, over and over she held it, till her breathing was doing strange things now, because he had his hands on the cheeks of her bottom and was pressing her into him, and his mouth was on hers and then he wanted more, more of her than he should sensibly want, because when he should be diving in he was diving down, pushing her on the bed and running his mouth up her thighs, and it was Nick in no rush now.

He kissed and he teased and he relished her throb in his mouth, but there was this strange moment, a warning almost, because though it felt like sex and tasted of it too, it was teetering into something more. A place where he had to *remember* to stop, to put on a condom, not just slide up and slide in as he so badly wanted to. A different place, because as he drove deep within her, why was he saying her name over and over?

And this was what he did, Alison reminded herself as she tried to hold back, tried and failed to cling onto that last bit of restraint.

This was what that smile promised, Alison told

herself, except her body didn't want to register dire warnings, it wanted to be free, and trapped beneath him, finally she was.

'It's the quiet ones you have to worry about.' She lay next to Nick and smiled at his voice as she came back to earth and when half an hour later, still neither were sleeping, she said yes when he offered to make a drink and lay there, just a little awkward as to what he was thinking as she heard him walk out to the kitchen.

What *was* he thinking?

Nick wasn't sure as he filled a glass with water and emptied it in one and then, rather than think, he flicked on the television as he waited for the kettle to boil. But there was no solace there, an armchair psychologist was telling him to face up to feelings, to be honest with himself—only Nick didn't want to.

'How many sugars?' he called down the hall, because *that* was how it should be, except he remembered before she even answered.

'Have you got any sweeteners?'

He didn't, so she settled for sugar then grumbled that it tasted different as he climbed in bed beside her, then admitted, as Nick lay there, that she actually preferred the real thing.

'It's bad for you, though,' Nick said, and he'd forgotten to turn the television off, so he padded back out and aimed the remote like a loaded gun, because honesty was not the best policy here.

It wasn't just Alison he was worried about hurting here.

It was himself.

# CHAPTER TEN

SHE could tell it was Tuesday the second she stepped inside. The slow cooker was on and the scent of beef stroganoff filled the house. Her heart was in her mouth as she waited for her mum to appear and say she'd been off sick and where the hell had she been all day, but the house was still and silent. Alison checked her mobile and the house phone and there were no messages, and *starving* Alison had some stroganoff between two slices of bread and butter then showered and headed straight to bed, to cram in a couple more hours' sleep, which she managed amazingly well. She was woken at six-thirty by her mum's knock on the door.

'Did you sleep well?'

'Really well,' Alison said, hiding her guilty blush.

'Good. I tried not to wake you when I came in. Dinner's almost ready.'

'How was work?' Alison asked as they sat and ate dinner. It was a nice dinner and a nice conversation and they even had a laugh. Alison would miss this and did love her so, it was just the little things that added up, like Nick wanting the crossword and Paul's garlic bread, that built and built until they became big things and change really was needed, because a row with her mother, hurting her mother, Alison would avoid at all costs.

Little things like Rose insisting she take leftovers for her meal break.

'I can put some in a container and you can have it on your break,' Rose offered.

'Put it in the freezer,' Alison said. 'I think I'll get something from the canteen.'

'From the vending machine?' Rose said.

'They do sandwiches and things and there are nice vol-au-vents.'

'Why would you pay for something when you can take it in?' Rose said, pulling out a container and filling it with Tuesday's beef stroganoff.

'I just fancy—'

'You need to be more careful—you've got a mortgage to think of now.'

She took the stroganoff.

Still, it *was* appreciated.

By Nick, who was sick of canteen sandwiches and mushroom vol-au-vents.

To describe a busy week of night shifts as the best week of her life would have once been laughable, but for the first time since the tragedy Alison actually glimpsed normality in upside-down week.

A gorgeous normality where work was busy, a happy normality where she ate dinner with her mum each night and packed leftover dinner for her evening break.

An easy normality, where she didn't have to lie, well, not outright, and she didn't have to race home at midnight. All she had to do was be.

Nick would drive her home. More often than not she'd see her mum at the bus stop or pop in just to check that she had gone, and, just to be sure, Alison would leave a little note on the kitchen bench that read something like, *Gone shopping*, or *At dentist*, which she'd tear up when she got home at four. Then she'd grab some clothes and race down the street to Nick's car, to him, to a gorgeous normality, where they shut the blinds on the world and lay in bed and talked and laughed, and made lovely love, or rather, she corrected herself, had torrid, wild sex and slept.

She knew from the start, though, that it couldn't last.

'Can I borrow you before you go, Nick?' Amy clipped in for her day shift at the end of the week, all scented, suited and gorgeous, as an exhausted Alison subtly hung back for her lift.

'I shouldn't be long,' Nick managed as he disappeared into his colleague's office, but no matter how many times Alison checked the staff roster, and no matter how chatty her colleagues were, by eight-fifteen she was starting to look as if she had no home to go to.

'Where is Amy?' Sheila barked from a cubicle, then marched out to the intercom. 'It's all very well swapping her shifts, but the occasional appearance on the shop floor would be nice.' Her voice was a lot sweeter when she pressed the button. 'Amy, we need you out here.'

'Is it urgent?' came Nick's voice, and Sheila rolled her eyes.

'Pressing, not urgent.'

'Let us know if that changes,' came Nick's firm reply.

'Good luck!' Alison smiled to Sheila as she heaved up her bag and headed for the bus stop, but despite a rapid run she missed it and despite the sun she shivered at the stop, tired and, as Nick's car pulled up a full twenty minutes later, just a little fed up.

'Sorry about that.'

It would have been childish not to get in.

'I was thinking…' Nick negotiated the early-morning traffic easily, even laughed when she grumbled about rush-hour, telling her she should try driving where he lived in England if she wanted a *real* rush-hour, and then he got back to thinking. 'How about we do the Sydney Harbour Bridge climb this weekend?'

'I can't even think about bridges and climbing at this hour.'

'It will be fun.'

Alison could think of other words to describe it and her eyes flicked to the clock on the dashboard—had she left on time and taken the bus, she'd already be in bed. 'What did Amy want?' It was a childish question to ask perhaps, or perhaps it was the edge to her voice, because Nick glanced over.

'There was something she needed to discuss.'

Which gave her no answer and the silence wasn't

comfortable as he stopped at the traffic lights and again he looked over at her.

'Don't ask me to betray a confidence, Alison, just because we're...' His eyes shuttered for a moment, perhaps ruing his near choice of words. 'Work's separate,' Nick said. 'We both agreed.'

It wasn't a row, it wasn't anything she could pin down, yet stupidly she felt like crying, relieved almost when Nick stopped at a corner shop and got out. 'I need milk.'

And it was a tiny time out, a welcome time out, because by the time he came out of the shop, all gorgeous and yawning, Alison had convinced herself she was tired, that was all, not questioning and jealous, just ratty, premenstrual and coming off a full week of sex and nights.

'Here.' He handed her one of two newspapers he had bought, gave her a kiss and then smiled. 'There's always a simple solution.'

There just wasn't to this.

And even if they were talking, even if there hadn't been a row, things felt different this morning.

Nick had a call from his boss in the UK then another from his mum, both reminding Alison there was a world that was waiting for him to rejoin it, and she was all too aware that next week she'd be back on days, which meant home by midnight, that the slice of freedom she'd carved for them was drawing to a close and it was either lie there and cry or just pretend to be asleep when a long hour later, damp from the shower, his tired body slipped into bed.

'Alison?' She heard his voice and didn't answer, lay with her eyes closed till she didn't have to pretend any more, didn't have to pretend that she could do this, but it was a fitful sleep, an uneasy sleep. She woke at two, and looked over at him and he really was exquisite.

Alison didn't generally prefer blonds—she just preferred Nick.

He must have felt her wake, because he stirred a bit beside her, rolled a little toward her and his legs trapped hers and pulled her in a bit so her face was closer to his chest. She'd been enjoying looking, but now she was enjoying feeling the sleepy body beside hers as she lay awake, exploring the sensation of his long limbs loosely wrapped around hers and the scent of him. There was more than just thought there, because it woke him, this energy, this want that hauled him from slumber, because he slid her up a little till their faces met.

'Morning.'

'Morning,' Alison answered, even if it was mid-afternoon and, better than a kiss, he answered what was still on her mind.

'Amy was offering me more work.'

'Overtime?'

'Extra time,' Nick said. 'She was just sounding me out, there's nothing definite...'

'Isn't Cort coming back?' Alison blinked, curious for other reasons. Cort had taken leave suddenly three months ago, and all the senior staff had been tight-lipped as to why—as Nick was being now.

'It's not that.' He closed his eyes. 'You can't say anything.'

'I wouldn't.' But Nick wouldn't reveal any more. Still, that he was considering staying was what she wanted to hear, but she knew his struggle, because hers was the same. 'What about Asia?'

'I can't do both.'

'Could you, though?' Alison asked. 'Could you take more time off?'

'They very reluctantly gave me this year.' It was too much to think about, too much to consider, so he pulled her closer instead and there were forty-seven minutes, give or take, till she had to up and leave, and they both smiled at that pleasurable thought.

Both awake, and even if their minds were racing with new possibilities, their bodies were still pliant and just a little lazy, because they moved in just a little closer, and his legs wrapped around hers a little tighter. The bed was so warm and it felt so nice, and Alison gladly kissed him back, which was so much better than thinking about Asia and careers and sky-high bridges, except the thoughts were in the bed with them too, because it wasn't fair, Alison thought, as his kiss deepened. It wasn't bloody fair, his mouth agreed as he pulled her in tighter. A little lazy, a little bit angry, a little bit reckless, or just greedy for a little bit more. When he pulled her even closer, Alison didn't move back, or away. She could feel his warm, heavy length between her legs, and she wanted him there, and he wanted to be there, because there he stayed a while.

She felt a low tremble in her body as he ran his tip over her moist place, she could feel his kiss deepen even more, feel the tightening of her throat and the flood of desire that bade him on, not consciously, more naturally, just a deepening kiss at both ends of their bodies, and he was just a little way in and her body willed him to go further, beat for him to join her. But sense hauled them back from that dangerous place, Nick rolling over and sheathing himself, Alison dizzy at what they had almost done but grateful for common sense prevailing. Then he was back and, yes, they were both angry, not with the other but at time that wouldn't pause. With every thrust she counted the days and her hips rose, defiant at the injustice.

She *was* angry.

And he let her be.

He let her be selfish and taste his mouth and his chest for as long as she wanted, he let her tension rise till she thought she might push him off, because she didn't know how to feel like this, she didn't know how far she could go. So he showed her, he pushed her, he waited for her, till she stopped counting the days and berating the past, stopped chasing the future till she was in an empty, silent space that was theirs alone to fill—with her scream and his release, with new sensations, deeper sensations than either had felt before.

And something shifted, something definitely shifted, because a little while later, when the alarm bleeped its warning, for the first time Nick grumbled, pulled her back when she said she had to go.

'Stay a bit longer,' Nick said.

And she did.

Alison reset the alarm and climbed back in, wondering if in a few weeks he'd do the same for her.

# CHAPTER ELEVEN

LIKE Louise Haversham's toothache, sometimes the agony woke her, but for a while, if she didn't push or probe, Nick's nearing departure was kept at a niggle, a gnawing in the background. Two months had never seemed long enough. In fact, by the time she'd met him, a week of that had already passed, by the time she'd decided to just go for it, another week, and since then she'd seen Sydney thorough the eyes of a tourist, had been on whale-watching trips and a jet-board ride, though she'd declined his suggestion for a tandem sky dive! With the keys to the flat soon to be hers, they were in the final countdown and it wasn't just her feeling it, at every turn she was reminded of the fact. But the hint that Cort's return might be delayed was her ray of hope on the horizon and Alison was determined to let it shine.

'These are for you!' David said. 'For all of you.' But he smiled especially at Alison as he handed over a large tin of chocolates and he was a different man indeed from the one she had met just a month ago. 'Rebecca's here for her outpatient appointment. We just wanted to stop by and thank everyone.'

'You're more than welcome.' Alison jumped down from her stool and accepted the chocolates. It rarely happened, but when patients came back, it was a treat indeed.

'How's the arm?' Alison asked, and she was thrilled to see Rebecca wiggle all her fingers.

'I'm doing loads of physio, but I'm getting there.' She smiled as Nick and Amy came over and she showed them her moving fingers again.

'I'm glad you're here,' David said to Nick. 'We thought you might be back on your travels.'

'A couple more weeks yet,' Nick said, and Amy rolled her eyes.

'What will we do without you?'

And that niggle was flaring. It was a line Alison was starting to hear far too often when she was around Nick, and it shot an arrow into her heart each and every time she heard it.

'We really are grateful,' David said, and Alison looked at his suit and his smile and the new-found confidence in this family and knew what was coming. 'I got that job, by the way.'

'Fantastic.' She could not have been more pleased. 'That's marvellous.' She was delighted for them all.

'Hello, there!' Ellie joined them and chatted for a moment. 'Has it really been a month?'

And it had been and it was, because just a couple of days later Alison had a mortgage and a set of keys.

'I don't remember the carpet being *this* green.' She

walked around with Nick and wondered if she'd bought the same place. 'Were the walls really brown?'

'It will look great with furniture.' Nick was optimistic and then realistic. 'And a coat of paint.' He saw her glance up at the grey ceiling and then blow her fringe skywards at the job ahead. 'I'll help you. We can go and look at paint this evening and get it done over the next few days.'

'You've got better things to do than paint a flat,' Alison pointed out.

'No.' He pulled her towards him. 'I like spending time with you—here.' He pulled out a present from the bag he had been carrying that had had Alison wondering, and she opened it and it was a plant in a bright red pot that he put on the tiny balcony table. 'That's the garden sorted.'

Then he pulled out champagne and, of course, he'd forgotten glasses, but as they had that night on the beach they sat on the floor and drank from the bottle. Though it was cool and fizzy, Alison just had a mouthful because, yes, the flat was hers and Nick was here and it was a great day, but somehow she was finding it hard to feel like celebrating, especially when Nick pointed out she should hold off getting her furniture delivered till the flat had been painted. It was practical, sensible of course, but she wanted to move in so badly.

'We'll get it done in a week,' Nick said. 'Then we've still got...' His voice trailed off, because then all they would have was a week.

And it just got ever closer—the future was fast

approaching and it caught up at six p.m. on the Friday. Alison was trying to wrestle damp legs into her stockings as her mum chatted to Nick in the lounge.

There was a seafood restaurant at the Quay Nick wanted to try and even if it was supposed to be gorgeous and the views and food to die for, Alison was exhausted and, frankly, a box of noodles and a DVD would have sufficed.

She peered at her slightly pale reflection and added a dash more blusher. She could hear the laughter from the living room, because even Rose seemed to have loosened up and was getting on with Nick. Everyone did. It just made it harder, that was all.

'Ready!' She was wearing high heels and a black dress with a sheer black blouse over it, and her hair was behaving. Nick's eyes lit up in pleasure as she walked in and Alison's did the same.

He was in dark trousers and a dark shirt, which accentuated his blondness. She wished her flat was ready and he had picked her up from there!

'What time's the table booked for?' Rose asked.

'Seven,' Nick said, 'so we'd better get a move on.' He kissed Alison on the cheek and he was clearly thinking along the same lines as she was because as Rose turned her attention to the television, he whispered the real time in her ear. 'Eight,' he said, and that made her smile. They were just about to dash off for their supposed seven p.m. booking, but really his flat, when his phone rang. He glanced at it, about to ignore it, then frowned. 'I'd better get this.'

Alison sorted out her bag and checked for lipstick and things as Nick went out to the little garden, and she could hear the restrained delight in his voice, hear him laugh, hear him talk. 'It's a huge surprise!' she heard him say. 'Thanks so much for considering me.' She glanced over at her mum and forced a smile, then poured herself a glass of water as Nick spoke for a little while longer and then came in.

'Work,' Nick said, and Alison gave a tiny frown.

'In England.'

'Oh.'

Rose suddenly remembered she had the iron on in the laundry and Nick must have remembered that he oughtn't to smile quite so widely, because he contained his delight just a touch. 'They've asked me to cut short my trip. Not this bit,' he added hastily, 'just get back from Asia a month early.' As she listened she found out that one of his seniors was leaving and there was a fast track to consultant, and she did absolutely everything right. Alison smiled and kissed him and offered congratulations, but it was the strangest feeling, because she was wishing him well for a time that didn't involve her.

'I haven't said yes,' Nick pointed out.

'It's still something to celebrate—so it's my turn to get the champagne!' Alison said, and she kissed him. She really tried, she did everything right, but Nick couldn't help but compare it to the more genuinely happy response she'd had to David's news, and it didn't irk him.

He got it.

Somehow they didn't dash back to his place for some alone time. Instead, by unvoiced mutual consent, they headed straight to Darling Harbour, walked around for half an hour and then shared a meal that should have been sumptuous, but there was just this sadness in the air and it was Nick who broached it.

'It's not looking hopeful for Asia.'

Alison forced a tight smile. 'You've got offers all round. What's happening with Cort?'

'Cort?' Nick frowned.

'Amy said there might be a spot…'

'That's still up in the air.

'It's going to be harder than I thought.' He took her hand, but it stayed in a ball beneath his. 'Saying goodbye.'

'It's going to be exactly as hard as I thought,' Alison said, and her eyes flashed with tears for the very first time.

'It doesn't have to end just because—'

'Oh, please…' She was almost accusing. 'I'll accept your friendship on Facebook.' Then she shook her head, because she wouldn't.

Because she could not stand the thought of following him, reading about him, and not having him. That at some point she'd have to block him, because he was taking with him her heart.

'We can still keep things going…' But he didn't push it, he paid the bill and though there was conversation, both were hurting.

'Alison,' Nick said as he pulled up at her house, neither having even suggested they go to his place for a while. 'I never intended… I mean…'

'Why couldn't you have been boring?' Alison turned to him. 'Why couldn't I have found you in high heels and my underwear?' And she started to laugh, but it was squeezed out with tears and Nick pulled her into him and held her for a moment.

'I'll pick you up tomorrow, we'll talk, we'll try and work something out.' His mind raced for solutions, and there was but one he could think of and that required deeper thought. 'Tomorrow,' Nick said, 'I'll pick you up.'

'I don't want to paint.'

'We're not going to paint,' Nick said. 'We're going to work something out. You just be ready at ten.'

'For what?'

'Eight letters,' Nick smiled. 'Starts with S, ends with E.'

'I hate surprises.'

He cupped her face with his hand and looked over to her, as if reading her for the very first time. 'You really do, don't you?'

And she pulled away, stepped out of the car and headed into her house—just a touch shaken by what he'd said, a touch unsure what he'd meant.

A touch worried that he'd stepped on a truth.

# CHAPTER TWELVE

'HI, MUM.' She was tired and confused and all Alison wanted was bed, but Rose seemed determined to chat.

'How was it?'

'Lovely,' Alison said.

'You're early.'

'I'm just tired.'

'You didn't go for a walk afterwards?' Rose asked. 'Or back to his place for coffee?'

'I told you…' Alison frowned, unsure what Rose was getting at, but she found out a split second later when her mother's hand slapped her cheek, and furious words erupted from her.

'You tell me nothing!' Rose snarled, and then she tossed a handful of little packages at Alison, like confetti to a bride. 'Strawberry flavoured…' Rose sneered. 'Banana flavoured—you tart!'

'Mum, please…' Shamed, embarrassed, shocked, still she tried to calm things down, but Rose would not let her speak.

'How could you, Alison?'

'I'm twenty-four!' She spelt it out, repeated it, said it again, but Rose would not relent.

'How could you?'

She was seventeen again, only there wasn't her dad or Tim to deflect her mother. It was ridiculous and they both knew it—and for the first time Alison told her mother so.

'You turned a blind eye with Paul.'

'Paul was serious about you!' came Rose's savage reply.

'So's Nick. He's not using me.' Alison's voice was rising, but she wasn't just arguing with Rose, she was arguing with herself. 'It's not some fling…'

'It's exactly what it is,' Rose responded. 'What? Do you think he's going to give it all up? You heard him tonight. He's got a promotion. It couldn't possibly work. And you're *sleeping* with him.' It was all too close to the bone for Alison and she sat there and tried to take it, but Rose would not stop. 'You were always trouble, always the one we worried about, always wild, and yet it was poor…' She stopped, but not in time. The words might just as well have been said—Alison had lived, Tim had died. It stung and it burnt and tears shot from her eyes, not just at her mother's thoughts but what she had done to her brother's memory.

'Tim was fun, Tim knew how to laugh. You've canonised him, Mum, you've turned him into some sort of saint. No matter what I do, I can never live up to him.'

'Alison…' Rose maybe realised she had gone too far. 'This isn't about Tim, it's about this man.'

'This man,' Alison said, 'is called Nick, and he makes me laugh and he makes me happy. And…' she threw the condoms on the floor '…you have no right to go through my things. I can't wait to move out!' In fact, she didn't have to wait now. 'I'm going.'

'With him?'

And Rose broke down then, just melted onto the chair. And Alison wanted to storm out, to go to bed, to curl up in a ball, but instead she sat with her arms around her mum, her own tears not helping her stinging cheek. Yes, it was a row that had needed to be had, but Alison knew what it was really all about.

'I was talking about the flat. I'm not going to England, Mum.' She stroked her mum's shoulders. 'He's not going to ask, and if by some miracle he did, I wouldn't go.'

She wouldn't.

She couldn't.

She'd had it confirmed now.

It wasn't about Nick, it wasn't about England. It could be Thailand, or a bungee jump, or a car, or a wave, and the row would have been the same. Even if cruel words had been spoken, she knew she was loved—it just stifled her.

'I'm not going to England,' Alison repeated. 'I may be moving into a flat, but I'm not going to leave you—I never would, Mum. But—' she was firm, really firm with her mum for the first time '—I do have to live.'

## CHAPTER THIRTEEN

IT WAS horribly awkward the next morning.

'Yes, please' to tea, and 'No, thanks' to toast.

And 'You should eat something.'

'I'm honestly not hungry.' Alison wasn't—she felt sick when she thought of the condoms, and just all churned up from their row. She had no idea what was happening today either. She had a bikini on beneath her denim skirt and halter neck and something a little more dressy laid out on her bed, in case…well, just in case Nick's plans were upmarket.

'Mum,' Alison tried, 'about last night…'

'Let's forget about that,' Rose said. 'It's sorted now.'

Except it wasn't, Alison knew that. She looked at her mum's strained face, at the panic that was always in her eyes, and it was more than Alison could deal with, more than she could help with, and she broached what she had once or twice before.

'Have you thought about talking to someone?' Alison swallowed. 'That grief counsellor you saw…'

'Can they bring them back?' Rose shook her head.

'Anyway, I'm fine. I am sorry about last night, I had no right to go through your things.'

'Mum,' Alison attempted, but the conversation was closed.

'What are you up to today?'

'I've no idea,' Alison admitted. 'Nick's planning something.'

And to Rose's credit she gave a bright smile. 'That sounds exciting.' But her smile faded as there was a low rumble in the street and as Rose went to the window she glanced anxiously at her daughter.

'Nick's here,' Rose said. 'On a bike.'

And, worse, he had two helmets.

'Hi, Rose.' Nick grinned. 'I'm taking Alison to Palm Beach—where they film that soap…'

'Nick…' She could see her mother's bleached face and knew she had to do something. 'I haven't been on a bike.'

'I'm the one riding it,' Nick said. 'All you have to do is hold on. Come on, Alison, I've got everything planned.'

The sun was in his eyes, so maybe he couldn't see her expression. Part of her knew she was being ridiculous, he was hardly going to go roaring off. It *should* have been the perfect surprise; it almost was. She wanted to grab the helmet he was offering, to climb on, to be the young woman she once had been, to spend a precious day with the man she adored.

So she tried.

'See you, Mum.'

'Alison, be ca—' And Rose tried too because she smothered down her warning. 'Have a good day.'

'I'll call you,' Alison promised, before her mum asked, and there was fear and trepidation but a certain exhilaration too as she took the helmet and did as he asked and just held on.

She held onto his back and felt the machine thrum into life, her lips tightly closed, breathing through her nose, utterly rigid as they made their way through the city and over the vast bridge. She wanted so many times to tell him to stop, to let her off, and yet there was a thrill, a thrill that felt almost like pure joy as they left the city behind. The bay glistened ever more beautiful with every turn, every incline, and Alison found out what it meant to leave her worries behind.

'Amazing, isn't it?' He paused the bike and they sat for a moment just admiring, and Alison waited for him to take a photo, but he didn't, he just sat and gazed out and drank it all in.

'We used to come here for a drive on Sundays,' Alison said. 'When we were kids,' she explained. 'If we go back a couple of kilometres, there's a nice picnic spot.'

'I've got it all worked out,' Nick said, turning the engine back on, and instead of going back they went on, further than she had been, and it felt faster too, but a faster that didn't unsettle her. She had her cheek pressed into his back, could feel the heat from his body and the blue of the water before her eyes and the wind on her legs and her hair whipping her mouth, and she wanted the road to last for ever.

Nick really had worked it out. He took the bike off the beaten path and he really had found the perfect spot. It was cool and mossy and a thick curtain of trees allowed no glimpse of the ocean, but you could hear the rumble of it in the background as they spread out the blanket and opened up the food.

'I couldn't sleep last night,' Nick admitted, opening up some wine as she scooped out rice onto plastic plates and shared out prawns. 'How about you?'

'It wasn't a great night…' Alison admitted, but she was reluctant to tell him about her mum, to bog him down with the endless problems, but *then* he surprised her.

'I couldn't sleep without you.'

And she tried not to let her heart leap, because then it would have to fall.

'I don't want this to end, Alison.' His eyes never moved, but his fingers found the knot of her bikini, his long slim fingers at the back of her neck, and she wanted to arch into them, but she just knelt there, felt the slight drop of her breasts as he unravelled the knot.

'Bet you say that to all your gals…' She tried to make a joke of it, but it petered out at the end. 'Here.' She pushed towards him a plate.

'I'm not hungry.'

Neither, suddenly, was she.

'Did you like the bike ride?'

'No,' Alison said.

'Liar.' Nick smiled, and it had all gone as planned, because that was supposed to be his lead in, something about bikes, he reminded himself, except his fingers had freed another knot now, and his train of thought was diverted as he peeled down her halter like the skin of a grape and saw the lovely plump flesh within, and maybe he was a little hungry after all.

'I couldn't sleep last night,' he repeated, but this time with different intent. And to others it might be tame, but to Alison it felt wild—she could feel the cool breeze on her breasts and she liked it, liked it more with each hot kiss he trailed because the breeze cooled her again. There was the hum of flies around neglected food and he kissed her off the blanket and away from them. She liked too the pillow of moss on her bottom as he slid her skirt up and in this, with him, there was no inhibition, and sometimes she wanted to explain, to tell him that this wasn't her, except in his arms it felt as if it was.

She slid down his zipper, slipped her hands inside and freed him, and such was her want she gave a sob of frustration as his hand slid to his trouser pocket, gritting her teeth and willing him to hurry it on, but it tore, and he cursed in frustration and dug in his pocket again. And she hated them so, with him, she hated them so, especially when they were in his wallet on the blanket, and there was a moment, not even a moment, where she looked in his eyes and there was a *Will we?* Only they never found out—a screech of brakes filled the warm air and a thud that had them both leaping up.

They were pulling at their clothes and Nick leapt on the bike and Alison did the same. 'It was that way,' Alison said, pointing left, and they headed along the cliff. She felt the slight wobble of the bike as his attention was diverted and her heart was already pumping faster before she saw it for herself—the front of a car crumpled into a tree and a man talking into his phone and waving frantically. Nick slowed down, pulling to a halt, and they both jumped off.

'I missed the bend,' the guy was shouting as they took off their helmets. 'I was going too fast, trying to get to the hospital, she suddenly wanted to push…'

It was so far better than it could have been, except Alison's heart wouldn't slow down.

'What's your name?' Nick asked as they ran to the car.

'Richard.' His wife's name was Carly and there was already an ambulance on the way, Richard told them.

Nick was assessing the passenger for injuries and apart from being in advanced labour, there appeared to be none.

'I'm only thirty-five weeks.'

'That's okay…' He was incredibly calm, unlike Alison. 'Thirty-five weeks is just fine. Alison, there's a first-aid box on the bike.' There was, the hire company had made sure of that, but her hands were shaking so much she could hardly open the clip, and in the end it was Nick who came over and waded through it. There wasn't much, but there were gloves and Nick pulled them on and told her to do the same then he headed back to the car and gave instructions.

'Alison.' She was aware he'd repeated it. 'Can you help me get Carly into the back?'

She helped the pregnant woman, rolled up a beach towel she found into a pillow and made her a bit more comfortable so she was semi-prone and though Richard was clearly beyond relieved there was a doctor present there was actually very little they needed to do, because nature was taking good care of both patients. All that was required from Nick were a few words of encouragement as he held the baby's head and guided the new life into the world.

'The head's out.' His voice was calm and Alison looked over his shoulder. She was holding Richard's T-shirt ready to wrap the babe, and it was all under control, except her heart was still thudding, she could feel the sun beating on her head and hear the distant blare of sirens. But the baby wasn't waiting for them—with just one final push the body was delivered and there was a bellow of rage from a rather small baby as Nick delivered it onto Carly's stomach.

'She's okay?' Carly checked, and Nick grinned.

'He's great.'

'I'm having a girl,' Carly insisted, pulling up her baby boy, but it was a happy mistake and from Richard's shout of joy, he wasn't complaining.

The arrival of the ambulance brought comfort rather than relief. Todd and his partner were wonderful with the new parents and baby. Richard cut the cord and then the paramedics transferred Carly to a stretcher.

Nick was on a high. There was a euphoria to him, and he stood with his arm around Alison as the stretcher was loaded into the ambulance.

'How good was that?' Nick grinned, with all the joy of someone who finally, absolutely, definitely loved their job. 'How good was that?'

Only Alison didn't answer, uncomfortable suddenly as Todd climbed out from the back and closed the ambulance door and she wriggled out of Nick's arm, remembering they were keeping things away from work.

She could feel Todd's eyes roam her body, feel her breasts loose without a bra, and as, embarrassed, she ran a hand through her hair she felt leaves and knew, *knew* how she looked, knew what Todd was thinking.

'Nice work!' Todd winked at Nick when he'd closed the ambulance and Alison stood with her cheeks flaming. 'Good to get an easy one.'

'Thanks very much.' Nick shook his hand and all she could see as the ambulance drove away was the car against a tree and all she felt was reckless, and Alison loathed it. All she felt was a tart Nick had taken to the hills—so very easily, as Todd had pointed out.

'Thanks very much!' she hurled at him. 'Did you not hear what he was insinuating?'

'What?' Nick frowned.

'"Good to get an easy one"!'

'Alison.' Nick shook his head. 'He was talking about the birth.'

'No!' She felt sick, she actually felt sick. 'He was talking about me.'

And coming down from the high of the birth Nick started to see it, but Alison didn't want to hear his apology.

'I want to go home.'

'You're going to let what he said ruin—'

'It's already ruined,' Alison said. 'And even if we do patch it up, it will be ruined next week…'

'That's what I brought you here to talk about.' He hadn't meant to say it like this, hadn't meant to just blurt it out, but she left him with no choice. 'I'm going to ring work and tell them I'm not coming back early.' For Alison hope flared, but it was fleeting, so fleeting it was gone before it was recognised. 'I want to do Asia.'

She could have slapped him.

'With you,' Nick said quickly. 'I do have to go to this wedding in New Zealand but, look, I've been thinking about it…' All night he'd been thinking about it. He saw the flash of tears in her eyes, but he hadn't finished yet. 'Why don't you come—just for a few weeks, however much annual leave you've got…' He was finding this awkward, he knew she was proud. 'I know you must be stretched with the mortgage and everything, I'll sort out the tickets and things…' Alison screwed her eyes closed. 'We can have a couple of weeks away, just us.' And it sounded perfect, almost.

But then she'd have to come back.

'It's not that easy.'

'None of this is easy,' Nick said. 'Alison, surely you can have a holiday, a few weeks of fun.' And that word jolted, because that was what this was to him, she reminded herself, fun and a holiday that he wanted to extend—take the good sex with him, and slowly dismantle her heart. She wanted to nod, to say yes, to carry on the crazy ride, but she was scared to.

'I can't.' She shook her head in fury. 'I can't just up and leave.'

'Won't,' Nick said, and the pounding pulse in her head stopped for a second and he said it again. 'You won't come.'

'You don't know what you're talking about.' How dared he? Except Nick did.

'You didn't even consider it before you said no.'

'You don't know how hard things are for me. I had a massive row with my mother last night…' Stunned, she watched as he pulled out an imaginary violin. 'You bastard.'

'You've had me pegged as one from the start.' Yes, he was being mean, but finally he was angry. 'I'm asking you to come with me, or at least to just think about coming with me.'

'And I'm telling you I can't.'

'You can't, can you?' Finally he got it. 'It's not your mum holding you back, Alison.'

'Just leave it.'

'No.' He couldn't and he wouldn't. 'It's not just your mum.'

'Let's just finish it.' If she was being unreasonable, well, she felt unreasonable. 'Let's just finish it here.'

And she did.

When the police arrived and summoned a tow truck, and a couple pulled over in their car and asked if there was anything they could do—actually, there was something.

'Could you give me a lift, please?'

# CHAPTER FOURTEEN

IT HAD to be better this way, Alison told herself as she ignored Nick's texts over the next few days and tried to get used to lugging around a broken heart.

The dazzling blond doctor was a just a little less so over the coming week.

Tired, a bit distracted and to the rest of the team just a little less fun, but he was thorough and kind to the patients and sometimes, quite a lot actually, she felt his eyes follow hers, and sometimes they frowned just a touch when their eyes met, because the Alison he had known simply wasn't there any more.

He was kicking himself, angry with himself about how he had handled it. But he was angry with her too—at how readily she could let them go, at how she just retreated back into her quiet, serious shell. Though she was polite and smiled and spoke when she had to, the Alison he knew was in there seemed to have gone.

'I'm getting nowhere.' Amy was unusually tense as she handed over her night to Nick. 'This poor man came in at three—he's an oncology patient with a brain tumour, but he's got acute abdomen. He had a scan last week in Outpatients that was apparently all clear, the surgeons don't want him to have anything till they've seen him, but they're doing an aneurism repair we had in—'

'So he's had nothing for pain?' Nick checked sharply.

'Five of morphine,' Amy said. 'I couldn't ask him to wait any longer, but it hasn't touched sides, and the second-on surgeons are in Theatre as well.' It was a regular scenario—the surgeons couldn't asses an acute abdomen if the patient was pain free, but the surgeons were stuck in Theatre. 'I can't get his notes, he was seen in Outpatients last week...'

Amy really was frazzled—and from the nursing handover it made sense. It had been an extremely busy night, but nothing usually fazed Amy. Still, Alison remembered she had swapped her nights with Nick for a family thing a few weeks ago and guessed that maybe it had something to do with things.

'If they're in Theatre it's not going to be this team that takes him.' Nick was completely reasonable. He looked up at the medical roster. 'I'll ring Howard's team—he's on take today and I'll get one of them to come down before they start rounds. I'll go and have a quick look at him now.

'Alison,' he added, because she was cleaning up the night staff's chaos, because she was the only one around, because he had to, 'can you come with me?'

'His daughter, Vivienne, is getting upset,' Amy added.

'I'll sort it,' Nick replied. 'Go home,' he ordered.

'Thanks,' Amy said. 'What will we do without you?'

Nick could have sworn he felt the roll of Alison's eyes, but chose to ignore it, heading for the cubicle instead. 'Hi, I'm Nick. I'm an emergency registrar...'

'So was the other one!' A woman, presumably Vivienne, snapped. 'Where are the surgeons?'

'I'm going to speak with today's team,' Nick said, 'but first I need to take a quick look for myself at your father.'

Jim was frail, thin and clearly in pain, and Nick didn't prod and poke him unnecessarily, but he agreed with Amy's finding that the problem was acute—because even if Jim's condition was terminal, an operation might be needed to relieve his pain.

'I need those old notes,' Nick said once they were outside the cubicle.

'The day receptionist is here,' Alison said, 'and Outpatients will be opening. I'll ask her to track them down.'

'Thanks.' He hesitated. 'Alison?'

'Yes?'

'Are you okay?'

'I'm fine,' Alison said.

'Can we talk?'

'About work?' she checked, and when he pushed his tongue into his cheek, she shrugged. 'Then sorry, no,' Alison said, and headed for Reception.

'How's the flat?' Another line she was getting used

to. Libby, the receptionist, asked the question as Alison popped in to check on the location of Jim's notes.

'Shabbier than I remember it,' Alison admitted. 'I'm painting before I move in and I don't remember a pea-green carpet when I bought it, but it must have been there.'

'Are you replacing it?' They stood making idle chit-chat as Libby tapped away on the computer and did her best to locate the notes Nick wanted.

'I was going to learn to live with it,' Alison said, 'but the more I paint, the greener it gets.'

'You'll get there,' Libby said, and then she shook her head. 'Those notes can't have come back from Outpatients.'

'They really need them,' Alison said. 'He's been seen by Gastro and the surgeons and they're all passing him on. He needs to be sorted. The family's getting really frustrated and frankly I don't blame them. Can you ring them again?'

'For all the good it will do.' Libby rolled her eyes. 'I'll go over now and have a look myself,' she offered. 'Could you just take these through for me?' She handed Alison a couple of rosters but as Alison walked through, the family caught her.

'Did you get his notes?'

'The receptionist is going to go over to Outpatients now—' She didn't get to finish. Jim's daughter let out several hours of frustration in a few caustic sentences, and Alison stood there, shaking her head a touch as a security man started to walk over.

'I know how hard this must be—'

'You know nothing,' Vivienne retorted. 'That's my father suffering in there, not that you care. Did you enjoy your coffee break? He hasn't had a drink since he arrived, he's sobbing for some water—'

'Vivienne.' Nick came over, gave Alison a tight, grim smile. 'Let's take this to an interview room.' He'd cut right in and Alison was grateful for it, annoyed with herself for not suggesting the same thing but glad that someone else was dealing with it. Alison glanced down at them as she popped the medical rosters on the bench. They were nothing to do with her, just the doctors rosters for the next four weeks, and normally she wouldn't have given them thought. Except today, she scanned the sheet and saw the absence of Nick's name, saw that Cort Mason was, in fact, coming back, and it just rammed home the truth. There it was, in black and white, as if she needed reminding, that in just a few days Nick Roberts would be gone.

'She apologises.' Nick came over to make a phone call. 'She's going to say it herself—'

'There's no need.'

She was close to tears all of a sudden but was determined not to let him see. 'Libby's gone over to Outpatients to try and find them—he was there last week.'

'He should have been admitted last week,' Nick said, and then, a little more tactfully, he told the voice on the end of the phone the same thing, and as Alison went to go he caught her wrist, which was the most physical he had ever been at work and the only contact in days. And she couldn't bear it, yet she took it, waited as he concluded his call, Nick doodling on the hateful rosters as he spoke on the phone.

'They're going to admit him.' He gave her the details and then there was just a slight frown as he looked her over and she didn't like his scrutiny.

'Are you really okay?'

'I'll get over you, Nick, don't worry.' She didn't turn round, because for the first time since his arrival, the first time in years in fact, there were tears, not just in her eyes but trickling down her cheeks, and Alison fled to the toilets, blew her nose and told herself she was being stupid, told herself she'd warned herself that this would happen.

'Alison?' Ellie was just dashing in before the start of her late shift, the surprise evident in her voice at catching her friend less than strong, because over the years she'd never seen her cry. 'Are you okay?'

'I'm tired,' she admitted, because suddenly she was. 'And there's this poor man, he's been shoved from pillar to post. He's been here since two this morning and we've only just found him a bed, his daughter just went off at me—'

'I know,' Ellie said, because anyone who worked in Emergency did know that families sometimes took out their frustration on the closest target, and even if Vivienne hadn't been that bad, some days it just hurt.

'All okay?' Sheila, the NUM, came in then and Alison even managed a wry smile that her *escape* to the loos had become so public and made a little note to herself not to go into meltdown till she was safely in a cubicle.

'A relative upset her,' Ellie explained.

'It's not just that,' Alison admitted. 'I don't feel so great.'

'You don't look so great,' Sheila said, and because it was Alison, who was always stoic, she knew it wasn't an excuse. 'Why don't you take a half-day? What are you on tomorrow?'

'An early.'

'Go home.' Sheila was firm and fair and knew how hard her staff worked. 'If you don't feel any better this evening, give us a call so we can arrange cover tomorrow.'

Alison felt more than a little guilty as she collected her bag, because even if she was tired and teary, there was another reason for it. The bus took for ever, it just crawled along and stopped at every stop. Maybe she was more than tired, she decided, trudging up the street to her house. Maybe she was getting the flu or something.

It was Tuesday, because the house smelt like beef stroganoff as she entered, though it smelt stronger today. Alison headed for her room, but the smell was in there too, permeating the whole house. She opened a window, swallowing a couple of times, and then fled to the loo, which was thankfully a lot quieter than the one at work.

'No.'

She actually said it out loud as she headed back to the bedroom, climbed into bed and very deliberately blocked that thought, and blocked it again when her mum came home and Alison had to fly back to the bathroom again.

'I think I've got gastro,' Alison said, and there were benefits to living at home, because she got some water, then tea and toast all brought to her, and her mum rang up Sheila to say that she wasn't well and wouldn't be in tomorrow.

*You okay? I heard you were sick.*

She read his text at ten p.m. and didn't reply.

Just turned on her side and tried to get to sleep.

She truly didn't know what to say.

# CHAPTER FIFTEEN

'YOU look terrible.' Ellie breezed into her bedroom on her way to a late shift. 'Or are you just not wearing mascara?'

'Both.' Alison tried to smile.

'Alison…' Ellie was tentative for once. 'I can see that you and Nick…well, you both look pretty miserable.' As quiet as they'd kept it, of course Ellie knew. 'I'm assuming it's over?'

'It was always going to be.'

'I'm sorry,' Ellie said. 'I feel like I pushed you into it…'

'I pushed myself into it,' Alison admitted.

'You can talk to me.'

'I know,' Alison said. 'Just not yet.'

'It's his leaving do on Friday. I just thought I should warn you…'

'I'm on days off Thursday and Friday,' Alison said, 'and I'm off sick today. I won't be seeing him again.'

And that was hard to say, let alone admit, and she couldn't really talk about it with Ellie—they were just different personalities, Ellie so light and breezy, she herself so serious. She'd been a fool to think she could do a relationship any other way. Surprisingly it was Rose who bought comfort, bringing her in some lunch and sitting on the bed for a while.

'I went and saw Anna,' Rose said, 'that grief counsellor…' The bite of scrambled egg stilled in her mouth as Rose spoke on. 'I was shocked by what happened, that I could hit you…' She started to cry a bit and Alison held her hand. 'I already had Tim by the time I was your age—and despite what I told your father, what I've told myself enough over the years, he wasn't actually my first.'

Alison was shocked, especially when Rose continued.

'Or my second.'

'Enough information!' Alison smiled.

'I've been holding you back for my own selfish reasons and you've been a wonderful daughter, Alison… but you need your life too.' And she told her what Nick had. 'You're holding back too.'

'No.' Alison shook her head and Rose, as she often did, rammed home her point. 'What's happening with Nick?'

'He leaves on Sunday,' Alison said. 'We had a bit of a row.' She took a deep breath. 'He offered to fly me out to Asia—do some travelling with him, just for a few weeks. It's not that simple, though.'

'Can you afford it?' Rose asked, and Alison was so proud of how she was trying—so relieved to have such a long-awaited *real* conversation with her mum.

'He offered to pay,' Alison said. 'It should be cheap—he's going right off the beaten track...'

'You'd need some immunisations...'

Alison shook her head. 'It's not the money, Mum. I don't want to feel like this again in a few weeks. I just want it over with, I just want him gone.' And she couldn't even cry because she wanted to be sick, which she was, dashing across the hall and just making it to the loo as Rose stood outside, fretting.

'Maybe just stick with toast.'

And Alison didn't answer, just leant over the loo and closed her eyes, because it wasn't scrambled egg making her sick, and it wasn't her mother or money stopping her from following her heart now, it wasn't even her.

She was in no position to be getting immunisations and going off the beaten track.

No position at all.

Of that, she was almost certain.

# CHAPTER SIXTEEN

SHE'D bought several pregnancy tests from this chemist without giving it a thought. Ellie panicked on regular occasions, but now that the test was for herself, she felt as if she knew half the shop and was sure the girl serving was the daughter of one of her mum's friends, though hopefully she didn't recognise her.

They'd been careful, Alison told herself as she took her little parcel home.

But not quite careful enough, Alison realised as she stared at the little blue cross. And maybe it was coincidence, but as her mind drifted to Nick, his must have drifted to her, because she felt the buzz of her phone.

*Can I see you before I go?*

*Still sick,* Alison replied.

*I can come over. Do you need anything?*

She was tempted to text back *Pram, cot, nappies,* but instead she wrapped all the evidence back up in a paper bag, put that inside a carrier bag and then in another one and then put it in the outside bin before she texted him back the absolute truth.

*I need space.*

## CHAPTER SEVENTEEN

'YOU missed a great night!' Moira was at her most bubbly, so too was everyone else as Alison dragged herself into work. 'Nick knows how to have a good time.'

It was all she heard all morning.

How great the party had been, how much everyone would miss him, and Alison couldn't face the staffroom on her lunch break, so instead she slipped outside to the little patch of grass behind Emergency, sat in the sun and tried not to think that this time tomorrow he would be on a plane.

There was no question that she must tell him.

The baby was his, he had a right to know, and their child had a right to know about its father too.

And, yes, Alison thought as she closed her eyes and the sun warmed her skin, it would be more sensible by far to have this difficult conversation face to face, but it would be so much easier another way.

She could plan what she said better, Alison told herself, tried to convince herself.

He needed to know that there would be no pressure on him.

It was her choice to keep the baby.

It would be better by email, Alison decided, then wavered. The truth was she couldn't stand to see his reaction as she crushed all his dreams.

'Am I disturbing you?' Amy sat on the bench beside her.

'Not at all,' Alison said.

'I just wanted a bit of peace.' Amy gave a tired smile. 'I've got so much going on at the moment and they're all…' Her voice trailed off for a moment. 'I'm going to miss Nick,' she said, and Alison looked, really looked, and saw a flash of tears in the registrar's eyes. Then Amy's phone bleeped and she looked down and smiled as she read the text.

'Speak of the devil.'

This time Alison made sure she was actually *in* the toilet cubicle when she had her little meltdown.

She was overreacting, she told herself, and yet…and yet… Amy had been acting differently lately and she and Nick did get on.

What? her angry brain demanded. When she had gone home to her mum's, had Amy come round?

Had Nick told Amy to keep things quiet too?

Oh, God!

Up came her coffee and half a slice of toast and down came the tears.

She needed her head straight, needed to *really* think this through before she told him.

Somehow she got through the rest of the day. Amy

shut herself in her office, no doubt to cry over him, Alison thought savagely.

By the time she was on the bus-ride home she had visions of Amy and herself stuck together in the same maternity ward.

Hell, maybe Moira would be there too.

'Alison!' She nearly jumped out of skin as she stepped off the bus and Nick was waiting for her. 'I was hoping we could talk. I don't want to leave with things as they are,' Nick said, as she walked along silently beside him. 'I don't want it to end on this note…'

It wasn't going to!

They walked down the road and he suggested something to eat, which was the last thing she wanted. 'Can we just sit?'

So they sat on a bench and watched the world go by for a moment.

'Alison, I don't know what happened,' Nick admitted. 'I know you think the paramedic insinuated something—I didn't see it as that. Alison, if I had thought for a moment… Do you really think I'd let someone speak about you like that?'

'How will you speak of me?' Her eyes glittered with challenge. 'When you're showing your photos, how are you going to describe me?'

'Confusing,' Nick said, 'because sometimes I feel closer to you than I ever have to anyone and other times…'

Nick was very easy to talk to, it was she that wasn't. She was concentrating so hard on not crying, on not challenging him, on just getting through, she hardly said a word.

'Will you please at least think about Asia?' Nick said to her silence.

'I can't go to Asia.'

'Alison, if it's the money…'

'It's not the money,' Alison gulped, 'it's…' And she bit down on her lips, because she needed to know how she felt before she shared it with him, needed just a moment's pause before everything in her life suddenly changed.

'Just go, Nick.'

'Just like that?' he challenged.

'Just like that,' she confirmed.

And because it had just been a few weeks, because there was no baggage, because he was just moving on, he took her at her word and stood, and so did Alison.

'Do you want to keep in touch?' Nick offered, because the poor man had no idea what was coming, no idea just how in touch they'd need to be.

And she didn't say a word, just nodded, and because she had to, it was Alison who walked away.

'You okay, darling?'

'Yes. Sorry I was late, I went to the flat.'

'You're not at work, Alison,' the new Rose said. 'You don't have to apologise for being late. How's the flat looking?'

'Orchid white.' Alison gave a wry smile. 'I've finished the lounge, I'm going back tomorrow to do a couple of other rooms, but it looks like an indoor tennis centre with that carpet.'

'It will be fine once it's got the furniture in,' Rose said, and then sat down. 'You know, I've been looking at some brochures...' She handed one to Alison and for just a second Alison wondered if she knew, because there were pictures of London and her mind jumped for a moment, then swung back as Rose faltered on. 'Your father and I always spoke about doing a trip to Europe, taking a couple of months...' And then Alison looked at the brochure, really looked, and, as she seemed to be doing rather a lot lately, tried to keep the tears from coming. 'It's for over-fifties, for widows, divorcees... It's not a meeting thing,' Rose said primly. 'They just sort out the accommodation, it's company...'

'It sounds wonderful,' Alison said.

'I want my life back too.' Rose was the one crying now. 'I want to do the things that I always said I would.'

'And you should.'

'There's a cancellation,' Rose said, and Alison realised then that her mother wasn't just thinking about it, she really was going to do it. 'But I'd have to go in three weeks. I've got enough annual leave stored up.'

'Go for it,' Alison said, and kissed her mum.

'You might need help with the flat and—'

'Mum!' Alison kept her voice light but firm. 'You have to go.'

And they spent an hour looking on the computer at all the places Rose would visit, all the things she would finally do, and Alison was pleased, more than pleased for her mother, but there was a hollow sadness there too. The conversation, the row that she had staved off for so long—now, she wished she could have had it sooner, because now everyone was moving on and *she* was the one who was…

Stuck.

She tried to reframe it, tried to rephrase it.

Pregnant, with a mortgage.

She tried and she tried and she tried once again, but no matter how she tried, as she walked into her new home the next day, there was only one other word she could think of—*trapped*.

Was it wrong to feel trapped?

Was *trapped* even the right word?

There was another word there, an emotion there that she didn't want to examine, so instead Alison slapped orchid-white paint on the walls and felt like the worst person in the world, because this wasn't how it was supposed to be, this wasn't how she was supposed to feel.

Except she did.

She stared at what was going to be her study, and even that had been a concession, a trauma course instead of a journey, but now even that was looking impossible.

A nursery.

She'd laughed when the real estate agent had said it, he had been so completely off track, yet just a few weeks later that was exactly what it was about to become.

And she stood in the little room and tried hard to picture it.

Staggering in for two a.m. feeds.

She actually could, she could see herself all dishevelled and exhausted and stressed, just like Shelly, could see a pink, screaming baby and a lonely flat and a fridge stuck with postcards from Daddy.

Or worse, far worse for Alison, would be the sight of Nick in the doorway, unshaved and annoyed, and trying to snatch some sleep because he was on call, and just so removed from his own dream...

She slapped the paint onto the wall.

She'd rather, far rather, far, far rather, do it alone.

Which she did.

She got the main bedroom done, and the kitchen and all the lights were blazing until late in the night. And despite what she'd said, a part of her hoped for a knock at the door, for the space she'd insisted on to be suddenly filled, but Nick had clearly taken her at her word.

The smell of paint made her sick, so late in the evening she walked the short walk home, along the foreshore, and she couldn't help what she did next. Maybe she was a stalker, but she took a little diversion past where Nick was staying and the lights were off and, yes, he could be out, but there was something about an empty home, and Alison knew then he had gone. She took a deep breath and thought about the little bean-sized thing in her womb, the baby he had unwittingly left behind.

'Can you do me a favour?' Her voice was a bit shaky and she should perhaps have apologised to Ellie for ringing her so late, but she was frantic.

'Sure.'

'Can you tell me your Facebook password?'

'It says never to reveal your password to anyone.' Ellie laughed and then promptly revealed it. 'Don't you want him to know you're watching?'

'You know me too well.'

There was a pause, a tiny pause. 'You know that he's...' Her voice trailed off and Ellie sat in silence on the phone as Alison, with a few short clicks, found out Nick was in New Zealand.

'Are you okay, Alison?'

'I'm fine,' Alison said, then relented, admitting a little of her truth. 'It just hurts more than it should. I mean, I knew it wasn't for ever, I knew it could only be short term...' She couldn't believe he'd gone. Okay, she'd asked him to, but he really was, grinning from the top of a rock in his profile picture, like that cat that had got the cream, and here she was, feeling as if she was on the top of a rock, but without the safety harness.

She waited till her mum went to bed then sat with a big mug of tea, and it felt different clicking on his profile without Ellie over her shoulder, peering into his life and scrolling through to find out more about the man she loved.

He was more social than her by far.

There were school friends, friends from med school and not just cyber friends. They were in his life, joking with him to get a job, asking when he'd be back, missing him at football and concerts and nights out, and that was aside from family.

And there was Moira.

Missing him already *and* she'd added a kiss.

*And* she hoped to catch up with him in Asia.

And there was Gillian, who still messaged him—pretty, funny and patient.

His status was single.

And that hurt.

So too was the fact he never mentioned her—that their ride to Palm Beach, their one massive row was just described as 'an interesting day'.

There was a life and a family and friends and a whole world waiting for him on the other side of the world, and on this side there was Alison and the little bean-sized thing growing inside that she was trying to get used to.

And maybe she really was a stalker, because she scrolled through Ellie's friends and then Nick's and there was no sign of Amy.

And then he updated.

*Back from sampling local delights. Great to meet cousins—loving it here.*

This probably wasn't the best place to announce a pregnancy, so she contained herself and clicked off and then she went up to bed and lay with her flat stomach and tried to be nice to it.

'We'll be okay,' Alison said, in a voice that didn't sound entirely convinced.

# CHAPTER EIGHTEEN

ALISON *was* sensible.

The world should have been back where it had been two months ago, except a blond English doctor had upended her life and now she somehow had to put it back.

She chose not to tell her mum, because she didn't want Rose not to take her trip.

But she took folate and saw her GP and then later an obstetrician, who scanned her and told her she was ten weeks pregnant, and she was about to correct him, because Nick had only been gone for two weeks, then remembered that it was dated from the start of her cycle.

And she had to tell him; she'd tried to tell him.

There were about fifty attempts in the draft box of her email and she'd rung three times but hung up before it could connect.

Tonight.

Alison decided as she put on her lanyard and checked all her pens. Tonight she would ring him, before he headed for Asia.

Or maybe, a little voice said as she smiled at Ellie, who was on her way home from night shift, she should wait till he's there.

'God, I hate nights,' Ellie said, and then she looked at her friend. 'You look awful.'

'I shifted my stuff yesterday and I'm trying to help Mum pack for her trip—sleep is a distant memory.'

'Here.' Ellie handed over her make-up bag. 'You'll scare the patients.'

She so could not be bothered with make-up, but Ellie was right—she did look terrible—so Alison retied her hair and put on some mascara and a bit of lip gloss, and when Ellie doused herself in perfume she squirted some at her friend.

'Still missing him?' Ellie asked, but Alison just gave a noncommittal shrug.

'The best way to get over a man is to get under another.' Ellie grinned. 'And you've no hope looking like that.'

'Thanks for the sage advice.'

'You *will* thank me.' Ellie beamed. 'Come on, you're late and I'm skiving off early.'

They walked out together, talking much about nothing, and then the world stopped because there at the nurses' station was Nick, smiling as she walked over. Her heart was in her mouth and her face must have paled but thank God for Ellie, who had ensured she was at least wearing mascara!

'Hi, there,' he said as she stood waiting for handover.

'Hi.' Alison could hardly get the word out, her throat was squeezed closed so tightly. 'How was New Zealand?'

'Great.'

And he just stood and she just looked and he just waited—and there were so many things that she wanted to say, to ask, and so much she wanted to avoid, so awkwardly she just stood.

'Nick!' Sheila was far more effusive. 'What on earth? It is so good to see you—we've had to battle through with the most miserable locum in the southern hemisphere.' She glanced over her shoulder just in case he was around, then shrugged. 'How long till you disappear?'

'Not sure,' Nick said. 'I've got a few things I need to sort out.'

He *did* change the energy of the place.

Moira squealed in delight when she came on at midday and though he was holed up an awful lot in Amy's office, Alison tried not to be jealous, or get ahead of herself and believe that it was *them* he had come to sort out. And yet, as she showed around a new group of student nurses, she was reminded of a certain matter that needed discussing.

'X-ray.' The familiar call came from Resus, and Alison moved the group back.

'Just be careful,' Alison warned. 'They do call out, but just be aware that there are a lot of portable X-rays taken here.'

'Is Resus lead lined?' a student asked, and Alison shook her head.

'You just need to keep your distance when they're shooting, and wear a gown.' She knew it was safe, had pored over all the information, knew that the safest place to stand was behind the radiographer, and that, really, the level of exposure was tiny, and yet, and yet... 'If you're pregnant, or think there's a chance you might be, it's best to let us know if you're not happy to be in there when they're taking films.' And then Alison realised just how futile those words were and offered the next best thing. 'Or just slip away...'

Which she tried to do when her shift ended, but Nick caught her as she slunk off.

'I want a word with you.' He was waiting outside the changing room. 'Several, in fact. If you want to, that is.' And she didn't know what she wanted so he spoke into the silence. 'I know a nice café that does ricotta cheese and cherry strudel—I'll be there at five.'

He was there before her again.

Only her teeth didn't feel like glass. Instead her mouth felt like it was filled with sand as she made her way over.

'I've already ordered,' Nick said as a waitress came over.

'I might not have come.'

'I'm always hungry.' They sat in silence as two lattés and two strudels were placed before them and Alison took a sip of her drink.

'What happened, Alison?'

And she had to tell him, except the words wouldn't come out.

So she toyed with her strudel, and went to take a bite, then remembered that soft cheese was on the list of forbidden foods her obstetrician had given her, and as she put the pastry down she saw him frown, almost saw the thought process in his eyes. And then two words were said, presumably by her, because it sounded like her voice and Nick's lips weren't moving.

And then she closed her eyes, because she didn't want to see all his dreams evaporating, didn't want to witness him realise that his twelve months of freedom had just delivered him every last thing he'd been trying to avoid.

'When did you find out?' His voice sounded normal.

'A few days ago.' Alison swallowed. 'When I was sick.'

'That was more than a few days ago, that was a few *weeks* ago, Alison.'

'I'm sorry.' Only Nick wasn't cross with her for not telling him.

'You shouldn't have been holding this in on your own.' He dragged a hand through his hair. 'I knew there was something wrong. I thought it was the promotion, me leaving...'

It was.

And it was a whole lot more too.

'You *could* have told me,' Nick said.

Not *should*, for which she was grateful. 'I was trying to sort out what I want.'

'And what do you want?'

'I don't know,' Alison admitted. 'I won't have an abortion so I guess it's not really about that...' She wasn't making much sense, but she didn't care. 'If you're feeling trapped, believe me, you're not alone.'

'I never said I was feeling trapped.'

'Oh, please.' She was angry, not at him but at the world. 'Well, I do. I haven't even left home and guess what—now I probably won't be able to. I'll end up renting the flat out. Mum can babysit while I work.' She could feel the walls closing in, she absolutely could see the walls closing in as she envisaged the future.

'You don't think I'd support you.'

That just made her crosser.

'Oh, yes, that's right, you're so Mr PC that you'll send a lovely cheque for his schooling and we'll fly over to you once year or you'll come here and we'll be all civil—'

'Alison,' he interrupted, 'did it never enter your head that I'd stay, that we could do this together?' And that just made her crosser still because, yes, of course it had entered her head, and now he was suggesting it, it just made it harder because she didn't want it to be that way, didn't want to force his hand, didn't want the man who had come here for fun and to find himself, a man who so clearly didn't want to settle down, to be forced to.

'You'll resent me,' she said, shuddered it out, the most horrible of all her horrible thoughts. 'You might never say it, you might never show it, but I'll know. I'll always know that if it wasn't for the baby...'

'Alison—'

She didn't let him finish. 'Please, do us both a favour, go on your adventure, have your trip, have your fun, and if you have an epiphany somewhere in Nepal—'

'Nepal?' For the first time he bordered on sounding cross. 'Are we talking about your dream holiday or mine? Alison, I'm not going to just get on a plane—'

'Please do!' She struggled not to shout. 'And if fatherhood and babies and maternity bras and nappies suddenly appeal, I'll still be here, getting bigger and fatter, and we can sort something out. Or you can head back to London and we can sort something out from there, but right now I want space, I want time, I want to work out my future, so please go and live yours.'

'You really want space.'

'Yes.' Could she make it any clearer? 'I want to get my head around this myself, and I can't do that with you.'

# CHAPTER NINETEEN

HE GAVE her space and she loathed him for it.

He spoke politely at work, and he didn't text, or ring, or email.

There was one room left to do in the flat and she couldn't face it.

Could not go in and again picture a cot, so she opened up her laptop on the disgusting green carpet and logged in as Ellie again and tortured herself with his latest postings.

He was back to earn more money, apparently.

And one of the many that jarred was a response to a question from Gillian.

*Bangkok here I come!*

'It's me and you,' she said to the slight curve on her stomach—and she slapped paint on her baby's wall and refused to wait for Nick's epiphany to come. She would keep on keeping on.

But when she had her first ever ring on her own doorbell, she didn't feel so sure.

He was blond and unshaven and looking just a bit fed up with his lot.

'Just how much space do you need, Alison?' he asked. 'Because this is driving me crazy. You can't just ignore it.'

'I'm not ignoring it.'

'No one knows—I saw you lifting a patient, all the X-rays in Resus…'

'I go out,' Alison said. 'I wear a lead gown.'

'Does your mum know?'

'Not yet. I'm not keeping it from her,' Alison said. 'Well, I am, but she's going on holiday, I don't want to ruin it.' And she burst into tears. 'Like I ruined yours.'

'You haven't ruined anything,' Nick said, and she couldn't even begin to believe him. 'I'm crazy about you. I have been since that bus ride.'

'Oh, please…' And out it came then, all the pent-up insecurity, all the doubts, all the things she'd stored up and tried to pretend didn't matter.

'You're single online,' she flung it at him. 'Off out, having *fun*—' she tossed that word up at him '—delivering babies up mountains, climbing bridges, and not a single mention of me…'

'Alison…' He was trying not to smile, and it incensed her. 'You're single, I can see that in the small part of the profile you allow to be visible, and you won't even be my friend…' He nudged her, tried to pull her from her tears as if they were in the school playground.

'No!' She was furious, close, dangerously close, to painting a gloss ochre strip on his suit with the paintbrush she pointed at him. 'I don't go on there.' Well, she did, all the time lately, but she wasn't actively on there was what she would say if challenged, but she was on a roll now. 'You say you're crazy about me, that you can't stop thinking about me, but you're on there every night, and I seem to slip your mind every time.' And then she burst into hears as she recited his latest posting. 'Bangkok here I come!'

He laughed.

He had the audacity to laugh, but not at her, Alison realised, because in the middle of hell she actually laughed too, a laugh that was laced with tears but a laugh anyway. 'You're such a bastard.'

'But I'm not.' He shook his head. He rued his words and the pain he had caused her, but he knew at least that he could put that bit right. 'I'm not a bastard, Alison, I'm not even a good backpacker, I'm the worst back-packer. That person you're reading about...' And she watched him struggle to explain it. 'Do you know how hard it was to justify taking a year off? Do you know how hard it was to end a very good relationship, for no good reason?'

And she did, she did.

'It seemed incredibly important to...' He raked his hand through his hair. 'To cram everything in, to have a ball, to validate...' Then he was completely serious. 'And I've loved doing all those things, but the bit I've loved most is the photos, is the afterwards, is sitting on the balcony with you. I can't tell her I'm no longer single on a computer, that's a face to face, or a difficult phone call at the very least, and I wouldn't do that to Gillian.

I honestly didn't know you were looking, or I'd have explained…' She shook her head, sick of his smooth talk, not wanting to be a woman who just believed because it was safer. It annoyed him, she could tell, so much so that he opened his laptop and she ignored him, carried on painting the wall as he logged on.

*Not sure about Bangkok. Alison is pregnant, but she hasn't told her mum yet and we're not sure what to do. That bloody ride to Palm Beach was awful. I had meant to tell her I was serious and we spend some time overseas to get to know each other more. She got all stroppy and hitchhiked a lift home, she was completely mental…*

'Do you want me to post it?'

She just stood there and read over his shoulder.

'Do you see that the person you've read about isn't all of me?'

She could.

'That there are other sides?' She nodded. 'I rang Gillian.' Alison felt her world still. 'I told her about you, because even though we're over, even though it ended more than six months ago—' and she got what he was saying '—she didn't need to read about it first.'

'I know.'

'And there's something else you should know,' Nick said, 'which you might not like and you might not understand. But I told her about the baby too. I know there are other people we need to tell…'

And she didn't like it, because it confirmed her darkest fears.

'It gives you the reason to stay.'

'I've already got a reason,' Nick said. 'I already had a reason.' He pulled her close. 'You.' Then he ran a hand over her stomach. 'This one just speeds up the decision-making process.'

'It's not what you wanted.'

'Not with Gillian,' Nick said. 'Alison, I don't believe in accidents.'

'So I meant it to happen.'

'I don't mean that.'

'You work in Accident and Emergency, you're going to be consultant when you get back…' Her voice was rising. 'And you're standing here telling me that you don't believe in accidents.' She was incensed now. 'What? Do you think my father and brother secretly wanted to die, that they deliberately—?'

'I mean *this* sort of accident…' He closed his eyes. 'I'm not saying this very well.'

'No, Nick, you're not.' She couldn't believe what she was hearing. 'You really think I set out to—'

'No.' He interrupted. 'No.' He said it again.

'Then what?'

'We knew,' Nick said. 'We, more than anyone, knew. And, yes, we were careful, but not *that* careful.'

And she opened her mouth to argue, but nothing came out, because she'd been over and over and over their oh, so careful love-making, except sometimes it hadn't been. Sometimes passion had overruled common sense and she was very cross with herself for that. With Paul she'd been contracepted to the neck, if there was such a word. With Paul she could have raged at the sky, at the gods, at the injustice, because she had been so very, very careful, but with Nick… She screwed her eyes closed, because the only person she was raging at was herself.

'I knew the risks too.' He caught her racing brain and sent it on a different track. 'Oh, I wasn't actively thinking…' The words weren't coming easily for Nick, but he was at least trying, this conversation incredibly honest, dangerously honest perhaps. 'I'm responsible, Alison, I've *never* not been careful except with you.' And it was raw and honest and the truth. 'And, yes, I should have taken more care, you can throw that at me too if you want to, but I guess for the first time passion won. There was someone, you, that I was willing not to be so practical and sensible with…' And he looked at her then and stated a fact. 'That's how babies are made, have been since the beginning of time. The chance was worth it at the time.'

'Is it worth it now?'

'Of course it is.' He sounded very sure.

'You want to travel.'

'The world will still be there, waiting.' And then he grinned. 'To tell you the truth, I'm sick of throwing myself off cliffs. You've saved me another bungee-jump, yet another sodding extreme sport to show I'm having a good time.'

'What will your parents say?' Alison asked.

'Trapped by a colonial!' He rolled his eyes. 'They'll

come round. I know you can't leave her, Alison, and I completely see why.'

'What about your job?'

'I've got a job! I've been offered a year's work when Amy goes on maternity leave next week.' And he gave a little grimace. 'Keep that quiet—I mean it. She's adopting a baby from overseas and she's beside herself— doesn't want to tell anyone till he's actually here.'

And someone *was* looking after her, because Nick would never need to know how little she had trusted him, how this gorgeous blonde sexy doctor somehow really was just that.

'What about your mum?'

'She'll be completely and utterly delighted.' And there was a wobble in her voice, a strange fizz of excitement that had, till now, when she thought of the baby been absent, a vision, a glimpse of a future, only now she could see Nick and herself and a beach and a baby…

And then she admitted something, something she hadn't dared admit, not even to herself.

'I'm scared.'

'I know.'

'No, you don't,' Alison said. 'It's not trapped that I feel, it's…'

'Scared,' he offered, and she nodded, sure he didn't really get it, except it would seem he did. 'Scared you might love it too much?' he said, and she nodded. 'Scared you might lose it?'

And he shouldn't say that, Alison thought frantically, because if he said it, then maybe it would happen.

'I think being a parent means you're scared for the rest of your life.'

'I can't stand what my mum went through.'

'Then you've got a choice,' Nick said. 'You can hold back, never fully live, never fully love, just in case…' Which was what she had been doing. 'But that doesn't work, because sooner or later living wins. Look at your mum,' Nick went on. 'Look at you.' He put his hand on her stomach, the result of taking a chance, and he was right because, cautious or not, life threw in surprises whether you liked them or not.

'I got you a present.'

And out of his laptop bag he produced not a ring but a rather tatty airplane magazine folded on one page. And it was nicer than a ring, nicer than anything actually, because it was a flight map showing all the destinations that airline went to, and Nick pointed a couple of them out.

'There's Sydney,' he said, 'and there's London, and there's an awful lot of world in between. You choose the stopovers.'

'Sorry?'

'Well, even if they are a pain, even if they are miserable and controlling, I guess I do love my family, and I'm going to be going home once a year, hopefully with you, or we can drop you off somewhere and pick you up on the way back. Me and the baby, I mean. It might take a while to complete your gap year…' he grinned '…but you can do it in stages.'

And it was the nicest picture. It would be the first on

her wall, one she would take to the shop tomorrow and have properly framed, because it wasn't the red dots, or the destinations, but the generosity that came with it—the acceptance, the space, the future they would create.

And she could do this, Alison realised.

She could love and she could live, and, yes, it might be scarier than safe, but it was nicer than safe, better than safe, and anyway Nick made her feel safe.

'Choose the honeymoon.'

'You don't have to marry me.'

'Actually, I do,' Nick said. 'Makes me feel more secure.' And then he grinned, and grinned even wider as a delicious thought struck. 'Oh, God,' said Nick, 'you know what this means…' He was grinning and sounding delighted. 'No condoms. Monogamy, here I come.'

They had to undress in the dark because there were no curtains and would have to be up at the crack of dawn if they didn't want to be on public display.

'I don't like the look of this,' he warned as he pushed at the inflatable bed. 'I think it needs more air.'

'It's been filling for ages,' Alison said. 'You go first.' Because she'd rather topple onto him than have him topple onto her.

'It's comfortable.' Nick sounded surprised and he took her hand as she climbed in beside him and lay a moment adjusting to floating on air—her first night in her flat and Nick was beside her, and she lay there for a moment, trying to fathom how in so little time her life had changed, was changing, and would keep on doing so.

He rolled towards her and she lay in silence, could feel him watching.

'Are you happy, Alison?'

'I think…' She thought and paused as she examined her heart. 'That I'm going to have to get used to being happy.'

'Hey!' Nick said. 'We could move in with your mum, save a bit of money—rent this place out…' She kicked him, which wasn't a great idea in that bed because he almost fell out, and he held on like he was climbing up onto a life raft.

'It's a bit awkward,' Nick said, and he was right. It was awkward, less then two months in and suddenly here they were, except, she realised, Nick was talking about the bed, because he toppled onto her with a touch more gusto than intended, his lips meeting hers. They were warm and firm as she had so often remembered and his tongue was smooth and warm and tasted of Nick. And he was here, and that was going to take some getting used to, that this gorgeous, stunning man was here, not for baby, not for duty, but for her.

'I'm scared,' Nick said, and she was about to admit again that she was too—scared of telling everyone, scared of the future, scared that what they had found was too good to last—except as he came up for air, again Alison realised that he was talking about the bed. 'That we're going to topple over.'

There was the difference. Nick was in the now, living

in the present, and for Alison grief and tragedy meant she lived with every scenario, every vision, knew how easily it all could change. And she wanted his faith and his presence in each moment, and she stepped into it as he moved deep within her, she let her mind still, concentrated on nothing more than the pleasure he gave her, focused on the now and all that they were.

And it was a precarious position, a shift to the left or the right and the passion that was building would crumble, but he locked his arms under her, cocooned her middle, trapped her where she wanted to be.

'I've got you.'

And she knew that he wasn't talking about the bed, that she was safe, and that they didn't need cartwheels. Just a dodgy bed and the other's body was enough for them.

# EPILOGUE

'WHAT are you doing?'

Nick woke up and found her standing in the dark kitchen on tiptoe. 'Looking at our ocean view.' It was the only room in the house you could see it from. Right there between a couple of buildings there was their glimpse of the ocean, and even if it was tiny and she had to stand on tiptoe to see it, every day Alison did so, and tonight she had to see it too.

Her mum had been absolutely delighted, of course. She'd be delighted to babysit so that Alison could work, but only a couple of evenings if Alison was on a late shift, because Rose was busy getting her own life back.

And, of course, Nick's parents hadn't taken it so well—this Australian hussy who had dragged their son screaming from his lovely structured life—but she and Nick had spent a couple of months in the UK and his parents had been over for a visit and were coming in three weeks when their grandchild was due.

'Come back to bed,' Nick said, because he'd worked the previous night and had been up all day, trying to turn what was surely a cupboard into a nursery. But more importantly he was loving this last trimester. Who would have thought pregnancy could be so sexy?

'My waters broke.' Just like that, Alison said it. 'Half an hour ago.'

'And you didn't wake me?'

'I just wanted…' Alison gave a little shrug '…a bit of time before everything happens.' And he heard the wobble in her voice and she was such a deep little thing, and he could see, even in the darkness, the sparkle of tears in her eyes, which meant she was scared. And though he never wanted her to be, he accepted that sometimes she was.

'You've got time,' he said, even when she bent over with a contraction. 'How far apart?'

'Ages,' Alison said.

'Come on,' Nick said, and he took her back to their bed, and he understood exactly where she was coming from because part of him didn't want the rest of the world right now, didn't want to ring the hospital or the excited, expectant families. He wanted just a little bit more time that was just for them.

And always he surprised her. Every morning, every night, every day he surprised her, because he was hers, because he got her, because he made her more of herself, and they surprised each other too.

Like this morning.

She had never trusted in them more completely, in him, in herself.

She had thought about labour, as to how it should be,

would be, might be, and had prepared, she thought, for every eventuality, was open to drugs and epidurals and a Caesar if it had to be. She had scared herself senseless while never imagining this.

To lie in their bed, with him beside her, with no rush and no haste.

To be held and kissed for that first couple of hours, because that wasn't in any of the books, and they certainly weren't sexy kisses, just confirmation, and then later, just to be held and stroked as the pains deepened.

And then later, to be locked so deep in pain and know he was there at the other end, to close her eyes and go with it and to hear his lovely silence. She didn't want to move, didn't want to leave their little nest.

And he thought about it.

Dr Nick, who had been, till that moment, had anyone bothered to ask, against home births, for all the obvious reasons, found himself outside the obvious and so deep in the moment that, yes, he thought about breaking the rules and having his babe at home.

'We need to go to the hospital.' He was reluctantly practical. 'We really need to go now.' He climbed out of bed and wanted to climb back in, but he went and got the car out of the garage and rang the hospital, and helped her down the stairs.

She could feel the salty air on her lips and the cool of the morning, and she knew they'd left it a bit late, because the sun was peeking up and she was so, so ready to bear down.

The first bus of the morning was idling, passengers

climbing in, and she hoped they all looked around to their fellow passengers and maybe met the person that bettered them, that every one of them could be as lucky as her.

'We're going to get told off,' Nick said as they pulled in at Maternity a little later.

'You'll get told off,' Alison said, really trying not to push. 'You're the doctor!'

But they didn't get told off, because everybody loved Nick.

And, yes, they'd spoken briefly about it once, but Alison had quickly declined. There was no way she'd let him deliver their baby, no way on earth, except the birthing suite was all dark and lovely, and if she closed her eyes she could almost be at home. The midwife was just glorious, just so calm and non-invasive, but Alison was glad she was there, and just very glad to hear Nick's voice.

'Come on, Alison, one more and the head will be out.'

It was the midwife holding her leg and Nick holding their baby's head, and it had all happened so naturally, far, far nicer than she could ever have envisaged. And she pushed as hard as she could till he told her to stop and, yes, it hurt, but in a moment her baby was there and it was Nick who had delivered her.

Her, because he couldn't help himself from saying it.

'She's perfect.'

She was.

Blonde and long limbed and completely her father's daughter, because with one look Alison's heart was taken, and like it or not there could be no holding back—she already loved her.

'Some souvenir!' Nick smiled a little while later, when holding his daughter for the first time.

'More than you bargained for?' Alison asked, but Nick shook his head.

'More than I could ever have envisioned.' He tore his eyes away from his daughter and towards Alison. 'And I did.'

'And in these visions,' Alison checked, 'did your daughter have a name?'

'Martha.'

'Martha?' Alison went to shake her head, but stopped because, as she was starting to trust, this was his dream too.

Here was their biggest adventure.

# FIRST TIME LUCKY?

## NATALIE ANDERSON

*For the University of Canterbury's Student
Volunteer Army – thanks for showing, in the
most fantastic way, that the brightest lights on
Christchurch's horizon not only have brains and
beauty, but also the most tremendous hearts.
You've been such heroes, and you've proved how
positive our city's future will be.*

**Natalie Anderson** adores a happy ending—
which is why she always reads the back of a book
first. Just to be sure. So you can be sure you've
got a happy ending in your hands right now,
because she promises nothing less. Along with
happy endings she loves peppermint-filled dark
chocolate, pineapple juice and extremely long
showers. Not to mention spending hours teasing
her imaginary friends with dating dilemmas. She
tends to torment them before eventually relenting
and offering – you guessed it—a happy ending.
She lives in Christchurch, New Zealand with her
gorgeous husband and four fabulous children.

If, like her, you love a happy ending, be sure to
come and say hi on facebook/authornataliea, on
Twitter @authornataliea, or at her website/blog:
www.natalie-anderson.com

# CHAPTER ONE

DR GABE Hollingsworth glowered at the bumper sticker on the car in front; the streamlined silver silhouettes reminded him that tomorrow was recruitment day. Half his team would be there to check out the possible additions to the posse of alluring females. But while the players saw the dancers as fresh game, Gabe reckoned the women were the *hunters*, not the hunted, with their sparkling eyes, suggestive poses and PhDs in serious flirting. They might officially 'support' the country's greatest rugby club, but they'd high-kicked more than one man's life right into touch. Including his. So he'd be light years away from the stadium at audition hour tomorrow.

He took the next left, while the silver-stickered car went straight on out of sight. Relieved, Gabe automatically glanced at the property on the edge of the park. He'd been curious so long it had become a habit. So he saw it immediately—the rough bit of board with 'To Let' and a mobile number scrawled on it that hadn't been there this morning. Gabe pulled over and put a hand to his pocket, let it drop again without retrieving his phone. He was right outside—there'd be no harm in walking to the front door and making enquiries in person, would there?

Assuming he could *find* the front door.

A decrepit garage stood on the edge of the footpath while the rest of the front boundary was marked by ferocious planting. He walked the length of the two-metre-high prickly 'hedge' of trees so intertwined you couldn't see through their thick evergreen foliage, then he peered behind the sign precariously tacked in front of the rusted letterbox. He saw hidden there what *could* be a narrow goat track between the branches—make that a single-file ant track. He winced as gnarled twigs scratched his bare arms. Pushing through, he figured it was an abandoned wreck of a house, probably in the midst of some development argument with greenies on one side wanting it to be absorbed into the park, while property tycoons fought on the other for consent to demolish it and put some apartment or office block in its prime central-city location. But the spiky green fortification intrigued him and the idea of having a central-city hideaway appealed given the fatal attraction nightmare his last fling had become. No chance of some unhinged ex-lover carrying out a home invasion here—a high-maintenance type like Diana would never risk her skin and nails to get through. Hell, *he* could barely get through. But he ignored the scratches and catches at his clothing and hair; the resistance made him all the more determined to see what was beyond. He snapped branches and stomped over the rough ground and suddenly was out in open space, blinking in the brightness of the summer evening.

He straightened, forgetting the zillion stinging scrapes on his skin as he stared. It wasn't an abandoned wreck at all.

Roxie only had the downstairs bathroom to do and the place was clean, empty and ready for occupation. She

picked up the spray bottle of foul-smelling chemical dis-
infectant and straightened her sore shoulders. She was
determined to get it finished tonight because the optimist
in her hoped people might call about renting the house
tomorrow. Flicking on the hot tap, she stepped right into
the shower cubicle. Getting wet didn't matter because
as soon as she was done she'd head to her studio, have
a real shower and flop into bed. She hunched down to
get into the corners, pointing the jet of water ahead, and
furiously wiped the walls. She'd spent most of the day
cleaning, had practised her routines as rest breaks to
stop herself dwelling on how different the place looked
without furniture. It would never be the same now, but
would always be home—her heart. This place was all
she had left.

She snorted at herself and went overboard with the
spray to stave off the OTT melancholic thoughts. The
shower was hardly dirty—hadn't been used in months—
but she wanted it immaculate, for prospective tenants to
see the perfect condition so they'd feel obligated to maintain it just so. Because, much as she didn't want them,
she needed tenants. Money of course, so she could finally get on with the rest of her life.

Her eyes burned as she scrubbed. Not from tears—
they'd long since dried up. No, it was the pungent fumes
of the industrial-strength cleaner setting fire to her
senses and not in a good way. She held her breath as she
swiped with the sponge but still the acidity swept over
her. She shook her head to stop the fuzzy hum, grabbed
the shower jet to sluice the suds away more quickly. But
the fumes grew overwhelmingly strong. Now, between
the suds and the steam and the stench, she could hardly
see. She couldn't hear properly either, because over the
sound of the running water she thought she could hear

someone calling out. But there wasn't anyone here to call for her any more.

Still holding her breath, she stumbled out of the shower, not bothering to turn off the taps, desperate to get to a window because she felt horribly faint.

'Are you okay?'

Roxie jumped, inhaled a last deep breath of chemical vapour and then screamed blue murder. For a method of stopping a faint, there was nothing better. Adrenalin flooded her system in a mad torrent, sharpening her mind and her muscles. Sadly not her vision. She kicked herself for leaving the bottle of cleaner in the shower. She could have used it like pepper spray or something. Instead she was the one temporarily blind. All she knew was some man she could hardly see was in the room with her.

'Hey!' he shouted over the top of her screeches. 'Calm down. I'm not here to hurt you.'

She went silent; the sound of streaming water ceased too. She tried to look but it hurt and she had to squeeze her eyes tight. 'Who are you?' she rasped, her throat raw from her ripped shrieking.

'You've got this stuff in your eyes?'

Roxanna's panicked senses were slightly pacified by the calm question delivered in such a cool, authoritative voice. 'I think the spray mixed with the steam or something,' she wheezed. Not that it was the more pressing point right now.

'It's a wonder you didn't pass out. Here.' He took her upper arm in a firm grip and walked her two paces. 'Sit.' He pushed her down so she was perched on the edge of the bath.

She blinked rapidly, desperate to regain her wits. She heard the tap running in the sink, felt the breeze as the window was opened. But no matter how much she blinked, the stabbing sensation in her eyes didn't ease. All she could see through the fuzzy agony was a tall figure, too close. 'Who are you?'

'Gabe Hollingsworth. I saw the sign and walked right in,' he answered in that same calm voice, but now he sounded as if he was smiling. 'Sorry if I gave you a fright.'

No one 'walked right in'. The hedge saw to that. Most people thought this place was an extension of the park, the gardener's disused cottage or something. She came in through the garage but that was securely locked. So she wasn't sure she believed him. Had he climbed the fence to steal something—or *worse*? But if he was a serial killer or sex offender, would he really be helping her now?

'Your eyes are really sore.' He truly seemed concerned. And, yes, amused.

'No kidding.' She couldn't keep them open they stung so bad. She gripped the edge of the bath with cold fingers and told the rest of herself to chill too. This Gabe guy didn't sound like a serial killer. Not that she knew what a serial killer was supposed to sound like, but she hoped that hint of humour was a good sign.

'We need to wash them out.'

*We* didn't need to do anything. 'I'm fine. It'll be right in a minute.'

'No, we need to bathe them. Don't worry, I'm a doctor.'

She half snorted. He might not be a serial killer, but she so doubted his ophthalmology qualifications.

'No, really, I am.' He read her sceptical mind. 'Put this over your eyes for a second.'

He pushed a wet and cold folded flannel to her face

and she raised her hand to hold it in place—had to admit it soothed. The taps ran again.

'Lift up.' As if he didn't think she was capable of following instructions, a firm, warm hand cupped her cheek. He took the flannel away and then tilted her face from one side and then to the other as he carefully poured cool, clean water across each eye.

'Try to keep them open,' he murmured. 'It'll help.'

His voice was right by her ear, meaning his face was right by hers. Roxanna's heart thudded. She hadn't been this close to another person in the best part of a year and last time she'd been the one doing the doctoring. This was beyond different. This was—

'Better?' he asked, another too-close murmur.

Goosebumps rippled across her skin as she suppressed a shiver, not that she was at all cold. In fact, she was all of a sudden burning. And all of a sudden she remembered she was only wearing a pair of ancient Lycra shorts and an almost supportive singlet. No bra. While water was trickling down her face and onto her chest. 'I'm getting wet.' She pulled back, wanting to cover up.

'No worse than you already are,' he said, a brisker tone this time.

'I can manage now, really.' She tilted her chin free of his grip. 'Thanks.'

The sting in her eyes truly had eased and she opened them widely to look at the man bent down before her. She blinked more rapidly than she had when they'd been chemical filled. Was she hallucinating her way through this? But no, she'd *felt* his touch, had *heard* his words and now, as her vision cleared, she *saw* him rise to full height.

The effect was something else. Bronzed, broad-shouldered, unbelievable. At least six feet with dark hair and even darker eyes that were gazing right at hers in an uncomfortably intense way. Peripherally she noted the blue jeans, red tee, skate shoes. The cool clothes merely served to emphasise the fit body, the tan, the muscles, the obvious strength that made her glad she was sitting because her knees had weakened from some patheti- cally female hormone-driven response. And given he had some foliage as decoration, it seemed he really had come through the hedge. But his eyes held her attention hostage—jet-black, bottomless, unwavering eyes.

'Thanks,' she croaked, to break the suddenly dense silence. She swallowed. 'How can I help you anyway?'

He put the glass he'd used beside the sink, then took a few paces backwards, shoving his hands into his jeans pockets. 'I saw the "to let" notice.'

'It only went up this afternoon.' She stood, trying to get some kind of equality in the situation. Fat chance when he was tall and she wasn't. When he was dressed and she all but wasn't. When he was devastatingly good- looking and she definitely wasn't.

'I know.'

'You want to rent this place?' He didn't look like a prospective tenant. He looked like the kind of guy who owned things. Lots of things. Working in retail, even her little-old-ladies-giftstore kind of retail, meant she knew fashionable, what cost lots and what didn't. She knew the watch on his wrist cost lots, so did the shoes, while the tee shirt was one of those priced ten-times too high just because of the label. He was definitely someone who held the cards in his hands.

'I want to buy it,' he said bluntly.

Yeah, definitely the owning kind.

'It's not for sale,' she answered equally bluntly.

He held her gaze for a moment, then dropped to look

at the puddle on the floor between them. 'Where's the owner?'

Roxie's spirit hardened. 'You're looking at her.'

His unfairly long lashes swept up and the deep, dark eyes studied her again—surprise had widened them.

'You don't believe me?' she asked.

'Well, you don't look…' He shook his head. 'Never mind.'

She knew what he'd almost said. He thought she looked too young to own a house? How old did he think she was? Clearly not much older than a schoolgirl. Did he think she was the teen cleaner? Great. But she was no kid, she was twenty-two and she'd cared for this house almost single-handedly for the last five years. Not that she was going to get all indignant and ram that down his throat, no matter how much his assumption annoyed her. And, yeah, underneath that, she smarted because this one-thousand-per-cent man-in-prime didn't see her as a capable adult, or a woman.

The unfairness of the situation riled her. This was her house, but he was standing in her bathroom with the upper hand, having rescued her from a mortifying moment. But she hadn't *needed* rescuing; she'd have been fine. She was always fine. And wasn't it just so typical that the one time in her life she met a spectacularly good-looking man, she had to be looking like a scruffy kid?

If only she had shoes on to give her the slightest chance of looking him straight in the eye—statement shoes, like six-inch stilettos. Instead she had to crane her neck to meet that focused, but depressingly impassive, gaze. She opted not to, instead walked as coolly as she could into the lounge. Not that easy when her heart was hammering faster than when he'd frightened the screams out of her minutes before—he really was something else.

'The house will never be for sale,' she said, aiming for polite but firm. 'I'm sorry you've fought your way through for nothing.'

'Not for nothing.' He followed her. 'I've always been curious about this place. If you don't mind, I'd love to take a look around it.'

She couldn't really say no when he'd just helped her out, albeit in dispassionate passing-medic style. So she nodded and spread her hands wide. 'It's known as the Treehouse. The reason is obvious.'

He walked into the middle of the large room, his gaze raking it with a wide sweep. 'It certainly is,' he said softly.

His obvious appreciation of it helped her forgive him—just a little—for not seeing her as an equal.

'Why are you renting it out?' he asked as he walked closer to inspect some of the detail carved into the picture rail.

'I need the money,' she answered honestly.

'You'd get a swag of money if you sold it.'

'I'm never selling it. I'm not worried about securing a tenant,' she lied.

Those dark eyes studied her again briefly, then his attention shifted to the room's features again. 'It's unique.'

Yeah. It wasn't a modern, floor-to-ceiling windows kind of place. And it wasn't big. Instead it really was a Treehouse—in one corner, an ancient, solid oak grew through the floor—both a support structure and design feature. Light poured in from the cleverly placed skylights, the windows were like frames for the beautiful living landscape of the park. The house itself was all hand-carved, polished wood. Built with the love, sweat and blood of her grandparents and, just as they'd put everything they had into the house, they'd put that same

level of time, love and energy into her. Until illness had
turned the tables and she'd become the carer for both
them and the house. She was never letting it go, but she
had to have some adventures now or she'd end up staying for ever and never moving forward. It was time to
fly free—but she'd keep the nest to come back to.

'Most people love it,' she answered him. The few
people who'd seen it in recent years had. 'My grandfather always said there was nothing like natural beauty.'

The dark gaze rested on her again for another moment. 'He was right.'

Roxie stared back. A frisson of something spiked her
goosebumps all the more—he was talking the *house*,
right? He'd turned away from her so she could no longer see his eyes—and they were unreadable anyway.

'How long do you want a tenant for?'

'Six-month lease initially, ideally a year,' she spelt out
her fantasy. In truth, she'd take what she could get.

He walked to the far corner, where that beautiful
gnarled tree literally grew through the floor. But Roxie's
attention was totally swallowed by him. His back view
was almost as good as the front—the masculine vee of
broad shoulders and slim hips reinforced that impression of strength again. She swallowed as heat flushed
through her. It was definitely time to move out and explore some of the world—some *men* of the world. She'd
clearly been waiting too long when she was this affected
by the first she'd come across in ages. He put a palm on
the trunk, his fingers smoothing over the bark. She remembered the feel of that palm on the side of her face.
Her face now burned.

He turned suddenly. 'I'll sign up for a year.'

Her eyes bugged and she momentarily forgot his hot
factor. 'You don't even know what the weekly rent is.'

'Doesn't matter. And I want first right of refusal if you do ever decide to sell it.'

He hadn't even seen the rest of the house, only the living area, but sometimes the house had an almost magical effect on people. For her it was a tranquil sanctuary—though not with him in it, he'd brought in an electrical charge that put her on edge. But she needed a tenant and if he was serious about a year's lease, then she had to get over that edge.

'There are a couple of things you don't know.' She felt it only fair to warn him, even though her heart was pumping even more crazily now with the prospect he was going to solve her financial problems.

'Conditions?'

She nodded. 'You won't have access to the garage or the little flat above the garage.'

His eyes narrowed. 'Someone's in the flat?'

She nodded.

His expression hardened.

'While I'm in town, I'll be living there,' she rushed to explain. It wasn't some random person he'd not met and she'd stay well away from him. Only her explanation didn't make him relax; if anything he tensed all the more.

'You're not usually in town?' he asked sharply.

'I'm going overseas.'

'When?'

'Soon.' As soon as she had the money, but she decided not to mention that getting all the money together was going to take a few months. 'I have some things to do before I go,' she fudged.

He nodded. Eventually. 'Okay.'

Sudden panic slammed into Roxie. It was going to be hard seeing a stranger live here, but it wasn't for ever and it would still be hers—this was the only way of ensuring it would remain hers. She breathed deep and pushed herself on. 'The garden will be maintained by the estate.' That was a plus, right? But she saw his smile of disbelief. 'You haven't seen the garden,' she pointed out defensively.

His hands spread and he looked down. 'I'm wearing half that hedge.'

She frowned at the number of leaves in his hair. 'I hope you didn't damage it.'

'Are you seriously telling me the hedge has a gardener?'

Yeah, he was teasing. And she so wasn't noticing how that smile shot him from hot to sizzling.

'Totally seriously,' she said. 'It needs a lot of care to maintain it.'

'It needs a chainsaw.'

'The hedge stays. As is. That's one non-negotiable condition.'

He walked back towards her, his smile curving his too sensual lips wider and in grave danger of distracting her. 'How am I supposed to get access to the house if I can't come through the hedge or the garage?'

'There's a hidden gate on the park side.'

'A hidden gate?' He chuckled then, an infectious, warm sound.

The surprise of it, the sexiness of it, almost rendered her speechless. She had to clamp her jaw to stop it from dropping, to stop herself drooling on the floor. She pivoted on the spot so she could no longer see him, so she could *think*. 'So much of what makes this house is its privacy. Isn't that what you like about it?'

There was a short silence. 'How astute of you.' No

amusement sounded now. 'All right, those conditions are no problem for me. I still want to rent it for the year.'

Roxie felt more dizzy than when she'd been in the shower accidentally inhaling industrial cleaner. 'I'm going to need references.'

'Sure. How about I give you a cash deposit now to secure it, and we can let our lawyers draw up a lease agreement tomorrow? You have a lawyer, right?'

'Of course. That's her number on the sign out there. I'll get her to put those conditions in writing.'

Gabe nodded and turned to walk back to the tree again, trying to keep his eyes up and away. Because Little Miss Landlady's white vest-top had not retained opacity in the shower-cleaning session. She might as well be topless. But she didn't know that and he didn't want to tell her. He didn't want to think about it a second longer than he already had. No, he didn't want to dwell on how completely gorgeous she was. Instead he lectured himself that she looked about seventeen. As if she'd just walked home from school. And he did not, *not*, not have raging lust for someone barely legal. She was a *kid*.

Except she wasn't. She had the most delicately feminine body he'd ever seen. He'd noticed it at first glance in the bathroom—her long legs, fine-boned shoulders, slender waist, sweetheart-shaped face, smooth, glowing skin, sensually full lips... And then her eyes had opened and stabbed him in the gut. The most vividly blue eyes. He deluded himself that they looked unnaturally vibrant because of that cleaner. That the chemical had some belladonna-poison effect that magnified the intensity of their colour or something. As if. They were just knockout powerful. And now her red-rimmed, stunning eyes were round.

Yeah, he'd have to be blind not to see how she looked

at him. It was a look he was used to and it didn't usually
affect him. Only he was working hard not to give her
that same look back. That surprised, almost dazed look
that had its roots in sensual appreciation and unexpected
desire.

Maybe he'd inhaled some poisonous fumes too because he couldn't be thinking this way. Her shorts were
old and worn and not any season's style. Her mouse-
brown hair was in a bedraggled ponytail that emphasised
that schoolgirl impression. And that damn thin white
vest-top had gone transparent. He was trying very hard
not to think about the pointed peaks jutting towards him.
Because he wasn't so out of control as to be turned on
by almost visible nipples, by imagining cupping those
mounds in his hands and bending before her to kiss the
pointed tips, to press his face to the softly curved sur-
rounds.

Okay, he was that out of control and his unruly imagination was making it worse. It'd been too, too long since
he'd got laid. Too long he'd been stuck on the straight
and narrow and boring. His heart hammered at an insane pace, ringing in his ears. The last thing he'd expected to find beyond that horrendous hedge was an
architecturally amazing home complete with some Snow
White or Sleeping Beauty or Rapunzel type impossibly
pretty Disney princess inside. He couldn't help wondering where the dwarves, beasts or wicked witches were…

Oh, he had to snap out of it. It was just frustration ad-
dling his reason. Going for a woman like this—one the
same age if not younger than Diana—would be insane.
She'd undoubtedly want more than he ever would. She'd
be emotionally immature, a dreamer with that happy-
ever-after fantasy that he was never buying into. It was
when he'd been forced to reiterate that to Diana that her

inner witch had appeared…intense, needy, a knife-edge to certifiable. Just the thought of that mess was enough to cool him off.

Almost.

Thank heavens this woebegone waif was heading overseas. It was only knowing she was leaving that he could take the place. No doubt she'd return from her trip all grown up and sophisticated and if serendipity saw their paths cross again, he'd dally with her then. Uh-huh, like in five years' time. For now he'd get himself this hideaway and then hide, right away. In a couple of weeks the team had that game in Sydney and he was so hitting the club scene and having a couple of nights all-adult action. Having fought so long to gain independence from family expectation, he was letting no woman hamper his freedom. So he definitely wasn't hot for Miss Skinny.

He turned back to face her and named a weekly rental price he figured should be almost on the money for the location.

'Actually I'd been thinking a little more than that. My lawyer will send you the details to set up an automatic payment.'

So Sleeping Beauty wasn't that sleepy. Good for her for knowing the high value of her property—and that he could afford it. Biting back all the flirt talk tingling on the tip of his tongue, he got his wallet and pulled out enough cash to cover the first two months. She took it from him with a steady hand and those wide, wide eyes.

'Don't you think you'd better tell me your name?' he asked drily, trying to hide how he was dying of desire inside.

'Roxanna Jones,' she answered, head high and unblushing.

'Good doing business with you, Roxanna.' So not thinking about the pleasure of it—of her—at *all*.

'When did you want to move in?' Roxanna gripped the wad of notes tightly to stop herself from touching him and easing her insanely curious fingertips. Since when had her fingertips *itched* like this?

'Tomorrow.'

She gaped. 'You're currently homeless?'

'No, but you were right, I like the privacy of this place.'

'I know.' She smiled, suddenly filled with excitement about her future.

He jerked a nod, turning abruptly away. 'Right, I'd better let you get on and finish.'

'You don't want to see the rest of the house?'

'I'll check it out tomorrow.'

'Okay, once the lawyer thing is done, I'll arrange access for you through the garage so you can get all your stuff in.'

'I'd appreciate that,' he said in a voice loaded with irony.

She tried to slow her out-of-control heartbeat with some sensible thought. The guy was now her tenant meaning she'd better put all her sizzle response in an ice-bucket. Not going to screw up this deal. Soon she'd be free to go overseas and discover all the way hotter guys out there…except she doubted there'd be a hotter male on the whole planet.

'Do you want to go through the gate or back through the hedge?' He hadn't seen the back of the house or the garden, and she wanted to witness his surprise.

'I'll go through the hedge, try to push some of those branches back into place for you.'

'You're sure?' She was disappointed; she'd been looking forward to a smug moment. It was likely to be her one and only with him.

'The hedge is your security system, right?'

Okay, so he was astute as well as gorgeous. 'I guess.' She shrugged as if it didn't matter so much.

'Then I'll cover up the stomping great path I just smashed through it. Wouldn't want anyone else creeping up on you in there and giving you a fright.'

'Good thing I didn't strip off to do the shower, otherwise it might have been you who got the fright.' She giggled, a high embarrassed sound that was embarrassing in itself.

To her surprise, his brief smile seemed as embarrassed and he moved quickly away from her and headed back into the prickly hedge.

Yeah, real clanger. Mortification cooled her right down as she was rudely reminded that Man of the Millennium didn't see her as a woman at all. Shaking her head at her gaucheness, she went back to the bathroom to rinse away the last of the cleaner. She glanced in the mirror and O-M-freaking-G. While her red-rimmed and bloodshot eyes were bad enough, her transparent-when-wet vest-top meant all-out wince city. Somehow the effect seemed more revealing than straight nudity, yet Gabe-the-gorgeous hadn't even blinked. Instead he'd been very particular to look at her face. She figured it had been born from courtesy or something. Or more like utter disinterest given her lack of spectacular in the boobs department. Yeah, that was it. Great. The first mind-blowingly handsome man to cross her path and she hadn't even been able to tempt him into a second look at her near-naked torso. She wondered what she needed to make someone like him do a double take.

She pulled her hair out of its dreary ponytail and

sighed at the straggly mess. No wonder he hadn't blinked. She tousled it with her fingers, imagining a new cut and colour. Then she looked at her chest and mentally fastened a cleavage-creating booster bra. Yeah, it was beyond time to glam up. No doubt the sensible thing would be to put that wad of cash in the bank tomorrow but she'd been without for so long and, damn it, now she had the certainty of a monthly rental income she could splurge, right? Just for once? She'd save all she needed in no time and this way she'd look great for her audition. She'd buy some other things to celebrate with too.

Re-energised, she put her music on and rehearsed one last time—danced hard out until she could dance no more. She slithered to the floor, resting her back against the old tree, and almost immediately thought of *him*. She heard the amused, low voice in her ear, felt the firmness of his touch. Then she remembered his impassive expression and determination seized her anew. No more would she be that *invisible*.

Her work at the Treehouse was finally done; now she deserved some fun. It wasn't just for the audition that she was going to look fabulous—the next time they met, she was so getting a second glance from her hot, built tenant.

Hell, make that a third.

## CHAPTER TWO

GABE got to work mid-afternoon, having spent the morning boxing up the few personal possessions he cared enough about and managing the shift in only two trips. Now, as he got out of his car he heard the music blaring through the speakers into the stadium. Damn, he'd hoped they'd have finished by now. He strode along the corridors to his office and shut the door. He flicked on his computer and checked his email. Excellent, the test results he'd been waiting for had landed. He settled more comfortably in his chair and started to work through them. But his door was flung open less than ten minutes later.

'Gabe, good you're here, I need you to take a look at one of these girls.' Dion, the stadium CEO. Dion who had no problem watching the wannabe dancers auditioning.

'No.' Gabe didn't even glance up from his computer.

'Seriously, I need you. Bee sting. Looks like she's allergic.'

'Oh, you've got to be kidding. A bee sting?' Gabe growled. 'That would have to rank as the most pathetic attempt ever.'

'But genuine. You really—'

'Dion,' Gabe interrupted, still staring at his screen,

'I've seen sprained ankles, sore calves, strained wrists. All fake. But a bee sting is a first. Certainly more inventive…if it weren't for the fact that there are no bees on that pitch. They're banned from play with chemical spray.'

'Gabe—'

'Come on,' Gabe sighed with weary sarcasm. 'I don't want to deal with another desperate-to-date dancer. Enough, okay?'

More than enough. After causing a cold war in his family for a few years over his refusal to conform to tradition, and the horror of an ex-lover psycho stalking him, Gabe had learned a couple of things. Firstly, he wasn't limiting his life by getting married and therefore having to compromise on his own goals for the rest of his days. And to be sure of escaping that noose, he knew he had to make his intentions clear from the start, to only seek company from the equally sophisticated and never mess with a woman who had anything to do with his workplace. Especially this workplace where temptation, exacerbated by all the travel, was too much for most men anyway. He'd seen it so many times—embarrassingly short marriages, even more embarrassing scandals.

'I should have told you I'd brought her with me.' With a wicked grin Dion stepped further in and too late Gabe saw the smaller figure behind him. 'And for the record, I had to drag her here. She reckons she's fine but I don't agree.'

Oh, great. Gabe winced. The girl had to have heard every word. Still, that was probably good—dispelling any ideas she might have had. He pushed out from behind his desk and shot the departing Dion a foul look. Dion merely winked.

Gabe looked at his new patient. Her head was bent so

he couldn't see her face. Naturally she was blonde. And naturally the blonde wasn't natural at all. He could see the myriad colours streaked through the long length that fell in gentle curves past her shoulders. She had the long, slim limbs of the dancer. And the extremely brief attire. Then she looked up at him. Her eyes were red-rimmed but challenging. Her cheeks flushed. Her mouth full but firm. All instantly recognisable.

Good grief.

Gabe just stared, his brain fuzzy, a humming in his ears. He had to be mistaken on this. But he wasn't. This was his under-age *landlady*? Sleeping Beauty from the wilderness?

'Hello, Gabe.' Despite the colour in her cheeks, the rest of her face was deathly pale.

'What are you doing here?' he asked.

'You mean you haven't worked it out already?' Her wildly blue eyes glittered. But not from tears. No, it was all defiance.

His gaze narrowed. No, he couldn't believe *his* eyes. The mouse-brown hair was now shot through with gold. And there was so much polish. She was wearing marginally more than she had been yesterday. Actually the shorts were even shorter—micro shorts, the exact colour of her eyes. And instead of a see-through old vest-top, she had a pink leotard on. The whole outfit too skin-clinging for comfort.

'I thought you said you were going overseas,' he said stupidly.

'I am.' She looked at him through lashes perfectly—but heavily—mascaraed.

'Then why are you trying out for the Blades?' He swallowed. Was this high-gloss vision truly the same sodden waif he'd met less than twenty-four hours before? Helplessly he glanced down her leotard-clad torso again. Not the slim waif at all. Curves had mushroomed magically. He bit his lip to stop the smile and the comment he so badly wanted to make.

'I'm going overseas at the end of the season,' she said. 'I want to dance first.'

'The end of the season?' He was appalled; his amusement fled. That wasn't *soon*. He'd thought she was shipping out in a week or so. How was he supposed to live in that house with her a stone's throw away for the best part of six months? Especially if she was going to be glammed up something gorgeous like this?

'Yeah, except that stupid bee just ruined my chances. And, no, I didn't stab myself with it just so I could get your face up close to my inner thigh.'

Oh, my. Gabe snapped his mouth shut, worked hard to bite back both the smile and the chuckle. His landlady had more fire than he'd given her credit for. He walked closer, watched even closer. Her transformation was something else, but he saw the hint of uncertainty in her expression as he deliberately breached her personal space. The girl was acting the grown-up. But some kind of madness raced in his blood when she lifted her chin and refused to break eye contact with him. Her audacious grit got to him. If she wanted to sharpen her kitten claws, well, hell, he'd play up to her—a *very* little. Frankly he couldn't resist seeing how far she'd go until she melted in a flush, until she got tongue-tied and lost her cool completely. He suspected it wouldn't be too far at all.

'Do some of the dancers really fake injuries to come and see you?' she asked outright.

Her obvious disbelief threw him instead. He cleared his throat, knew he'd sounded like the most arrogant a-hole ever. 'It's happened a couple of times.' More than a couple. But still.

Roxie giggled, suddenly delighted as she saw her tenant steal another quick look at her outfit—at least she'd achieved one objective today. Maybe it was the bee poison running through her system, or she was intoxicated by his proximity, but she couldn't resist baiting him—his arrogance was incredible. 'But you're not a rugby star. Surely the dancers have bigger fish to fry in this place? You know, all those *fit* young rugby players?'

He met her gaze with his dark one and a spark flickered in the depths. 'Maybe some of them prefer my qualifications.'

Heart racing, she breathed carefully to keep her answer cool. 'I'm sure more prefer the status and short-term income of the real stars.'

His smile was all shark. 'Maybe I have some other factors in my favour too.'

She figured he meant his looks. Yeah, so good-looking her toes were curling. All kinds of muscles clamped down—mostly in her nether regions. As if they were trying to dampen the inferno blazing there. 'Well, you don't need to worry about me, you're not my type,' she lied, feeling sassy and amused and surprisingly in control.

'No?'

She froze. She hadn't expected that direct challenge—his tone as loaded with tease as hers had been. She narrowed her gaze. 'Definitely not. You're too arrogant.'

*Way* too arrogant.

He leaned closer, his smile even more wicked. 'Lots of girls like arrogance. Confidence.'

'Lots of girls like bad boys too. I'm not like lots of girls.'

'That's true.' All of a sudden he frowned. 'Roxanna, *what* are you doing here?'

'Auditioning,' she cooed, to maintain the tease. 'And it's Roxie.'

Yeah, it was fun flexing flirt muscles that had been dormant so long. Really, it was easy. Because she could see the reaction—the glint in his eyes. And she could feel that pull between them; it was out-of-this-world strong.

'You told me Roxanna yesterday.' He stepped that little bit closer, his voice dropping.

'You caught me by surprise yesterday,' she breathed softly, holding eye contact. Nerves squeezed down tighter in her lower belly.

His gaze travelled across her face—eyes, lips, then dipped to her chest. 'So now you're Roxie.'

'Yes.' She tossed her hair defiantly and lifted her chin at him. 'I've always been Roxie.' Inside she had anyway. And 'Roxie' was certainly having an effect on him. She wasn't a total innocent. She'd had a boyfriend—one who had let her down in her hour of need, for sure, but she knew the look—and there was no disguising the look Gabe was giving her now. Oh, it had been worth every cent, every never-ending minute in the salon this morning. Poor Roxanna had never stood a chance, but add a little blonde, a little oomph to her assets? It was a different story. She couldn't believe men could be so shallow. But right now she didn't care, she was just basking in the heat in those eyes. The novelty was heady.

He shook his head very slowly. 'Well, Roxie, we'd better take a look at it.'

Look at what? Oh, her bee sting. She looked down at it and sighed; seemed as if the fun moment was over.

'I want you on the bed.'

Roxie almost gasped at that instruction, until she

quickly looked up and caught his too-bland expression. He was baiting her right back.

But he frowned when he glimpsed the circle of red, swollen skin on the inside of her thigh when she moved and sat up on the narrow bed against the wall. 'You weren't kidding.'

'Of course not,' she grumbled. As if she'd make up a bee sting just to get within cooee of the team doctor. He had such an inflated opinion of himself. 'Hurts like hell.'

He bent to look more closely. 'You can see the mark, but it looks like the actual sting is out. You've always been allergic?'

She nodded. 'But I haven't been stung in years. I thought I might have outgrown it.'

'Shame,' he murmured with evil intent, his breath a warm cloud brushing her thigh. 'When you've gone to such effort to grow up in other ways.'

She felt a very un-grown-up urge to throw something at him and his patronising attitude.

'Never mind, Roxie.' His bedside manner came out more like a taunt. 'Maybe you'll get to dance overseas.'

'Maybe.' She shrugged like as if she didn't mind, as if it wasn't the disappointment of the year.

'Spread your legs wider,' he instructed casually, but with that dangerous glint back in his eye.

Externally she froze, internally she melted. 'How wide?' she managed to ask.

'Wide enough for me, of course.' His expression was now pure challenge, purely expectant of...*what*?

She saw the barely suppressed smirk. He was amusing himself at her expense? Well, two could play at that game. Roxie determinedly imagined diving into Antarctic waters, cool—*freezing*—waters. Anything to keep her blush at bay. She was not going to go all girly embarrassed here, even though she felt it. Instead, she leaned back on her hands, tossed her head so her hair flicked out of her eyes. And she—who'd never spread her legs for any man—spread them as wide as they'd go. Which, given she could do the splits three ways, was actually quite wide. 'This okay?' she asked huskily.

He looked. Down then back up. Opened his mouth. Closed it. Swallowed as he looked down again. 'Just about,' he murmured and stepped right into place—mere inches separating them.

She ignored the flush she knew just had to be covering every inch of her skin and smiled the smile of total success. 'I didn't know you promised to flirt with your patients when you took the Hippocratic oath.'

'You're not a patient.' His gaze snapped up to her face.

'No? Aren't you tending to me, Mr Physician?'

'No. Not as a medical professional. I'm just going to hand you some cream and you can rub it on that sting yourself.'

She didn't know what had come over her, but the need to tease more was impossible to ignore. For the first time in her life she was flooded with confidence. She could say anything and not give a damn—the more provocative, the better, because his rapid response—desire mixed with defence—fuelled her wicked excitement. 'You're not going to rub it on for me?' she purred.

'No.' He stepped back. 'I am not.'

'Oh.' She looked down innocently. 'Do you only like rubbing cream on those big rugby boys?'

'Roxie.' He came back close, too close, his expression goaded. He studied her silently, ensuring he had her attention, then deliberately looked down her body in a blatantly sexual appraisal. 'Your hair isn't the only thing about you that's changed.'

He was looking at her chest. And, yes, he knew the truth for sure.

She lifted her chin, refusing to let embarrassment rise. 'It's amazing what supportive underwear can do for a girl.'

'Quite amazing,' he agreed drily. Suddenly he chuckled, that wholly amused sound that stirred that instinctive response in her to draw closer—and the temptation to tease further.

Yeah, she couldn't help but giggle back, despite the tension that still threaded through her. If anything the shared amusement pulled that thread tighter. 'You don't think my rack's real?'

'We both know it's not.'

Yeah, they did both know that. She angled her head down but peeped back up at him, batting her lashes to totally ham it up. 'But you have to admit, if you didn't know better, you'd be completely fooled.'

He took a moment to study her again, slow, deliberate consideration. 'Completely.'

She decided to push for more. 'And even though you know the truth, you like the effect anyway?'

The deep breath he drew in seemed to be painful, because he grimaced at the same time. Then he shook his head. 'It's false advertising. What happens if you pull one of those rugby boys—how you going to cope when he finds out the truth? Or are you going to offer to cook the chicken fillets for supper after?'

She wrinkled her nose but appreciated the attempt to shoot her down. 'Not chicken fillets. They'd stink something awful.'

'What's in there, then, cotton wool?'

'Gel pads. Much more comfortable. Natural feeling.'

'They feel natural?'

She shot a look into the deep, dark eyes that were only a few inches from her own. 'You want to find out for yourself?'

Oh, the challenge was out now. She could see him thinking, deciding…

'Roxie…' He cleared his throat and turned away quickly, went to a cupboard and pushed packets around in it with fierce concentration.

Disappointment burst her fantasy bubble. She looked down at her leg, suddenly the pain that had been muted screamed. She saw how the red was spreading, the swelling thickening.

'The reaction is getting worse,' she muttered, biting her lip because her thigh was hot, itchy and sore.

'It certainly is,' he answered abruptly, returning from the cupboard, still not looking at her directly. He pierced the seal on the small tube, squeezed some of the white cream onto the tips of his fingers. 'I'll give you a couple of antihistamine tablets as well. Have them when you get home—they might make you drowsy.'

She nodded, not able to speak any more. He'd gently spread her legs wider again and with fingers was smoothing the cream across the hot, tight skin. Seemed he'd forgotten he was going to make her do that herself. She looked at him as he watched what he was doing. Now she knew exactly why all those dancers faked injuries to get him to tend them—he was fun. And he truly was gorgeous with his perfect features and height. So very male. So very close. Touching her in a way that suggested other kinds of touch might be even more moving. Her lashes lowered as the tips of his fingers circled carefully, narrowing in on the sting site. She shouldn't be feeling it so sensually, but she was. She shouldn't be imagining those fingers gliding higher, but she was. She shouldn't be heating, melting, wanting—but she was. And she couldn't help the small shudder as he stroked in that smooth, regular rhythm.

He looked up; his eyes bored into hers. All tease gone and nothing but banked fire in the black eyes. 'You need to do this yourself.' Honest, raw—faint sheen sparkled on his skin as if he too felt a fever.

Her throat tightened, rendering her mute. So she nodded. But even that took effort. It was as if he'd some spell cast over her. Her heart wasn't racing, it was thumping so slowly, and every beat was so huge it hurt. She thought her eardrums were going to burst with the pressure. Both his hands rested on her now, no longer rubbing the cream, but holding her thigh. He could tighten his grip any moment.

*If he wanted.*

His gaze dropped a couple of inches south of her eyes. She knew what he was thinking about. She was thinking about it too. Wanted it. Her lips tingled, dried, she was desperately trying not to lick them. Suddenly he was closer, so close that—

'Hey, Gabe, how's our new girl?'

Gabe moved so fast Roxie didn't have time to blink before he was at the sink, running taps and scrubbing his hands.

'You mean me?' Roxie stared at the vivacious blonder than blonde who'd just burst into the room. Chelsea, the leader of the dance troupe.

'Yeah, are you okay?' Chelsea came up close to look at Roxie's leg. 'Looks ouch.'

'It's okay.' Seriously, she'd forgotten it in that over-

powering moment with his hands on her. 'Really, I'm...
just fine.' Just breathless.

'Great. Because up to the bee thing, you blew us away.
We want you in.'

'You do?' Roxie gaped. 'Really?' She'd thought she'd
blown it with the whole allergic-reaction-and-screams-
of-agony routine.

'Yeah, you're classically trained, right?'

'It was obvious?' She was stunned; she hadn't been
to a ballet class since she was sixteen.

'Not in a bad way, but I thought I could spot that un-
derlying technique a couple of times. Your freestyle was
amazing and I totally want to raid your moves. I've not
seen a girl break the way you do. We need some edge
and you definitely have it.'

Wow. No one had ever said she had 'edge' before.
Then again, no one had seen her dance in years. She'd
gone into that all but empty stadium today and just given
it everything. And she'd done it.

Elation added to the excitement that had already been
flooding her. She couldn't resist glancing at the tall, dark
torment now standing a few paces behind Chelsea. But
in the split second she looked, she saw the naked emotion on his face.

Anger.

His thunderous expression momentarily crushed her
mood. Why did he look so *bothered*?

'I'll leave these pills for you here.' He brushed past
Chelsea and brusquely put a small pill pack on the edge
of the table. He left the room faster than a streaker ran
the length of the pitch in an international match.

'Hottest thing on two legs, isn't he?' said Chelsea a
few seconds after he'd shut the door one decibel short
of a slam.

'I'm sorry?' Roxie blinked, still absorbing his massive mood swing.

'Gabe,' Chelsea explained. 'Hotter than any of those players. Fit plus brains plus wads of old money.'

'Really?' Roxie hoped her suddenly ravenous curiosity wasn't too obvious.

'Yeah but don't bother looking. See how he shot out of here the second he could?'

Roxie just nodded.

Chelsea sighed almost sadly. 'He used to be so outrageous, dated a different woman every night. Absolute slayer.'

Roxie carefully picked up the tube of cream he'd left on the narrow bed beside her and concentrated extra hard on screwing the cap back on. 'What changed that?'

'His ex Diana went crazy for him. Literally crazy.' Chelsea stepped nearer, her bubbly voice dropping conspiratorially. 'She was a dancer here, they didn't even date all that long but she tried to move in on him. I mean, she really did move in one weekend when he was away. It almost got to restraining-order point, but she had a breakdown and her family got her some help.' Chelsea looked awkward about sharing the info, but she talked on anyway. 'It wasn't his fault, she was delusional. Everyone knows he's never going to put one of these on a girl's finger.' Chelsea waggled the fingers of her left hand, and the flash of her massive diamond engagement ring temporarily blinded Roxie. 'Gabe's a playboy to the grave. Or he was. Now he's a repressed playboy.' Chelsea frowned and fixed Roxie in place with a searching look. 'When he smiles—too rare these days—all females instantly melt. There's not a woman in the world who wouldn't fancy him.'

Roxie knew denial would be too revealing and Chelsea

was looking as if she could see straight through her anyway. 'Well, he is very attractive.'

'Yeah, but he's unattainable,' Chelsea warned. 'Which
makes him all the more attractive to so many women.'
She half laughed and then instantly sobered. 'But don't
waste your time. He's signed off from the game. Look,
I've been with my man so long the others call me ma-
tron, but I still know how it works in this place—you
get a bunch of fit guys together with a bunch of fit girls
and it's all going to happen. There are twenty-odd gorgeous young things on that team who'd love to play. So
if you want, go for it with one of them, just be sure to
play safe.'

Roxie swallowed and stood up from the bed, letting
her hair fall forward so the blush in her cheeks wouldn't
be so obvious. Now probably wasn't the time to admit
she'd never played at all—well, not all the way through
a game. And she hadn't looked twice at any of the players—but their doctor? She stepped to get the pills so
Chelsea couldn't see her face as she asked, 'Why did
that girl go so crazy for Gabe?'

'You've got eyes, right?'

'Yeah, but sometimes good-lookers don't think they
have to make any effort.' She'd read that in a magazine.
She turned to get Chelsea's answer.

'Rumour has it his technique is even better than his
body. I don't know the truth of that myself but I'd believe it.' Chelsea looked worried. 'Look, so many girls
have tried it with him and failed in the last few months
since Diana. Save yourself the humiliation—I've seen
them fall but he rejects *harshly* and then they resign. I
don't want to lose another dancer, especially one as interesting as you, so *please* don't go after him.'

Roxie laughed—she'd never gone after a guy in her

life; she wouldn't know where to start. 'Don't worry, I won't.'

And she didn't want to jeopardise her spot on the Blades—she'd wanted that for too long. But a part deep inside her flamed because Gabe had *wanted* to kiss her. She might not be all that experienced but she'd known that. Which meant he wasn't entirely unattainable. Oh, yes, temptation whispered—tantalising her with the fantasy. She wanted that experience—to finally take a lover and a damn good one. If Gabe was that great, couldn't he be the one to do it all with? Clearly he didn't want commitment—none of that lovelorn, clinging stuff. But nor did she. She had no intention of being pulled into a relationship. Her freedom had been a long time in coming and she wasn't giving it up for anyone.

Hours later, as he drove to his new home Gabe rationalised. It didn't matter, the Blades only rehearsed on site once a week and he was well used to avoiding them at that time anyway. She'd be there during the games, but he was busy with the boys for all that time. He didn't attend the after-match functions at the home stadium as a rule now. So while he might glimpse her every now and then, that would be it. He could live with that for just this season. Sure he could.

But when he got to the Treehouse he couldn't help looking at the window above the garage. The curtain wasn't drawn; there was no sign of life. The garage was locked but a wall of boxes blocked the back window so he couldn't see if a car was parked in there. He had no way of knowing whether she was home or not. Unless he knocked on her door.

The tablets he'd given her could cause drowsiness. He sighed. So what? That was no reason to bother. She'd be fine. Only there were probably druggies and vagrants in that park in the dark of the night. And she was on the edge of it, alone. In a room above a rickety garage that had to be the size of a postage stamp. Yeah, the niggle turned into a nag and then into a frankly disturbing level of worry. The only way to get rid of it was to see her for himself and thus be sure she was okay. And that was the only reason he wanted to see her. Medical—a professional capacity. But he wasn't her doctor or anything. He was determined *not* to be that. A concerned acquaintance?

Oh, bugger it. He thumped up the stairs, hoping to make enough noise to ensure she'd hear his arrival. He rapped hard on the door. Rapped harder. Shouted out her name. It was at the point when he was considering smashing the lock that he heard a grumbling response.

Finally the door swung open.

At first all he saw was the tee shirt. Less than a second later realised that all she wore was the tee shirt. Cute, cotton, white thing. Maybe there were knickers, but maybe not. His tongue gummed to the roof of his mouth.

'Is everything okay?' Drowsily she tucked her hair back behind her ears.

'That's what I was coming to ask you,' he muttered, barely more intelligible than a grunting Neanderthal. Even sleepy her eyes sparkled. He then made the massive mistake of glancing down. Thighs, calves, ankles. Her long, tanned legs that were slender but also hinted at strength. Yeah, supple muscles were shown off under the gorgeous stretch of golden skin and he wanted to reach out and run his fingers down their warm length. Wanted them to spread again for him.

'I think it's okay,' she said huskily. 'It doesn't seem to be any worse.'

He flinched. He'd totally forgotten about the sting, he'd just been checking her out and wondering about the undies. And now she held her leg slightly outstretched meaning he caught the glimpse of lace-edged silk covering her crotch. His tongue actually tingled as the urge to drop to his knees hit him. He wanted to lick her there. Oh, hell, everywhere.

Cotton tee shirt. He frowned, forced himself to think on the cotton. Not the lace knickers. Sweet not sexy. Not sophisticated. Not appropriate. She was his landlady. This would be mess-up central if he followed the path his body was determinedly dragging him towards. He swallowed, furious with his rapid descent into peeping Tom territory. 'Make sure you reapply the cream.' He snapped more than he meant to.

Her sleepy blue eyes widened. 'Why are you so grumpy?'

He glowered. 'I'm not.'

'Oh, you so are.' She grinned, undaunted. 'But I think it's still there, buried beneath the frown.'

'What's still there?' He couldn't resist asking.

'The ability to have fun.'

The tiny tot was back at flirting? 'Oh, I have fun,' he said deliberately slowly. 'But I'm selective about who I have fun with.'

'That's very wise.' She nodded guilelessly. 'I'm very selective myself.'

Oh, really? His muscles sharpened. 'How much fun have you had?'

Her lashes drooped; she almost pouted. 'Not enough.'

He determinedly looked past her so he wouldn't be tempted to touch those full lips. 'Looks like you've been having a bit.' He nodded towards the empty bottle in the middle of the dining table.

She turned to see what he meant. 'Oh, that…' she swung back, her smile impish '…was good.'

He took the opportunity of her movement to step past her into the room. And was dead unimpressed with what he could see. Furniture from one corner to the other. Furniture on top of furniture, boxes above and below. A tiny single stretcher crammed under the window was her bed? He winced at its obvious discomfort—hard and definitely too short for him. How could she stand it?

'You can't be serious about living here,' he said, all grump again.

'Why not?' she answered coldly.

'There's no *room*.' There wasn't an inch of spare floor space. A half metre square in which to get in from the door and then, bam, *stuff*.

'There's more than enough room for me.'

He looked down at her—too close—in the too small space. Quickly he looked back to the table, anything to stop himself taking rampant advantage of the lack of space. He noticed an 'H' written in permanent marker in the top corner of the wine label. 'What's the H for?'

She glanced at the table and her expression turned guilty.

*Why?* 'Got any more?' he couldn't help teasing.

He glanced round; behind him was a fridge. He shot her a look and reached out a hand. It was literally a bar fridge—and, yes, filled with alcohol. He hadn't actually expected that. The only other item was an oversized container of hummus. 'How many bottles you got in here?' He held the door open, amazed.

'Five,' she said defensively. 'And they're only half bottles.'

He drew one out, saw the single capital letter on the label, bent and saw they each had different letters. 'What do they stand for?'

Roxie folded her arms, never going to admit that she'd blown his rent advance on getting her hair done, some new underwear and half a dozen half-bottles of champagne. 'None of your business.'

'No, go on, they obviously mean something.' Relentlessly he waited.

'All right, H was for getting my hair done.' She defiantly ran her fingers through her hair, flicking it so it fell over her shoulder, almost long enough to cover her breast. Almost. 'I'd waited ages for that.' And she'd drunk it early—to celebrate getting her tenant and the money *for* the haircut. She watched him drag his gaze from the ends of her hair back to the bottles in the fridge.

'What about the P?' he asked.

'For my first public performance.' She stepped forward, quickly trying to explain them all so he'd leave. Trying to think up something for the one whose purpose was flashing neon-sign style in her head. 'T is for when I book my ticket overseas. D is for when I get my driver's licence.' She winced when she said that one—now he'd really think she was a kid. 'A was for the audition—getting through to the Blades. I'm going to have it later.'

'Who are you going to have it with?' he asked.

*You?* Roxie slammed her mouth shut on the instant-response answer and took a half-second to come up with something sassier. 'It's only a half-bottle. I'm going to have it all by myself.'

His brows lifted. 'Did you have the first all by yourself?'

'Absolutely.' She smiled, pleased with her ability to keep talking in the face of his gorgeousness.

'Didn't it have a bit of a kick?'

'Fantastic.' She nodded.

He finally grinned back. 'No headache?'

'That's why I got the good stuff.' And she was feel-ing far more of a kick from the way he was smiling. She was positively giddy and she certainly hadn't been giddy from the champagne last night.

'Have enough of it and you'll still get a hangover.' He actually laughed then. 'You should share them with someone.' His voice dropped.

'Never,' she dismissed him instantly. Dismissing the outrageous invite on the tip of her tongue too. 'Do you know the price of each one of those bottles? It's mine, all mine.'

He chuckled and looked back at the fridge. 'And V, what's that one for?'

Damn, she'd hoped he might have forgotten about that last one. She swallowed, wished her addled brain would come up with something—anything to get her out of this embarrassment.

'Victory?' he asked.

'Yeah.' She nodded enthusiastically. So not going to admit to this guy that the last bottle of Bollinger was for when she finally lost the virginity she'd been dragging round for far too long. 'For when the Knights win the trophy.'

'You drink champagne all the time?'

Uh, try never before last night. 'On special occasions.'

He closed the fridge and eyed her, looking serious now. 'Mind if I ask you a personal question?'

'Go right ahead.' She waited, wondered.

'How old are you?'

She hadn't expected that. 'Twenty-two.'

His mouth thinned.

'That surprises you?' *Unpleasantly?* Why was he looking so unimpressed?

'I thought you were younger.' He swallowed.

Uh-huh. 'How young?'

'Eighteen or so.'

At the most, she reckoned. What was with the putting her in a child's box? 'Well, how old are you?'

'Thirty-one.'

'There's less than a decade between us,' she pointed out with extreme pleasure.

'I'm still a lot older than you.' He seemed determined to labour that one.

'Yeah, but you're hardly old enough to be my father. Unless, of course, you were *very* advanced for your age,' she taunted softy, pleased to see him wince in horror.

'I was very advanced for my age in some areas,' he said, quickly reverting back to his blunt arrogance. 'But, no, I was nice and normal and didn't start fooling around 'til my teens.'

She gritted her teeth. A nice, *normal* teen life. She hadn't had that. She didn't resent the reasons why she hadn't, she had loved caring for her grandparents, but it was time now for her to have the freedom and fun she'd missed out on as an eighteen-year-old. Not to mention the fooling around. Better late than never and she was damn well determined it wouldn't be never. Maybe it could be soon. 'Well, as you now know, I'm more than old enough to be living on my own, in any way I like, drinking whatever I want.' And she'd do whatever she wanted too.

There was a moment's silence. He glanced at the fridge again. 'Do you eat anything?'

She knew he'd noticed the lack of oven. But there was the microwave and a single gas ring. Okay, she was pretty much camping. But it wasn't for ever and it was worth it. 'I usually make a salad or something.'

'From the garden big enough to feed a small island nation?' He turned away, his smile twisting. 'Well, make sure you eat a load tonight and don't have the champagne, given you've had those pills.'

She followed him to the door and leaned against the jamb, well aware that as she lifted her hand her tee shirt rose higher. Sure enough, she saw his eyes dart down. Her thighs burned, not because of the bee. She brushed her hair back from her face with her other hand and watched his gaze flicker first to her hair, then to her chest where her tee shirt had tightened across her bra-less breasts. Emboldened she answered him softly, full of feminine taunt. 'Gabe, I thought we'd just established that I'm not a child.'

His gaze shot to her eyes, intensified—the black pupils expanding to obliterate any hint of the molten colour. The muscles in his jaw were delineated as he clamped his mouth shut. Then he suddenly drew breath. 'You might not be a child, Roxie, but you are a bit too much of a babe for comfort.'

Roxie froze, her body so hot she was on the brink of incineration.

His gaze swept over her one last time before he turned away. 'So I think it's best we steer clear of each other.'

She watched him take the stairs three at a time as if he was escaping some terrible threat. She went back into her studio and smiled. In so many ways Gabe Hollingsworth was a challenge. And Roxie, for all her inexperience, had never backed down from a challenge.

Not even the most impossible.

# CHAPTER THREE

GABE pounded round the park. If his apartment hadn't been leased already he'd have moved back into it. Because finding out her age had not helped. She had that extra five years he'd thought she'd get overseas. She had enough sophistication to tempt him to tease. But it was still wrong—with the landlady thing and the dancer thing.

But then there was the water torture. Every damn morning.

After the first night he'd slept at the Treehouse, he'd been woken by the gentle sound of running water. He'd peered out of the window, then *stared* out of the window. His eyes wide, his wayward cock gaining width too. Yeah, at five o'clock in the freaking morning he'd found out who the gardener was. And how well she danced. Now every morning he was literally *roused* by Roxie watering the garden, doing some kind of insane yogic stretching while the tomatoes got their drink. She warmed up her barely covered body while watering the damn plants. A music player clipped to her hip, headphones in her ears, her whole body swaying. It was enough to drive any man to drink straight spirits. By the gallon. From the way she moved—too sensually— he suspected she knew he watched. Of course he bloody

watched—what man wouldn't? And her deliberate provocation was working—despite his attempt to defuse it
between them and tell her keeping some distance was
best.

Yeah, he was dying of lust. Not only did she disturb
his dreams, but conscious moments when he didn't have
a tight leash on his imagination. He *ached*, hungry every
damn minute of the day.

So now, every morning, Gabe escaped by running
round the park, supposedly sticking well out of temptation's way. Only today, a week after he'd moved in, he
ran faster and harder than ever. No time at all before he
was back at the hidden gate and the giant padlock. And
behind that fence, watering the vegetables, Roxie was
bent over in those short, short shorts. He could see the
headphones in her ears as she bopped round the place,
thinking she was completely alone.

Yeah, okay, he'd known she'd still be there.

Breathing hard—and not because of the forty-minute
run he'd just been on—he walked closer and watched
her legs in action. Thanks to the headphones she had no
idea he was there. It was dangerous. Anyone could sneak
up on her. Anyone who saw the way she danced in her
backyard would be all over her. She needed to be taught
a lesson—that the headphones had to go, the shorts had
to be longer, the dancing needed to stay indoors.

He walked behind her, not bothering to be quiet, because he could hear the thumping beat of her music from
here. In a sudden movement he wrapped his arms around
her. He'd anticipated she'd jump, so he tightened his arms
so she couldn't flee. The hose did a snake dance on the
ground spraying them both, until he kicked it away with
his foot. The cold burst of water didn't cool his insanity
at all.

He let her twist round, feeling her fury, feeling his own fire as her breasts were brought flush against him. He almost growled with the satisfaction of finally having her this close.

'What are you doing?' she shrieked at him.

He plucked buds from her ears. 'No need to shout, I'm right here.'

'Well, why are you right here, sneaking up on me like this,' she panted.

It was sick how much he liked feeling her breathing hard against him. How hard he was breathing too. Oh, her eyes were blue this morning. And her hair in that loose plait with those recently shorn, blonder bits wisping round her face...

'Teaching you a lesson,' he muttered, putting both arms securely around her again. Tightening them.

'What lesson's that?' She looked stunned.

'That when you're alone in the garden, watering whatever and doing your workout, that anyone could sneak up on you.'

'Only some sicko.'

Yeah, like him. 'That's right. So you need to be more careful.'

Roxie was caught between fury and desire. In the first instance, fury won. She brought her knee up between his legs fast. Only slowing at the last possible second.

His eyes widened and he jerked—too late—she just brushed his balls.

'I could have got you really badly then,' she said severely.

He nodded. 'Thanks for not. I've never wanted kids but retaining the physical ability to have the option would be good.' He repositioned himself out of harm's way, but still didn't release her. 'But what if I'd had a weapon?'

'What exactly are you trying to do?' she confronted him. 'You're telling me I can't feel safe in my own backyard? What kind of a kick-in-the-teeth lesson is that?'

'I didn't mean that.' He suddenly frowned. 'I just think you should be careful.'

'I am careful, Gabe. And you know what? In the entire year that I've been living here alone, not one person has bothered to break in.'

No one had bothered to visit either. Honestly? No one had in years.

The silence lengthened. She was vaguely conscious of her rapid breathing, of his, of how close they were pressed together. But the main thing sucking all her attention was that deepening emotion in his eyes. She didn't know what it meant.

'I did,' he eventually said. 'I wanted to.'

Roxie just didn't know what to make of that. Her breathing deepened—so did his, until they were inhaling in sync. It finally occurred to her that she was staring. But she couldn't stop. Randomly she realised he'd been out running. She hadn't known he did that. She also had her palms wide on his shoulders. She wasn't moving them away. The warm, solid strength was wonderful. And arousing.

'You train every morning?' she asked softly, not wanting him to move either.

He nodded his head. 'I find it difficult to sleep in. Here.'

'Does my doing the garden bother you?'

'Yes.'

'Oh.' Too bad. She wasn't going to stop.

'You've always done it?' he asked quietly, inching even closer.

She nodded slowly.

'That's why you have the tan, why you're fit.' Oh, his voice was mesmerising, he was *all* mesmerising.

'That and the dancing.' She relaxed against him a fraction. Felt his tension increase.

'The dancing,' he repeated in a low mutter. 'Yeah.'

'I wear the headphones because I don't want to disturb the neighbours.' She looked up at him with eyes that hadn't blinked in so long they ached.

'You disturb the neighbours anyway. *This* neighbour.'

At her waist, his grip tightened. Then his fingers moved—pushing, creating a space between her tee shirt and waistband—accessing bare skin. She shuddered—an uncontrollable spasm of pleasure as one anticipation was fulfilled. More rose fast. Oh, this was good. This was very, very good.

'This is bad.' He seemed to be talking exclusively to her lips. 'This isn't happening.'

'Why not?' She slid her tongue across her excessively dry lower lip.

He tensed more. 'I'm not in the market for a relationship.'

'Nor am I,' she assured him.

He was silent.

But with his grip this firm on her, his gaze this firm, she grew bold. 'But I do want you…'

He remained silent, but the heat in his expression flared.

'To do me a favour,' she expanded, her voice even softer.

'What?' His gaze remained glued to her mouth.

She didn't know if he was really listening—but she was about to find out. 'Sleep with me.'

His focus shot to meet hers. She lifted her chin a notch, not retreating from her challenge.

His lips twisted. 'Have you had champagne for breakfast?'

She wished she had—it might make this easier. She repeated her new mantra. She was a free spirit, floating through life now. Unafraid to do what she wanted. And she'd take neither acceptance nor rejection to heart. 'I want you to be my lover.' She drew her lip in with her teeth and breathed the last. 'My first.'

His eyes widened. 'What?'

She waited, knowing full well he'd heard.

His hands gently shook her. 'Your *first*?'

A different kind of tension rolled off him now.

Okay, so maybe mentioning the 'first' had been a mistake. But she'd wanted him to know. Thought it was better to be honest. Thought it might tempt him all the more. Only a look of sheer panic scrunched his face. Now he dropped his hands and took a step back.

'Isn't it every man's fantasy?' she asked, suddenly a lot less confident.

'Not mine.'

'No?'

His jaw clamped for a moment; she saw the deep breath he dragged in. Then he lifted his chin. 'No. I don't want some total novice who doesn't know what she's doing. Who'll lie like a log expecting me to do all the work.'

Ouch. How to shoot her down. 'I'm not a total novice. The actual virginity bit is a mere technicality,' she flung at him, furious that he could go cold so quick—and be so damn brutal about it. Chelsea had been right about him being harsh; he had a really offensive kind of defence. But it was an act—she knew it. She'd felt the need in his body. 'I know you're interested,' she said defiantly. 'I've seen the way you look at me.'

'How do I look at you?'

'Like you want to touch.' She moved forward, her boldness returning when he didn't walk away. And damn it, she'd come this far, there was nothing left of her dignity to lose. So she wasn't just flirty, she was shameless. 'And I do know how to touch. Won't be any kind of cold stone.'

'Really?'

She nodded. Hoping her hammering nerves weren't obvious.

He stood like an immovable mountain. In fact she didn't see any part of him move as he murmured, 'Prove it.'

Part of her wanted to tell him to go to hell for playing her so hard. But victory surged through her veins too. Yes, she'd known. She might be a virgin but that didn't mean she was an idiot. He wanted her.

She got to within kissing distance. But she wasn't going to go for the obvious. Nor was she going to make it that easy for him. Somehow she was going to make him suffer for this humiliation.

She looked down his body—as freely, boldly, brazenly as he'd looked at her before. Then she stepped closer, angling her head so her face tucked in near his neck—her own neck exposed to him. She blew, very lightly, on the pulse she could see beating madly just beneath his jaw.

He flinched.

With one, light finger she stroked his forearm, feeling the heat of his skin, the tenseness of the muscles beneath it. She moved, licked her lips, then very lightly pressed them against his salty skin.

He stood like a statue. A very hot, breathing hard one.

'I have had a boyfriend. I know a few things,' she whispered against his throat. 'Done a few things.' Her hand moved to his chest, circling the tight nipple beneath his tee. 'And I'm keen to learn some more.'

She felt the rise and fall as his breathing quickened from just that little touch. And then he seemed to stop breathing altogether.

She moved her hips closer to his. Dancing just that little bit in front of him. Bringing her mouth closer to his throat again. She'd wanted to taste him for so long. She wrapped one arm around his lean waist, her other hand flat on his chest, fingers smoothing.

She felt his response. Rocked her hips closer to the thick erection but pulled back at the last millimetre— *almost* touching, *almost* thrusting against him. But not quite.

She snuck a very quick look at his face. His eyes were shut tight. The muscles in his jaw stood out. His fists clenched at his sides. She felt heady pleasure at seeing how she affected him. But she didn't want him to be in such rigid control. Her instinct was to soften more against him. To come closer, to drape like silk over him. But she sensed that this slightest of distances between them was doing her cause some good.

She rose on tiptoe and gently scraped his ear lobe with her teeth, then whispered, 'I won't just be lying there, Gabe.'

It would be impossible anyway. Her hips had a mind of their own, circling near him in that rhythm that was ancient and instinctive.

He moved, hands slamming her body against his. His fingers digging into her hips. His erection doing the same to her belly. He held her firm, clamping her to him so she couldn't move. Pressed together like this, with only the fabric separating them, she didn't want to. His hardness, her softness. She let her head fall back to meet his fiery gaze, her position wholly submissive as he took her weight. But her eyes and mouth teased.

'Why now?' he asked through tightly clamped teeth.

'It's a good time.' And that was the truth.

'Why me?'

'Isn't it obvious?' she asked breathily. 'Just as it's obvious you want me as much.'

'Only a gay man could fail to react to this stunt of yours,' he growled. 'Even then I reckon he'd rise to it. But that doesn't mean I'm going to follow through.'

Cold seeped into her skin, stiffening her. She straightened as she felt his physical withdrawal. 'Why not?'

'I'm flattered, Roxie.' He stepped back and let her go. 'But this isn't the right thing for you.'

Who was he to judge that? Only she knew what was right for her. 'I'm not a child.'

'No, but you are a lot less experienced than I am. I don't think you've thought this through.'

'Don't insult me.' She'd thought of nothing else for days. 'I've not been hanging onto my chastity for the one and only. It's been more circumstance than design.'

'What, you're an accidental virgin?' he said sarcastically.

'Yeah, for want of a better description, I guess I am.' Jake, her ex-boyfriend, hadn't understood her situation at all. Had run out of patience when she'd said she couldn't go clubbing or partying with him. Yeah, she'd learned years ago that people didn't want to hear about her life— that it made them uncomfortable. After he'd dumped her, she'd gotten so busy at home it was the last thing on her mind. But it was there now.

'That's what that other bottle of Bollinger is for, isn't it?' Gabe said slowly. 'The V bottle. Good grief. You can't be so premeditated about this.'

'Why not? Isn't it better to be prepared with someone suitable rather than have some impulsive experience with someone who might not be able to deliver.' She wanted a good lover and she *knew* Gabe would be more than good. Her physical reaction to him was so intense and an absolute first. She wanted to follow through on it— just knew it would be incredible.

'This isn't impulsive?' He ran both hands through his hair and then bent to pick up the hose and turned it on the garden.

'I thought you might appreciate my honesty. That was clearly a mistake.' She pushed out a deep breath, trying to expel her anger. 'I won't make that one again.'

'What do you mean?' He jerked back to face her.

'Next time I proposition a guy I won't mention the "v" word.'

His jaw dropped. 'Are you planning to proposition another guy?'

'Maybe not today, but hopefully soon,' she bluffed, wishing she could meet someone even more attractive first thing so she could get over the ache she had for the impossible one in front of her.

'You have to tell him you're a virgin,' Gabe snapped.

As if she'd ever do that now. 'Why? It shouldn't make any difference.'

'Of course it makes a difference,' he said, looking angrier than ever. 'You should want someone who's in love with you and who you're in love with.'

She gaped at him. Who'd have thought the supposed ultimate slayer had a romantic streak? 'Were you in love with your first?' she asked.

'That was different.' He turned back to the garden, spraying the hose wildly over the paths rather than the plants.

'Why? Because you're a man and it's different for men?' She glowered at him. 'Why can't I have sex just for the pleasure of it, for the curiosity. Why did you have sex that first time?'

He growled. 'It's not the same.'

'Why not?' Her voice rose. 'Why can't women have the same kind of sex drive? is it somehow wrong to admit to it?'

His knuckles were white on the hose. 'No, but don't throw it away on some skunk. It's a gift you should give someone who'll appreciate it.'

Roxie groaned in frustration, too cross to care about how indiscreet she was being. 'I never thought you'd be so old-fashioned. Your reputation is so wrong.'

He tossed the hose and grabbed her arm instead. His grip so hard his knuckles remained white. Not that she minded that much, truthfully—her skin sizzled from his touch, and her insides melted.

'Is that why you picked me?' he asked. 'Because of something you heard, something you think you know?'

His anger made her own flare again and she pushed even closer to his tense fury. 'I asked you because you're hot. And, yeah, rumour has it you're good and you're not interested in commitment. All three are on my essential list.'

'Most women have commitment-friendly on their essential list,' he snapped back, his black eyes incandescent. 'Why don't you?'

'Because I don't want to be tied down. *Ever.*'

His brief bark of laughter was filled with disbelief. 'So there's going to be no marriage, kids and people carrier for you?'

'Never.'

He grinned savagely but his grip on her eased. 'Never is a very long time for a young woman.'

'Don't patronise me.' Jerk. 'I know what I want and what I don't want.' She wasn't going through the heartache that family brought again. She just wasn't ever. She had the need-to-be-free gene and she wasn't going to screw it up as her mother had by having a child or any kind of lengthy relationship.

'What you want is someone who'll do right by you,' he said, harsh again.

'And you won't? You're saying you're not up to the challenge?' She leaned so close she nearly kissed him as she whispered in a low taunt, 'You're not good enough as a lover?'

'Don't try to tease me into it,' he said through gritted teeth, letting go of her completely. 'It won't work.'

'Won't it?' She looked down his body, brazen in her assessment of his aroused state. 'You're only human, Gabe.'

'That's right, I'm human. I'm not an animal. I have self-control and free will. Choice.' He drew in a deep breath and then pushed back her braid from her shoulder with a surprisingly gentle hand. 'Are you going to use your innocent wiles to try to tempt me into losing that control?'

Silent, she just looked at him. Because, hell, yes, she wished she could do just that. It would so totally serve him right.

A wicked, patronising grin made him look like a smug satyr. 'You think you can play with fire, Roxie?'

'You're the fire?' she scorned. 'You're so not the blaze I'd heard about. All you are is insufferably arrogant.'

'Well, haven't you just given me more reason to be?' he drawled back, before snapping, 'I'm doing what's best for both of us. And, honey, you're not hot enough for me.'

She knew what he was doing. Pushing her away by putting her down. Bastard. 'Making me mad with you isn't going to make me want you less,' she said brazenly. If anything it made it worse. Yeah, now she wanted to see him shaking with desire for her—on his damn *knees* for her. 'I'm more than hot enough for you. I might be a virgin but I'm not stupid.'

His grin died an instant death. 'And that's another reason to say no.' He walked further away that time. 'This conversation is over. We'll pretend it never happened. Landlord, tenant, vague acquaintance at the stadium. That's all we are.'

Roxie remained where she was, feet apart, skin burning, senses screaming to be back in touch zone. 'Let me remind you, Gabe, that you were the one who started this.'

Gabe stopped and turned, his body howling at him for doing this hatefully 'right' thing in such a rubbish way. Being chivalrous really wasn't all it was cracked up to be and it was almost impossible. But now there was no choice—no matter her age or intelligence, learning Roxie was that inexperienced ruled out any kind of thing between them. He refused to be the cause of another girl's emotional—and mental—meltdown. And he was an absolute fool for taunting her into touching him just then; it had brought nothing but more torture for himself. 'I think we could debate that one for some time too. But for now, okay, I'll take the blame. I'm not too filled with self-worth to be unable to admit I make mistakes. This was a huge mistake. We're not making it worse.'

Yeah, as if he could really think that. Honestly?

It couldn't get any worse.

# CHAPTER FOUR

'SEEN the new dancer?' Dion asked him as they watched the boys doing their drills that afternoon. 'Your bee-sting girl got in and she's good.'

She wasn't his bee-sting girl. And he was trying very hard not to watch the women doing the warm-ups down the other end of the pitch. Usually they made it a rule not to practise when the girls were around—it was too distracting. But it was the day before the first big game of the season and everyone wanted extra pitch time.

'Foxy Roxie.' Dion's smile was pure evil.

Gabe nearly jumped out of his skin. 'Who's calling her that?' He consciously tried to relax but his body had been nuked and he was boiling from the inside out.

'Jimmy, couple of those new kids. Got their eyes trained.'

Foxy Roxie wasn't that at all. She might have her hair blonded and her eyelashes blackened and her breasts pushed up front and centre, but that was all surface. The suggestion of sophistication was merely skin deep. She was an innocent at large. Admittedly she didn't want to be innocent but that was beside the point. She still was. And he didn't want any of those louts taking advantage of her. No, truth was, he wanted to take total advantage himself.

'She's just a kid.' He tried to act dismissive and completely blanked Dion's snort of laughter.

Inevitably the two groups met up as practice ended. It was brief, management were watching close to make sure the boys didn't get up to bad the night before a big game. She stood on the edge of the circle of dancers, not saying anything, a little distanced. Probably because she was new. But it was only a matter of time before one of the guys would strike up a conversation with her. Sure enough, one of the young bloods took a buddy as back-up. Shook her hand and everything. But Roxie had a back-up too, another dancer who was doing all the talking while Roxie had a Mona Lisa smile on.

Gabe didn't like her standing that near to any of them. As he watched she flicked a glance at him. Her blue eyes burned brighter—and she smiled wider at the guy beside her. Gabe knew she was doing it deliberately to tease him. Because every few moments she glanced back at him, saw him watching and her blue eyes burned brighter.

So, yes, he was staring. And, no, he couldn't stop. The thought of her hooking up with someone else ate him whole.

When she went to put her empty electrolyte bottle in the recycling bin he took the chance to talk. 'Don't do anything dumb.'

He'd been a jerk to her—several times over—and he deeply regretted it. But he didn't want her making a worse mistake out of hurt pride. Of course, complete louse that he was, the thing he regretted most was not kissing her.

'Didn't think you cared,' she said with an annoying level of composure.

He hesitated.

She smiled, drawing his attention to her glossed lips. Yeah, he totally regretted not kissing her. It was all he'd been thinking about since—how soft and hot she'd been in his arms, how vibrant, how beautiful. Fresh as a damn daisy.

'You had your chance,' she said with a smugness that suggested she could read his mind.

'You'd go off with just anyone?' he asked snarkily.

'Not just anyone. I'm sizing them up. You know them well, got any recommendations for me?'

'Not funny.'

It really wasn't. But she chuckled anyway.

'Not one of those guys would be any good,' he said firmly. Would it be bad if he told her they all had STDs? Yeah, defamatory and enough to cost him his job.

'None as good as you, right?' Her eyes sparkled. 'Oh, Gabe, ever heard of the dog in the manger?'

'I just think you're making a mistake.' Massive mistake. And the idea of it was killing him.

'No, I'm getting on with my life. There are lots of things I want to do. This is just one of them.'

'Well, do some other things first.' He thought half desperately. 'Go swim with dolphins or something—wouldn't that be good?'

She put on a thoughtful pose and her eyes went bluer than that fantasy ocean he wanted her to dive into—alone. 'I guess that would be good. I'll add it to my list. But right now I'm enjoying flirting.'

He put his hand on her arm to stop her, couldn't resist that smallest touch. 'Some of these boys don't know how to do slow,' he warned.

She turned back to face him, her smile slaying all his good intentions. 'Who said anything about slow?'

She pulled her arm free and sauntered back to the

group of girls and their hangers on, and Gabe was left
with his jaw hanging mid-air. Yeah, he couldn't leave.
Just stood, ostensibly laughing at some of the jokes with
the guys, but, really, watching her like a damn hawk and
mad with himself for obsessing. It was only because he'd
put her out of bounds that he wanted her so much, right?

The boys started to go, keen to get an early night. But
those two talking to her were still here. Then she moved.
So, naturally, Gabe did too.

'You're leaving?' He caught up to her as she headed
towards the corridor.

'Yes, I'm leaving,' she confirmed sarcastically.

'Alone?' Oh, he was so enthralled he had to ask more
to be sure. It was pathetic.

'Gabe, it's the night before the first big game of the
season. You really think any of those boys are going to
go for an up-all-nighter with me now?'

Actually he wouldn't blame any of those boys for picking pleasure with her over being sensible the night before
the season starter. But it seemed they were more professional than he was. Had more self-control. He glanced
back at the group of them and saw several watching her.
Yeah, she was the new crush. He walked out with her,
happy to let them see it. If they thought he had a claim,
that was fine by him. He didn't give a damn about maintaining his no-dating-in-the-stadium distance this second.

He walked with her to the car park, watched when
she stopped and pulled a key from her pocket. 'This is
your car?'

Roxie paused—he was all wide-eyed and animated
as he took in the gleaming metal—and she couldn't hold
back her smile any more. 'Sure is.'

He blinked a couple of times before running a hand

over the bonnet. 'Wouldn't have expected that.' Only then he frowned. 'But doesn't one of your Bolly bottles have D on it? For *driver's…*' His gaze narrowed and he whirled towards her. 'Show me your licence.'

'Only when you show me your badge, *officer,*' she drawled, finding such pleasure in mocking him. She was in way too good a mood because he hadn't wanted her to flirt with those others. That in fact he'd followed her out and hadn't seemed to care that everyone had watched him do it.

'You're driving illegally.' He looked amazed and suddenly laughed. 'I can't believe that Miss Goody Two-Shoes is driving illegally.'

She steeled herself to resist her melt reaction to his laughter. 'Why do you think I'm Miss Goody Two-Shoes?'

'Oh, come on.' He met her gaze with that warm humour glinting in his own. 'You're totally good. You *told* me how good.'

She sighed and exaggeratedly rolled her eyes. 'I really don't think virginity ought to have anything to do with whether a girl is "good" or not. You need to get over your outdated stereotypes of women.'

His grin went totally wicked. 'You're right. But you dare take me to task about stereotypes? What about your new hairdo, your fake breasts, your sudden decision to shimmy and shake it all in public? Truth is you live in a hideout and garden instead of partying. You're Roxanna not Foxy Roxie, you're playing at being a sophisticated vamp go-go dancer. Question is why?'

*Foxy Roxie?* Oh, she wished. 'I'm not playing at anything. What do you think I am, some toddler who's got into her mother's make-up drawer? So you saw me before I had my hair done, so what? I'm capable of more bad than you can ever imagine.' And she was thinking *such* bad thoughts this second. And just because she'd never acted on them much in the past, didn't mean she wouldn't in the future—or *now*.

The glint of humour got lost in the brilliant blackness of his eyes. 'Actually I can imagine.' His voice dropped. 'Believe me, I can.'

She turned her back on him and his damn flip-flop, flirt-or-not attitude. Just to breathe for a second. But he took the step right up to her car, right beside her, so close she couldn't actually open the door.

'So if you're capable of all that bad,' he muttered low in her ear, 'why didn't you have sex with your boyfriend in the back seat of this baby?'

Burning from the inside out, she gave his shoulder a shove—but he didn't move. 'Because it would have been disrespectful,' she answered honestly—and breathlessly.

He spun, leaning back on the door, and getting his face right in hers. 'No more disrespectful than driving round without a licence. How come the cops have never pulled you over?'

She shrugged, battling the urge to lean in the inch that would bring her mouth into contact with his. 'It's a vintage car in mint condition. I think they assume that the dame behind the wheel cares for the car way too much to be doing anything illegal. I always drive carefully.'

'It must be heavy to steer,' he said almost absently, his gaze not releasing hers. 'Who taught you to drive?'

'My grandfather. It was his pride and joy and I respected *him*, so, no, I wasn't going to get spunk stains on the leather.' She'd never have done that to her grandparents. Especially not when her mother had disappointed them with the whole 'baby out of wedlock and left them to hold it' thing.

His smile deepened at her crude reference. 'So why haven't you got the licence?'

'I haven't had the opportunity.'

He looked sceptical. '*How* can you not have had the opportunity?'

'I've been busy,' she fudged. 'Besides, L-plates would ruin the look of the car.'

She'd needed to be able to drive at any time—to get to the urgent pharmacy or wherever when her grandfather's meds ran out. Sure, she could have done it in the last few months, but, yeah, there was that one bit of her that wanted to stick it to the authorities. The institutions that had abandoned her and her family. They'd been left alone to deal with everything. There'd been no support structures. A social-worker visit a long time ago. No follow up. Because by then she was no longer a child— she'd just turned seventeen, her grandmother had just died and left her the sole carer for her grandfather at the beginning of what ended up a long illness. The time she'd needed someone—anyone—to help, there'd been no one.

'You have to get your licence. You can't keep driving without it.'

Who was the Goody Two-Shoes now? Struck her that Gabe had more of a conservative element than anyone had guessed. 'I'm working on it.'

'Getting the celebratory Bolly isn't exactly working on it.' He eyeballed her and looked dead serious. 'Give me the keys.'

She sighed dramatically, covering the hiccup in her heartbeat. 'Who do you think you are?'

Somehow he broadened his position, blocking her from the car door. 'Give me the keys or I'll call the cops and dob you in.'

She gasped at the unmistakable menace in his tone. 'You wouldn't be such a nark.'

'Try me.'

She curled her fingers round the keys so hard they marked her skin.

He just waited, his hand outstretched. 'Give.'

Her nostrils flared as she smacked the keys down hard on his upturned palm.

He straightened and spun, unlocked the car and got into the driver's seat with a wicked grin on his face as he unwound the window to talk to her. 'I've always wanted to drive one of these. Can I drive home?'

She glared at him looking so at home in her 1954 Mark 1 Zephyr with its powder-blue base and gleaming chrome. No way was he driving her baby. 'What about your own car?' It was one of those sporty convertible things that cost an absolute fortune. Parked only a few spots away from hers, it was too flash for daylight.

He reached into his pocket and threw his keys at her. 'You drive it.'

She was so shocked she failed to catch them. 'No way.' She picked the keys from the ground, balled her fists and stuck them on her hips.

'Why not?' He laughed, annoyingly. And, yes, reheating those parts that always leapt to life in his presence. The melt was almost impossible to prevent now.

'Because it's worth eighty times what mine is,' she fumed, trying to stay mad with him, trying not to like him all the more for teasing her so hard. 'I drive that and you're not insured. I can't afford any bill to fix a dent in your baby.'

He leaned back in the seat, a smug expression all over. 'Goody Two-Shoes.'

'Fine, so what if I am?'

'You *stay* that way.' His eyes flashed as he got out of the car and handed her keys back to her. 'You know, you really should get your licence,' he said condescendingly. 'You're not covered by insurance without it. One day you'll get caught and then you'll get done. You don't want a conviction to ruin your chances of getting an entry visa into the US or wherever it is you want to go travelling to, do you?'

She frowned, not pleased by that idea. 'Could that happen?'

He shrugged. 'Dunno. Maybe.' He held the door for her, way too close again as she took up position in the driver's seat. 'Guess you'd better drive carefully...' He trailed off and then dipped down to murmur slyly, 'Unless you want me to drive you?'

Oh, now there was no holding back on the flirt of it. Not when he couldn't help himself either. She turned her head and peered up at him, fluttering her lashes. 'Gabe, you know I want you to drive,' she cooed. 'Just not my car.'

He chuckled as he shut the door, then reached through the window to gently brush her jaw with his knuckles. 'Keep working on the sass, I'm sure one day you'll graduate to fully frisky vixen.'

She glared at him and started the engine. 'Better stand back, the steering on this beast can be tricky sometimes, wouldn't want to run over your toes.'

He followed her home, making her so hot and bothered she missed a couple of gear changes. A glance in her rear-view mirror showed the flash of his smile in the car too close behind hers. She turned into her place, got out to drag open the heavy old garage door, then parked her car inside.

He'd parked on the street, so she left the garage door

open for him. He walked in and shut it with annoying ease. Then he walked to where she was trying to straighten the blue tarpaulin that barely covered the towers of cardboard boxes she'd stacked along the back wall.

'You have so much stuff,' he commented as she turned towards him.

'Yeah, but at least it's all sorted now.' She glanced back at the boxes with displeasure. 'I'm not sure what to do with it.'

'You don't want to keep it?'

'Not all of it. But if I let it go, then it's gone for good.' All the memories, the stories, their lives. She'd been through every inch and not found the answers she wanted. 'Same with the furniture.' She sighed and walked to the small door that led out to the garden. 'I got rid of a few things, but you've seen the rest all jammed in up there.' And she couldn't bring herself to get rid of it.

'There's no one else who might want some of it?' he asked as he followed her.

'No. My mother was an only child. So was I.' No aunts and uncles, no cousins. She was the only one left in her little family.

'What about your father?'

Roxie hardened her heart enough to be able to answer lightly. 'I don't know anything about him.'

'Not even his name?' he joked.

But she couldn't do more than answer baldly then. 'No.'

'Oh.' He cleared his throat and looked anywhere but at her. 'Sorry.'

'It's okay.' Now she felt sorry for making him feel awkward. She shouldn't have said anything but she felt as if she had to explain more now—to ease over the moment. 'There aren't any records. No clues in any of those boxes. Naturally no bureaucratic department is able to help either.' She forced a smile. They never seemed to be able to help her.

He met her eyes and half smiled back. 'So this was your mum's house?'

'No, she lived in the UK. I was raised by my grand-parents. This is their house.'

'And they left it to you?'

She nodded.

'When?'

Oh, man, hadn't they covered enough already? He didn't know it but he was dragging the conversation to even boggier ground. But she maintained her smile and quickly recited the facts. 'My grandmother died when I was sixteen. My grandfather died just over a year ago.'

'I'm sorry.' He turned slightly away and looked at the beautiful house, which was good because holding her smile was causing mouth ache. 'Where's your mum now?'

Roxie closed her eyes for a split second. 'She died when I was eight.'

'Man,' he muttered softly. 'That's rough.'

Roxie shrugged and downplayed it. 'She lived over-seas. I grew up with my grandparents so I didn't know her that well. I've lived here all my life.'

Long ago she had mourned for what could have been, as a kid she'd been filled with the idealistic hope that her mother would one day return to her and would answer all her deep-held questions. But that hadn't happened and any chance of getting those answers had been bur-ied with the last of her family. She'd spent the year sort-ing through papers, sorting through those feelings. Now she'd put them all into boxes and sealed them away.

She glanced at him and saw the one thing she'd never seen from anyone else. The one thing she *didn't* want to see from him.

'I don't need sympathy, Gabe,' she said, annoyed by it. 'A year or so ago, it would have been nice.' And she couldn't help throwing him the challenge that one last time. 'What I need now is some fun and adventure. It's been a long time coming.' There was no soft coo, or coy look this time, she spoke with hard, raw honesty.

'I don't think diving off the deep end is the way to go,' he answered with clipped finality.

Roxie couldn't believe it—so the flirt of mere minutes ago had just been that? He was still denying this? So much for him being the ultimate slayer. He'd come over all old-school gallant because of that one stupid word—virgin. She had no idea how he'd got that playboy reputation; it truly was misplaced. And she was mortified because she'd thrown herself so hard at him.

'You don't think I can handle it? I've handled more than you can ever imagine.' But she sure as hell wasn't going to give him the fine details of her sob story to gain points like some try-hard on a reality TV talent show. She was mad with herself for saying the bit she had already. Sympathy *really* wasn't what she wanted.

He looked at her too intently for another too long moment, his stance rigid. 'I'll see you at the game tomorrow.' His parting words came over his shoulder as he strode away. 'Dance hard.'

# CHAPTER FIVE

Roxie pulled on her costume, engulfed by embarrassment. Gabe was avoiding her. She'd seen him duck his head back from the window when she'd been out in the garden this morning and he'd immediately zipped the other way when he'd seen her down the corridor at the stadium as she'd arrived half an hour before. So, yeah, she'd made a huge mistake. He wasn't interested at all— had merely been flirting for amusement. And now he knew some of her history he was probably afraid she was all fragile and about to go crazy like his ex.

'Almost ready?' Chelsea asked with a bouncy flick of her hair.

Roxie nodded and bent to smooth her outfit so she could hide her face. Yep, she should have paid closer attention to Chelsea's warning. If it weren't for the fact that she didn't have her funds together yet, she'd be on the next plane.

And now there was this. Her first night dancing as a Silver Blade. She stared at her reflection, trying to tell herself that if she didn't recognise herself, no one else would, and therefore it wouldn't matter if she made a total dork of herself on the pitch. Only she was terrified—all her confidence and self-belief sucked away. *What* did she think she *was* doing? She was going to make a total fool of herself. She didn't have the experience or the training for this. And as she frowned at the mirror she realised she couldn't remember the start of their first routine. She'd gone totally blank. She tried to breathe but she needed fresh air—not the clouds of hairspray in the Blades' change room. The fumes were stinging her eyes.

Gabe was almost ready for the game. He'd strapped a couple of players' knees for extra support, had his kit ready for sideline duty. But his head was somewhere else altogether—repeatedly banging on the brick wall of desire. He was out of his mind for that provocative, beautiful woman so out of bounds. He went for a walk, determined to claw back the necessary focus. Striding along the corridor, he almost missed the shadow lurking at the back of a remote stairwell. He did a double take, but his body recognised her immediately. 'Roxie? What are you doing here?'

'Nothing. Having a moment. Go away.' The last of her breathless comments rose. Kind of like a question but more like hysteria.

'No.' He moved closer, answering her firmly. 'You're upset. What's wrong?' Adrenalin surged, his muscles flooded with aggression-filled strength. 'Has one of the players done something?'

'What? No!'

He believed her, but he also heard the raw emotion cracking her voice. He'd seen plenty of fear in his job and he saw it in her now. The way she was clutching her hands together, as if she was trying to stop herself fleeing. Beneath the silver glitter her eyes were wide with terror.

Concern gripped him. 'Please tell me what's wrong.'

He couldn't breathe, holding himself back from drawing her hard against him so he could keep her safe from whatever, wherever, the danger was.

'I'm fine. Really. Just having a breather. Lots of perfume in that room, you know?'

She was babbling. Why was she babbling?

'I wanted a walk. You know. Clear the head.' She looked at him with eyes so huge they were manic. 'I'm nervous.'

Finally he could release the screaming tension in his lungs. He was so relieved, but he knew better than to laugh at her. 'You're a great dancer. You'll be fine.'

She shook her head violently, her hair streaming out like a gold and bronze waterfall. 'I've never done it before.'

He groaned. 'Roxie, now is not the time to talk—'

'No.' She actually managed a laugh. 'Not that. I've never danced in front of an audience.'

*'What?'* She had to be kidding. Never danced before an audience?

She was still talking—faster and faster. 'The stadium is full. And there's the broadcast—all those viewers at home. I've not been to a dance class in *years*. I did ballet as a girl but when Grandma had the stroke, I gave up classes. I'm self-taught from dance vids and music clips. I'm not good enough to be alongside those professionally trained girls with all their experience. Who am I kidding? I can't do it.'

'Yes, you can.' Gabe's head was spinning with all that info, with a ton more questions.

But she just shook her head wildly, her body trembling, on the edge of making a run for it.

'Just imagine you're in the garden and there's no one there.' He stepped closer and kept his voice calm. 'You dance incredibly in the garden.' He'd watched her so often, he knew how damn well she moved. A million times better than any of those other girls—she totally had edge.

She looked even more panicked. 'I can't do it.'

Fear was irrational. And it was obvious his rational attempt to reassure wasn't going to work. But he wasn't about to tranquillise her, which left only one course of action—distraction.

And this was purely to offer comfort, right? There was comfort in a cuddle. That was all it would be. He could manage that and only that. For sure. Because there was no way he couldn't touch her now. He didn't have the strength not to. Didn't have the desire not to. All that mattered was making her feel that little bit better.

Roxie was almost in tears. Trying so hard to blink them back because she was going to ruin her make-up if they spilt over. And she hadn't cried in months—she couldn't cry over something as silly as this. She held her hands together, pressing them tight just below her ribs. Wanting to stop shaking, unable to control her agitated movements. The more she tried to calm down, the more upset she got. And having him here wasn't helping. She'd been getting a grip 'til now. Now she was all over the place. She wanted him to clear off. Only now he'd moved right in front of her.

'Roxie.' He gripped her shoulders hard.

Startled, she lifted her head to look into his face.

'Roxie,' he said again, the tone of his voice totally changing.

Her whole system froze for a moment and then slowly focused on him. But he didn't say anything more, just the smallest of smiles appeared on his face. Fascinated, she watched, because that smile wasn't one she'd seen from him before—that smile was full of naughtiness, full of promise. His eyes reflected it, darkening with only a slim gleam shining from the very centre. She held her breath as his expression deepened wickedly. It looked as if the rake in him had been released.

One hand released her shoulder, moving close to cup her jaw, his broad palm pressed almost the length of her throat. He held her firmly. Her breathing slowed as she watched him move so slowly nearer. His touch seemed to drug her, replacing the anxiety twitching through her veins with a sluggish warmth instead. She couldn't move—not to encourage, or to run away. She could only wait. And want.

His thumb moved, stroking, the pressure of his fingers increasing on the vulnerable pulse point in her neck. She felt the release of his breath over her face. Her eyelids fluttered, blocking the visual overload from him being so close, so her body could focus on the touch, the scent.

His kiss was soft and not anywhere near enough to her lips. She felt the pull deep within—the ember that had been smouldering for so long was blown into a flame with just those too few touches.

'You're going to be amazing,' he whispered, almost crooning, as his lips touched her skin. 'Just amazing.' He kissed along her jaw. 'You are amazing.'

Heat flooded her system, galvanising her again—only this time the energy pulsing through her was born not of fear, but of desire. She wanted closer, wanted to cling. The one thing she'd wanted for days was now in front of her. Teasing, tormenting, captivating—just out of reach.

'Go out and have fun,' he said.

She didn't care about the damn dancing any more. The fun was right here.

'Kiss me,' she said softly.

He did, but not where she wanted. Another series of kisses down her throat. He brushed the swathe of hair from her neck, clearing the path for his lips with skilful strokes of his fingertips.

She leaned closer, felt one hand at her back as he adjusted to take her weight, crushing her to his length. She threw her head back, abandoned, as he pressed ever more passionate kisses across her skin. His teeth nipped, his tongue flickered to soothe the tiny scratches, his hands held. She discovered just how much she loved to be held by him. How much she'd wanted it. She yielded to him completely.

'Roxie,' his tone warned, his voice rasping.

Her body burned for more. 'Kiss me properly.' She wanted his mouth on hers. She wanted to be absorbed entirely in his embrace.

She could feel the acceleration in his breathing as his abdomen was sealed to hers, could feel the hunger rising as his kisses swooped lower, across her chest, down to the curve of her amplified breasts. He licked down the deep vee of her Lycra top. She felt the hardening in his body as hers softened—his bulging erection insistent against her belly.

'Gabe,' she begged.

He dragged his mouth from her skin. 'I'll kiss you properly after the show.' A hot, rough mutter.

Her heart banged. 'No.' She rolled her hips against his, teasing the only way she could. 'Now.'

Both his hands gripped her butt, holding her still— flush against his strained jeans. 'After.'

'No,' she sighed, rubbing against him. The tiniest of

movements that his grip allowed, but enough to send her to the brink of ecstasy. 'Please.'

'You're going to be late,' he groaned, his mouth dropping to her collarbone again, his pelvis rocking powerfully against hers. 'You can't be late.'

'Don't stop.' She didn't care how desperate she sounded.

He moved against her once more, his kisses frantic on her skin, his groan harsh in her ears. Her nipples screamed for his mouth to cover them, the hunger in her womb was all heat. Oh, she wanted him, wanted, wanted, wanted.

'Please kiss me,' she begged. 'Please.'

But then, with a set jaw he stepped back. '*After* the show.'

Panting, she couldn't believe it. She shook her head, but was too breathless to plead more. He took her upper arm in a firm grip and walked, swiftly guiding her back down the corridor towards the changing room. He pushed the door open but kept walking—leaving her.

'There you are!' Chelsea called from inside. 'I was wondering.'

Roxie had no choice but to go in. So warm, so excited, so amazed. Slowly her smile spread. He'd changed his mind. He was hers. No way could he deny them now. She'd felt the way he shook for her, how hard, how strong his hunger was.

'Ready?' Chelsea asked. 'You look great.'

A quick glance in the mirror showed sparkling eyes, her cheeks glowing. Blood racing. Every cell singing in excitement. And her make-up still perfect.

'I am *so* ready.' She beamed. She couldn't wait for it to be over.

In the distance, the music thumped, amping the crowd

higher. She heard the calls, the whistles. She laughed aloud as they ran through the tunnel and out onto the pitch. The noise burst into her. It was crazy, it was fun and it was only the beginning. She moved fast, her body fluid, free, totally relaxed, zinging on the anticipation. She'd never loved dancing so much. Never felt so aware of her body.

She wasn't aware of anyone watching her, the crowd a distant blur, and inside her mind she saw only him, his breathlessness, his dark eyes gleaming beneath half-closed lashes. She danced thinking of nothing and no one but him, of his expression as he'd moved closer, of the way he'd seemed to savour every touch of her skin. Being that desired was incredibly intoxicating. And the heady pleasure released her from any anxiety, any self-consciousness. She danced only for him and for herself.

During the game she knelt on the sideline with the other dancers. For this part they held pompoms, which they were to shake and shimmy at high points in the game—i.e. when the boys scored. Which they frequently did. She was loving it now—looking forward to dancing more at half-time. All nerves eviscerated.

She knew exactly where Gabe was—impossible to miss him with his neon green vest over his jeans and DOCTOR printed in large lettering across the back. Far sexier than the numbers on the rugby pitch. He ran on a couple of times to deal with blood injuries. She saw him moving to ice a couple of boys' knees and ankles when fresh players were subbed on in the second half. She was so aware of him, felt such a connection, it was a wonder the world couldn't see the string attached from her eyes to him.

After the game—which naturally the Knights won— she wriggled out of her costume and into her new dress.

The kind of thing she'd never have worn when her grand-father was around to see it. Not that it was low cut, but it clung in all the right places—to the curves that she'd let go back to almost normal in just a booster bra rather than all-out padded. False advertising wasn't necessary for Gabe, he already knew what was on offer and, to her great pleasure, he still wanted. There was an after-match function within the stadium and then most of the players and dancers went to a particular club in town. Her first time to attend. But she'd happily skip it. She couldn't wait to be alone with Gabe—to finally get the kiss she'd been waiting for for ever. And then everything else.

She walked into the crowded room with a couple of the other dancers, her smile impossible to contain. She searched, her eyes flickering from one tall man to the next. Her heart beat louder, drowning the noise of talk and laughter and clinking glasses. Icy awareness slith-ered down her spine. She was certain before she'd even finished her sweep of the room.

Gabe had gone.

# CHAPTER SIX

ROXIE ran up the stairs to her tiny bedsit above the garage, too defiant to bother about being quiet. There was no light on in the house so maybe he was still out. Maybe she'd missed him somehow and he was still at the bar waiting for her.

But she knew he wasn't. She'd stayed for the drinks, gone on to the club and danced her heart out in the crowd, pretending she didn't care that the coward had chickened out of following through with her. He was still treating her like someone not old enough or cool enough or sophisticated enough to be with him.

So now, nearly two in the morning, she unwound the wire cage on the P-for-performance bottle of Bolly. Stood in her open doorway and fired the cork towards his house. Then was crass enough to drink straight from the bottle.

It tasted good.

She was hot and thirsty, both angered and excited, sleep was utterly impossible. So standing on the landing out in the warm night air, swigging from a bottle that was emptying surprisingly quickly, seemed like a damn fine idea. She glared over at his house, mentally rehearsing what she was going to say to him as soon as she saw him again. With every sip she grew more riled, more defiant, more confident.

Damn the man.

She had a key to his house. After all, it was *her* house. And he was so going to get a piece of her mind. He owed her. Why shouldn't she go in now and let him know all about it?

She ditched the drained bottle and grabbed her keys, kicking off her shoes before skipping down the stairs and along the path that led to his back door. She unlocked it and stepped inside. Realised then that she didn't know which room he'd taken. No matter, the house was hardly huge.

She walked into the master bedroom downstairs. The one with the en suite where he'd washed out her eyes. Nothing.

Which left only the bedroom upstairs on the mezzanine floor—her old room. The door was ajar; she nudged it open. He hadn't drawn the curtains and living in the central city meant there was a lot of light pollution, so she could see quite well—especially with the full moonlight streaming in as well.

She stared at the bed. The bastard was sound asleep. How the hell could he be sound asleep when she was being eaten alive by fantasies of everything she wanted to do to him—and for him to do to her?

Without thinking she walked closer, because it was a hot night and he was sleeping with just a sheet covering him. No pjs or tee shirt or vest or anything. Just a sheet that was currently resting low round his hips. She drank in the sight of his bare chest, breathed deep as she scoped his ripped abs.

He stirred and opened his eyes. Took a glimpse of her

and groaned, closing his eyes tight. 'F...in' dreamin'...
Rox...'

Enthralled, she watched as he groaned her name
again, watched his hand slide below that sheet to where
it was seriously rucked up. He sighed then, frustration
seeking satisfaction.

O-o-okay-yay-yay-yay.

She smiled broadly, thrilled to know she wasn't alone
in dealing with explicit dreams. She reached forward and
trailed a finger down his sternum towards his belly button. 'I'm right here.'

'What the...!' He sat bolt upright, his hand slamming
on top of hers, squashing it against his chest so she could
feel his heart thumping right through her fingers.

*'Roxie?'* His eyes horrified wide. 'What the hell are
you doing here?'

She tried to tug her hand free but he didn't let it go.
He glared, his chest rising and falling as if he'd been
sprinting.

She glared back. 'You ran out on me.'

'Roxie...' He flung her hand from him. 'You can't
just break into someone's house.'

'For the record, this is *my* house. But don't panic,' she
drawled sarcastically. 'I'm not here to attack you or move
in on you. I just want to give you a piece of my mind.'

He puffed out a big breath. 'It couldn't wait 'til morning?'

'No, because you acted like a jerk.'

'No, I didn't,' he snapped back. 'I was very nice and
helped calm your nerves.'

'Oh, like they taught you that in med school? Don't
try to act like it wasn't something *you* instigated. And
don't try to pretend it wasn't something you've wanted

·for days. And don't you dare try to pretend nothing more personal isn't going to happen.'

He shifted. The sheet slipped. He hastily pulled it back.

Yeah, his 'personal' reaction was only getting bigger. And she was beyond sure of him now. Anticipation licked her nerves and made her laugh. 'Did you know there's over two hundred and fifty million bubbles in a bottle of champagne? Which means there are about a hundred and twenty-five million bubbles zinging through my veins now.'

Gabe leaned back and rested his head back on the headboard, his pulse still settling from the shock of waking to find her in his room. But this reality was no nightmare, just pure fantasy—a too-pretty girl laughing at him, daring him, tempting him. 'Someone bothered to count?' he drawled, trying to feign some cool—some control.

'Apparently so.'

'You've had your bottle, then?'

'All by myself.' She sniffed. 'You should have had some with me.'

He shook his head slowly, ruefully smiling. He'd lick the last drops from her lips given half the chance. But the trouble was he *liked* her. And that was where the complications arose. He sensed hurt beneath her determinedly sunny exterior, was certain she was denying loneliness and who knew what other needs. But he couldn't ever be the guy to give security. His lifestyle would never accommodate a serious relationship and he didn't want emotional hassle. It had taken him too long to feel his own freedom. And he couldn't trust that she wouldn't think she wanted more if they became fully intimate.

'No matter.' She sashayed closer. 'You promised me something.'

Oh, the temptation was extreme now. 'I didn't promise,' he muttered weakly.

'After the show.' She ignored his denial. 'I danced how you said to. Did you see?'

His gaze dropped to the sheet as he tried so hard to expunge the image that had sprung to mind. 'Yes.'

'Did you like it?' Her voice went husky.

He swallowed. This was torture. Utter torture.

'You're afraid to answer that?'

'Yes,' he admitted.

'Why?'

'I don't want to hurt you.'

'You won't. So long as I'm warmed up—and I do believe I am.' She chuckled. 'It shouldn't hurt that much at all, should it? I always figured the pain thing was a way of trying to put a girl off. Trying to keep us "good".' She gurgled with laughter.

'Roxie.' He felt strangled as heat consumed him. 'I didn't mean physically.'

'Oh.' She bit her lip but the giggle continued anyway.

'I'm serious.' He sat upright, angry and frustrated and so, *so* painfully hard. 'Can you really do a one-night stand, Roxie? Can you really stay emotionally disconnected? First lovers usually go hand in hand with first *love*—involving more emotions than you intend simply because you don't have the experience to control them. I don't want emotional entanglement. I don't want commitment. If we did this it would matter more to you than it would to me.'

'No, it wouldn't,' she denied it. 'All that matters to me is having it good and I know it'll be that way with you.'

He screwed his eyes shut tight, because he knew it

would be so much *more* than good. 'You're a virgin. A *drunk* virgin,' he reminded himself. 'What am I thinking trying to have this conversation now? Get the hell out of here.'

'I'm not drunk,' she asserted bluntly. 'I want you. And I don't want anything more than tonight.'

His eyes shot open and he took a deep, pained gulp for sanity.

'Isn't it every man's fantasy to initiate a woman in the art of sensual pleasure?' She sighed with the most witchery smile he'd ever seen. 'Why not show me how good it can be?'

He'd been hard for her since the moment he'd found her red-eyed scrubbing the shower—long before she'd told him her secret. But her devastating frankness—that mix of innocence and carnal desire—made him want her all the more. Hell, yes, he wanted to show her how good it could be. But he couldn't. He just couldn't.

Wild with both her and himself, he threw off the sheet and swung out of bed.

Open-mouthed, Roxie gazed as he stood up. He was hotter than she'd imagined. His abs rippled beneath golden skin and a smattering of dark hair that arrowed down to emphasise the huge hard-on he was packing. He advanced towards her with aggression inked all over him. Some of her bubbles popped. 'What are you doing?'

'Frogmarching you home. Leaving you there. Alone.'

But his body gave him away. And they both knew it.

She shook her head. 'I never should have told you.'

'No, I'm glad you told me. I can stop us both making a big mistake.'

Emboldened by that skyscraper of an erection, she walked up to him. 'How can it be a mistake, Gabe? When we both want it? I'm not a complete novice. I know how to stroke this.'

This time she went straight for the kill—couldn't resist the chance to hold. She cupped his balls, let her fingers feather up his shaft, let her thumb rub over the broad tip. Oh, she felt dizzy now.

His hand tangled in her hair, fingers twisting in the strands and then tugging to pull her head back. Mouth open, breathing hard, she gazed up at him through half-closed lids. Unashamedly his to manipulate however he wanted.

She heard him swear, the words so violently uttered she felt the wind gust over her face. Then he crushed her mouth beneath his.

*Finally.*

She'd been dreaming of this for days. And for once reality was better than dreams. No soft caress, it was all erotic, all consuming and carnal. She shook with the violence of need that erupted within her, with the violence of his kiss. She pushed through the initial shock of passion to move closer, deeper into him. Not wanting him to think she couldn't handle all he could give. Because she knew she could, now she wanted it all—with a fury that might have frightened her had she been one hundred per cent herself. But the last hint of caution had been drowned—bubbles flowed through her veins, effervescent, exhilarating, exquisite. And not the champagne; not the alcohol. Pure joy at being this close to someone. This one person, whose simple presence could set off an uncontrollable, instinctive reaction within her. And now he was where she'd wanted him most—pouring his fiery energy and focus on her. Desperately she strained, her tongue lashing with his, shivering in his embrace yet wanting closer. She curled one leg around his, bringing her pelvis into direct contact with his. But it wasn't enough. It still wasn't enough.

Gabe's hands clenched hard on her body when he felt her leg slide around his, when he felt her core. Even through her knickers he felt the dampness. The evidence of how ready for him she was.

He nearly lost his mind. And it really didn't help that she was lapping up the kiss that he knew was too rough. He forced himself to ease off, to be a little more gentle. At the very least he could do that for her.

But she mewled, her chin lifting, her lips catching his again—her tongue assaulting his mouth, her hands taking him in a too tight clutch. She was as rough as he.

'Gabe.' It was a demand for everything.

Frustration made him shake, until he grabbed her butt in his hands and lifted her, carrying her to his bed. He lay her back on it, lay on her. Taking pleasure in the groaning sigh she gave as he let her take the bulk of his weight. He rose a little on his elbows so his pelvis ground harder into hers.

Her pupils dilated. He saw the blood beating its rosy path to her cheeks, her lips. There was no denying she wanted it—*him*. She arched, her hips thrusting. Inexperienced she might be, but she had all the right instincts.

Gabe bent his head and kissed her, letting them both drown in the powerful pleasure of it again. His head spinning at how good it felt to be with her like this. But the alarm in the back of his brain was ringing louder and louder and louder. If he did this now, he wouldn't be able to live with himself. She'd been drinking and he hadn't. But he couldn't not touch her. He ached to satisfy her. Ached to satisfy himself. Only the former was allowed.

Even then he enforced limited options on himself. He wasn't going to take advantage of her condition. She wasn't sure of all she was offering. Her defences were totally down—thanks to some expensive champagne. It was not okay to take her at her word.

But the way she moved was just killing him. The way she kissed. Passionate and hungry. She rubbed against him, hitching her dress so they could lie skin to skin.

He buried his face in her neck, all his weight pinning her now, his cock straining to push through the thin barriers between them. He could feel her tiny movements, the friction an intense, intolerable tease.

How was he supposed to resist her sighs and pleas and writhing body? How was he supposed to deny her the pleasure she sought?

He shifted, forcing himself away, keeping her in place with a heavy thigh rather than his whole body. He kissed her and swept his hand up under her skirt, finding those lace-edged knickers so quickly, sliding beneath them with even greater ease. He moaned into her mouth as he felt the hot wetness. Then he focused. Stroked. The lightest brush with the tip of his finger against the small nub that would send her into orbit if he did it right.

Seemed he did it right because her moan then, was the pure sound of sensual pleasure. He felt the throb as blood pulsed, swelling her sex, feminine moisture slicking her more—preparing her for his invasion. He ached to plunge his fingers deep, his shaft, his whole damn self. So desperately he wanted to bury deep inside her and ride hard and furious to an orgasm he knew would be out of this world. Because *she* was out of this world, the most beautiful, passionate woman.

His frustrated passion found release in her mouth. He rammed his tongue deep and rhythmic. Barely a kiss,

more a brutal display of unbridled desire. But she took
it, her neck arching, her whole body arching, making
herself more accessible, more vulnerable to him. Even
more impossible to resist. But he did—refusing to pos-
sess her sex, just touching her sweet spot so, so lightly.
He pulled back the urgency of the kiss too—worked hard
to play more, to tease her more. As she arched higher
still her hands raked his back. He almost burst out of
his skin, had never felt lust as painful as this. His heart
hammered, his skin coated with sweat even though he
was barely moving. Holding back required the most extreme effort of his life.

He felt her scream as those exquisite sensations shuddered through her, but he wouldn't release her from his
kiss, nor from the soft strokes of his finger back and forth
and round and round. Not entering her, just rubbing,
rubbing, rubbing, teasing that pulsing nub mercilessly.
She shook, her body taut and then trembling as the orgasm tumbled her into those moments of mindlessness.
He persevered, relentless in his need to wring it all from
her, to exhaust her. Her fingernails scratched hard. He
pressed her deeper into the bed. His mouth pleasuring
hers until she went completely lax.

Only then did he ease back, pulling her to her side to
cradle her from behind, trying to regulate his breathing
and the unbearable agony inside.

'Oh, Gabe,' she breathed. A sound filled with satisfaction.

'Shh.' He stroked her hair, pulled her dress back down
over her thighs and waited for sleep to claim her.

Mercifully it wasn't long before it did. And then she
was a warm soft bundle in his bed. And he couldn't
move. His swollen cock was so sensitive even the brush
of the cotton sheet above him hurt it. He gritted his teeth,

willing it to subside. But lay awake for hours tormenting himself with visions of what he could have done, once would have done without a second thought.

Having a conscience really sucked.

# CHAPTER SEVEN

WHEN Roxie woke she was alone. She blinked at the familiar walls. She was in her room—she'd woken up every morning here for almost her entire life.

Only now she remembered. Now it was all different.

She lifted the sheet, saw she still wore her dress, her underwear. She dropped the sheet and slumped back down on the pillow. Gabe wasn't there, of course. And she remembered it all. The ferocious kisses, the feel of his weight, the way he'd touched her until she'd come.

But that had been all.

But, damn it, it wasn't going to be all any more. Now she knew he dreamed of her just as she did him. So there was to be no more pretending otherwise. She wriggled out of her dress, knickers and bra. She refused to leave his bed until he'd come as hard as she had. It was only fair, after all. So she lay back and waited. Trying not to lose her nerve.

Fortunately, she didn't have to wait long. He appeared in the doorway in dark jeans and nothing else. She figured he'd taken a shower given his hair was damp, his jaw clean-shaven. But he still managed to exude edginess—the grump was back.

'Have you got a headache?' he asked roughly.

'No,' she answered sweetly, stifling the butterflies in her stomach. 'I wasn't drunk, Gabe.'

He cleared his throat and looked to the left of her. 'Are you hungry?'

'Yes,' she said with determined sass, totally not meaning what he'd meant.

He shot a heated glare at her.

She smiled wider, because she wanted to get to him, she wanted to push him over his damn boundaries. 'I remember everything.'

He looked so uncomfortable then that Roxie's anger began to bite. If he dared apologise she was going to have to hurt him.

'You were tipsy,' he said firmly. 'I'm sorry. I shouldn't have...' His voice trailed off.

Her turn to send a glare—an unforgiving look from top to—*oh*.

Yeah, that was when she noticed that he was hard. That the bulge in the front of his jeans was nowhere near normal size. That his lickable nipples were taut. That despite the heat of the morning, there were goosebumps peppering his skin.

Her flash of anger fled and amusement—*elation*—emboldened her. She sat up, clutching the sheet to her chest for a last second as she got out of the bed. Once standing, she let the sheet fall.

'Gabe,' she murmured. As she walked towards him she ran her hands down her sides and let her hips sway. Her whole body was ready to sway with his.

He stared, his mouth open, frozen to the spot.

That reaction was all she needed to lose every last inhibition. 'You really don't need to feel bad about doing something that I'd already done to myself.'

His eyes widened, darkened, heated. His mouth shut

then opened again before shutting a final time. Clearly rendered speechless. Dull colour washed over his cheek-bones. It was the first time Roxie had seen a man blush.

She got within touch distance and let her amusement warm her whisper. 'I've been thinking about you a lot.'

'What were you doing when you were thinking about me?' he answered, completely hoarse.

She ran her tongue along her lips and smiled.

Almost helplessly, he lifted his hands, held them just in front of her. 'What did you imagine these were doing when you were thinking of me?'

She took them in her own and guided them towards her body. Placed one on her breast. His fingers automatically moved to cup her flesh, to graze over her tight nipple. His other hand she placed palm down on her belly and covered it with her own. Slowly she pushed their fingers down and down.

'What did you dream I would do?' he whispered.

'Everything,' she murmured, shifting so her feet were slightly further apart. 'I imagined everything.'

'Hell, Roxie,' he muttered. 'How am I supposed to resist you?'

She smiled. 'You're not.'

'Every time I close my eyes, you're here,' he confessed. His fingers teased—her nipple, her sex.

Her eyes were half closed now as she shivered. 'Does the reality live up to the dream?'

'I'll make it,' he promised. 'I'll do that for you.'

'You did last night,' she said. 'But I'm taking it all today, Gabe.'

She threaded her fingers through his hair and held him still as she reached up and kissed him.

In a second he claimed dominance, crushing her mouth beneath his. Instantly as carnal and passionate and furious as last night. His tongue impolite, demanding, his hands hauling her closer, the denim rough on her naked skin.

'Are you sure you can handle this,' he demanded, breathing heavily.

She leaned closer, resting her weight on him. 'I want more.'

She wasn't afraid of the strength rippling through him. The way he'd shown her that passion unleashed last night. She liked it. Her mouth felt huge from the pressure of the kiss just now. All she wanted was another one.

'More,' she muttered again, reaching onto tiptoe to press her lips to his again. More, more, more.

Sunlight streamed through the windows. There was no need for the duvet. He threw back the coverings leaving only the sheet-clad mattress and pillows beneath them. She reached round his waist from behind and unfastened his jeans. She pushed them—and the boxers beneath—down. Her hand cupping him for only a second before he spun to face her, to seize her wrists.

She liked seeing him naked in broad daylight. Able to watch the movement of strong muscles beneath golden skin. To feel the focus in his now pure-black eyes. To taste the sparkle as sweat slicked his skin. And she was so hot.

He tumbled her to the bed—thankfully, because her legs had lost all boldness now. He kissed her mouth, her face, her neck, then back to her mouth again as if he couldn't bear to leave it for long. His hands swept down her body, stroking every over-sensitive spot with teasing touches—alternately light and firm. She couldn't bear to wait much longer. So wanting—so wanton—and ready.

But he peeled away from her. She gasped, panicking. 'Don't leave me now. Don't you dare stop.'

'I'm not strong enough to stop,' he muttered, his gaze fiercely scraping down her naked body. 'Not again.'

The passionate look in his eyes sent tremors along her nerves. 'Gabe.'

He swiftly reached under the bed, struggled to rip the plastic wrap sealing the box of condoms. She sat up and watched as he rolled it down his erection. He glanced up and caught her. She smiled. He smiled back.

Yeah, happiness surged as she realised he'd laid down his weapons. He couldn't deny it any more and she no longer had to fight him for it.

He pinned her to the bed with his weight. 'There's no going back now.'

'Good.' She wasn't afraid.

He kissed her, his knees pushing her legs further apart as he settled over her. Excited, she wriggled closer. She could feel him, heavy, thick, just out of reach. Her heart thudded and she clasped his shoulders, pressing kisses on his jaw. He put his other hand between them, his fingers seeking her first, teasing in circles, while he kissed a burning trail from one breast to the other, until she was breathing hard and wet and rocking to an ever-increasing rhythm, urgently needing that satisfaction.

'I don't want to come without you,' she panted, desperate for him to take her.

He grazed the soft swell of her breast with his teeth. 'You can come again with me.'

She arched, rigid, on the brink of release. 'No, I want all of you now,' she begged.

'Don't limit yourself,' he muttered. 'Indulge.'

It was too late to deny it anyway. Ecstasy slammed into her. She shuddered, lost in the intensity of the tumbling sensations. Her fingers curled into his broad shoulders as she convulsed, desperate still to draw him closer.

As her screams ebbed he encouraged, his voice thick with satisfaction, his words hot and thrilling. 'Now you're going to come again.'

Panting, she shook her head, certain it was impossible.

'Yes,' he muttered. 'Think yes.'

He shifted, so he was no longer touching her intimately, lifting his hands to toy with her nipples instead, pressing kisses to the vulnerable pulse points on her neck. Keeping her in the moan zone but carefully not touching where she was too sensitive. Not yet. And slowly that hazy giddiness receded as she became aware of need knifing through her—even more urgent than before.

'Yes,' she repeated his mutter. Anticipation, energy flooded back—nothing but erotic hunger in her body. She rocked her hips up to his, seeking his touch there again. Now.

Wickedly he smiled. 'Oh, yes.' He kissed her, his mouth and tongue staking the claim the rest of him was about to.

His hand moved between them again. She felt him gently rubbing, only this time it wasn't his fingers, but the head of his erection sliding back and forth at the entrance of her slick folds, spreading her damp signs of delight, almost, almost becoming part of her. She sucked in air but it did nothing to cool her. She rocked harder, trying to force him to hurry, but he just chuckled. She ran her hand down his back, clutched his butt, urging him closer, while her other hand pushed into his hair, pulling him back for another of those possessive, passionate kisses. She moaned, so excited by his teasing strokes, so on the edge of her next orgasm.

His hands framed her face and he captured her gaze

with a searching one of his own as he slowly, smoothly claimed her.

She closed her eyes at the intensity of it. Tremors racking her body, her mouth opening in an involuntary, silent sigh.

His movement ceased completely.

'Gabe?' She looked at him, startled by the expression of pain on his face.

'It's not right that something that feels so good for me should be hurting you,' he whispered gruffly.

'It's not hurting,' she breathed. 'Honest it's not. It feels…' She paused to consider whether saying 'overwhelming' would be wise or not. But as she deliberated he tensed, and suddenly all thought fled. 'Do that again,' she demanded.

'Do what?' He looked agonised.

'Move like that again.'

He tensed, pressing that touch closer, then released.

'Like that,' she breathed, smiling. 'That's amazing.'

Gently he thrust closer. 'Yeah,' He smiled back. 'Amazing.'

His hand splayed across her bottom, pushing her pelvis towards his until she grasped the rhythm. She wound her arms around him, holding tighter as his movement became faster, more fluid, stronger as he was sure of her pleasure.

'I knew it would be like this,' she murmured, almost mindless with bliss, wanting it never to end.

'Like what?' he asked raggedly.

'Perfect.'

He combed his fingers through her hair, his palm cupping the side of her face, holding her still so he could kiss the soul out of her. He broke it, looked into her eyes with those bottomless pools. She gazed back at him, their breathing mingling, meshing as one as their bodies did the same.

But she hadn't known it would be this intense. That she would feel this close to him emotionally as well as physically. She brushed a kiss across his shoulder so she could break that heart-stopping eye contact. When she glanced back at him he too had closed his eyes. She smiled when she saw how good it felt for him too. She ran her hands down his back, pressing him closer.

He surged harder, faster. 'Okay?' he muttered.

'Just don't stop.' Her eyes opened, wide, her vision suddenly acute as sensations shuddered through her. She ran her hands over him. Suddenly understanding that he was hers to touch now. That there was so much to explore and that until that moment she'd been doing exactly what he'd jeered he didn't want—just lying there.

So now she touched, now she hungered. She spread her legs wider, wrapping them round his hips to trap him in place while her hands swept south, searching out all his masculine secrets.

'Roxie,' he choked. He grabbed her wrists and pinned them above her head.

'I thought you didn't want someone just lying there,' she gasped. 'You don't want me to touch you?'

'Oh, I do. Later. But I won't last if you touch me like that now.'

She arched anyway, her body exposed and vulnerable to his. It struck her that at this one moment she was in his total possession. But she was also in his complete care. And he was taking such wicked, wonderful care as he bore down on her over and over and over until she convulsed beneath him, her body finally finding its long-sought completion.

His jaw was locked, his eyes burning as he watched

her, ensuring her physical fulfilment. She wasn't just fulfilled, she was all but delirious with ecstasy.

Gabe didn't think he'd ever breathe normally again—he seemed to be playing an impossible game of catch-up with his pulse. He'd always cared about whether his partner had a good time with him, but he'd wanted it to be better than good for her. He knew it would be unforgettable—it was her first time after all—but he'd wanted it to be unforgettable for so many more reasons than that.

So now he faced the uncomfortable truth. He hadn't had sex with her. He'd made love to her. Just a very little love—which was as new to him as it was to her. And in those moments in her arms, connected with her, he'd have done anything for her. A loss of free will he'd never before experienced. She might have lost her virginity, but he'd lost something too. Some part of himself was now locked within her and he wasn't sure he was going to get it back. A chunk of his heart he only now realised he'd actually had. He figured it served him right.

He also figured he could live without it. After all, he'd only just discovered it anyway so he could hardly miss it now. Besides, he was too busy wondering how soon until she'd be ready to take him again, or whether she was too tender—emotionally as well as physically. He frowned. He really had to keep a lid on this somehow. Stop her from wanting too much other than the physical. Because he really wanted her to want some more physical. But how the hell did he balance it?

'You like sleeping in here?' She broke the silence lazily, stretching out on the bed beside him with a little moan that made his blood rush all over his beat body.

'It has the best view,' he answered without thinking. From his bed he could see straight out that one window across the floor—its view encompassed the garage, and that other window in the flat above.

'Have you been watching me?'

He could hear her smile. 'I've seen you in the garden a few times. But you know that.'

She rolled towards him, then he felt her smile kiss his shoulder. 'Yes, I know.'

He cleared his throat. Hoped she didn't think he'd been watching because he was besotted or anything. She wore the skimpiest shorts and vest-top combos ever—of course he looked. Any man would. Oh, man, how did he handle this now?

But she rose up onto her elbow and peered, reading his expression. 'Stop looking so worried, Gabe. I'm not going to fall in love with you,' she scoffed.

He stared at her. Since when was he that much of an open book?

She smiled—easy and amused and happy. 'I told you last night, I'm not going to want anything more from you.'

Good. 'Cos he didn't want that either—right? Only now, contrarily, he did want more. More like right now.

She leaned right over him, brushing her hair back behind her ears, her blue eyes looking earnestly into his. 'You know I'm not interested in a relationship, right? As fantastic as that was and as gorgeous as you are.'

He managed to nod. She'd just spoken words he'd said so often in the past.

'This was just a one-off.'

A one-off? *Really?* 'Sure.' He faked a grin.

She smiled wider, clearly genuine. 'Great. The minute the whistle blows on the final this season, I'm out of here. I'm booking my ticket as soon as the bank lets me.'

'You really are?' He'd been wondering about those plans of hers.

'Yeah, so don't renege on our rental agreement, will you? I need the money to pay for it.'

He shook his head slowly. 'I won't.'

'Great.' She slipped out of the bed with a way too energetic wriggle. 'I really appreciate your effort today. Thank you.'

So that was it? He'd helped her lose the virgin tag and she'd appreciated his effort in doing so? It was like getting a report card from school. His *effort*? Where was the bloody award of excellence? Didn't she know out-of-this-world sex when she had it?

His heart seized. One day she'd learn that that hadn't been average sex. He tried to stop that direction of his thoughts—because the idea of her being in some other guy's arms, of some guy not doing it good enough for her? Oh, now he was beyond grumpy. His freaking *effort*? The more he thought about it, the more it stung. The more he wanted to roar.

She glanced back, brows lifting at his silence and her skin suddenly washed beet red. 'Oh, I'm sorry about...'

He glanced down, then quickly covered the stained sheet. 'Forget it.'

But it was as if she had already. Oh, the irony. *He* was the one feeling like the emotional innocent. As if sleeping with someone made you feel something more than mere physical fun. Intimacy. Caring. As if it all should have mattered so much more to her than to warrant a good *effort* sticker. Damn. He couldn't be feeling used because he'd known exactly what she'd wanted. It was what he'd wanted too. Those desires had finally converged and now it was finished. Right? Sure.

She was slipping her dress over her head, not bothering with either bra or knickers. He was trying hard not to get turned on by that. And failing.

'You're going?' he asked.

It was obvious doofus. Did he have to make his unexpectedly massive disappointment just as obvious?

'Yeah, you've got to get to work later, right?' she answered breezily. 'And I need to do some work in the garden.'

She wanted to *garden* over spending more time in bed with him? That was a kicker. To his bemusement she walked out of the room. A minute later he sat up, watching out of the window as she took the trail through the tomato plants to the rickety flight of stairs along the garage's rear wall. He peeled his aching body from the bed. No way was he going to spend the afternoon watching her shaking it in the garden.

He drove to the beach, pushed through the physical exhaustion to run a mile along the shore. The entire time he thought of nothing but her—wanting nothing more than to be snuggled with her and sound asleep. And the doubts started, the worries. He found himself walking instead of running and chewing on his blasted thumbnail. Because now he wanted to know for sure that she really was okay. Maybe she was back at that house feeling all anxious. Maybe her casual goodbye this morning had been all façade—an attempt at sophistication like her hair and her lip gloss and her damn fake chicken fillets. Maybe she was up in that horrendous bedsit of hers bawling her eyes out and about to go scary emo on him.

Oh, hell. Hadn't he better go make sure she was okay?

# CHAPTER EIGHT

ROXIE breathed deep and smiled—to keep her good vibe even. She knew all about laughter therapy—that if you were down, even just putting on a smile lifted your mood up a few notches. Not that she was down, of course. No way could any kind of sadness sink her now—after all, she'd gotten what she'd wanted. The most incredible experience. Now it was finished and that was fine. She wasn't going to fall for him. No, if anything, what she felt was *gratitude*. He'd given everything she'd ever wanted—fun, courtesy, ecstasy. She knew it all now. And sure, she could see why some girls went crazy for the guy who gave that kind of absolute joy. But *she* wasn't going to lose it.

Having said that, it had to be a one-time-only. Once definitely had to be enough. And honestly it was—she was so exhausted she could hardly move. No way could she manage a replay anyway. She stepped out of her hot shower and pulled on a fresh tee shirt. She curled up on her camp bed, pulling her pillow under her cheek, and relaxed as tiredness overwhelmed her. Tiredness and satisfaction—that tiny hint of forlorn determinedly forgotten. She forced herself to focus on upcoming European destinations. But as she drifted to sleep it was him she dwelt on—his smile, his tease, the comfort of his arms.

'Roxie.'

She moaned and rolled over. Dreaming of him, of the way he'd groaned her name as he'd surged inside her.

*'Roxie!'*

Okay, he didn't usually shout like that—not in her dreams.

'Open the damn door!'

She pushed her hair back from her face, blinking rapidly to try to bring her brain back from the sensually charged sleep state it had been in the last couple of hours. She stumbled to the door.

'Is everything okay?' he asked as soon as she opened it. 'I've been knocking for ages.'

He was wearing shorts and a fitted tee and had clearly been out running. She could hardly drag her eyes up to his face. Her dreams broke their boundaries, sending images—some real memories, some utter fantasies—scrolling through her mind. All involving him *without* those shorts.

'Sure,' she mumbled. 'I was sleeping.'

She looked into his face; his eyes were focused on her and a heavy frown had obliterated his earlier satisfied expression.

'Is there something you wanted?' Her question trailed off. There was something going on with her body; she could feel it priming again. She breathed in, her senses filled with nothing but him—his height, his scent, the harsh sound from his throat as he'd hit his release. She squeezed her pelvic floor muscles to try to stop the melting sensation. It only made it worse.

'You were really asleep?' The dark centres of his eyes swelled.

'Sure,' she said, starting to laugh. 'I was tired—it was a late night.'

'You've really been asleep this whole time?'

'Well, I had a shower…' She stepped back as he pushed past her and hunched down by her bar fridge. He drew out the bottle with the V marked on it.

'Why didn't you come back here this morning and have a champagne brunch to celebrate your new non-virgin status?' Now he had the smile on—that rakish one.

'I was waiting to have it with dinner tonight.' Truthfully she'd forgotten about it. 'But maybe I'll open it now.'

Her mouth was so dry, the drink would help. She held out her hand for it.

'You know, you don't deserve it yet.' He stood and held the bottle out of reach.

'I'm no longer a virgin, Gabe, as I do believe you know.' She couldn't resist the husky reminder.

'I disagree.'

She gaped at him. 'Tell me I didn't dream it.'

'No,' he chuckled. 'But there are so many ways in which you are still a virgin. So you've had a little vanilla sex. Missionary style. Shouldn't you be trying out all the options?'

'What other options did you have in mind?' Fascinated, she moved closer.

'Strikes me you have an interesting mind of your own, Roxie. What have you thought about?'

The heat flushed through her body. She didn't know if she should answer that.

His eyes gleamed and he leaned closer so they were almost, almost touching. 'Don't try and tell me you haven't thought about a few things.'

Okay, so it was going to be more than once. He was

right, there was a lot she'd yet to experience. And she wanted to try it all with him.

'You might regret asking this,' she breathed. 'Because the whole time you've been out exercising, I've been sleeping. You might not have the stamina to keep up with me.'

'Somehow I think I'll cope.' He swallowed. 'So you want to investigate this further?'

'There isn't a "this" between us.' There couldn't be. She was *free*; that was the whole point.

'No, I meant *your* sensual nature. Don't you want to explore that some more?'

Oh, she did. She really, really did. With him.

'And which was more fun?' he asked. 'The fantasy or the reality?'

'This is all a kind of fantasy,' she said honestly.

'Okay.' He nodded. 'But while you can pretend your hands are mine, there are a couple of things you need me in the flesh for, right?'

Oh, yeah, she needed that flesh. Badly. She moved another step towards him. 'I'm going away at the end of the season.'

'We'll be done before then anyway. Easy, right?'

'Really easy.' Oh, just so easy, so nothing more.

He walked closer to meet her. 'So what other ways, Roxie? Standing, sitting, doggy, on a table, in the shower?'

'Reverse cowgirl.'

*'What?'*

'Reverse cowgirl.'

A distracted look crossed his face. 'Sure, that too.'

'Shall we draw up a list?' 'Cos she had a large number of ideas in her head already.

'By all means write up a list. So long as I can add to

it. Hold this.' He thrust the bottle into her hands then swooped and picked her up. She giggled as he strode out of her little flat, down the stairs, not stopping 'til he'd barged into his own bedroom. 'And there has to be some room for spontaneity.'

It seemed sometimes spontaneity involved a champagne shower.

When Gabe woke the next morning—alone—he spotted a single sheet of paper Blu-Tacked to the wall. On it was a neatly written list. Bullet points and everything. He both blushed and chuckled as he read it. Seemed Roxie had a flair for fantasy—or had some tantric sex manual stashed somewhere, because even he wasn't sure what she meant by some of those suggestions. But, man, was he happy at the thought of finding out. On the negative side, it meant his day at the stadium dragged unbelievably slowly.

She was in the garden when he got home. But he thought he should try to hold off for at least five minutes, to prove to himself that he could more than anything. He made a show of looking at the ridiculously huge, abundant green garden, trying not to explode at the way she stroked his chest in explicit welcome.

'You have enough vegetables here to feed the team three times over,' he said.

Roxie gave the beds a fleeting glance, really not caring about them that second. 'There's not that many. I can eat a lot.'

She saw him glance over her sceptically.

'When you only eat plant, you eat a lot of plant,' she pointed out.

'Is now a bad time to admit that I come from generations of farmers? With several farms. Beef, dairy and sheep.' He even looked sheepish as he said it.

'Meat central, huh?' She shrugged. 'I guess we do live in New Zealand—fifty sheep per person and all that.'

He chuckled. 'I don't think it's that many. And I didn't follow the plan, did medicine instead. That make me more acceptable?'

Oh, the man was so much more than acceptable. But she couldn't afford to admit that, and his ego didn't need fattening. 'Marginally.'

'Marginally?' He looked affronted. 'Doctors save lives.'

She shot him a teasing look. 'How many lives do you save, Gabe? You're a sports specialist.'

'I save a lot of lives, actually,' he said, quite seriously. 'Think about it. You're a dancer, right? So you know something of what it's like to spend every minute of every day training for that one goal. Of making all kinds of sacrifices to try to meet that goal. So what happens if you get an injury and it threatens to snatch it all from you in a second? Don't you want a doctor on hand then?'

Okay, so she could give him that. 'Didn't your family want you to do medicine?'

He shook his head. 'The firstborn son must grow up and take over the farming empire. It's written in stone. That archaic belief in primogeniture.'

Oh, her curiosity was piqued. 'You're the firstborn son?'

'Uh-huh.'

'Of how many?' Yes, totally curious now.

'Just my sister and me.'

She wondered what his sister was like. What his parents were like. Wondered a ton of things she had no real business wondering. That didn't stop her asking. 'And you didn't want to farm?'

'Do I look like a farmer?' he joked.

In his on-trend jeans, tee and trainers, she had to admit he didn't. 'Is it too much hard work for you?' She couldn't resist teasing him some more.

'It's too far out in the country for me.' He matched her tone. 'I love to visit but don't want to live there. I like the city.'

'Because you like to be near a high-density female population? I'm guessing there aren't nearly enough women in the countryside for you.'

'Exactly.' He grinned. 'I need the variety. But of course the family doesn't approve.'

'Of all the women or the lack of farming interest?'

'Both.' He winked. 'I'm a wayward terror.'

Roxie shook her head. The guy was over-egging it. 'You're not that much of a terror. Look how hard I had to push you to take me to bed. I don't think there's much substance to your rogue reputation.'

'Ah, but that was because I was trying to reform my wicked ways.'

He had her absolute attention now. 'And why was that?' She watched him close, curious to see if he'd answer.

It seemed he'd decided to give the nearest tomato plant a thorough inspection, bending down to see if the cherry-sized reds were ripe for picking. 'I get the feeling you might already know about it.'

'Diana,' she confirmed softly.

He snapped off the first fruit. 'What did they tell you?'

Roxie decided to be completely honest. 'I'm a new dancer for the Blades—first thing they did was warn me away from you.'

He swivelled to look at her, his brows impossibly high. 'But you ignored them.'

She shrugged. 'I'm not as vulnerable as it seemed she'd been.'

He looked uncomfortable and turned back to the plant, started a picking frenzy. 'She wasn't exactly healthy, no. I didn't know that when we started dating.'

'So what happened?' She moved up beside him and held her hands out so he could put his growing collection of tomatoes into them.

He avoided answering by popping a tomato into his mouth—putting one into her mouth too. She ignored the sweet sensation that flared deep inside—not just from the sun-warmed sweet fruit, but from the feeling of intimacy in him having fed it to her. Determinedly she kept looking at him—her brows raised as she waited for him to spill it.

'Okay, we dated,' he said after finally swallowing. 'Just normal dating—which for me is usually fairly short term, right?' He gave her a keen look.

Roxie grinned. 'Yeah, but I'm guessing she didn't take that on board?'

'I ended it—way soon even for me. But she'd got it into her head that we were supposed to be soul mates or something. It got very awkward and she became increasingly hysterical. She was on my doorstep, she'd turn up at events I attended. I went away with the team and when I got back she'd actually moved into my apartment. All her stuff, everything, and was acting like… I don't know. It had gone from awkward to ugly to dangerous. She threatened all kinds of things. I called a friend who's a psych. We called her family. But it was bad, it was really bad. And after that I decided to take a break from dating altogether.'

Which was why he'd been so grumpy? Because a dating break wasn't his natural style. Yeah, she knew he
wasn't entirely the heartless playboy he had the rep for,
but he did like to have some fun. She moved to put the
tomatoes on the outdoor table, pleased he'd been honest enough to tell her about it. She liked that he'd been
bothered someone had been hurt—even if it wasn't really his fault. She guessed Diana had other issues too,
it had all just come to a head with Gabe. Poor guy, she
didn't think he'd deserved to put himself into penance
for months like that. She smiled at him as he followed
her and added yet more tomatoes to the collection.

'You do know I'm not going to go stalker on you,
right?' He had nothing to fear from her.

'Yes, I do know that.' He broke eye contact—staring
across the garden instead.

There was an oddly fixed silence.

'So what does your family think of your career now?'
she asked, just to break it. 'You *can't* be a disappointment, you're a doctor.'

That brought a slight smile back. 'Even just a sports
doctor?'

'You know I was only teasing.' She'd seen for herself
how highly regarded he was at the stadium—the team
totally relied on him.

'Yeah, well. You're not the first to make an issue of
it. No, my dad didn't want me to do medicine. You're
looking at Andrew G. Hollingsworth the sixth and the
first to betray the family and walk off the land.'

'Andrew?' That threw her—Andrew didn't suit him
at all.

'Andrew Gabriel,' he explained. 'Gabe.'

Gabe was so much better, with those heavenly connotations and all—she knew just *how* heavenly he felt. 'Did that go down badly too?'

'Unbelievably,' he answered briefly, picking up another tomato and munching on it.

'Were you written out of the will?' she joked.

'For a while.' He nodded and answered out of the side of his mouth. 'But I wasn't going to back down. I'm not having my entire life dictated by other people's expectations.'

Freedom was important to him too, huh? Roxie walked over to the tap at the back of the garage so she could rinse the plant scent from her fingers. 'So how did you break free?' she asked when he came beside her, waiting for his turn under the tap.

'I ran away to the city, which wasn't the smartest move, but at the time it was all I had. It's not that easy to go against the wishes of your whole family when you've been groomed from the moment of conception—"one day this will all be yours, your responsibility" blah, blah, blah.'

'Did they come after you?'

He shook his head. 'I was seventeen and we didn't communicate for over a year.'

'That's awful.' How could they do that to a son who was everything any sane parent would want? Not just fit and healthy but bright and super successful and *everything*.

'It wasn't so bad.' He smiled when he saw the expression on her face. 'I had friends. Studied, played rugby. And I kept in touch with my sister because she was at boarding school. Honestly, the things I missed most were the lambs I'd reared and my dog.'

'You had lambs?' She was momentarily diverted by that cute mental image. Was even more diverted when

Gabe cupped his hand under the still running water and then sipped from it.

'Took the orphans in each season,' he explained after he swallowed.

She refused to ask if they'd had them for Christmas dinner.

'No, I didn't eat them, they were pets.' He read her mind as he turned off the tap. 'Anyway, Mum got steadily madder and madder with Dad. In the end they had a massive blow-up.'

'Hooray for your mum.' Roxie really hoped she'd withheld conjugal rights and everything.

'She insisted Dad and I get together. I told him what I was going to do with my life and if he wanted to be a part of it, he had to accept it.'

Take-no-prisoners Gabe—the man was tough—but then it seemed he'd had to be to get free. That was something she could understand. And admire. 'And he did?'

'Eventually.'

Wow. Roxie knew how conflict within families could change people. That lack of support must have affected him—and his ability to trust.

'What about your sister? Did your dad have some grand plan for her too?'

'Well, here's the ironic thing—she loves farming. But she's a girl.'

'Don't tell me girls can't be farmers?' Roxie caught on quick.

'Never. No such thing as a lady farmer,' he joked.

Roxie felt as bad for his sister as she had for Gabe. It was only circumstance that had held Roxie back from doing all she'd wanted to—her grandparents' health, but they'd been supportive and caring in every other way possible. They'd always believed in her, in fact she'd downplayed her disappointment at having to stop dance lessons so as not to distress them. 'That's just crazy.'

'Isn't it?' He wiped his mouth with the back of his hand. A couple of drops still remained just below his lip. Roxie wanted to kiss them away.

'So there was the guy wanting an heir to take over the place and he had one chomping at the bit and he couldn't even see it,' Gabe continued. 'I told her to get out of there and do her thing and I'd back her up.'

Roxie felt a bit sorry for his mum now. Must have been hard having both her kids feeling as if they had to *escape*.

'My sister, the natural-born farmer, did an agriculture degree. Won top honours of her year. You should have seen Dad at her graduation. So now they're working together on the farms and everybody's happy and the big bust-up is all in the past and done with.'

Was it? Roxie heard that slight edge in his voice and knew she was right—wounds like that left scars. 'But it was worth it?'

'No one was telling me what to do with my own life. I won't be hemmed in,' he said firmly. 'And I guess it's why I like working with the team, helping those guys achieve their ambition. Everybody should be free to chase their own dreams.' He shot her a suddenly embarrassed look. 'That's really cheesy, isn't it?'

'No, it's not,' she said honestly. 'Your sister must have liked having you in her corner.'

He laughed—full of self-mockery. 'I was totally selfish. I just wanted to stay at med school and live it up in town. It was in my interest to see them sort it out. And now they can finally cope with my job because I get them VIP tickets to all the big games.'

'But I'm guessing they could afford to buy their own tickets if they really wanted to, right?'

His expression completely sobered. 'Yeah, there's a lot of money. And I'm back in the will—am a shareholder in the estate. The Hollingsworth clan has finally landed in the twenty-first century. That's the reason women say yes to me—they know the value of my surname.'

Roxie froze for a split second and then roared with laughter.

'Gabe,' she gasped when she could, wiping a tear from her eye and breathing deep to ease the stitch in her tummy. 'That's *not* why they say yes.' She smiled up at him as her amusement threatened an uncontrollable return.

But he wasn't smiling back. He was just watching her, a slight knot between his brows, as if some thought up in his brain was uncomfortable. His gaze dropped, zoomed in on her mouth. She knew exactly what he was thinking now. Only instead of acting on that urge, he turned away. The frown crease deepening on his forehead. Disappointed, she watched him walk towards the house. What, were they not going to tick an item off her list tonight? Well, that was disappointing—she'd been hanging out for it all day at work. Had she offended him somehow? How did she bring back the play in him?

'Want to know one of my favourite things?' she called, suddenly hit by inspiration.

He wheeled on the spot.

'Wait there, I've got to get it.' She raced up to her flat, fearing he'd go into the Treehouse and leave her all hot and bothered and alone.

But instead he followed her up the stairs. 'Let me guess, champagne?'

'No, this.' She turned and brandished the bottle.

Maple syrup. Gabe looked at the label and whipped his head up to read her face. 'Oh, my.' Goosebumps smothered his skin. 'What are you planning to—?'

'You know already.' She smiled that totally audacious smile.

He adjusted his stance because his body was rioting. And he just gave in to it. Anticipation blasted away the sting he'd felt from her saying she wasn't going to go stalker on him. Why it had kicked he didn't know, and why would he fight the vision of seduction in front of him now? He didn't have to fight it any more; they wanted the same thing—nothing but fun frolics for a few weeks...

She paused from unscrewing the lid of the bottle. The amusement flashing in her eyes undermined the innocence of her smile. 'I thought you liked spontaneity.'

'I do,' he muttered, suddenly breathless.

Mere minutes later Gabe was flat on his back on the floor and wondering if he was about to have a cardiac arrest. It sure as hell felt like it. 'Where did you learn to do that?' he gasped.

'A magazine, where else?' She sat up, her hair tumbling down her back, her cheeks rosy, her lips still slick from the syrup she'd licked and sucked from him. 'The article said it would send you cross-eyed. Did it work?'

Well, his head was spinning and his heart reeling. And seeing her look like the ultimate hedonistic nymph, he had to screw his eyes shut tight again.

'Long live women's magazines,' he muttered fervently. Another realisation dawned as he absorbed her words. 'Was that your first time?'

'Mmm hmm.' She sounded very pleased with herself.

He sat up in a hurry, fully focused on her now. She'd never gone down on a guy before and she did it like that?

Such a natural it was unnatural. As she licked her lips he took her by surprise and pushed her back, settling his body over hers so she couldn't escape. It truly was sick how much he liked having her beneath him. He tugged down her shorts, then slid so his face was where they'd just been. His hands held her wrists to her sides and he looked up her belly and between her breasts to her very wide blue eyes.

'What about the situation in reverse?' He brushed the lightest kiss across her upper thigh. 'Has anyone ever done this to you?'

It took her a moment, then she slowly shook her head.

His instincts burned. 'I thought you said your virginity was a mere technicality, that you were no novice. But you haven't even had oral sex?' Hell, that was the thing lots of teen technical virgins did, right? How they got off without going all the way.

Her flush deepened. She shook her head again.

He paused, too late to go back now—and now he needed to know it all. 'So why me?'

'You know what you're doing?' she answered in a small, uncertain voice.

He figured that was a partially honest answer, he looked at her steadily waiting for more. Hoping there *was* more.

'And I think you're very nice,' she added in an even smaller voice. 'I'm very attracted to you and I trust you to do what I need you to do. *All* I need you to do.'

He watched more closely. 'Why do you trust me?'

'Because you already have.'

Done what she'd needed? Shown her a good time in bed and let her keep it so casual they didn't even spend ten minutes together out of the sack?

All of a sudden it wasn't enough.

'Tell me about the boyfriend,' he prompted. 'Did he even exist?'

'Yes, he did,' she answered. 'We dated for a few months.'

'A few *months*?' Gabe was amazed. How on earth had she stopped herself from shagging him? She was insatiable. And curious. And determined. 'He'd taken a celibacy vow?'

'No.' She pulled a wrist free and mock-slapped him. 'There just wasn't the opportunity.'

'You could have found an opportunity.' She so could have.

'I didn't want to.'

And that was the answer he'd been seeking. Yeah, contrary to his keep-it-casual intentions, it pleased him no end that she was hot for him in a way she'd not been hot for anyone else. But he wanted her to appreciate some of his other skills too. Oh, he did not want this to become some sordid, nothing but sex-travaganza. There were other things he wanted—like a little more of her respect, to soothe that little chunk she'd taken out of him.

Yeah, his ex-*non*-accidental-virgin was about to get a little more than she'd bargained for.

# CHAPTER NINE

ROXIE sent him packing, using her minuscule shower as her excuse. Truly, she'd just needed to breathe. No, she hadn't slept with Jake, because Jake had never turned her on to the point that she was a writhing, panting, incoherent mess of sensation—as she'd just been on her cold, hard floor. She couldn't believe she'd let Gabe do all that boundary-breaking intimate stuff. Or that she'd done it to him first. Or that she'd liked it so much she was hot again already. But she was hanging onto this new-found audacity. This was fun—so long as she could keep it all within her control. And her flight instinct told her that meant maintaining some distance.

She pulled on some clothes and realised she was hungry for food. She snuck down the stairs to get some greens to add to her dinner. He was on the deck, sticking his knife into a giant steak. Masses of potatoes encircled it. He was clearly both carbo-loading and replenishing muscle. That would be useful—later—when she was ready to deal with him some more.

Gabe swallowed a smile at the dirty look she gave his dinner, but she said nothing. It amused him that she'd had no idea of what his name meant. It really was the reason so many of those dancers had set their sights on him rather than a rugby boy. His name—and family—was synonymous with farming wealth. So she was wrong about the sex-stud thing, and there were a few more things it wouldn't do her any harm to learn about him. Except she didn't seem to be interested in doing anything with him but the salacious. But he planned to change that.

'Why not sit here to have your dinner?' he asked casually. 'You can't sit at your table up there with all that furniture and crap crammed around it. Have it down here. I promise I won't bite.' It was more a dare than an invitation.

She didn't answer immediately. Interesting how at ease she was with him when they were physical, and how uncomfortable she was at the thought of spending more simple, sex-free time with him. Was she actually *shy*? That didn't make sense when she'd been nothing but smart'n'sassy and strong from word go. Assertive beyond belief. He thought about it more carefully—about how she'd hung on the edge of the group of dancers at the after-practice drinks, how she'd hidden in the dark instead of confiding to anyone about her nerves before the game, how she lived behind a giant hedge no one would be mad enough to fight through. Suddenly, the idea of her being shy made more sense than anything.

'I'm nearly done anyway.' He tried to make it easier for her.

She shrugged. 'I have to get the rest of it.'

'So go get it,' he said, as if he didn't care. Wished he didn't care half as much as he feared he could.

Three minutes later she perched on the edge of the seat opposite his, her plate full of rabbit food. No wonder she was so slim. He kept the conversation light. Stadium-related stories mostly, until she warmed up and laughed. Until she started talking back. Topping some of his tales with mad-old-lady shopping tales of her own. Turned out her day job was at the gift store at the corner shops, a store no one from their generation would ordinarily enter. He couldn't understand why she worked there—if she wanted to work in retail, why not some high-dollar fashion place? She had the physique to wear those expensive, slinky numbers and have all the customers desperate to look just like her. That was just one of several things he was biding his time to ask her. But for now, he just talked—nothing too personal or too heavy, but enough to entertain and keep her there until it was late and dark and the bedroom beckoned.

In his big bed in her old room, Roxie stretched. It really was time for her to slope across the garden and curl up on her own hard, narrow stretcher that reminded her of reality. But Gabe's big arms encircled her. He lifted her, repositioning her so his chest was her pillow, his hand worked through her hair and he rubbed the base of her skull. She let it happen—it felt too good to pull from. Just a few more minutes. No harm would come from that little bit of closeness—right?

'Why haven't you gone travelling sooner?' he asked lazily.

'I needed to get this place ready.' The repairs after the earthquake had cost money that had taken her a long time to earn.

'But you've never got round to trimming the hedge?'

She laughed gently. 'No. At first it was just because I was too busy to get to it. Then I noticed it kept people out. I liked that, keeping my privacy.'

She felt the vibrations in his chest as he chuckled with her—it made for a wonderfully relaxing kind of massage.

'So what are you going to do once the champagne runs out?' he asked. 'Is there a new list or are you just going to travel indefinitely?'

She breathed in deep and sighed as she answered. 'There's a new list. I'll have to find some champagne over there.' There had to be a new list—her life would just be beginning over there, right? The start of her freedom.

'Where's there? What's first on the list?'

She smiled up at the ceiling as she thought about it. 'You're going to think it's lame.'

'No, I won't.'

Oh, he so would. 'I want to go to the ballet in London.'

'The ballet? That's number one?'

She chuckled. Yeah, he wasn't that wowed. 'Don't knock it. I studied for thirteen years, started when I was three. I've been dreaming of going there for ever.'

'If you loved it so much why'd you give up?' He firmly slid his hand down her back, pulled her lax body even closer. 'You couldn't afford classes any more?'

'Actually my teacher offered to waive the fees, but it was the time more than the money. There were other things I had to do.' Her grandmother had just had the stroke; her grandfather had needed help caring for her.

There was a small silence, as if he was waiting for her to say something more. Which she didn't.

'So the ballet—in London?' he finally prompted— with a distinct lack of enthusiasm.

'Yeah, the Royal Ballet at Covent Garden. To see one of the classics. Not your thing, huh?'

She felt his laughter again. 'All those blokes leaping about in tights and no one saying anything? Nah.'

She nudged his thigh with her knee and teased. 'I knew you were going to comment about the tights. Why do guys always feel so threatened by them? Hell, the rugby players wear almost as little—their shirts are skin-tight.'

'Well, it's not just the men I'm not so keen on. All the girls are bony. They've got no shape, no boobs, where's the attraction in watching them? They're not exactly sexy.'

Roxie sat up indignantly and twisted to see his face in the moonlight. 'You don't like skinny dancers? Then why have you dated so many?'

'Not *that* many.' He went on instant defence. 'And I didn't date them because they were dancers—it was just that they were who I happened to meet.'

Oh, so it was a circumstantial thing, not that dancer girls were his 'type'? She was fairly surprised—and surprisingly miffed. 'So you don't like the ballerina body?'

He paused, a grin suddenly flaring, and he reached up to pull her back to him. 'I think you know how I feel about your body, Roxie.'

Yeah, that wasn't good enough. She resisted his tug closer and waited, fingers tapping on his chest.

'It's not just beautiful.' His grin widened as he unashamedly back-pedalled. 'It's the way you move. You know what you're doing, but it's like its unconscious at the same time. Total natural grace and not like anyone else I've met. Ever.'

'You need to keep the compliments coming because I'm still feeling insecure about the no-boobs bit.'

He laughed harder; she felt his body harden too. 'You do great in that department.'

'With my booster bra.'

'I like them best with no bra, as well you know.' He slid a broad, warm palm up over her stomach, towards her ribcage, as if to prove it. 'In fact, you'd be fantastic at burlesque,' he teased. 'You know, with those nipple tassles?'

'Oh, you would know all about nipple tassles,' she huffed, twisting away to leave him.

Except he grabbed her so she couldn't, pulling her back and rolling so he had her pinned, oh, so pleasurably. Admittedly she didn't put up too much of a fight.

'You want to dance full time?' His mouth hovered above where he wanted those damn tassles.

'When I was a kid I did,' she answered breathlessly, getting distracted by what his tongue was now doing. 'Reality is, not many people can make a viable living as a dancer. Even if you can it's not for long—you're arthritic at thirty. That's why scoring the gig with the Blades was such a thrill—even for just a short time I'm a pro.'

'You shouldn't settle for only a short time. Why not go the whole hog?'

'It's too late for classical,' she moaned. 'I'm over the hill already.'

His grunt of laughter was muffled against her breast and his fingers teased further south. 'There are other forms of dance.'

'I'm sorry to disappoint you, Gabe,' she panted. 'But I don't think burlesque is for me.'

He flexed, teasing her more exquisitely. 'You could teach or make up the Blades' routines or have your own shop—you like retail, right? Why not dance gear?'

She actually quite liked that idea. Having a retail space with a studio above it to teach or something. 'I used to love going to the ballet shop and looking at the costumes.'

'You love a costume, Roxie?'

'You bet I do.' Yeah, she had a soft spot for sequins and Lycra.

'Well, I really think you should try the tassles.' His voice deepened with laughter as she wriggled against him. 'Not many women could, you know. That's a real compliment.'

She muttered an adjective so colourful he instantly reared up and took her hard.

She had no idea how much later it was when he lifted her back with her head resting on his shoulder. All she knew was that she was utterly relaxed and bone-deep exhausted. She closed her eyes, her own breathing falling into sync with the deep, regular rise and fall of his broad chest. So very vaguely the thought pinched—she really *ought* to go back to her own place. But she was so tired. And so warm. And she'd never been held like this by anyone…so finding the energy to leave this haven was going to take a few minutes.

'You miss your grandparents?' he asked softly, gently rubbing her shoulders with the tips of his fingers in light, slow circles.

The question was so out of the blue she answered without even thinking about it. 'Every day.'

'And you've never tried to track down your father?'

That brought her back from the brink of sleep, but his fingers kept up the rhythmic kneading. She sighed—so damn tired and, while he was soothing, he was also holding her in an embrace she'd have to push hard to break free of. So she just gave in and told the truth. 'No information to go on,' she murmured, her eyelids drooping.

Time drifted and she floated deeper into the warm, velvety darkness. She felt so comfortable it had to be a dream…and, yeah, she wasn't sure if she really heard the next question or not.

'You really know nothing?'

'There's no one left to ask, nothing in the papers.' As she slipped into that half-sleep state the futility was the last thing she remembered. 'Day after I was born she left for the UK and never came back. Asked Grandies a couple of times but I didn't want to hurt them. *They* were my parents.' For years she hadn't pushed it because she'd known it had distressed them. 'They always told me the same story—Mum was young and hadn't wanted to be tied down. She'd had an affair but didn't want an abortion, but didn't want to be an involved mother either. They wanted to keep me in the family. So I never went off the straight and narrow 'cos I knew how much Mum's mess hurt them. And me. So I was a total good-girl. Almost. Dated Jake. But did nothing that would devastate them if they ever found out. But he didn't understand why I never went out for a drink or clubbing. Never stayed out late, never swore. Never did any normal teenage rebel things. Grandma got sick and needed me.'

She burrowed deeper into the warmth, seeking to escape. But her mind skittered through the memories relentlessly. She'd grown up in ways her more experienced friends hadn't. And those friends had been too busy with their own parties and teen issues to deal with her own sombre ones. She'd learned not to talk about her life at home—too much of a downer. Too unrelatable. And it was easier not to talk because she could hardly bear to face it herself—the inevitable loss that had loomed. First one, then the other. Until she was left alone.

'They were older parents when they had Mum and she'd been headstrong and wilful. I couldn't do that to them too. But now they're gone and I can do whatever.' She was answerable only to herself—free. While she didn't resent a minute of her life up to now, now was *her* time. Maybe that was what she'd inherited from her mother—that need never to be tied down. 'I always wonder why she didn't want me. Why did she leave me and go overseas if there wasn't something that hurt her to even look at me?'

The high-pitched, harsh question woke Roxie. She swallowed and felt the roughness in her throat. That was when she realised it had been *her* talking. And she was being held in a tighter-than-tight embrace. She was awake—and, even worse, *he* was awake and she'd just been spilling all this stuff *aloud* and she'd never said it to *anyone*. Eyes flashing wide open, she froze in position, her skin goosebumping, her heart hardening. Oh, hell, this had been dumb. She couldn't let the happy-after-orgasm hormones confuse her into thinking there was *intimacy* here. And she most certainly didn't want him feeling sorry for her or thinking she was some kind of stuffed-up, incapable, needy person. She was totally capable—and totally embarrassed. All her internal alarms clanged—way past time to go back to the garage and get this non-relationship back to its clearly delineated fun-only status.

But she had to make her exit smooth and unpanicked-like. As if she hadn't just confessed some of her innermost turmoil or anything. She pressed a couple of kisses to his shoulder and slipped out when his hold eased the tiniest amount. Then desperately tried to think of something completely safe to discuss. Glancing out of the window at the dark shadows of the garden outside, she landed on it.

'Do you mind if I use your kitchen to make some things with the tomato glut?' she asked as she felt on the floor for her clothes. Because the last thing she wanted him thinking was that she was trying to move in on his space by stealth. 'I'll do it when you're at work.'

'Course I don't mind.' Gabe minded that she felt she had to ask. Damn, for a few minutes there he'd thought he'd been busting through her reserve—which was more prickly than that damn hedge outside. But obviously not, given she was now asking permission for the simplest of things, given she'd suddenly stiffened as if she hadn't re-alised what she'd been saying, given her voice had gone from sleepy-slurred to shrill and given how quickly she was escaping from him now.

'It's just that my kitchen's not big enough.'

He made a deal of pulling up the duvet to stop himself glaring at her. She even felt as if she had to explain?

'You don't *have* a kitchen.' He couldn't resist the dig. She had a gas ring, a microwave and a fridge half full of champagne.

She merely smiled and waved as she left.

Gabe slumped lower in bed and tried to kick away the disappointment and dissatisfaction. He had absolutely no fear of Roxie walking in and taking over his home à la Diana. If it weren't for the scent of her lingering on his sheets, there'd be no clue that she'd been there with him at all. And now, not for the first time, he wished she'd stay in the house with him. He'd even had the mad thought of doing something to the garage so she'd *have* to move in. Because those rickety stairs made him shud-der. So did her isolation.

When he got back from the stadium one afternoon a few days later, it was to find the windows open and the relentless beat of dance music vibrating through the hedge. He rubbed his knuckles over his chest—first time in his life he felt his heart literally lift.

The Knights had had another home game. Roxie had

danced, he'd doctored. They hadn't attended the after-match celebrations. They'd gone home and had one of their own. Every night since they'd had separate dinners together on the deck. He'd engaged her in more—easy—conversation, even managed to get her to watch movies with him. The first night he'd had to surrender to her choice of those awful dance flicks—but it had been worth it when she gave him her own demo of the theme moves. Now they alternated—dance flicks, then thrillers. Gabe was pleased about it. He didn't like to think of her being in that tiny studio alone—no reason why they couldn't hang out together a bit. Still easy, right?

She was in his kitchen—looking more Roxanna than Roxie with her hair pulled back into a plait, not a sker-rick of make-up, and swamped in an apron. But then she saw him—and there was a flutter of eyelids and a flash of blue that was pure Roxie.

He strode over—it smelt good. 'Let me try it.'

She pulled a spoon from the drawer and dipped it into the oversized pot that scarily resembled a witch's cauldron.

'Mmm.' Impossibly, it tasted better than it smelt.

'No salt, no egg, no dairy, no oil, no gluten, no meat—'

'No fun,' he inserted.

'You liked it before you knew all that.' She turned a cold eye on him.

'True.'

'And all organic, no GM ingredients.'

'I am truly impressed.'

Her eyes narrowed.

'Honest,' he surrendered with a laugh. 'It's amazing.'

She nodded, satisfied. 'I make a mean salsa.'

He hadn't been talking about the sauce. But he leaned

back and watched her work, listened, more interested than he'd thought he'd be as she went on about the nutritional value of the ingredients. 'How do you know all this?' he finally interrupted the never-ending flow of facts as she poured ladlefuls into the masses of sterilised jars that waited on the table.

'I did lots of research about cancer-fighting superfoods and stuff. Tomatoes are up there.'

'Was your grandfather sick for a while?' Gabe held his breath as he waited for her answer. It was the first directly personal question he'd asked since that night when she'd sleepily muttered too few secrets.

She nodded briefly, her mouth closing, and she got very busy filling the jars. Totally shutting that topic of conversation down again. He tried not to frown, went for the obvious distraction instead.

'What do you want?' That flash of blue again from under the fluttering lashes.

'Payment for letting you use the kitchen,' he said in his worst lecherous-landlord tone.

'What kind of payment?' She smiled but he also saw the spark.

It was so easy to excite her. But so damn hard to open her up in other ways.

'Three bottles of that sauce.' He watched, his body helplessly winching harder when he saw the hint of disappointment in her eyes. He just couldn't resist. 'And...'

'And?' Her mouth tilted.

Gabe slapped a booklet on the table in front of her after dinner. 'Ever seen this?'

Roxie read the title. And frowned.

'It's the road code,' he drawled. 'And you need to study it, because you're going for your theory test tomorrow.'

'Am not.'

'Are too. Or else.'

She narrowed in on his naughty vibe. 'Else what?'

'We won't be checking any more items off your list.'

She gasped at his 'I mean it' expression. 'You're bluff-ing.'

He sat back, patted his lap for her as if she should come sit astride it. 'Come try and tempt me.'

The heat began to rise upwards, her chest, her neck, her face. But she wasn't going to let him tease her into saying yes to his bossiness. 'Don't need to. I can figure some fun for myself.'

'Think you'll find going solo isn't nearly so sweet now, Roxie,' he taunted.

She swiped up the damn book and opened it on a random page. Just so she could bury her burning face in it. Because she knew he was so right.

'You can do the practical in my car if you like.' He resumed the conversation as if he knew full well she wasn't concentrating on the printed words. 'Might be easier? I can get you covered on the insurance.'

Ugh, insurance. She hated that word. 'Thanks, but no, I couldn't.'

'You're too scared to drive something that actually goes fast?'

'I think you know I'm not afraid of fast.' She shot him a look over the boring rule book.

'Everything comes back to sex with you, doesn't it?'

'Are you *complaining*?' she mocked, tossing the road code aside. 'We *are* sex, Gabe. We're a shag team.' But she wasn't being completely honest—not even to her-self. She got up from the table quickly. 'I've got the most awesome dance flick ever for tonight.'

'Oh, I can't wait.' Gabe didn't sound any less sarcastic than he had a moment before.

But the opening theme had barely started when his phone beeped. He glanced at the message and groaned.

'What's wrong?' She pressed pause on the remote, the opening number wasn't one to be missed.

He was studying the screen intently, scrolling through some lengthy missive. 'One of the boys has gotten into trouble. Cheating while on summer tour. Pretty sordid too, going to be all over the front pages tomorrow.' He shook his head and tossed his phone to the floor. 'This is why they shouldn't get married. Commitment doesn't work with this lifestyle.'

Roxie giggled. 'Are you serious?'

'Absolutely.' He met her smile with censure in his dark eyes. 'The pressure these guys are under? They're away so often. There's all that adrenalin—they need a release. Distance relationships never work and in this business there are even more factors to make marriages fail.'

Roxie gaped at his earnest expression. 'You call this lifestyle working with a *distance* relationship?' she mocked. 'Gabe, you're not talking being away months or even weeks at a time. You're talking *days*.'

'You don't understand the temptation they face.'

'Oh, please. Temptation passes *you* on the street every day. The number of women who give you that *look*.' She shook her head. She'd seen it so many times at the stadium. 'The guys who give into temptation on a short trip like that would give into it at home just as quick if the opportunity arose,' she said bluntly. 'It's not the lifestyle that's the problem, it's that the guy doesn't know how to keep his zipper up.' She chuckled again. 'I mean, really, Gabe, you're away for what, a week at most?'

'When we go on tours it's weeks at a time,' he said defensively.

'Oh, come on, it's a big fat excuse and you know it.' She leaned closer, getting into the stride of her argument now. '*You* don't want to give up your freedom in case something better swings along. That's okay, you don't have to. Just don't try to hide behind your job as some lame excuse for being unable to make a commitment. If you wanted to, you would. But you don't want to.'

That was right. He didn't. Gabe was stunned with how she had him pegged. And that she'd just shot him down with a couple of snappy sentences. Yes, he liked the convenience of the short-term fling—and the out-of-town bender was even better. No mess in his backyard. 'Okay, you're right. It took a lot to get my freedom and, no, I won't give that up for anyone. I'm not willing to compromise on the most important things in my life.' That was still his view, right?

She nodded, apparently all understanding now. 'I know exactly how you feel. I don't regret any of the time in the last few years. I'd still be doing it if I could. But now? I want my time. I want *my* freedom. I don't want anybody holding me back.' She grinned impishly.

Strangely, even though she was now agreeing with him, Gabe didn't feel any better. 'So you're really serious about the no-marriage-and-kids thing?'

'I think I take after my mother,' she said, settling more comfortably on the sofa. 'She didn't want me despite going ahead to have me. I'm not doing that to anyone. I'm never having any in the first place.'

'No permanent man either?' He had no idea why his pulse had just picked up.

She shook her head. 'Playmate every now and then. That's the way forward.'

She was quoting his own philosophy but it sounded so wrong coming from her mouth. He didn't like her turning her back on the idea of being with someone for good. She should be cherished and treasured and adored—the prize, the heart, of some guy's life. And any guy who even thought of straying from Roxie would need his head read. Who'd ever want to give her up?

Gabe really needed to bury this line of thought—it was weird. He pressed the pause button on the remote she still held so the movie started running again. But a dance flick was hardly the kind of movie to completely absorb him, so those damn thoughts kept circling. Had he been hanging back from doing anything more with any of his exes in case someone better came along? Surely not, he'd just thought he had it sussed. Even after the Diana debacle he'd merely figured all he had to do was fling it with the right kind of woman. But Roxie wasn't that kind. In fact he now wondered whether that kind of woman even existed.

Yet here Roxie was basically trying to walk in his foolish footsteps. That just didn't sit right with him.

Damn it, none of this was right.

# CHAPTER TEN

As ROXIE drove towards home she saw Gabe jogging through the park. He signalled and she pulled over. He raised a brow at the P-plate on the rear window. She'd known he'd spot it straight away.

'I didn't just do the theory, I passed my practical. First time,' she said smugly.

'I should hope so,' he answered drily as he got in the passenger seat. 'You've been driving on the roads long enough.'

Roxie giggled and drove the final few metres to the garage. It had been a brilliant day: she'd taken the afternoon off work and done her test, gone to practice with the Blades, they'd asked her to do some freestyle—to help work out a new routine. Now she'd come home and found *him*. And he'd just gotten out and opened the heavy old garage door for her to park the car and was waiting to close it once she was in. First time ever anyone had done it for her. Life just couldn't get better. Her smile widening, she stepped out to meet him. And her foot sank into a puddle. Several inches deep and lapping—water was flowing in from somewhere. She headed straight for the boxes sitting in the new lake.

'Maybe we left a hose on.' Gabe disappeared out of the side door. He was back in a nanosecond but the sound of running water hadn't ceased. 'Probably a burst pipe, won't take anything to fix,' he said, pulling his phone from his shorts pocket.

Only money she didn't have. She should have been saving everything—not having her hair done or buying multiple bottles of Bollinger. She should have waited until she had more resources to deal with these seemingly inevitable setbacks. The house had eaten all her resources over the last year; she'd really hoped she'd hit the end of it. This was supposed to be her new start. Angered with her idiocy, she splashed forwards to lift the first of the boxes to safety out in the garden. The contents of the ones at ground level must be sodden already.

Gabe had his phone to his ear; she could hear the 'on hold' music as she walked. 'You should move into the Treehouse while this dries out,' he said.

She shook her head. No way would she move in with Gabe. Her instinct had been whispering a warning to pull back on the time she spent with him and at that suggestion it shrieked. 'It's just a flood. Upstairs isn't damaged, only the stuff stored down here. It won't take long to dry.' She hoped. She also hoped like hell the plumber wasn't going to cost a bomb.

'You might want to transfer some of this stuff to plastic boxes for longer-term storage, especially the paperwork,' he said.

Did he think she hadn't considered that first time round? Of course she should have used better storage when she'd originally sorted all the stuff, but the banana boxes had been free from the supermarket. She didn't bother answering—the man was made of money, he had no clue what it was like for those not born with silver spoons.

'Don't do that.' He frowned at her. 'I'll lift them for you—' He broke off as someone finally took him off hold.

Roxie kept lifting and lugging—they were her boxes after all. Gabe's frown deepened as she marched back and forth past him carrying the worst affected out to the deck. She listened to him issue instructions to the plumber with his innate lord-of-all authority. Which annoyed her even more. She couldn't ask him not to make the call, didn't want to reveal her proximity to the poverty line, but she couldn't let the entire property flood either. As he wrapped the call she bent down for the next box—the bottom one of the first tower. The water was already at the one-third mark. She hoisted it up, cold wet running down her arm.

'Oh, hell,' she muttered, quickly changing her grip, but it was too late—the box simply disintegrated and its contents splashed everywhere. Glancing down at it all, her blood froze. She immediately looked for his reaction. Tension twisted his usual good-humoured expression. She could see him thinking, his face hardening as his jaw clamped, his eyes darkening.

Did he doubt her?

Defensiveness rose, intensified by tortured memories and the frustration from this latest fix-it job the house demanded. Truthfully she'd forgotten that box was even there. She'd had to. But his icy attention was fixed on the stuff now scattered, half submerged, over the floor and that defensiveness burst from her in a bitter torrent. 'I'm not a junkie, Gabe.'

He went all the more rigid. 'I know that,' he said roughly.

Given the number of plastic-wrapped syringes, blister packs of prescription-only painkillers, bottles of morphine and who knew what else, she wouldn't really have blamed him for wondering.

'They were your grandfather's,' he said shortly.

She bent, scrambling to get it all together. 'I meant to take it to a pharmacy to get rid of, but I just boxed and forgot it.'

'I can drop it off.' He bent down beside her and gathered the needles.

'He was diabetic,' she felt compelled to explain. 'Injections a couple times a day. Then pain relief too. Some of the pills were Grandma's.' It really did look as if she were running some kind of drugs lab. 'She had so many they took an age to dispense.'

'Why did it have to be you?' he asked. 'Where were the district nurses?'

'Busy.' Her defensiveness resurged—higher. '*I* could manage. Grandad didn't want to die in hospital so at the end I didn't call anyone. I gave him the painkiller the doctor prescribed and I held his hand and I watched him. In the end I called an ambulance because...' Because she couldn't bear it any more. She paused and tried to suck back her emotion. 'By the time it got there, he'd gone. That's a decision I made and I live with.'

She'd fought so damn hard with her stupid garden with her organic everything, and trying to make him laugh and do everything and anything anyone said might help battle that bastard disease. And for a couple of years there she'd succeeded. She'd thought it would go on like that indefinitely—what a dream that had been. Because all of a sudden he'd deteriorated and there had been no coming back from it. She looked up from the dirty puddle. 'It happens all the time. Cancer is the country's number one killer. People cope.'

'Most people don't have to cope alone,' Gabe answered gruffly, his hands full.

She shrugged, fully regretting revealing the little she just had to him. 'There was so much bad stuff happening in the city at that time, the medics were run off their feet.'

Gabe nodded but said nothing more. His pallor surprised her—for a doctor he looked a little shaken by all the medical guff. Tight-lipped, he stood and got a plastic bag to tip it all into. Then came back and viciously chucked the remainder in too.

Roxie blinked at the energy crackling off him. He was angry? Well, so was she. She didn't want to deal with this—least of all in front of him. She was so sick of fighting to keep this place okay. She picked up the box that had her mother's letters and papers in. She'd put it down here after it had given her nothing but disappointment. Not a single clue as to who her father had been. That dream had died a year ago too. 'I'll take some of these boxes upstairs,' she said dismissively.

'You don't want me to help you carry them up?' he called after her.

'No, I'm fine.'

Really? Gabe wasn't so sure about that—he heard raw emotion in her bitten-off words. 'It wouldn't take me a minute.'

'You've already done enough calling the plumber.'

Yeah, and she didn't exactly sound grateful about that. Gabe gritted his teeth, feeling extremely pissed off and it was worsening with each second. 'It really wouldn't take a minute.'

'I can manage.' She had her back to him, box in arms, stomping up the stairs already.

'I can help,' he argued. He hated her stubborn insistence on managing all by her damned self. She'd had to manage all kinds of hell as the primary carer, for not one, but two terminally ill elderly people. Alone. Why couldn't she say yes to a bit of muscle to help lug some bloody boxes now? Why couldn't she smile and say 'sure' and 'thanks'?

She looked over her shoulder, shooting him a quelling look. 'I don't need you to.'

*Don't want you to*, was what she really meant.

Gabe flung the bag of drugs into the corner of the garage. He could hear her stropping around up in her postage-stamp-sized studio. His fists clenched. There'd been no need for her to get snippy with *him*—the pipes weren't his fault, despite his random wish that she'd move in with him, he hadn't tampered with the plumbing like some sick stalker. But from years of working with finely balanced athletes, Gabe knew that a bad mood was often aggravated by not enough food. She must have gone straight from work to her driving test and then to the Blades practice. She had to be hungry. So he'd feed her. He wanted her to accept *something* from him tonight—and not merely sex.

He knocked on her door an hour or so later. For once she answered almost right away but that wasn't what made him blink so rapidly. No, she'd changed into the most hideous trackpants he'd ever seen, and, given he worked with sportsmen, he'd seen some ratty trackies. These were thick, massive and shapeless and he really just wanted to remove them then and there. But he reminded himself that wasn't the first priority.

'I'm guessing you probably haven't made dinner so I made enough for you too.' He refused to be offended if she said no to him. Even if he had gone to a stupid amount of effort.

'You have?' She blinked at him.

He nodded. 'It's on the deck if you want to come and get it.'

She hesitated.

'It's getting cold and I've gone to a lot of trouble.' He put on some pressure with a wicked look. He wanted to see her smile.

And she did smile—all sceptical, as if she didn't believe he'd ever go to any trouble. Oh, the irony.

'Okay, give me a second.' Roxie stepped back inside and shut the door. Gabe had gotten over his snappy temper flare, surely she could too. Hopefully he'd forgotten her angst moment in the garage. She was too tough to let a blasted pipe get her down—so it would delay her trip another couple of weeks perhaps; worse things had happened. She grabbed the half-bottle with the D on it— that and Gabe back in stud mode would help bubble her out of the funk.

'Wow,' she said, taking in the laden plates on the outdoor dining table. 'Not sure the Bolly is good enough for this.'

'Don't get too effusive.' He pulled out her chair. 'It's only burger and chips.'

'Not your average burger and chips.' She sat, breathing in the yum display. They were home-made bean patties, ripped-from-the-plant salad and freshly dug new potatoes cooked then crisped up something yummy. Her mouth watered, her appetite suddenly screaming. 'You cooked all this?'

'I'm a single man, living alone,' he drawled. 'You didn't think I could cook?'

'But it's—'

'Veggie, I know. Not bad for a beef-farm boy, huh?' He popped the cork and poured the champagne into two glasses—frowning when that was enough to empty the bottle.

She picked up her fork and took a bite of the patty poking out from the toasted roll. Oh, wow. 'You really made this from scratch?'

'Your amazement is insulting.'

She chuckled, warmth trickling back into her chilled body. 'I've never met anyone who makes veggie burgers like these. From scratch. Not even me.'

He pulled his phone from his pocket and swiped the screen a few times. 'Okay, I got the recipe online. Here.'

She angled her head to read the page he'd pulled up. 'The *Heganator*?' She didn't just giggle, she squealed. '*He*gan?'

'Yeah, cool recipes for the hot vegan male.' He turned the phone back to study it, oh, so intently. Then he peered over the top of the phone, eyes twinkling. 'I think it's really written by a woman. Apparently hegans like burgers and barbecues.'

'You're hot but you're not a hegan,' she said, almost all her old flirt tone back.

'But I can cook like one on occasion.'

'It is amazing. I mean that in a good way.' She looked at him and her teasing smile died. 'Thank you.'

Her heart was beating too hard. She couldn't remember when someone else had cooked dinner for her. When someone had gone to so much trouble and thought. Someone who bothered to understand what she preferred to eat and not eat. Certainly not her lame ex-boyfriend. The joke died from his eyes too—leaving them warm and gentle and so deep...

She dropped her knife so she had the excuse to break away from that acute, wordless communication. Surely she was reading the wrong messages. It wasn't caring she was supposed to see in him, it was supposed to be all carnal. But for a weird second there everything had gone upside down and inside out.

'While I have this out, I want your number,' he said.

She looked back up at him.

'Mobile number,' he elaborated at her blank expression. 'I'm away for the next week, so I need your number. In case.'

In case of what? 'I don't have one.'

'You don't have a mobile?' He leaned forward.

'Don't have any kind of phone.' She chased a bit of patty round the plate with her fork. 'Don't need one.'

'Of course you need one,' he said, still sounding amazed. 'Everyone needs one.'

'Well, I don't.' It was an expense she didn't need. The very few calls she had to make were usually local, so she made them from the gift shop.

'Roxie, it's a safety issue as much as anything. What if your ancient car breaks down when you're on some back country road?'

'I don't drive back country.' She smiled.

'You know what I mean.' He didn't smile back. He growled. 'You should have a phone.'

She didn't have a phone because she didn't have anyone to call. And that was the way it was going to stay.

'If I hadn't been here tonight, how would you have gotten hold of a plumber?' he asked, still holding his phone mid-air as he waited for her to answer.

'I would have figured something out,' she answered frigidly. She always had before. Tonight if she'd been alone she'd have turned off the water at the mains and waited 'til she had the money to deal with it. She stabbed a potato and stuffed it in her mouth. Having to chew stopped her saying too much more about her ability to manage just fine and about her funding issues. She didn't want him to know all that. He put his phone down and mirrored her actions, attacking his burger as if it were alive and about to scuttle off the plate away from him.

Several minutes later, both meals almost entirely eaten, Gabe spoke. 'Want to go out tonight?' His humour-laced attitude was back; so was his sinful smile. 'I'm guessing you haven't had nights and nights out on the club scene. I know a couple of places.'

Roxie's blood burned, but the melt from ice to fire was so rapid it hurt. Maybe dinner with Gabe hadn't been such a great idea—she felt wobblier now than when she'd first seen the water washing over the garage floor. As if her world were more on the edge of danger in this seemingly easy instant. 'I went dancing with the Blades after that first game. You know, the night you decided to go home early.' She matched his light'n'teasy tone.

'Another time.' He shrugged, that smile widening. 'But I confess I saw these poking out from that last box on the garage.' He bent and picked up something under his side of the table.

'Oh, I remember those.' She studied the couple of old records he held up and felt the ice threaten her heart again. She'd played those to her grandfather in the last few days as he'd slipped in and out of consciousness.

'No doubt you have a player up in that overcrowded antique shop you call your studio.'

'Somewhere under a million other things.' She didn't want to dig it out.

'No matter.' He put the vinyl records back by his seat and picked up his phone again. 'Because I found a couple of tracks online and downloaded them.' He tapped the screen and the intro started. 'Come on, you can't deny me when I cooked you that *amazing* dinner.'

In the end Roxie pushed her chair out and took his hand because it was herself she couldn't deny—she ached for the pleasure of his touch. She wanted a return to that simple, mindless, *uncomplicated* pleasure. Her bare feet were mud-splattered, her ugliest trackies hung shapelessly from her hips and her hair was a tangled mess. But he held her as if she were Cinderella herself in all her finery—only extra firm, as if he wasn't about to let her run away.

He danced smooth and natural and strong. Clearly not intimidated by her ballet background, he was in charge and not afraid to let her know it. She liked it more than she'd thought she would. She'd danced alone for years, but being partnered, guided like this? It was surprisingly good. The song was a big-band swing number from the nineteen fifties, one she'd always loved, one that brought happy with the sad in her mind's eye. But there was no room for memory, there was only now. He swept her from one side of the deck to the other, turning her on a coin-sized spot and all with the ease of a professional. Breathless, she pulled back to look in his face.

He shook his head ruefully. 'You didn't think I could dance either? Don't think I'm capable of anything much other than sex, do you?'

There was an edge to his comment that pushed Roxie's caution button. She thought him capable of a hell of a lot actually—thought he was more magnificent than was good for either of them. She didn't need to be wowed further by his cooking and dancing talents. It wasn't fair of him, not when this was supposed to be a trifling fling.

'Are you fishing for compliments?' she murmured lightly. 'You, the doctor who has all those dancers faking injuries to get near you?'

She felt the slight movement in his chest, guessed it

to be a grunt of amusement. He pulled her closer to keep her moving. Another song automatically played from his phone. Another swing number, slower this time. She let her lashes droop as he swayed with her, felt the stresses from the flood ease. So easy to lean against him, so easy to let him take all her weight, to take all this and more from him... But he didn't want to give more. And if she did that, if she let herself *depend*, then she'd want more. And wasn't she determined *not* to want that from anyone? It would only end badly. Being too close always brought loss and that was what she wanted to be free of most of all.

'Do you want to talk about it?' he asked softly, his smooth voice inviting every confidence.

Roxie stared over his shoulder at the top of the trees. What *man* ever wanted to *talk*? Men hated that emotional 'talking' thing, didn't they? They were all action over words. Then she realised—this wasn't Gabe acting like a *man*, this was Gabe acting like a *doctor*. Was he taking care of her because he felt sorry for her, because he'd found out something more about her time with her grandfather's last days? Was he cooking for her and offering to counsel her too? Was he afraid she was fragile? That she might go deep depressive as Diana had? It was nice he was concerned and all, but *medical* concern wasn't what she wanted from him.

Ever.

So no, she didn't want to talk. She didn't want anything from him. She pulled free and stepped out of his arms. 'Actually I'm pretty tired,' she said coolly.

'Okay,' he said. There was a silence as she took another step back and didn't meet his eyes. He stood exactly where she'd left him, as if he was waiting—for what? There was nothing she could bear to give. And she couldn't take anything more tonight either.

'I have some dishes to do,' he said eventually, quietly.

That hit her conscience. 'Oh, I should—'

'No, my mess, my shame,' he answered with a brief facsimile of a smile. 'You're not seeing it.'

Now she looked at him—and with superhuman effort refrained from asking him to come up with her. For now, contrarily, she didn't want to be alone. Now she wanted back in his arms. For a second there she'd glimpsed something so sweet, but it was a mirage lasting only while the music played. If she took him now, she'd be vulnerable to investing too much as he'd warned her before their first time together. She couldn't chase a dream that would disappear in a blink and a smile. Her bruised heart would be battered worse than ever. Exactly what she didn't want. So she turned and took the stairs alone.

Frustrated, Gabe let her go, at a loss as to how else he could try to break through the defensive barriers that she could erect in the blink of an eye. Lying alone in bed, he watched the light at her window. It was after two in the morning before she switched it off. Less than four hours later he heard her flick the hose on in the garden. He was due at the airport soon and he'd be in Sydney for the next five nights and, damn it, he wanted to reach out to her.

He walked out of the house, saw her pallor and the dark rings beneath her eyes. She couldn't completely hide her stress. The pipes would be nothing to fix, he'd already paid the plumber to come back later today and finish last night's temporary patch, but as for the other hurts he suspected went deep? He didn't know how to

help with those, not when she wouldn't admit to them—
least of all to him. But he wanted to. He really wanted to.

She tossed the hose and strode to meet him. Her
bruised eyes burned, feminine aggression made her
slim frame strong—and made him unusually weak at
the knees. She didn't give him the chance to say anything. No, she led the dance and reverse cowgirl rocked.
It really did. He loved watching her half-lightened, half-
natural coloured hair swinging over her back. Loved
tracing the curve of her butt. Loved sliding his hands
around to her breasts, down her slender ribs and beyond
to her hottest spot, teasing the ecstasy out of her. But he
wanted to look into her eyes too. Wanted to *know* her—
to connect so much more completely than this.

He knew she was determined and today more ag-
gressive than ever—more hungry, more driven, more
demanding. Her hands were so tight on his thighs he'd
bear her fingermarks for days. For someone so slight
she had gut-wrenching strength and she ripped what she
wanted from him. He growled through gritted teeth, desperately holding back as she rode him. Glad there were
no neighbours overlooking them—given they were outside, given it was six in the morning, given this was all
screaming, sweaty, animal sex. But the best sex of his
life wasn't enough any more.

She arched as her orgasm hit, her piercing shriek loud
enough to make the sparrows fly from the trees. As soon
as she crumbled he moved, flipping her over and then
rolling again so she was back above him, but facing him
this time. He held her face so he could see into those sex-
dazed eyes and pushed as deep as he could go.

He waited, breathing hard while he got it together.
Because he refused to have sex with her now. Now he

was making love. Now he was giving everything he
could.

Her eyes widened, she shook her head, but he firmed
his grip, holding her so she couldn't escape his kiss. And
slowly, so slowly he started all over again. Every movement, every touch filled with care and passion. His hands
sweeping, fingers drifting, his heart bursting. He ached
for completion, contentment—hers. He wanted to fill
her, to treasure her.

She lay limp above him—as if she was sated already and could move no more. So he was gentle, slow.
And then he felt the subtle change, her skin warming as
muscle beneath became energised. She draped like silk
now—her limbs curving, embracing. Her hands cupped
almost shyly. And then he heard her breathy sob—it
wasn't an entirely sexual plea. He cradled her and kissed
her, the simplest of caresses. Until that moment when she
moaned, until she clung, until she murmured his name
brokenly just that once. Until she was soft, warm, ac-
cepting. And his.

He groaned as words failed, emotion overwhelming
him—the need for her, to care for her. But also, for her
to care back. He wanted it *all* back from her. Oh, now
he felt it—the yawning need that had never before been
realised, let alone exposed. So vulnerable.

He pulled her closer, buried his face in her warm soft
skin, and gave in to it.

Afterwards her eyes remained firmly closed.
Apparently she was asleep. He sat up, managed to hook
one arm under her legs, while supporting her back with
the other. He carried her to the comfort of a soft mattress
and cotton coverings and space. To *his* bed, not hers.
She didn't open her eyes as he covered her and told her

to sleep. But he knew she was awake. He could feel the aware tension emanating from her body. But there was no time left to call her on it.

# CHAPTER ELEVEN

GABE sat in his hotel room in Sydney and ruefully laughed about the plans he'd made only a couple of weeks ago about coming here and having some seriously debauched nights on the town. Had he honestly thought he could sate his sexual appetite with a one-night stand? The idea of sex with a stranger left him cold—and flaccid. He pulled out his phone and went online. Pointless given she didn't have any kind of a phone, let alone a computer. So he did a search to find clips from Blades' shows. Naturally some fan had uploaded the Blades' on-pitch performance from the first week. He watched it. Watched it again. After three replays knew exactly when each shot of Roxie was with her long, slender legs lifting and her hair wild and her cheeks flushed and her smile huge. Roxie dancing only moments after he'd been pawing her in the corridor. The sexiest woman ever.

Not so flaccid now.

He might have dated a couple of dancers before, but he'd never been reduced to watching vids of any woman over and over. He pushed the button so the screen went black. Lay back on his bed, the phone pressed to his chest. He hated that she'd not said a word this morning. That she'd used him. He had more to offer her than that and he wanted her to realise it, want it, accept it.

Only now distance brought doubts. Had he imagined the warmth and caring in her return embrace? He needed to know her emotions were as entangled as his.

He sat up, frustrated with his impotence. Surely there was something he could do? He glanced at the phone in his hand and smiled at the obvious. He scooped up his wallet and hotel keycard, thankful that the shops in this city were open all hours.

Roxie worked late at the shop, avoiding the emptiness back at the Treehouse. She knew the science of it. The way humans were programmed to respond to a prospective mate. Women the world over—regardless of their culture or background—displayed the same available signals to the potential male—innate, instinctive, unstoppable. So why wasn't she having any of those normal responses to any of those other guys? There were a ton of them in that stadium, several were gorgeous, certainly virile and fit. Couldn't get fitter. And yet there was none of that softening deep inside; she didn't catch herself giving any a second look. Hadn't been *compelled* to. Not that she'd been compelled to with Gabe. He'd been the right guy in the right place at the right time, that was all. There was nothing any more special about him than anyone else. Right?

But then there'd been this morning. And there'd been nothing scientific about this morning. It had been all terrifying, out-of-control magic.

So she was relieved he'd gone away. She had time to remember her goals for her future—to travel and be independent. A free spirit with an unencumbered heart.

Finally she walked home, bypassing the heavy machinery that had trucked into the street some time during the day—diggers making mud and noise as they

replaced broken waste water pipes. She understood the
need, since the earthquakes that had decimated so much
of the city, the repair and renewal work had been intense.
She'd got off relatively lightly—her home mostly okay,
her workplace mostly okay, so she wasn't going to complain about the roadworks now.

She went through the garage, planning to go straight
upstairs, except she was drawn to the Treehouse. It
looked sad somehow, as if it knew it was empty. Even
the windows seemed sad. Then she realised that was
because the one at the front was on a lean—sagging towards the tree. She put her head on an angle; it didn't
help. She reached for her keys and opened up. Walked
into the main room, to that window nearest the tree.
Three quarters of the way there, the floor creaked alarm-
ingly. She could see the tipping angle of the floor with
her bare eyes. Under her weight it actually sagged an
inch more.

She jumped back to a more secure part of the room.
Oh, that could not be good. She raced outside again. She
didn't need a spirit level to be certain that corner of the
house had sunk. She couldn't believe it—not when it had
survived all those earthquakes. Why was it crumbling
now?

She looked up at the three-quarter-century-old
branches and then down at the roots. She didn't know
how bad it was yet, but she already knew she didn't
have the money to fix it. She went back to the gift shop
and called an engineering firm. They sent an engineer
first thing next morning. She stood beside him, trying
to keep a grip as he did his assessment. The foundations
had gone. The tree roots had rotted, causing a giant hole
beneath the house. It was possible the vibrations caused
by the heavy machinery out on the road had exacerbated

the rapid sink, but it would have happened soon anyway. And if it wasn't fixed, the whole house could come crashing down.

Roxie looked up at the branches—the thing that gave the house its beauty, its point of uniqueness, was the thing that would ultimately cause its destruction.

The engineer apologised as he explained—especially when she asked how much repairs could cost. He promised to send another engineer for a second opinion, but for now he was classing it as unsafe—*uninhabitable*—until the remedial work was done. Roxie's blood froze as she processed the info. Uninhabitable meant she'd lose Gabe as her tenant. Which meant she'd lose her income. The engineer left a brief report for her then and there. Black inked words leapt off the blinding white page—extensive, damage, cost…

Anger surged. She'd fought so long and still been defeated—in everything. She turned to the garden she'd tended for so long in the hope it could help her grandfather. But it had ultimately failed her too. The tall, fruitful plants mocked her, growing so strong when there was nothing left in her life. Furious, she lashed out with her bare hands. She tore the nearest tomato plant, swearing when the leaves ripped through her palms. She clawed until the whole thing was out, leaving a square of bare brown earth. She stopped, breathlessly stared at the small empty space that had been exposed.

Yeah, that was better.

Gabe frowned as the taxi drove alongside the park; there was something different about Roxie's place. When the car pulled over he saw the problem clearly. The hedge had been cut so there was a wide *path* through. He sprinted along it. 'Roxie? What's going on?'

He stopped, shocked, as he got to the garden.

'You're here sooner than I expected.' She clattered down the stairs from her studio in crazily high heels and met him with a smile, her hair flicking round her face. Only her eyes weren't sparkling to match.

'What the hell's happened?' Gabe all but gasped.

She carefully brushed her hair back behind her ears. He saw a long thin, scratch on the back of her hand. 'The vegetable garden was too big. No potential buyer would want it like that.'

Gabe still couldn't breathe. 'Potential buyer?'

She nodded blithely and stepped closer in her pretty dress. 'I'm selling.'

*'What?'* His heart stopped altogether.

'It's the right thing to do.' She smiled. 'I should have worked that out sooner.'

He stared back at the neatly turned over, empty soil—every abundant bed now completely cleared. She'd ripped out that entire magnificent garden. It was all gone. 'Oh, Roxie, what have you done?'

'Tidied up.' She laughed as if his reaction was over the top. 'It'll be bought by a developer anyway and the place will be skittled.'

*'What?'* Now his heart raced, thudding so hard in his ears he couldn't be sure what he was hearing—or what he was seeing.

'It's okay,' she reassured, sounding all confident. 'Take a look at the house.'

He stared at her instead. Because it wasn't okay. She could smile as much as she liked but she was never going to get him to believe this was okay.

She didn't fill the silence he left for her. Instead she waited and finally he turned and saw an official notice taped on the door. He'd seen a ton of them in the months post-earthquake. 'Why have they stickered it?'

'The foundations have gone,' she said matter-of-factly. 'It's sunk already. It could fall down any time.'

He could see the worst spot now, right by the tree. 'Foundations can be fixed.'

'Not this time.'

He couldn't believe this was happening. He couldn't believe she was acting so calm when he knew, he just knew she was being eaten up inside. He whirled to face her, to look into that too perfectly *made-up* face. 'You don't have to sell it.' She really didn't.

'I can't afford to fix it.'

He coughed away the tight feeling in his throat. 'What about insurance?'

She smiled again, that awful smile that was nothing but a meaningless twist to her mouth. 'There is no insurance, Gabe. We couldn't afford it. I was only working sporadically because—'

She broke off, but Gabe knew why already. Because her grandfather had been sick and she'd been needed at home with him here.

'There's no insurance for the car, the house or the contents and I don't have any savings.' She still wore that synthetic smile. 'We were lucky in the earthquake that there wasn't much damage. I've spent the last year fixing the superficial stuff. I tried to get insurance after but the companies weren't exactly running to cover any houses then and honestly I still couldn't afford it. I can't afford the repairs.'

'Roxie—'

'I'm sorry about your tenancy,' she interrupted him. 'Not much of a welcome after your trip away. You can't stay in there tonight.'

'If I can't stay there, you're not staying either,' he said. He'd take her somewhere with him and work on her until she broke down and let out the agony he was sure was hidden behind her dull eyes.

'No, I'm not. My flight goes at three p.m. tomorrow.'

*'What?'* Oh, no, no, no. This was worse than anything.

'I've brought my trip forward.'

It was more of a shock than seeing how she'd decimated her beloved garden. 'What about your job?'

'I've resigned already.' Still that smile.

'What about the Blades?'

'That's why they have an extra in the squad. They're used to losing dancers partway through the season.' Now the smile had the slightest of edges.

*What about me?* Gabe wasn't going to ask that. 'So you're going to run away?'

'I'm not running away.' Finally there was a spark in her eyes—a flash of temper. Good, he wanted more of that honest kind of emotion.

'I'm getting on with my life,' she said. 'There's nothing here for me any more.'

Okay, maybe he didn't want *that* honest. 'I'm nothing?'

There was a moment. One moment when something else flashed before that damn smile came back, that caricature of Foxy Roxie sass. 'Not nothing, Gabe, you've been an education.'

His head went all funny, his breathing fast and shallow, he couldn't *think* properly. She still saw him as nothing but a good-time guy? An *education*—with his sexual *effort* and all? 'I think there's a bit more to us, Roxie. Maybe you're too inexperienced to know that.'

She shook her head and added to that sassy smile with a vixen shimmy of her shoulders. 'I'm not too inexperienced to know that this isn't anything more than a fling. Neither of us ever wanted anything more.'

The Treehouse wasn't the only thing with shaky foundations. Gabe's world was sinking with every word she spoke.

'I could buy it,' he said, latching onto the house rather than facing the implications of his tumbling emotions.

'Please don't feel like you have to help me.'

'I don't. I want the house. I've always wanted the house.' And he wanted what belonged in it too.

She laughed. 'You don't want the house *now*. It's ruined.'

'It's not, it just needs new foundations.' He saw her stiffen and tried to fight it—he had to break down her damn defences somehow. 'I'm not doing this out of sympathy, Roxie.'

'You can't help yourself, Gabe,' she said patronizingly, maintaining that bloody smile. 'You're a *doctor*. Helping people is in your blood. It's so much a part of you, you don't even realise. But you help those players, you helped your sister. You pulled back from your social life because you were so bothered about hurting someone. You're a good guy, Gabe. But I'm not going to let you get all chivalrous over this just because you took my virginity. We're having sex because it's fun and it's all we want from each other. You don't need to do anything more for me, okay?'

How could she see that good in him—more than he deserved—and not want more from him?

'Don't try to dictate to me what I can and can't do,' he snapped. 'If I want to buy the house, I'll buy it.'

Even in the face of his temper she kept her cool, angling her head and looking up at him from beneath those darkened lashes. 'This is *my* problem, Gabe, not yours. You'll get your bond money back.'

'I don't care about the bloody bond money.'

She shook her head and laughed. 'Only you can afford not to care about money.'

'What's that supposed to mean?' His anger mounted—how could she maintain this veneer?

'You're so used to doing whatever you want, achieving what you want, getting whoever and whatever you want. Have you ever really had to fight for anything, Gabe?' Oh, now there was an edge, the slightest hint of cut in her tone.

'I've had my battles.'

'Breaking out from family expectation?' she teased.

Well, that wasn't as nothing as she made it sound when you were talking five generations of expectation, of being the sixth Andrew G. Hollingsworth and the only one to turn into Gabe. Of never feeling as if you could have your own voice. At the time, as a teen, it had been all but everything.

She laughed and answered her own question. 'All that did for you was get you even more used to having your own way.'

Yeah, he was totally used to getting what he wanted. But he was miles off getting it now. This was a first. This was not nice.

'Gabe, when you've fought some really tough battles, you know when something's worth that effort or not. And this place isn't worth my fighting for any more,' she said. 'It's right for me to leave it.'

He just didn't believe she meant that. 'Roxie—' He broke off when he saw her stiffen.

And that was when he knew. She might be bleeding to death inside, but her mind was made up and she was the strongest person he'd ever met. She'd chosen her path and she was running for it. So why try and stand in her way? If this was what she truly wanted, and apparently it was, why argue and make it harder for her? He'd only fail at it anyway.

She looked as if she hadn't slept at all the last couple of nights. Probably worrying and breaking her heart over losing the house. Now he was furious—she should have bloody gotten in touch with him. It hurt that she hadn't. Instead she'd made all these decisions already. On her own.

Was that because he wasn't important enough to her to talk to about it? He was merely a bedmate, nothing more than a toy for her? He had the horrible feeling it was. And there was one way of finding out for sure.

'I got you a little something when I was in Sydney,' he said, lightening his tone completely.

Her eyes widened in genuine surprise.

He dug the new phone from his pocket and handed it out to her. 'We can stay in touch. If you ever need any-thing...' He trailed off, momentarily floored by the fro-zen expression on her face. 'You don't need to worry about the ongoing costs or anything. I've got that cov-ered.'

'Gabe, I can't accept this from you.'

Just the phone or anything he might offer? 'Sure you can.' He forced a smile. 'It has a great camera—you'll need that on your travels. I've downloaded some apps for you already, set up an account so you can get more, whatever you want.'

'Gabe...'

'You live in the mobile age, Roxie, you need one. It's a safety thing—see it can be a torch, an alarm, a GPS navigation system...' He was selling it too hard. Only

because she looked more and more distanced. Not wanting to be rude to him, but clearly not wanting to even
touch the thing. Oh, hell, he'd been right. The distress
he read in her had nothing to do with him. She didn't
want to know him once she'd gone.

'You can text me any time, send me a photo or something.' He pushed one last time for a reaction.

And at that she smiled and took the phone from him.
'You just want a sext pic, right?'

It was the worst attempt at humour he'd ever heard.

'Honestly, I just want you to be able to get in touch if
you need to,' he said.

If she *wanted* to. Which clearly she didn't. He got it
now. Oh, yeah, she was hurting, she was a mess inside.
But not about *him*, it was all her house. He'd seen her a
bit shaken up only last week over a simple burst pipe;
he knew how much work she'd put into that garden, into
keeping the place in shape, the furniture that had all that
history. And she was gutted about losing it all.

But not about leaving him.

'I'd like to get in touch now,' she purred, stepping
closer. 'There are still a few items on my list that we
haven't ticked.' She actually pulled it out from her pocket
and unfolded it.

Gabe didn't see the sheet for the red fog of fury that
suddenly materialised before his eyes. 'You risked your
neck going in there to get your sex list?' And she'd
stashed it in her pocket so they could work through it
together tonight? Irate, he glared at her make-up and her
pretty dress and her fancy shoes—she'd got dolled up for
her last debauched night with him? He really was just a
tool to help tick off her list?

She looked slightly apologetic. 'Well, I would have

got your stuff but I didn't want to pry into your personal things.'

Oh, of course she didn't. The dinners, the movies on the sofa, the laughs, that last time they'd been together? All had meant nothing to her. It really was just a physical fling. A feel-good-for-the-moment thing. She was keeping her innermost emotions at a distance and using him as some kind of take-the-edge-off crutch?

'I think it'll be okay if you just zip in and out to get your personal items quickly,' she added, spreading her hands wider over his torso. 'But you should probably get the construction guys in hard hats to retrieve the furniture and stuff.'

As if she were really that concerned for his welfare? She just wanted his damn body.

'Come up to the studio with me,' she murmured. Her lashes dropped as she watched her fingers sliding across his chest. 'I've got that last bottle of Bolly we can share.'

He couldn't believe she really wanted that now. She wanted to use him so she could forget the hurt of losing her house?

Hell, no. She wasn't getting everything her own way. Not any more.

He tipped up her chin and looked into those mascara-framed, listless eyes. Bent and kissed her. Her arms slipped around him instantly, her lithe body melting, twisting, teasing against his already. It'd be so easy to fall deeper into her delicious heat, to take what was being offered. But what was on offer wasn't enough. He wasn't doing it to himself. If it was over, then it was over *now*. He had some pride. He wasn't going to be a boy-toy for her right up to the minute she was ready to discard him and step onto some plane. He had some self-respect.

And he was angry.

'Those bottles aren't really big enough for sharing,' he said, trying to keep a lid on it. Trying to ignore how badly his body wanted him just to give in. 'And I don't think there's anything more I can teach you now.'

Roxie watched him stalk over to the house. Her pride reared up, she knew what Gabe liked and wanted. It was what she wanted too. To be free to have some fun. And she'd wanted to get through this last horrendous night having fun with the one guy she knew in the world capable of doing just that. Hell, she thought it was the *only* way she might get through tonight—in a state of mindlessness. And she desperately, desperately wanted to feel him that one last time. Because she wasn't doing this ever again.

Only he'd just said no. And she was devastated.

She ran up the stairs to the garage to hide before the hit registered and she lost some of her tightly held composure. She faced the almost empty room. She'd sold all the furniture to an antique store—cheaply as she was in such a hurry. And she'd sold the car. That was how she'd gotten her airfare.

She looked down from the emptiness to the phone in her hand. The same as his, fancy and beautiful only he'd gotten hers a sleek silver case. Girly and gorgeous. Unable to resist, she pressed the button to turn it on. He'd loaded a picture of the Blades as her wallpaper. She tested the ringtone. It was the song they'd danced to just the other night. She opened up the contacts. There was only one programmed already. Gabe Hollingsworth. There was a picture and everything. One he'd obviously snapped himself—with a more self-conscious grin than she'd ever seen on him in the flesh. More handsome than ever. She couldn't bear it.

Glancing up, the first thing she landed on was the

fridge. It mocked her with its remaining half bottle of Bolly. She opened the fridge door and chucked the phone in the ice-box in the top. Slammed the door and backed away from it as if it were some bomb she had to freeze to disarm.

Which was how she had to deal with him all over.

Gabe had hit a new low of voyeurism. Standing at the window in his darkened room in the damaged house, he watched her put the phone in the fridge and slam the door. His jaw dropped. Not exactly what he'd expected. But why was he surprised? She was putting all her feelings on ice. And didn't she do everything to the extreme? She wasn't just vegetarian, she was vegan. She didn't just have a vegetable plot, she had a vegetable paddock. When she'd decided to get a gig dancing, she went for the biggest, flashiest show in town. When she'd decided she wanted him as her lover, she'd been fearless in her pursuit. But when things were finished, they were totally finished. No looking back—like her decision to sell the house, the car, everything. No phone, no contact. All or nothing.

And she'd put him in the nothing box.

Too many long hours later, he waited at the bottom of her stairs. She appeared mid-morning. Looking awful but beautiful, hiding the lack of sleep damage beneath a layer of make-up thick enough to withstand a nuclear detonation.

'I'm giving you a ride to the airport.' He stood to let her past, his body stiff from sitting so long.

'That'd be great.' She cracked a smile through the warpaint.

So that was how they were playing it, as if it were all still fun and friendly and meaningless. He'd take her to the airport and let her go, right? It wasn't fair to try to hold someone back—he knew just how much resentment could build when someone tried to clip your wings.

'Got your phone?' he asked as casually as he could given he had shards of glass in his throat.

The smile stayed fixed as she nodded. He saw her gripping her hands together tightly, her fingers locked into each other. He made a thing of starting the engine and then clapped a hand on his forehead. 'Oh, I forgot something, hang on a mo.'

It took less than a minute to jog through the garage and up the stairs. He used the keys she'd just given him to hand to the lawyer. Apparently he could be trusted with that minion task. Her studio was all but empty—that furniture had already gone, and he'd noticed the car was gone from the garage too. It cut to the quick that she'd chucked the stuff that only days ago she'd held so tightly to her. Sure enough, the phone was there in the ice-box where she'd left it. She had no intention of keeping in touch with him. Gabe forced his blood to freeze, stopping the surging anger from flooding the deep wound she'd gouged inside him. He had to stay cool on this. So she was the first woman to dump him—maybe that was why he was so bothered. Maybe it was all just hurt pride.

Out of the corner of his eye he watched her stare straight ahead as he drove her away from the house she'd loved.

She didn't even blink.

Roxie didn't say a word the entire drive to the airport. Her throat had seized. It was too much to hope he'd just drop her in the two-minute car parks right outside the terminal. Of course he didn't. He parked in the expensive parks, insisted on carrying her bag in and even filled in a luggage tag for her while she checked in.

She was going straight through the security clearance; she couldn't delay getting away from him. She was about to lose it entirely. She folded her arms tight around herself, gripping her upper arms with her hands, holding all the agony inside.

It hurt to see him so at ease about her leaving. Which was yet more proof it was the right call to have made. She couldn't believe it when his expression warmed to tease-level as he cupped her face and tilted it up towards him.

Yeah, thank goodness he'd said no to her last night. From this one touch now, she knew she'd never have been able to pull off a last night of nothing but passion. She'd have clung to him, begging for everything he never wanted to give.

He'd meant the phone as a friendly gesture. It was kind of him. But she didn't want kind or friendly. He was supposed to be her *lover*. It was supposed to have been *once*. Only it had been once every which way and then some. And there'd been the fun, the conversation, the laughter, the way he'd held her, that had all led to… something she couldn't bear to define.

But he was redefining them in a way that was even worse. Concerned and caring, wanting to stay in touch as a *friend*. It was humiliating when what she really wanted was…

*No.*

She knew—to her *bones*—that she couldn't stay in touch with him. She was leaving this part of her life behind. If she really was going to live light and free, then she had to sever all connection.

'Your lawyer will be in touch about the sales of all

the assets,' he said quietly. 'But you know I'll keep an eye on it for you too.'

She nodded, mustered a slight smile to show her damn gratitude. Her throat was so tight with unshed tears she couldn't speak.

She looked for one last time into his beautiful almost black eyes. His teasing look gave way to a small smile that sawed through her nerves. She was a total block of wood, couldn't kiss him back, could barely manage to take the sweetness of his light, gentle caress. Gripped her sleeves even harder to stop herself shattering into a thousand little pieces of nothing.

'I hope it's everything you want it to be,' he whispered.

She barely nodded because now she knew—uselessly—that what she truly wanted was right in front of her. She wanted *him*—to love her, to want her, to hold her and keep her... But he didn't want to keep or be kept. And she couldn't bear the inevitable hurt of his rejection and her loss.

Motionless, she stared up at him. Stared so hard she could no longer focus. Her last sight of him blurred—he was that fuzzy outline she'd first seen in the bathroom that day. She blinked but it didn't make it better. She couldn't say a thing, her throat burning hot but, like the rest of her, paralysed.

She heard his deeply drawn breath. Felt his hands hard on her shoulders. 'Go.' Forcefully he turned her away. Pushed so she took a stumbling step in the direction of security clearance. Her frozen cold feet automatically took the next step. And the next.

She didn't turn, didn't raise a hand as she heard him harshly instruct her that one last time.

'Go.'

# CHAPTER TWELVE

THE flight lasted a lifetime. The droning engine hurt her head. The air-conditioning left her eyeballs even drier. The chilled blood in her veins made her stiff and cold. After a hell-on-wheels stopover and yet another long, frozen flight they began the descent, except the lights of London stretched for ever. And hard as Roxie tried, she couldn't stop thinking about Gabe. Surely he'd seen it in her face? In that one moment her heart had been exposed, there for him to take. If he'd asked, she'd have stayed, she'd have literally fallen into his arms. Only he'd told her to go.

So go she did—to all the tourist attractions: Buckingham Palace, The Tower of London, Madame Tussauds... And at the end of her first, miserable week, mad with herself for still feeling wretched, she queued for tickets at Covent Garden to see the Royal Ballet, as she'd dreamed of doing for almost two decades.

The theatre itself was beautiful, the audience was beautiful, the ballerinas beautiful. But Roxie's heart wasn't in it. She watched the dancers—the incredibly talented dancers—and hated every second of it. In the interval she walked out through the well-lit foyer, out into the crowded, famous square. And that was when she drew up short, not knowing what the hell she was doing or should do or wanted to do. She was in the middle of a foreign city, utterly alone. Just as she'd thought she'd wanted to be.

Only to find it *sucked*.

She'd made the most massive mistake.

'Roxie.'

She turned. No one in this city knew who she was. No one in the world knew *where* she was. So who was calling out to her?

Okay, now she was seeing ghosts—because there was a guy standing just by the theatre entrance who looked exactly like Gabe. But he couldn't be a ghost because Gabe wasn't dead, he was back in New Zealand. So she must be hallucinating. Delayed jet lag was sending her crazy.

It was a pretty good hallucination, though, because now the Gabe-non-ghost was walking, his gaze trained on her. She blinked but he was still there, striding towards her, faster now, until he was almost upon her. And he was in the most gorgeous suit and clutching a glossy red programme.

'You don't like the ballet,' she said when he got within earshot, because what else *could* she say to this unreal creature?

'Yeah, but you do.' He stopped a mere ten centimetres away from her, his expression searching. 'Why have you walked out halfway through?'

'I didn't think it was realistic.' Although it seemed she'd lost her grip on what was real altogether because here she was talking to a hallucination and, incredibly, it was talking back.

His brows nearly hit his hairline. 'A girl gets let down by a guy so she dies of a broken heart. Then she comes back as a ghost and protects that guy from other supernatural spurned women. Which bit's not realistic?' The corner of his mouth rose in the smallest of grins.

Okay, so now she was sure she was dreaming. 'You *hate* ballet, so how come you know the story of *Giselle*?'

'Because I've sat through three performances already.' His smile widened to rueful and he stepped just that bit closer.

'Three?' Her voice almost failed as she felt the warmth of his breath on her icy skin.

'I'm sure the woman in the ticket office thinks I'm a stalker. Which I kind of am.'

Roxie stared at him, her mind spinning. He really wasn't a ghost. He really was here. Oh, Lord, *why* was he here?

'So which bit did you think was unrealistic?' he prompted her.

She was shaking inside, outside, all over. 'I didn't like how she died of a broken heart just because that guy let her down,' she whispered.

'No, that wasn't exactly brave of her,' he agreed softly. 'What should she have done instead?'

Roxie was still digesting his appearance, so she didn't answer. She just stared at him some more and tried not to think too closely about *why* he was here.

'What would you have done?' He waited for a while. Then offered an answer himself. 'Should she have packed her bags and gone adventuring instead?'

Roxie shook her head, spurred into a sturdier response at that. 'No, she should have confronted him and told him what for.' That was what she should have done. She should have told him what she really wanted—been honest and to be unafraid of the consequences.

'Fair enough.' Gabe's eyes were fathomless inky

pools. 'But you know, I think you'd find the second half better.'

'Why?' Her throat had seized so tight again she could barely answer, and the trembles were graduating to shudders.

'Because in that half she proves her strength,' he answered, still quiet. Still unfathomable. 'She does everything in her power to protect that guy because she loves him so much. And to be able to love someone that deeply, that passionately, is beautiful. It's rare and it's a gift.'

Her heartbeats boomed like cannons. She refused to believe this might be what she wanted it to be. She wanted it too much—she was still too scared to be honest and to be unafraid of the consequences. So she tried to joke, just in case. 'Are you saying you *enjoyed* the ballet?'

'Well,' he answered seriously, 'I saw some parallels.'

'I'm not about to die of a broken heart,' she said, suddenly indignant. She hated him thinking she was weak.

'I am so aware of that.' His grin flashed, even his melt-inducing laugh sounded briefly. 'That wasn't what I meant.'

Roxie couldn't take much more without losing it. 'Well, what *did* you mean?'

'That you're like her in that you have the capacity to love that deeply, that profoundly.'

Oh, now she felt hurt—and so, so vulnerable. 'What makes you think that?'

His expression softened. 'You showed it in the way you cared for your grandparents. You did everything and anything you could for them.'

'Nothing anyone else wouldn't have done.' She tried to minimise it; she was no saint.

He shook his head. 'You *give*, Roxie. You give everything.'

She didn't say anything to that. Couldn't.

He leaned nearer, bending slightly so their faces were almost touching, whispered, 'Aren't you going to ask me why I'm here?'

'Should I have to ask?' she basically wailed, her nerves finally shredded. 'You don't just want to tell me?'

'I shouldn't have let you down.' He too suddenly sounded rougher round the edges.

'You've *never* let me down.' Every cell inside her hurt from the effort of trying to stop trembling. To stay standing. He'd been wonderful to her in all the ways he could.

He closed his eyes. 'Yes, I have.'

Did he mean that final night when he'd refused her stupidly desperate advances? 'You were allowed to say no to me.'

'No.' His eyes flashed open, his gaze pinning her. 'I let you down, and myself down, when I let you leave without telling you how I felt. I should have told you, but I was proud. And hurt. Now I'm just so miserable I'm prepared to grovel as much as I have to.'

Roxie's shaking became uncontrollable. 'G-g-grovel?'

'You asked if I'd really had to fight for something. That if I had, I'd know when a fight was worth the effort. Well, I'm fighting now. You know what for?'

She shook her head. The boulder that had just gotten lodged in her throat prevented her answering verbally.

'I'm fighting for you.'

Gabe watched the colour wash out of her face—leaving her paler than when she'd first seen him walking towards her. 'I didn't want you to go,' he said roughly. 'I should have told you that, but I didn't want to *stop* you from going. I didn't want to stand in your way and I didn't think you wanted—' He broke off. She was still staring at him as if he were an apparition or something. He'd been holding back, not wanting to overwhelm her but it wasn't working. And he needed to hold her. He put his hands on her waist, about to pull her close, but she put her palms on his chest. Defensively. And, worse, she still looked disbelieving.

'I know you, Gabe,' she said, her voice harsh. 'You're a healer, not someone who hurts other people. You hate the thought of hurting someone. But I'm strong, I'm not like Diana, I'm not going to crumble.'

'You know, I bloody wish you would,' he said, tightening his grip on her and pulling her closer despite her hands blocking him. 'I wish you'd open up and tell me how you're feeling. It's okay to admit to being upset. It's okay to ask for help. It's okay to need something from someone.'

From *him*. He wanted her to want everything from him.

But she shook her head. 'When you were a kid you looked after the orphan lambs. I don't want to be another orphan lamb for you.'

'Roxie, you're not listening to me. I *know* how strong you are. The strongest person I've ever met. You're all steel, able to make whatever sacrifice necessary. So I don't feel sorry for you, I feel sorry for me having to try and match your courage. I don't think you're some orphan lamb who needs rescuing. Quite the opposite.' He was determined to prove it to her—even if it took him the rest of his life to wear her down enough to accept what he had to give. 'You're brave and terrifyingly independent. You learned how to load syringes so you could administer pain relief to the people you loved most. You cared for them, helped them, fought to give them the best chance. You grew that massive garden, filled with wonderful goodness, made all that food with such love. You put your own dreams on hold for so long and I know you did that gladly. And I know you said this was your time now—to have your adventures and fun. And I don't want to hold you back. I don't want to stop you doing the things you want to do. But I do want a place in your life and I'm going to fight for it, Roxie. I think you're blocking yourself from the biggest adventure of all, with *me*, and that's not true to *you*. You're an all-giving person.'

He could feel the constant tremors racking through her. Could feel her trying to stop them. To resist.

'I don't want to be,' she whispered.

And he heard the fear.

'You can't *be* any other way, and I want it for me.' He cupped her cheek and looked into the beautiful blue eyes that were filled with a hurt he ached to ease. If only she would give him the chance. 'And you deserve someone to give it all back to you too. That would be me.' He smiled. 'You're not meant to be alone. I felt the way you held me, Roxie, I felt that need in you and I hope like hell I'm not delusional on that. You know I never wanted to commit, never wanted to compromise. I thought I had my life plan perfect. But then I met you. And now? I'd do anything for you. So be with me. Lean on me. That's what people who love each other do.' He bent his head nearer, his heart hurting for hers. 'I'm sorry you lost your family. But you can't protect yourself from loving any more. That's not living. You, more than anyone, are supposed to love. You need your connections, your history. You need your home and I'm sorry if being with me there spoilt that place for you. Is that what happened?' He'd had the awful fear that he'd somehow ruined it for her.

'Oh, no,' she breathed, her eyes full of distress. 'I just couldn't bear it any more—everyone I loved I lost in that house.' She bit on her lip, then whispered, 'Including you.'

'You never lost me.' He lifted her face with gentle fingers. 'But don't leave me in the wilderness now, Roxie. I want you. I want everything with you.'

He swore he could see her heart reflected in those pure blue eyes—glistening, vulnerable, beautiful. And as he watched the smallest curve to her lips grew and she blinked—her gaze suddenly stronger, direct, true.

'Everything?'

That hint of undaunted tease, of Foxy Roxie, made his bones liquefy.

'The works,' he promised.

She moved closer, snuggling right against him. Gabe's blood fizzed as her fingers curled into his shirt. Holding him close now—she clutched as if she was never going to let him go. She rose on tiptoe, her heart bursting, and whispered, 'But you know I've got quite an imagination, right?'

'I can't wait to see what you're going to add to my list,' he breathed, bending to brush her lips.

'*You* have a list?' Her lips curved against his.

'Come with me now and I'll show you it,' he invited, then swooped.

Roxie's spirit soared to the heavens like a cork fired from a bottle of champagne. She lifted her hand, feeling his warm jaw with her cold fingers, holding his head to hers. Deep, yearning, passionate. Her tired eyes closed as he filled her senses, pouring warmth and love into her cold bones. She did as he'd invited—leaned on him, drawing on his heat and strength and heart. His arms tightened all the more around her, pulling her closer and closer.

'Please don't ever let me go again,' she muttered.

'Never.' He kissed her fear away. 'Come on, let's get some place else before we get arrested.'

He kept her close, tucked in right beside him as they walked to flag a cab. She wasn't letting him go either, one hand still curled into his shirt. 'Shouldn't you be helping the team prep for the next game?' she asked, once they'd gotten in the back of a taxi. Suddenly she was nervous of the future that only seconds ago had seemed easy and perfect. 'It's only early in the season.'

'I've got this one covered but, you're right, I can only stay a few days unless I resign.' His arm tightened around her shoulder as she tensed in rejection of that idea. 'I know you want to travel and I don't want to stop you doing that. So maybe I could come over every couple of weeks. Even for just a few nights. I can meet you wherever.'

Every couple of weeks? She vehemently shook her head. 'You can't fly all this way and back again all that often. You'll get too tired and it costs too much.'

He opened his mouth to argue but she pressed the backs of her fingers against it. Because no way was she being apart from him for that long.

'Maybe we could travel together for a while when the season ends.' She smiled when she saw his frown, pushed her fingers more firmly against his lips when she felt them move. 'I could come back and dance for the rest of the season. Even as just the substitute. I feel bad for running out on Chelsea.'

His eyes widened and the rest of him went very still.

'I want to come back with you,' she whispered. 'I don't want to do this trip on my own. I want to go to all

the fun places, but I want to do that *with* you. I'm not
letting *you* go either.'

He pulled her back into a tight embrace. She felt his
face, hot and hard pressed against her neck. He said nothing for a while. Didn't kiss her. Just held her close. The
way she needed to be held. His muscles bunched. What
she'd just said meant something to him. As she began
to understand that he really meant it. That he loved her
and wanted her. And, scared though she was, the beauty
and magic of it overruled that fear.

He pulled back and looked in her eyes. 'You know
I'm going to buy the Treehouse.'

'Oh, Gabe, I can't let you do that. It's not worth it.'
Her lawyer had been in touch, the offers from develop-
ers had started—an insane amount of money was on the
table because of the location.

'Then you'd better take it off the market and let me
use the money I would have spent buying it, fixing it. It
*can* be fixed. I love it and so do you. We're not letting it
go.'

The emotion bursting within her rendered her immo-
bile—so far beyond happy, she was speechless.

His smile just broadened. 'We'll get the tree fixed,
we can replant the garden and let the hedge grow back.'

She inhaled deeply and managed a nod. He cupped
her face with both his hands and drew closer to kiss her.
Kiss her and kiss her and kiss her.

Thanks heavens his hotel was a mere five-minute
drive from Covent Garden because in those few magic
minutes the cab's windows were fogged and she was
frantic to be alone with him.

'This is a bit flasher than my hostel,' she said vaguely,
blinking as they walked through the gleaming, posh
lobby.

'Wait 'til you see my suite,' he murmured, guiding her to the lift.

Anticipation shimmied through her veins.

He caught her eye; a wild look entered his. 'Just give me a chance to unlock the door, okay?'

She skipped alongside him, but once in the room he didn't stop by the massive bed—instead he led her the twenty steps further into the enormous en suite. And in the doorway, Roxie stopped—stunned.

The bath was huge, full of steaming water and billions of white, sparkling bubbles. There were soft scented candles lit, there was all indulgence to be had.

He caught her jaw-to-the-floor moment and winked. 'Know you like your bubbles.'

Indeed there were two champagne flutes on a tray, but Roxie's eyes were glued to the thing standing beside them. 'That's not a bottle, that's practically a keg.' She walked over to it, touching the dewy glass, the coldness assuring her this was all real—not her mind presenting the most incredible fantasy ever.

'You get kegs of beer,' he jeered lightly. 'That's a jeroboam. There are more in the fridge. For *my* list.'

His teasing talk kindled her own, easing her through the emotion of seeing the effort he'd gone to for her. 'Must be a massive fridge.' She'd never seen such a giant bottle of champagne.

He chuckled. 'I thought this was a better size for sharing.'

'Because you've invited the whole rugby team here?' She pretended to look around the room for the crowds. But less than a second later she sobered, because she truly couldn't believe he'd done all this. For her. 'How did you get this organised so quickly?' They'd only been in the hotel a minute.

Gabe reached into his pocket. 'I don't know if you've come across these things much, Roxie. They're called mobile phones.' He'd pulled out two of them—his and her silver-clad one.

Horrified, she stared at the two gadgets. And then she couldn't see them any more because her eyes flooded with tears denied too long. Rivers and rivers of tears.

The phones hit the floor with a clatter and in a second she was pressed tight against his hard strength.

'You're going to cry *now*?' he asked, aghast. 'Over a stupid phone?'

'Not the phone,' she sobbed. 'Because *I* was stupid. And scared. And I nearly lost my future as well as my past.'

His arms tightened more.

She cried more. 'You came after me. You found me. You love me.'

Oh, she believed it now. Needed it now. Was so happy she couldn't possibly hope to express it.

He thrust his fingers through her hair, massaging the base of her skull and tilting her head back to meet his kiss. Her whole body was one big shiver. He peeled the clothes from her, then pretty much ripped his own off. A haze of husky words, whispers of love and trust, promises, and touches that led to absolute ecstasy.

And many, many minutes later, even though her skin had been thoroughly warmed, it still tingled when she stepped into the bath. She stretched out and smiled at the sight of him opposite her, his glorious body half hidden in the mass of pearlescent froth.

'What if you hadn't found me at the ballet?' she asked, unable to bear the thought that he mightn't have found her. 'How many nights were you going to go there?'

'A few more, then I was going to bribe your lawyer

into giving me your address, or contact the embassy or something. Anything.'

'And what would you have done if I'd been fine? If I'd been off at a nightclub pulling some random guy?'

Gabe's dark eyes sharpened. 'I'd have punched his lights out.' But then his grin flashed. 'I told you I'd do anything, was totally up for a fight. But I never thought for a second you'd be off with someone else. Not you.'

'I was never going near another man,' she admitted. 'Too busy breaking my heart over you.' She'd been so stupid and scared. 'I should have said something to you.'

'You had to go,' he said softly. 'You'd been dreaming of it for so long, you had to go and see what if it was really what you wanted. I didn't want to try and stand in your way.'

Roxie's blood chilled, despite the warmth of the water. 'I knew I didn't want to go at the airport,' she admitted sadly. 'I couldn't turn away from you. But I didn't think—'

He stopped her rising distress by pulling her to him and planting a kiss so passionate and perfect that she knew there was such a thing as paradise on earth.

'Worst moment of my life,' he muttered against her skin. 'I really believed you wanted to go. But I knew right away I'd made an awful mistake. I should have gone with you then and there. Instead it took me four hours to get everything organised so I could follow you.'

She gave a watery chuckle and wrapped her legs around his waist, her arms around his shoulders, embracing him. In return he held her, caressed her, fulfilled her. She rested her head on his shoulder, at home.

'I love you, Gabe,' Roxie finally admitted. And in that instant, she'd never felt so free.

# EPILOGUE

*12 Months Later*

HE WAS waiting for her when she came out to lock up.
Her store had been open a month—dancewear supplies,
costumes, theatre make-up, pointe shoes. At this stage
she didn't stock nipple tassels but she knew Gabe held
hope eternal.

Tonight they'd have their first night back at the
Treehouse. It had taken months for the remedial work
to be completed. They'd rented a small apartment nearby
and Roxie had spent her days supervising both the repair job and the outfit of her store, her evenings choreo-
graphing new routines with Chelsea for the Blades. After
the big digger work had finished at the Treehouse, she'd
replanted the garden—not completely vegetables this
time, but the occasional amazing flower as well. Now
Gabe parked in the refurbished garage and with a flour-
ish opened the front door for her. She literally danced
in, so happy to be home.

'Oh, look, you have mail already.' He took the enve-
lope pinned to the tree-trunk and handed it to her.

'Specially delivered.' She took it with a smile and
a kiss that threatened to go wild—loving him so completely.

'Not yet.' He broke free and stepped back from her, his hands up in the surrender position. 'Open it first.'

She did and drew out the gilt card, reading the beautiful script. 'Tickets to the Paris Opera Ballet?'

'*Giselle*, of course.'

She was going to *Giselle*, in Paris, with Gabe? 'You mean you're coming with me?' She almost squealed, this day just couldn't get better.

'Nothing I like more in the world than coming with you.' He waggled his brows. 'And seeing we'll be in France, I've booked a trip to Champagne. To the House of Bollinger.'

'No,' she screeched. 'As in like the factory? Where they grow the grapes and bottle the bubbles?' That would be too much fun.

'Well, it is the only thing you drink,' he teased. 'But maybe we could try some others too—you know, Moët, Veuve, Taittinger? We could bubble around the region, don't you think?'

'Absolutely!' She wrapped her arms around him and squealed. 'That would be fantastic.'

He chuckled as he hugged her. 'I love you and I love this place.'

Oh, ditto, ditto, ditto.

She reluctantly eased out of his kiss. 'But there's still something wrong with the house you know,' she whispered, shyly hiding her face in his neck.

'What's that?' He waited, quiet, to catch her answer.

'There are only two bedrooms.' She leaned back so she could see into his eyes and took hold of some courage. 'I don't want to have an only child.'

His eyes widened and his arms tightened. 'You're pregnant?' He lifted her and twirled and positively shouted. 'Oh, darling, that's brilliant!'

'No!' She laughed, her heart soaring at his ecstatic response. 'I'm not pregnant *yet*. I just thought I might like to be. One day. More than once.'

He stopped spinning her, but kept his hold super tight as he lowered her to the ground. His eyes glowed, his growl of amusement warm, then he smiled the most heartfelt smile she'd ever seen. 'Roxie, you can have as many children as you want, whenever you want.'

Relief tumbled through her. 'Are you sure? You never wanted—'

'I was wrong about so many things I thought I didn't want. And I couldn't be happier about that.' He suddenly stepped back and tugged her hand. 'Though I have to admit, I'm just a little glad you're not pregnant right *now*, because I have something for you.' He led her to the kitchen.

She stopped in the doorway. 'What is *that*?' Her shoulders began to shake.

'A Nebuchadnezzar of Bollinger,' he answered drolly.

'A *what*?' she spluttered with laughter.

'A Nebuchadnezzar. Fifteen litres. Just *imagine* how many million bubbles.'

'A *gazillion* bubbles. Did you hire a crane to get it in here?'

'Yeah, because there are three of them—the others are in the bath. And this time I actually did invite the team to share it with us, as well as all the Blades. But they're waiting for my signal.'

'Really?' She glanced out of the kitchen window and saw the juvenile plants were festooned with fairy lights. 'Are you going to give them the signal?'

'In a minute,' he said deeply. 'Something to do first.'

She turned to look at him. He wound his arms around her waist and tugged.

'You know that trip to France?' he said. 'There are a couple of conditions.'

This time Roxie's heart soared so high so quick it broke the sound barrier. 'What conditions?' Oh, she was so breathy.

He held her so close, his eyes so full of love they made hers water.

'On *my* list, Roxie,' he whispered, bringing his face to hers. 'Before we have the babies, we have the wedding. And in between the two, we have the honeymoon. In France.'

There was only one thing she could say to that. 'Okay.'

'Okay?'

'Oh, yeah. That's really okay.' She laughed as much as she cried and then could manage neither as he kissed her—out of control, adoring, explicit.

'Did you really invite the team?' She tore her lips from his in part despair.

'For the engagement party. That's the thing on the very top of my list. That's tonight.' He breathed hard. 'But we could steal a few minutes before I sound the horn. Right?'

'Well, you always did like room for spontaneity,' she teased, inside totally desperate herself. 'Why not a few minutes now, then hours together after when they're gone—okay?'

'For *ever* after.' He smiled wickedly as he swept her in his arms and charged up the stairs to their room.

And Roxie knew the happiness bubbling inside her now was never, ever going to burst.

\* \* \* \* \*

# HOW TO MEND A
# BROKEN HEART

**AMY ANDREWS**

*For Carita. Who knows.*

**Amy Andrews** has always loved writing, and still can't quite believe that she gets to do it for a living. Creating wonderful heroines, gorgeous heroes and telling their stories is an amazing way to pass the day. Sometimes they don't always act as she'd like them to— but then neither do her kids, so she's kind of used to it. Amy lives in the very beautiful Samford Valley, with her husband and aforementioned children, along with six brown chooks and two black dogs. She loves to hear from her readers. Drop her a line at www.amyandrews.com.au

# CHAPTER ONE

THICK grass spiked at Tessa King's bare knees as she sank to the ground beside the tiny, immaculately kept grave. Large trees shaded the cemetery and birdsong was the only noise that broke the drowsy afternoon serenity as she laid the bright yellow daffodils near the miniature marble statue of a kneeling angel.

Grief bloomed in her chest, sharp and fresh, rising in her throat, threatening to choke her. She squeezed her eyes shut and sucked in a breath, reaching for the headstone as the tsunamilike wave of emotion unbalanced her.

She let some tears escape. Just a few.

*No more.*

Even on the anniversary of his death she rationed her grief. It was ten years to the day since Ryan had died. Ten years of living life in greyscale.

The memories struggled for release but not even on this day did she allow herself the luxury of remembering too much. She rationed the memories too. His little body squirming against hers, his boyish giggle and that perfect little bow mouth.

The double cowlick that had refused to be tamed.
*It was enough.*

Tess opened her eyes, the simple inscription she knew as intimately as she knew her own heartbeat, blurring in front of her.

*Ryan King.*
*Aged 18 months.*
*Gone, and a cloud in our hearts.*

She reached for the letters, the smooth marble cool beneath her fingertips. She didn't let them linger. She wiped at her cheeks, blinked the remaining moisture away.

*Enough.*

Fletcher King ground his heels into the luxurious carpet of grass, resisting the urge to go to her as she sagged against the headstone. His butt stayed stubbornly planted against the bonnet of his Jag. She'd made it perfectly clear when they'd separated that it had to be a clean break. That she didn't want to see him or talk to him, and every overture he'd made the first year to keep in touch, to check on her, had been resoundingly rebuffed.

Frankly, after nine years of watching this ritual from afar, he didn't even know how to approach her. She seemed as distant today as she had for that awful year after Ryan's death when their marriage had slowly shrivelled and died.

He hadn't been able to bridge the gap back then and

he doubted almost a decade of distance would have improved things.

It didn't mean he was immune to her grief. Even from this distance the weight of her despair punched him square in the solar plexus. Took him right back to the dreadful day as they'd frantically tried to revive their son, hoping against hope, trying to ignore the portent of doom that had settled over him like a leaden cloak.

His frantic *'Come on, Ryan, come on!'* still echoed in his dreams all these years later.

A lump rose in his throat, tears needled and stung his eyes and he squeezed them tightly shut. He'd already cried a river or two; hell, he was probably up to an ocean by now, but he couldn't afford to succumb today.

He was here on a mission.

*He needed his wife back.*


Tess put one foot in front of the other on autopilot as she made her way to her car. Whether it was because of the dark swirl of emotions or the jet-lag, she didn't see him or at least register the identity of the tall, broad man leaning against the car parked in front of her rental until she was two metres away.

Then, as her belly did that almost forgotten somersault and her breath hitched in the same way it used to, she wondered why the hell not. She may not have been interested in a man in ten years but she obviously wasn't totally dead inside.

And Fletcher King in dark trousers and a business

shirt that had been rolled up to the elbows and undone at the throat was still an incredibly impressive man.

In fact, if anything, the years had honed him into an even more spectacular specimen.

He looked broader across the shoulders. Leaner at the hips. There were streaks of grey at his temples and where his dark, wavy hair met sculpted cheekbones. His three-day growth, black as midnight last time she'd seen it, was lightly peppered with salt. There were interesting lines around his tired-looking eyes, which were the silvery-green colour of wattle leaves.

Did he, too, still have trouble sleeping?

The indentations around his mouth, which became dimples when he laughed, were deeper. Even his mouth seemed fuller—sexier. His lips parted slightly and she caught a glimpse of his still-perfect teeth.

'Hello, Tessa.'

Tess was surprised by the prickle of awareness as his soft voice rumbled across the void between them. The latent attraction was unexpected. She was so used to locking down anything that had an emotional impact on her she was amazed she could still feel a pull at all.

But this *was* Fletch.

'Fletcher.' So much lay unsaid between them she didn't know where to start. 'It's been a long time.'

Fletch nodded, stifled by their formality. 'How have you been?'

She shrugged. 'Fine.'

Fletch suppressed a snort. *Hardly.* Each year she seemed to have faded away a little more. Gone were those curves that had driven him to distraction. There were only angles now. The legs sticking out of her above-knee, cargo-style pants were slender, her collar bones visible through the V-opening of her modest T-shirt were like coat hangers.

'You've got very thin.'

She shrugged again. 'Yes.' Tess ate as a matter of survival. Her pleasure in it had been sucked away with all the other things that had once brought her joy.

He regarded her for a moment. She was still a striking woman despite the angles. And the uber-short hairstyle. She'd cut it some time in that first year after they'd separated. She'd once had long white-blonde hair that had flowed down her back and formed a perfect curtain around them when they'd been making love. He'd spent hours stroking it, wrapping it around his hands and watching the light turn it incandescent as it had slowly sifted through his fingers.

It was darker blonde now, more honey than snow—a direct consequence of moving far away from the sunshine of Brisbane to the drizzly English countryside. It was cropped closely to her head, the back and sides razored severely in. The slightly longer locks on top were brushed over from a side parting, blending in with the jagged edges.

His sister had called it minimalist. He'd preferred the term butchered.

It did, however, draw attention to her amber eyes. They sat large in her spare, make-up-less face, dominating prominent cheekbones that fell away to catwalk-model hollows. They looked at him now, shadows playing in their sherry depths.

Her composure reached across the space between them and squeezed his gut hard. She projected calm detachment but he knew her well enough, despite their time apart, to see beyond. There was a fragility about her he'd have not thought possible a decade ago.

The impact of it rattled the shackles around his heart.

Tess weathered his probing gaze, waiting for him to say something more. Finally she could bear the silence no longer. She cleared her throat. 'I have to go.'

Fletch's gaze was drawn to her mouth. Her wide, full lips were devoid of any cosmetic enhancement, just as he remembered them. The same mouth he must have kissed a thousand times. That had travelled over every inch of his body. The same mouth that had desperately tried to breathe life into Ryan, that had begged a God she'd never believed in to spare their son.

Tess took a step towards her car. 'I have to go,' she repeated.

Fletch blocked her path, gently snagging her wrist. 'Could we talk?'

Tessa recoiled from his hold as if she'd been zapped, crossing her arms across her chest. 'There's nothing to talk about.'

'It's been nine years, Tess. You think we have nothing to say to each other?'

Tess bit her lip. *Nothing that hadn't been said already—ad nauseam.*

Fletch glanced at her white-knuckled grip as her fingernails dug into the flesh of her bare biceps. Her wedding ring, *his grandmother's ring*, snagged his attention. 'You still wear your wedding ring.'

Tess, surprised by the sudden direction the conversation had taken, looked down at it. The rose-gold band with its engraved floral pattern, thinned with age and wear, hung loosely on her finger, only her knuckle preventing it from sliding off. She absently twisted it around with her thumb a few times before returning her attention to him.

'Yes.' She wasn't going to tell him it was her deterrent against unwanted advances from men. She glanced at his bare left hand. 'You don't.'

Fletcher glanced at his hand. It had taken a year after the divorce to take it off yet sometimes he was still surprised by its absence. The white tan line that had remained after he'd removed it had long since faded.

'No.' It had got to the stage where he hadn't been able to bear the memories it had evoked.

Tess nodded. What had she expected? That he would choose to hide behind his as she had hers? That grief would torpedo his libido as it had hers?

Tess dropped her arms to her sides. 'I really have to go.'

Fletch held up his hands. 'I just need a minute, please.'

She felt exasperation bubble in her chest. In less than twenty-four hours she'd be back on a plane heading to London. The same as last year. The same as the last nine years. Why had he chosen to complicate things now?

'What do you want, Fletch?' What could he possibly want to say to her after all this time? After all these years of silence? Silence they'd *both* agreed on despite his lapses early in their separation.

Fletch blinked as her familiar name for him finally slipped from her lips to claw at his gut. 'It's my mother…she's unwell. She's been asking for you.'

Tess felt her stomach drop as concern for her ex-mother-in-law caused her heart to leap in her chest. Fletch looked so grim. 'Is she…? What's wrong with her? What happened?'

'She has Alzheimer's.'

Tessa gasped, her hand coming up to cover her mouth. 'Oh, Fletch…' She took a step towards him, their baggage momentarily forgotten, her other hand reaching for him.

'That's terrible.' Her hand settled against his arm, her fingers on the sleeve of his business shirt, her palm against the corded muscles of his tanned forearm. 'Is it… Is she bad?'

Jean King was one of the sharpest women Tess had ever met. She was funny, witty, insightful and super-smart. Tess's mother had died when she'd been eight and Jean had filled a very deep void. They'd been close right from the get-go and Jean had been her anchor— their anchor—in the dreadful months that had followed Ryan's death. Even when she and Fletch had separated and then divorced, Jean had been there for her.

Fletch nodded. 'She's deteriorated in the last couple of months.'

'When… How long has she had it for?'

Tess had dropped in on Jean on her yearly pilgrimage home those first two years after she'd moved to the UK. But it had been too hard on both of them. Jean had wanted to talk about Ryan and Tess hadn't been able to bear it. So she'd stopped going.

Fletch, aware of her nearness, of her faint passion-fruit fragrance, of her hand on his arm, waged a war within himself. Tess looked as devastated as he felt and it was as if the intervening years had never happened. As if he could walk right into her arms and seek the solace he so desperately craved.

It was a dangerous illusion.

He couldn't hope to execute what he'd come here for if he let emotion take over. He just hadn't been prepared for how hard it would be, seeing her again, talking to her again. He'd foolishly thought it would be easy.

*Well...easier.*

He gave himself a mental shake and rubbed the back of his neck. 'She was first diagnosed five years ago. She's been living with Trish for the last two years.'

'Five years?' she gasped. Tess couldn't even begin to comprehend a world where Jean King was anything less than her larger-than-life self. 'Why...why didn't you tell me?'

Fletch raised an eyebrow. 'Seriously, Tess? I rang you practically every day for a year after you went to England.... You made it pretty clear that no correspondence would be entered into. Anyway, what were you going to do?' he asked, surprised at the bitterness in his tone. 'Come home?'

Tess bit her lip. He was right. She had been ruthless with her no-contact request. 'I'm sorry...'

She searched his silvery-green gaze and saw appre-hension and worry and for one crazy moment almost took another step forward to embrace him. But a decade of denial slammed the door shut and she dropped her hand from his arm, shocked at the strength of the impulse.

She shook her head. 'It's just so wrong. Your mum has always been as fit as a fiddle...'

Fletch felt her withdrawal from their intimacy as keenly as if it had been ten years ago.

*Damn it.*

Did she really think because she hadn't moved on that things weren't going to change around her? 'She's seventy-four, Tess. She's getting old. Did you think she was just always going to be here, frozen in time, waiting for you to come around?'

Tess recoiled as if he had slapped her, colour draining from her face. 'I doubt your mother has been sitting around waiting on me,' she retaliated.

'You're like a second daughter to her, Tess,' he dismissed impatiently. 'She's missed you every day.'

*I've missed you every day.*

Fletch blinked at the thought. *He had.* Standing here in front of her, talking to her for the first time in nine years, he realised just how deeply he had missed her.

Tess felt the truth of his starkly delivered words wrap around her heart and squeeze. She wanted to deny them but she couldn't. He was right. They had been close. And Jean *was* getting older.

Fletch sighed as Tess gnawed on her bottom lip, looking utterly wretched. He raised his hands in a half-surrender.

'I'm sorry, I didn't mean to...' To what? Get angry

with her? Make her feel guilty? 'Will you, please, just come and see her? She gets anxious easily these days and you're the one she wants to see the most.'

Tess was torn. She'd love to see Jean again. Had missed her wise counsel and warm hugs over the years. And if it helped ease some of her mother-in-law's anxiety to see her then that was the least Tess could do. But would it be Jean? And would it build an expectation, make it harder to walk away?

*Because she was getting on that plane tomorrow. Just like she did every year.*

And most importantly, what if Jean wanted to talk about Ryan? What if she didn't remember he was dead? Talked about him as if he was alive and just down for a nap?

Tess looked at Fletcher. 'What about…?' She cleared her throat as a lump formed there. Even just saying it was beyond difficult. 'What does she remember from…?'

Fletcher watched the shimmer of emotion in Tess's amber gaze as she struggled with her words. He shook his head. 'She doesn't remember him at all, Tess.'

It had been a particularly difficult thing for Fletch to cope with. After Tess had refused to hear his name, his mother had been the only person he'd been able to talk openly with about Ryan.

*Now it was as if his son had never existed.*

'Her memory seems to stretch to about a year after we were married. As far as she's concerned, we've just got back from Bora Bora.'

Fletch had taken Tess to the tropical paradise for

a surprise first wedding anniversary present. They'd lazed in their over-water bungalow all day. Making love, drinking cocktails and watching the multitude of colourful fish swim by their glass floor.

He shrugged. 'There's an occasional recall of an event beyond that but it's rare.'

For a brief moment Tess envied Jean. The thought of forgetting how Ryan had felt in her arms or at her breast, forgetting the way his hair had stuck up in the middle from his double cowlick and how his giggle had filled the whole room. Forgetting that gut-wrenching day and all the empty days that had followed since.

It sounded like bliss.

The fantasy was shocking, wrong on so many levels, and she quickly moved to erase it from her mind. Jean was suffering from a debilitating disease that was ravaging her brain and would rob her of her most basic functions.

There was no upside to that.

And no justice in this world.

*Although she already knew that more intimately than most.*

Tess nodded. 'Okay.'

Fletch blinked at her easy capitulation. 'Really?'

'Sure.' She frowned, his disbelief irksome. 'For Jean.' He should know she'd do anything for his mother. 'Did you think I wouldn't?'

He shrugged. 'Yes.'

His bluntness hurt but she pushed it aside—it was, after all, a fair statement. She *had* been sneaking into the country once a year for the last nine years with only two paltry visits to Jean to defend herself against his conviction.

But they'd agreed on a clean break.

And she'd stuck to it.

Eventually, so had he.

She gave him a measured look. 'It's Jean.'

Fletch nodded as the husky note in her voice didn't mask her meaning. She wasn't doing it for him.

*And that was certainly what he was counting on now.*

'Thank you.' He gestured to his car. 'Do you want to follow me?'

Tess shook her head. 'She's at Trish's, right? They still live in Indooroopilly?'

Fletch shook his head. 'No, she's at my place for the moment.'

Tess blinked. 'You have a place in Brisbane?'

Since their separation Fletch had moved to Canada, where he'd been heavily involved in research and travelling the world lecturing. Or at least the last time she'd heard, that had been where he'd been. It was suddenly weird having absolutely no idea where he lived—or any of the details of his life for the last nine years.

She honestly hadn't cared until today but it somehow seemed wrong now to know so little about someone whose life had been so closely entwined with hers for so long they may as well have been conjoined.

When she thought about him, which she still did with uncomfortable regularity, it was always against the backdrop of their marital home. The ninety-year-old worker's cottage they'd renovated together.

Polished the floorboards, painted the walls, built the pergola.

The house they'd brought Ryan home to as a newborn.

'I'm renting an apartment on the river.'

'Oh. Okay.'

Tess tamped down on her surprise. Fletch had always despised apartment living. Had loved the freedom of large living spaces and a back yard.

But, then, a lot of things had changed over the last ten years.

'Right,' she said. 'I'll follow you.'

Fletch nodded. 'It's only about a ten-minute drive. See you soon.'

'Sure,' Tess murmured, then walked on shaky legs to her car.

Nine minutes later they drove into the underground car park of a swanky apartment block. She pulled her cheap hire car in beside his Jag in his guest car space. They didn't talk as he ushered her to the lifts or while they waited for one to arrive.

Tess stared at the floor, the doors, the ugly concrete walls of the chilly underground car park—what did one say, how did one act around one's ex? An ex she'd deliberately put at a fifteen-thousand-kilometre distance?

A lift arrived, promptly derailing her line of thought. He indicated for her to precede him, which she did, and then stood back as Fletch pushed the button for the nineteenth floor. More silence followed. Surely at least they could indulge in inane conversation for the duration of their time together?

A sudden thought occurred to her and she looked at him leaning against the opposite wall. 'How did you know I was going to be there today?'

Fletch returned her look. 'Because you're there every year on the anniversary.'

Tess blinked at his calm steady gaze. 'How do you know that?'

'Because I watch you.'

Another silence descended between them as her brain tried to compute what he'd just said. 'You *watch* me?'

He nodded. 'Nine years ago you were leaving as I was arriving.' He remembered how close he'd come to calling her name. 'I thought you might come back the next year. You did. And the year after that. So now I… wait for you.'

The lift dinged. The doors opened. Neither of them moved. The doors started to close and Fletch shot an arm out to push them open again. 'After you,' he murmured.

Tess couldn't move for a moment. She stared at him. 'Why?'

'I know you think that your grief is deeper than mine but he was my son too, Tess. I also like to visit on the anniversary.'

Tessa flinched at the bitterness in his voice. And then again when the lift doors started beeping, protesting their prolonged open state. She walked out, dazed, conscious of Fletch slipping past her, leading the way down a long plush hallway with trendy inkspot carpeting. She followed slowly, still trying to get her head around Fletch's revelation.

She drew level with him, glancing up from the floor. 'I meant why wait for me? Why not just visit for a while and leave?'

*Like she did.*

Fletch wished he knew the answer to that question. It was the same thing he told himself every year as he set out for the cemetery. Go, talk with Ryan for a bit, then leave.

But he didn't. He'd sit in his car and wait for her. Watch her kneel beside Ryan's grave.

Torture himself just a little bit more.

He shrugged. 'To see you.'

# CHAPTER TWO

'Mum, we're home,' Fletch called as he opened the door, checking behind him to see if Tess was following or still standing in the hallway like a stunned mullet.

He wasn't sure why he'd said what he'd said. Except it was the truth. He just hadn't realised it until right that moment. He'd kidded himself that it was to check up on her but now he knew it was more.

That there was part of him, no matter how hard he'd tried to move on, that just hadn't.

He walked into the apartment, throwing his keys on the hallstand. 'Mother?'

A voice came from the direction of the bathroom. 'I'm in here, darling, there's no need to shout.' Jean appeared a moment later with a spray pack in one hand and a mop in the other.

'Mum, you don't have to clean the apartment,' Fletch said, trying to keep the exasperation and relief out of his voice as he unburdened her of her load.

He didn't like to leave his mother alone for too long these days. She seemed so frail and unsteady on her feet and he worried she might fall and injure herself while he was out.

*Especially if she was mopping floors.*

'I have a cleaning lady for that.'

'Nonsense, darling, I have to make myself useful somehow. Now, is Tess working late or shall I put something on for tea for her tonight?'

Tess stepped out of the shadow of the entranceway where she'd been frozen since Jean had entered the room. Jean, who had once been a towering Amazon of a woman and was now white-haired and stooped and looked like a puff of wind would blow her over.

She sucked in a breath at the absurd urge to cry. 'No, Jean, I'm here.'

Jean looked over her son's shoulder and smiled. 'Oh, Tess! There you are!' She hurried forward and pulled Tess into an effusive hug. 'Goodness, you're getting so skinny,' Jean tutted, pulling back to look at her daughter-in-law. 'And your hair! Did you have that done today? I love it!'

Tess swallowed hard at the shimmer of moisture in Jean's eyes as her mother-in-law wrapped her in another hug. She shut her eyes as she was sucked into a bizarre time warp where the last decade and all its horrible events just didn't exist. She held tight to Jean's bony shoulders.

Her mother-in-law had become an old woman while she'd been away. Guilt clawed at her.

'How about a cuppa?' Jean said, finally letting Tess go.

'Great idea, Mum,' Fletch agreed. 'Why don't you take Tess through and I'll get the tea?'

Jean smiled and nodded. She turned to go then

stopped, her smile dying as a look of confusion clouded her gaze. She looked at her son blankly.

'Over there,' Fletch murmured gently as he pointed to the corner of the open-plan living space where a leather three-piece suite, a coffee table and a large-screen television formed a lounge area.

Jean's gaze followed the direction of Fletch's finger. It took a moment or two for the set-up to register. 'Of course.' She shook her head. 'Come on, Tess. Tell me all about work today.'

Tess moved off with Jean but not before her gaze locked with Fletch's. She saw his despair and felt an answering flicker. No wonder Fletch had looked tired earlier—this had to be killing him.

Jean patted the cushion beside her and asked, 'How was the unit today, dear? Busy as usual?'

Tess sat beside Jean, bringing her thoughts back to order. 'I...' She glanced at Fletch for direction.

Since moving to England Tess had changed her speciality to geriatrics so nursing Alzheimer's patients was part and parcel of what she did every day. But each patient was individual and responded differently to having their misstatements corrected.

He nodded his head encouragingly, which didn't really tell her very much. 'I didn't go to work today,' she sidestepped. 'It was my day off and I had...some business to attend to.'

'Ah, well, no doubt Fletch will know. Fletch?'

'It wasn't too bad, Mum,' Fletch said as he placed a tray with three steaming mugs on the coffee table and apportioned them. He sat on the nearby single-seater.

'Still a lot of kids with the last of the winter bugs getting themselves into a pickle.'

Tess picked up her mug and absently blew on it. So they were validating Jean's false sense of reality? At this stage of her disease it was probably all that was left to do. Too many dementia patients became confused and distressed when confronted with their memory loss, and to what end? They were too far gone to realise what was happening to them.

Jean sighed and looked from one to the other. 'I'm so proud of both of you. It can't be easy going to work each day looking after such sick little kiddies.'

Tess squeezed Jean's hand in response. What else could she do? She and Fletch hadn't worked at St Rita's Paediatric Intensive Care Unit together for ten years. Not since Ryan had died there. In fact, she hadn't been able to return to that field of practice at all, hence her move to the other end of the spectrum altogether.

Fletch changed the subject to the weather and they let Jean lead from there, navigating a maze of patchwork conversation—some lucid, some not so lucid. They got on to the spectacular view from the floor-to-ceiling glass doors, with Jean teasing Fletch about his fancy apartment. 'I can't believe you two got this thing. What happened to that gorgeous little cottage you were renovating?'

Fletch smiled at his mother. 'We sold it. Too much hard work.'

'Oh, pish,' Jean said, swatting her hand through the air. 'As if you're afraid of hard work.'

Tess swallowed a lump as Jean, despite the dementia, looked at her son the way she always had, like he could hang the moon. Fletch's father had died when he and his sister, Trish, had both been very young and Fletch had been the man of the house for a long time.

'Gosh, Tess,' Jean remarked, shaking her head. 'Look how skinny you are! And where did that lovely tan go? I can't believe how quickly that gorgeous tan of yours has faded. It hasn't been that long since you've been back from Bora Bora.'

Fletch felt the bleakness inside ratchet up another notch. *The tan had gone to England and never come back!*

Jean held up an imperious finger. 'Hold on a moment.' And she scurried off towards the direction she'd originally come from.

Tess felt exhausted with jet-lag and trying to keep up with Jean's meandering conversation and rapid-fire subject changes. But not as exhausted as Fletch looked. 'What medication is she on?' she asked.

Fletch rattled off a series of the most up-to-date dementia pills on the market. He shrugged. 'They've held it at bay for many years but—'

Jean bustled back in, interrupting them. 'Here it is,' she said, brandishing a book of some description. When she sat down and opened it Tess realised it was a photo album. The one she'd put together all those years ago after their return from Bora Bora.

Fletch frowned as a hundred memories flooded his mind. He shook his head slightly at Tess's questioning look. He'd had no idea his mother had this album. It, along with all the others, had been stored in one of the many boxes that he'd packed their marriage into after he and Tess had separated and she'd run away to the other side of the world.

Maybe when he'd asked his mother to get rid of it all just prior to his move to Canada, she'd decided to keep a few souvenirs? He hadn't really cared at the time how she'd made it disappear, just that it had. God knew, he hadn't been able to bear the thought of going through it all himself, deciding what to keep and what to discard.

Getting rid of it all, holus bolus, had been a much easier option.

And yet here was a part of it, turning up like the proverbial bad penny. A full Technicolor reminder of how happy they'd been.

'See, now look at you here,' Jean said, pointing to Tess in a bikini on the beach. 'Brown as a berry!'

Tessa stared at the photograph, shocked by the sudden yank back into the past. She'd taken three photos from the ruins of their marriage—all of Ryan. Not that she'd been able to bear to look at them. They lived at the back of a cupboard she never opened.

But it had been a long time since she'd seen ones of Fletch and herself.

A stranger stared back at her. Yes, she *was* very tanned. She was also deliriously happy, obviously in love and blissfully unaware of the giant black hole hovering in her future. In fact, the woman in the photograph looked nothing like the woman she was today.

*And it had nothing to do with the tan.*

For a fleeting second, Tess wished she could jump

into the photo, like Mary Poppins had jumped into that pavement painting, and give herself a good shake.

If only she'd known then what she knew now.

If only…

'I think this is my favourite one,' Jean said, flipping to one of Fletch, towel wrapped around his waist, elbows on the balcony railing, looking back over his shoulder and laughing into the camera, crystal waters behind him.

Tessa stilled as she remembered she'd been fresh from the shower and naked when she'd taken that picture and the series of intimate photos that had followed—ones that had not made it into this album! She remembered making him lie on the bed and loosen his towel, snapping shots of every glorious inch of his body.

Then he'd grappled the camera from her and returned the favour, asking her to pose for him and taking a set of photos a professional photographer would have been proud of. To this day the one on her stomach, looking over her shoulder with her hair flowing down her back, the sheet ruched around her bottom revealing only the slight rise of one cheek, was the best picture ever taken of her.

She remembered being so turned on by their nude photo session they'd made love for hours afterwards, rolling and sighing and moaning to the gentle swish of the waves.

She glanced at Fletch—did he remember?

His gaze locked with hers, turning almost silver as heat flashed like a solar flare. It dropped to her mouth and she watched as his throat bobbed.

'It's my favourite too,' Fletch murmured.

*Oh, yeah, he remembered.*

Tess sat through the rest of the album, desperately trying to claw back some control of her brain. Bora Bora was in the past—a long time in the past. She hadn't come here to take a walk down memory lane, although she guessed to a degree that had been inevitable. Neither had she come to rekindle the sexual attraction that, prior to Ryan's death, had always raged like an inferno between them.

She'd come for Jean. To alleviate some anxiety and then turn around and go back to her perfectly fulfilling, asexual, far-away existence.

Jean closed the album. 'I think you two need to go back to Bora Bora. You're both too tense.' She patted Tess's hand. 'And pale.'

Before Tess could answer, an alarm blared out and she jumped slightly at the same time Jean clutched at her chest and looked at Fletch anxiously.

'It's okay, Mum,' Fletch reassured her as he reached over and turned off the alarm on the clock that was sitting on the coffee table. 'Remember, that just means your show's about to start.' His mother continued to look at him blankly. 'Wheel of Fortune,' he prompted.

'Oh.' Jean sagged a little and dropped her hand to her lap. 'Oh, yes, oh, I love that show!'

Fletch nodded as he picked up the remote and flicked on the big sleek screen to the channel that played non-stop 1980s television shows. 'There you go, just starting,' he said as the game-show music rang out.

'Tess.' Jean bounced like a little girl on Christmas morning. 'Do you want to watch it with me?'

Fletch watched the play of emotions mirrored in Tess's eyes. She was obviously shocked by the many faces of Jean. 'Actually, we're going to go out on to the deck and have a chat,' he said.

But his mother wasn't listening, engrossed in the show, her invitation to Tess already forgotten. He inclined his head at Tess, indicating they move away, and she eagerly complied, following him to the kitchen.

'Would you like something a little stronger?' he asked as he removed the mug she'd brought with her and placed it in the sink.

Following a period after she'd moved to the UK when she'd drunk a little too often, Tessa didn't drink much these days. But if ever she needed alcohol, it was now. Being with Jean was heartbreaking. And being with Fletch, seeing those pictures, was…disturbing.

'Yes, please.'

Fletch pulled a bottle of chilled white wine out of the fridge and held it up. 'All right?'

Tessa nodded. 'Sure. Thanks.'

He poured them both a glass and handed her hers. Normally he'd clink glasses with someone in this situation but nothing was normal about right now so he took a mouthful then led the way to the deck.

Fletch, conscious of her behind him, put his arms on the railing and inhaled the late-afternoon river breeze. He took another sip of his wine then turned to face her.

'Thank you,' he said.

'I'm so sorry, Fletch,' she murmured. 'It's…it's so unfair.'

Fletch's lips twisted into a bitter smile as his mobile phone rang. 'Since when has life ever been fair?' he asked as he located his phone and answered it.

Tess nodded. *Truer words had never been spoken.*

She moved to the far side of the railing to give Fletch some privacy. She had absolutely no desire to eavesdrop on the conversation but it was hard not to when he was standing two metres from her.

It was Trish and Tess gathered Fletch's little sister was asking after Jean. Then she heard Fletch tell her that he'd been to the cemetery and reassured her three times that he was fine. Like Jean, Trish had been a tremendous support for them after losing Ryan. She'd worried about them, about her brother particularly, like a little mother hen. Tess knew that if Trish had been able to turn back time for them, she would have.

Her name was mentioned and Tess wondered how Trish was taking the news that she was here. They'd been close once, like real sisters, but Trish was loyal to a fault and while she'd been supportive for that horrible year, she'd been angry with Tess over her desertion of Fletch.

It had hurt at the time but blood was thicker than water and it was only right that she should stand by her brother.

Fletch hung up. 'Sorry, that was Trish.'

'So I gathered,' she murmured, swishing the wine in her glass absently. 'How's she and Doug doing these days?'

'Great. Doug started his own computer repair business five years ago. It's thriving. Trish gave up the childcare centre a few years ago to work full time taking care of the books side of things and managing the job schedule. They have Christopher, he's almost two. And she's seven months pregnant with number two.'

Tess stilled, the swirl of the wine coming to a halt. She glanced at Fletch. Trish had a child? A little boy. A little boy only a few months older than Ryan had been when he'd died?

And another on the way?

She and Fletch had been trying for another baby just prior to Ryan's accident.

The ache that was never far from her heart intensified. In a split second she both envied and despised her ex-sister-in-law with shocking intensity.

Fletch watched Tess's face as a string of emotions chased across the taut face, which seemed suddenly paler. 'She always wanted babies, Tess,' he said gently.

Tess breathed in raggedly. She nodded her head vigorously. 'Of course.' Trish had absolutely doted on Ryan. 'That's great,' she said, forcing words past the husky lump lodged in her larynx. 'So, you're an uncle, huh?'

Fletch nodded. 'Yes.'

Of sorts. He hadn't had a lot to do with his nephew given how often he was out of the country. But he was a dear little boy who adored him. And if it was hard at times to hold his wriggly little body and not think of Ryan, not see the similarities between the two cousins, then he erected another layer around his heart and sucked it up.

Tess heard the grimness in his response and knew that it couldn't have been easy for him. She hesitated for a moment, went to take a step towards him until a shout of 'Buy a vowel!' coming from the lounge area halted the reflex before her foot had even moved.

She smiled at him as the sound of Jean's excited clapping drifted out. 'How's Jean with him?'

Fletch felt his answering smile die. 'She doesn't remember him most days. It's hard for Trish. Especially as Mum's been living with them since just before Christopher was born.'

Tess frowned. 'How come she's living with you now? I don't mean to tell you how to manage Jean's condition but I don't think changing her living arrangements at this stage in her disease is such a good thing, Fletch.'

'Trish had problems with her first pregnancy. She went into early labour at twenty-four weeks. They managed to stop it and get the pregnancy through to thirty-four weeks. A month ago she went into early labour again with this one. Which they also managed to stop. But given her history and her age, her obstetrician ordered bed rest and no stress for the remainder of the pregnancy.'

'Ah,' Tess murmured. 'Not very easy when you're looking after a toddler and your high-needs mother.'

Fletch grimaced. 'No.' He rubbed the back of his neck. 'Trish tried day respite but the unfamiliar setting distressed Mum, made her anxious, which flowed on into the nights. Mum stopped sleeping and she started to wander. She had a couple of falls.'

'Oh, no,' Tess gasped.

Fletch shrugged. 'Lucky she has bones made of concrete.'

Tess laughed, remembering the time that Jean had slipped and fallen down a flight of stairs with not even a bruise to show for it. Fletch smiled at her laugh. It was as familiar to him as his own and yet not something he'd heard for a very long time.

Another thing he'd missed with surprising ferocity.

'We got a day nurse in but the same thing happened. An unfamiliar face just aggravated the situation. So…I took a leave of absence from Calgary and came home to step in and do my bit. Look after Mum until after the baby's born.'

Tess understood the conundrum he and Trish faced. The familiar was important to dementia patients, who clung to their repertoire of the familiar even as it shrank at an alarming rate around them. But, still, uprooting yourself from the other side of the world was a big ask.

Although she guessed not for Fletch. He'd always been very family orientated, always taken care of his responsibilities.

'It's a good thing you're doing,' she said softly.

He looked at her. 'It's family, Tess. Family sticks together.'

Tess shied from the intensity of his silver-green eyes. Was there an accusation there? Sure, she'd asked for the divorce but he hadn't exactly put up a fight. In fact, he'd been pretty relieved as far as she could recall. Did he really blame her for wanting to get as far away from it all as possible?

She took a deep breath. She wasn't going to go there. She was finishing her drink. She was going back to her hotel room.

Tomorrow she was getting on a plane.

'So you're not working, then?'

Fletch shook his head. He looked into his drink. 'That was the plan but St Rita's approached me with an interesting proposition and I've accepted a temporary contract…'

Tess blinked as the information sat like a lead sinker in her brain. 'St Rita's? In the…PICU?'

Fletch glanced up into her huge amber eyes, flashing their incredulity like a lighthouse beacon. 'In both the adult and kids' ICUs. They want someone to head up a study on the application of hypothermia in acute brain injury. They've asked me. I didn't come here to work but…how could I refuse? It's a marvellous opportunity.'

Tess was quiet for a moment while she processed the startling information. 'Oh.'

She knew that since their separation and his move to Canada, Fletch had become an authority—*some might call it an obsession*—on cold-water drowning, undertaking several world-renowned studies. In fact, he was probably one of the world's foremost experts on the subject. She'd read everything he'd ever published from the impressive studies to journal articles and every paper he'd ever given at a conference or a symposium.

*None of them had brought Ryan back.*

'It's part time, only a few hours a day with no real

clinical role. I can do a lot of the work from home, which is perfect, leaves me a lot of time for Mum.'

Tess nodded. It sounded ideal. She just wished she could understand how he could go back there. She knew, although she didn't pretend to comprehend, why he'd chosen that particular field of research but how he could handle the subject matter was beyond her. And how he could enter St Rita's without breaking down she'd never know.

Her eyes sought his. She remembered how he'd told his mother earlier about the kids with the last of the winter bugs. She'd thought he'd been fobbing Jean off but obviously not. 'You've…you've been into the PICU?'

Their gazes locked. 'Yes. Several times. In fact, I called in there on my way to the cemetery.'

Tess let out a shaky breath. 'Right…'

What did she say now? How was it? Have you been into room two? Did it bring back memories? Was Ryan's presence still there or had it been erased by years of other children and hospital antiseptic?

Instead, she said nothing because she really didn't want to know.

Fletch's stare didn't waver. 'It wasn't easy, Tess.'

She looked away. *Had he thought it would be?* Did he expect her sympathy? An embrace? Applause? Some kind of a shared moment where everything was suddenly all right because he'd confronted some ghosts?

A surge of emotions knotted in her belly and she knew she had to leave. Get out. Far away from Fletch and all that reminded her of that dark, dark time.

*Denial had been working for her just fine.*

She just wanted to go to bed and sleep off the jet-lag and not have to think about any of it.

'Well,' she said, downing the contents of her glass in one long swallow. 'It looks like you have everything worked out.'

'Tess.'

She ignored the reproach in his voice. 'I've gotta go.' She placed the wine glass on the table and headed for the door.

'Tess,' he said, catching her arm lightly as she brushed past him.

Tess stopped. 'Let me go,' she said, staring straight ahead.

'Tess, please, stay for a while.'

She squeezed her eyes shut. 'Fletch.'

'I want to talk to you, Tess.'

'I think we're all talked out.'

'It's about Mum.' He felt her arm strain against his hand. 'Please, Tess, just hear me out. For Jean.'

Tess sighed, and her muscles relaxed, knowing she was defeated.

*Damn it.*

And damn him.

# CHAPTER THREE

Tess sat at the table, staring out over the Brisbane River, while Fletch was in the kitchen fixing them both a top-up of their glasses. A light breeze ruffled her utilitarian locks and she had to shake herself to believe she was actually sitting on her ex-husband's deck, drinking wine.

The whole scene felt surreal. Jean's dementia had dragged her reluctantly into her past. A time when things had been simple and she'd truly believed that love could get a person through everything. It was a strange reality that warred with her present-day situation.

What did he want to talk to her about regarding Jean? Surely he had better access to the medical side of Jean's condition than she did? He probably had half a dozen gerontologists up his sleeve he could talk to. Or maybe he was after practical advice? How to care for his mother on a day-to-day basis? Or a recommendation for a good home-care agency, maybe?

Whatever it was, she hoped he made it snappy because when she got to the bottom of her second glass she was walking away.

Fletch paused by the sliding door, watching Tess's

profile for a moment, and wished he was sure of her. He needed her help. Once upon a time he could have counted on it. But a lot of water had flowed under the bridge since then and she was so very, very skittish.

Plus he wasn't so sure of himself now. His plan had sounded fine in theory but being with her again was confrontational on many levels. He'd thought he could handle it but standing two metres from her he realised it would be physically and emotionally harder than he'd ever imagined.

Still…he was desperate and Tess was perfect.

He took a deep breath and stepped out onto the deck. 'Here you go,' he said, placing her refilled wine glass in front of her.

Tess glanced down at the offering and murmured, 'Thanks.'

She picked it up and took a decent mouthful, the smooth, fruity crispness against her palate not really registering. She placed the wine back down as Fletch sat opposite her, hearing the clink as it met the smoky glass of the tabletop. 'You wanted to talk about Jean?' she prompted.

Fletch sighed. Obviously there wasn't going to be any small talk. Which he'd have preferred. He had no idea how she was going to react to his proposition, although instinct told him it wouldn't be very well…

'I need to get someone in for Mum. Someone who can be here while I'm out. When I accepted the contract I thought I'd be able to juggle it and her. It's only part time and Mum doesn't need constant care and attention. But the truth is I don't feel comfortable leaving her at all. I just don't think she's safe enough and I'd feel a hell of a lot better if she wasn't here by herself.'

'Like a home-care nurse?'

Fletch shook his head. 'No. I'm not after someone to help with her physical needs because she's still capable, so far, of taking care of that. Although having someone who understands Alzheimer's is a definite plus… I'm thinking more like a companion.'

'You mean someone closer to her own age?'

'I mean someone who knows her. She's not great with strangers—they distress her.'

Tess's brow wrinkled. 'That would be ideal, of course. Are you thinking of one of her old friends?'

Fletch didn't take his eyes off her. 'I'm thinking of someone closer than that. Someone she knows really well who has experience with the elderly and with dementia sufferers. The best of both worlds.'

Fletch watched and waited—waited for his meaning to sink in. It didn't take long.

Tess narrowed her eyes. Was Fletch thinking what she thought he was thinking? She shook her head at him. 'No. No way.'

'You're perfect, Tess.'

She shook her head again, mentally recoiling from the plea in his wattle-leaf gaze. 'No.'

'I know this is kind of out of the blue—'

'Kind of?' Tess spluttered.

'I wouldn't ask if I wasn't stuck.'

Tess stared at him, wondering when he was going to grow a second head. 'Putting *everything* else aside, I'm leaving for the UK tomorrow.'

'It's just until after Trish is back on her feet. A couple of months.'

Tess blinked. 'I have a *job,* Fletch.'

Fletch snorted. He'd always thought Tess squandering her critical care skills in a geriatric facility was such a monumental waste of a highly skilled nurse, even if it was to his advantage now.

She glared at him. 'That I love. Where I get an enormous amount of respect and job satisfaction.'

It might just be a little nursing-home in the middle of the Devonshire countryside but people depended on her. The staff and the residents. When she'd needed a place to hide and lick her wounds they'd taken her in and given her a direction for her life. They'd helped her function again.

'I'm sure they'd understand if you explained the circumstances. I can recompense you if it's money you're worried about.'

Tess shook her head at his utter gall. Had he thought she'd just agree? They'd been virtual strangers for the past nine years and he expected her to just…comply? And that splashing some money around would sweeten the pot? Sure, she loved Jean, he knew that. He knew how close they'd been. But it was still a big gamble for him to take—betting the bank on her.

*The woman who had already turned her back on his family.*

'So this is it?' she demanded. 'This is your brilliant plan? Ask your ex-wife? Who just happens to be here at the same time you need someone to look after your mother? That's crazy! What would you have done if I hadn't been in town?'

'It's not crazy. It makes absolute sense. You're the perfect person to ask. And, yes, the timing has been perfect too but, frankly, Tess, I would have gone to England to get you.'

'To *get* me?' Fletch held up his hands in a placatory manner.

'To ask you,' he amended.

Tess wasn't placated. 'How about this, Fletch? How about you give up *your* job and look after *your* mum instead? Trish's been doing it for two years. Surely you can take a lousy couple of months off to do your bit.'

Fletch nodded. 'And I will. If you won't…I will. But studies like this are so important, Tess. The results can help the way we treat acute head injury. What we learn from them can make a real difference to neurological outcomes. This is critical stuff, Tess.'

'Someone else can do it,' she snapped.

'Yes.' He nodded. 'Someone else could…but this is what I do.' He placed his hand on his chest. 'This is my field of expertise.' And his passion—Tess could hear it lacing every syllable. *But chasing after medical rainbows wasn't going to bring Ryan back.* She stood up, the metal chair legs scraping against the terracotta tiles.

'No, Fletcher. I'm sorry about your study, I really am, but I do not want to do this.'

He rose too and opened his mouth to interject and she held up a finger, silencing him. She looked into his determined face, his jaw set, his hand thrust on a hip, and she knew he didn't get it. Didn't understand why she'd be rejecting his perfectly rational plan.

He didn't understand how just being around them—him and Jean—would be like a hot knife to her chest every day. How the reminders of Ryan that she was able to keep rigorously at bay on the other side of the world would be torturous.

It was suddenly vitally important that he understand. Vitally.

'I get by, okay? I make it through each day and I sleep at night and my life is on an even keel. It may not seem very exciting to you—I'm not setting the world on fire with my cutting-edge research, but it took a while to reach this place and it works for me, Fletch. I don't want to undo it.'

Fletch felt his breath catch as the fierce glow of her amber eyes beseeched him. He held her gaze, ignoring the anguish he saw there. 'I came home the other day to a blaring alarm and smoke pouring out of the oven. She'd baked some biscuits and forgotten about them.'

He refused to look away, refused to back down. His mother was his priority and Tess was the answer. He needed her.

*Whatever the emotional impact.*

He was pushing her, he knew that, but listening to her talk had him thinking that maybe this was exactly what Tess needed also. Maybe she needed to start living a life where she more than just *got by.*

It was criminal that she was living this half-life stashed away in the English countryside where nobody knew her past and she could eke out an existence by pretending nothing had happened. That her whole world hadn't come crashing down and sucked her into the deepest, darkest despair.

Maybe it was time for both of them to confront the past and deal with it. To talk and grieve together instead of separately. He'd let her deny and avoid all those years ago because her sorrow had been all-consuming and he'd been walking through a minefield he'd had no idea how to navigate whilst suffering his own debilitating grief.

He hadn't pushed her back then.

*But maybe it was finally time to push.*

Tess swallowed as his intense look seemed to bore a hole right through her middle. It made her feel ill thinking about Jean almost burning the place down but her ex-mother-in-law wasn't her responsibility.

*She was ex for a reason.*

And she didn't want to get sucked back into lives that were too closely entwined with the tragic events that had defined all their lives since.

It just would be too hard.

She shook her head and turned away. 'Goodbye, Fletcher.'

Fletch shut his eyes as she whirled away, heading for the door. *Damn it!* He'd felt sure he'd be able to convince her. He opened his eyes, resigned to letting it go. He'd tried. But he had to respect her decision.

Tess stalked into the apartment. *Wheel of Fortune* had finished, the show's theme song blaring out. Jean was nowhere to be seen.

'Jean?' Tess called, reaching for the remote. Nothing.

Not that anything could be heard over the roar of the television. 'Jean?' she called again, hitting the mute button.

'Tess?'

Tess walked quickly towards the feeble, panicked voice she could hear coming from the kitchen area. 'Jean?'

'Here…I'm here.'

Tess rounded the bench to find Jean sitting on the floor, her back propped against the fridge, staring down at two raw eggs, one in each hand, the shells crushed, yolk oozing between her fingers. She looked at Tess with red-rimmed, frightened eyes, the papery skin on her cheeks damp.

'I don't know what these are,' she said to Tess, holding them up.

'Oh, Jean…' Tess sank to the floor beside her and put her arm around skinny shoulders. 'It's okay,' she murmured. 'It's going to be okay.'

Jean shook her head, pulled away to look at her daughter-in-law. 'I'm frightened, Tess,' she whispered, and started to tear up again. 'Something's wrong. H-help me, please.' Her voice cracked. 'Please…h-help me.'

Jean dissolved into soft tears and Tess felt her heart swell up with love for this woman who had been like a mother to her as she snuggled her into the crook of her shoulder.

'Shh,' Tess crooned, rocking slightly. 'Shh, now.'

Tess heard footsteps and looked up to find Fletch staring down at her with solemn eyes. He crouched beside them and Tess saw that all-too-familiar look of sadness sheen his eyes to silver. She watched as he reached for his mother's shoulder, placed his long brown fingers over her pale, waxy skin and gently rubbed.

'It's okay, Tess,' he whispered over his mother's bent head. 'I'll fix it.'

Tess shut her eyes as Jean's plea tugged at her. *She was almost out the door, damn it.* She didn't want to be needed like this. Not by Jean. And certainly not by him.

*Not fair. So not fair.*

But, as Fletch had only just pointed out, when had life ever been fair?

Could she really turn her back on Jean who had never asked her for anything? Fletch maybe, but Jean?

She opened her eyes. 'Let me see if it can be arranged…'

Fletch felt his heart swell with relief and something else far more primal. He sagged slightly as what seemed to be the weight of the entire world lifted from his shoulders. 'Thank you,' he mouthed. 'Thank you.'

Tess pushed the 'end' button on the phone thirty minutes later. Her boss at Estuary View Nursing Home had been very understanding of Tess's predicament and had urged Tess, her best employee who only ever took the same two weeks off every year, to take as much time as she needed.

*So, that was that.*

She kept her elbows firmly planted on the balcony railing, staring out over the river darkening to liquid mercury. The city's first lights winked on the polished surface and shimmered in the wake of a City Cat as it fractured the surface. She was surprised at the tide of nostalgia that crept over her.

Brisbane was her home town.

And she'd been away for a long time.

In recent years it had been a place to dread, a place of terrible memories, a heinous pilgrimage. But a sudden strange melancholy infused her bones.

Irritated by the path of her thoughts, Tess turned her back on the river. Through the open doorway she could see Jean sitting happily once again in front of the television, sipping a fresh cup of tea, her incident with the eggs forgotten. Fletch sat beside her, holding her hand, his dark wavy hair a stark contrast to the thin, white wisps of his mother's.

He looked up at her at that moment and for a second they just stared at each other. Tess felt the melancholy sink into her marrow. Then Fletch raised an eyebrow and she nodded at him and he once again mouthed, 'Thank you,' before kissing his mother gently on the head and easing away from her.

Tess moved inside, following Fletch into the kitchen. 'All sorted?'

She nodded. 'Yes.'

They were standing a couple of metres apart and Fletch took a step towards her as a well of gratitude rising inside him propelled him forward. In the old days he would have swept her into his arms. 'I know this is a big ask, Tess…'

Tess shook her head. If he truly knew, he wouldn't have asked. 'You have no idea, Fletch.'

Just looking at his face caused her chest to ache. It

took her back to times she'd spent ten years trying to forget. Ryan had looked so like his father it had been ridiculous. He took another step towards her but she held up her hand to ward him off.

Fletch stopped. 'You think this is any easier for me?' he asked.

Tess dropped her gaze at the honesty in his. It was a horrible situation for them both. 'What time do you want me here in the mornings?'

Tess had no idea where she was going to stay for the next couple of months but she'd figure it out. In the interim she could extend her stay at the hotel. But there was no way her budget could stretch to such luxury for more than a week.

Fletch frowned. 'I don't just want you here in the mornings, Tess, I want you here twenty-four seven.'

Tess's gaze flew back to his face. 'What?' Her heartbeat kicked up a notch as his meaning sank in.

'Mum's wandering more during the night and can become quite agitated when you try and get her back to bed. She's particularly disorientated when she wakes up in the morning since moving from Trish's. She sees me and the first person she asks for in the morning or if she wakes at night is you. It'll be good for her to have you right there when she's so distressed.'

Tess held his gaze. 'And when I go?'

Fletch had always believed in not borrowing trouble. He had it covered for the next two months and that was all he was worried about for now. 'We'll cross that bridge when we get to it,' he said, his expression grim.

'Your mother's condition needs a little more forward planning than that,' she said waspishly.

Dealing with families of dementia sufferers, Tess knew that those who had planned for every contingency coped better with the curve balls the condition threw them.

Fletch nodded. He couldn't agree more. 'Another reason why I need you here. Forward planning.' He looked into her shuttered gaze. 'It makes sense for you to stay here, Tess. And where are you going to find short-term accommodation at such late notice?'

*Anywhere but here.* 'I have friends in Brisbane…'

'Do you? Do you really, Tess? Kept in contact with the old crowd, have you?'

Tess broke eye contact. He knew she'd severed all links when she'd moved overseas. Before that even, when concerned friends had been too much for her to handle. She'd withdrawn from all her support groups, from her life really, as grief had consumed her utterly.

'I can't pretend happy families with you, Fletch,' she said, the marble surface of the kitchen bench cold beneath her hand. 'Too much has happened. Living with you again…it'll bring too much back.'

Fletch nodded. He knew that. And after only a couple of hours in her company he knew it would be harder than he'd originally thought. But sometimes the greatest gain came at the greatest cost. Ten years ago she'd shut down, shut him out—shut the world out—and he'd let her. With her here and committed to the task she wasn't running away any more and maybe, just maybe, they could face head-on what they hadn't been able to a decade ago.

'You think it's going to matter where you lay your hat each night,' he asked her downcast head, 'when we'll be seeing each other day in and day out?'

Tess knew he was right. It was going to be difficult whether she stayed here or not.

Fletch willed her to look at him. 'We have to prepare ourselves for the fact that this isn't going to be easy, Tess. It *will* bring back painful memories. But if we keep our focus on Mum then I'm sure we'll get through it.' He shrugged. 'Who knows, we might even become friends.' He gave a half-smile. 'I hear that's possible.'

Tess speared him with a look. 'We're not an ordinary divorced couple, Fletch.'

He nodded, acknowledging the truth of her words. 'Still…I never wanted it to be like this between us, Tess.'

Fletch tamped down on the guilt that he kept in a box labelled 'Tess', knowing that ultimately it was he who had severed their relationship. He wished he could go back and undo what he'd done that night nine years ago. That his actions hadn't made their already shaky marriage untenable and guilt hadn't driven him to grab hold of the out she'd given him.

Yes, their relationship breakdown had been multi-factorial and, yes, she had been the one to ask for a divorce, but when it had come to the crunch, he hadn't fought for it.

Or her.

He'd run away—just like she had.

Tess still remembered her surprise at his easy capitulation when she'd asked him for a divorce. 'We don't always get what we want,' she said testily.

He held up his hands in surrender. He didn't want to get into this now. He really didn't.

'This apartment is big enough for all of us, Tess. It would really help Mum and me if you stayed here for the duration.'

Tess would have liked nothing more than to walk away and never see Fletch again. But there was no way she could turn her back on Jean now, and Fletch was right—it was easy and convenient for her to stay here.

She hadn't fought with him nine years ago as they'd calmly ended their marriage—why waste her breath doing so now? She'd do what she had to do then leave— just like she'd done before.

'Fine,' she muttered. 'I'll go and get my stuff.'

An hour later Tess was back from checking out of her hotel and following Fletch as he showed her to her room. *Which looked suspiciously like his room.*

'This is your room,' she said bluntly, looking at the signs of his habitation strewn everywhere.

His watch and one of those crime novels he loved to read lay on the bedside table. A desk by the large floor-to-ceiling windows housed a sleek laptop and a tottering pile of papers and medical journals. A tie was thrown over the back of the chair. A pair of socks lay discarded on the thick, expensive-looking carpet.

'Yes. It is.'

Tess stared at him incredulously. 'I am *not* sharing a room with you.'

Fletch clutched his heart in mock injury. 'You wound me.'

'Don't you have another room in this luxury riverside apartment?' She ignored him, crossing her arms. 'And don't you dare lecture me about being adult, about me not having anything you haven't seen before or about keeping the pretence going into the bedroom because this is not negotiable!'

Fletch smiled as her eyes hissed fire at him like a lava flow of molasses. She looked so much like the old Tess for a moment that his breath caught.

Even if he hadn't seen any of what she had in a very, very long time.

'The only other bedroom I have, my mother lives in.'

'This is a two-bedroom apartment? Only two bedrooms?'

Tess hoped that the squeak she could hear in her voice was just being distorted through the layers of confusion in her brain.

'It's okay, Tess. I'll sleep on the couch. It's perfectly comfortable. Probably better with Mum tending to wander during the night anyway.'

Tess felt a wave of relief wash over her as she sagged against the doorjamb. In fact, she felt a little silly at her reaction that could be seen as being slightly over the top. But, honestly, sharing the apartment with Fletch was bad enough—she didn't even want to contemplate sharing a bed with him too.

She already knew how good that was.

And guilt had driven all the good out of her a lot of years ago.

'I think you're going to need to get yourself some clothes,' Fletch said as he plucked her overnight bag from her fingers and strode across his room, dumping it on his bed.

She nodded. 'I hadn't exactly planned on staying. I'll slip down to a department store in the next couple of days and pick up a few outfits.'

His eyes met hers as he tried not to think about the time she'd dragged him into the change room at a department store on a slow Sunday morning and had had her way with him in front of three mirrors.

*He failed.*

And if the sudden smoulder in her eyes was anything to go by, so had she.

'I'll let you get settled in,' he said, withdrawing quickly—because he knew from bitter experience that down that path lay no good.


Tess was in bed by eight-thirty. The jet-lag, the wine and the tumult of emotions from the day had well and truly caught up with her. She'd tried really hard to stay awake with Jean and Fletch but in vain. Fletch had nudged her awake and ordered her to bed. She hadn't even bothered to shower or change—just kicked out of her cargo pants and collapsed onto the bed in her knickers and T-shirt, barely getting the covers over her before she sank into the blissful depths of dreamless slumber.

She wasn't sure how many hours had passed when she first heard the commotion. It took Tess a while to realise Jean's sobbing wasn't coming from inside her head as it usually did but externally, outside the room somewhere.

*And it was actually real this time.*

She sat bolt upright as the shackles of heavy slumber fell from her eyes. The clock said two a.m. as she kicked the covers aside and stumbled out of the room, her heart pounding like a gong.

'Jean?' she called as she hurried down the hallway to her mother-in-law's room.

Nothing. *The bed was empty.*

'Jean?' she said again, louder this time as she headed towards the source of human anguish getting louder and louder.

'Out here, Tess,' Fletch called.

Tess entered the lounge area. The lamp near the television threw weak light into the room and she headed to the lounge where Fletch sat comforting his weeping mother.

'Everything okay?'

Fletch nodded over his mother's head as Jean sobbed.

'It's no good, Fletcher,' Jean sobbed. 'No good.'

Tess, her lack of clothing eliminated from her subconscious by nagging fatigue and her pounding heart, crouched down in front of them. 'Hey, Jean, don't cry, sweetie. It's okay.' She rubbed her palms against a pair of bony knees. 'What's the matter?'

Jean turned wet cheeks on Tess. 'You should never let the sun go down on an argument. Never spend a night apart. Fletch's dad and I never spent a night apart.' She grabbed Tess's hand. 'You never know how long you have with each other.'

Tess murmured, 'Of course not,' not entirely sure what was going on.

'I was just telling Mum that I got in late from the hospital and didn't want to disturb you so I collapsed on the couch.'

*Ah.* Now Tess got the reason for Jean's distress. And it was *acute* distress. She was crying, her movements agitated.

'It's still wrong,' Jean sobbed. 'You don't care about being disturbed, do you, Tess, darling?'

Tess looked at Fletch. He was at his disturbing best. Shirtless and trouserless, his big, bare chest and long, bare, dark-haired legs exuding a masculinity that was almost overwhelming in the intimacy of the little circle they'd formed. He rubbed the back of his neck in a helpless gesture and the lines of worry and tiredness around his eyes and mouth seemed to deepen.

She wished like hell they cancelled out the scruffy sexiness of his tousled hair and unshaven jaw.

'This is how people get divorced,' Jean continued, worrying at the fabric of her nightgown, rolling it between her fingers. She suddenly clutched Tess's arm. 'Oh, no…you're not getting divorced, are you?'

Tess felt her heart sink. Jean's level of anxiety was distressing to watch. As fanciful as it might seem to them, she was worrying herself sick.

And for that there was just one thing she could do.

She took a deep breath and slid her hand onto Fletch's knee and then up a little further to his thigh. 'Of course not, Jean,' Tess murmured, not acknowledging either his harshly indrawn breath or the tensing of his firm, bulky quadriceps. 'Fletch and I are fine, aren't we, darling?'

She looked at him then and smiled, sincerely hoping he could act better than she could.

# CHAPTER FOUR

FLETCH was too stunned to say anything for a moment. His body, on the other hand, wasn't as reticent. Her hand searing into his flesh took him back to the days when they hadn't been able to stop touching each other and in an instant he was hard.

A decade ago she'd have sensed his arousal in a flash with that weird sexual ESP they'd shared. She would have smiled at him, moved her hand slowly up his leg and kept going until she'd hit pay dirt.

'Fletch?'

He blinked as Tess's voice yanked him back to the here and now. To the startling reality of the present—Tess hadn't wanted him in a very long time and his mother was sitting right beside him.

*His very distressed mother.*

Grateful he was sitting down, Fletch grappled with what exactly the question had been.

'We're fine, aren't we?' Tess prompted, squeezing the firm, warm muscle beneath her palm.

Fletch saw the *keep up* look in her amber gaze as he fought against the automatic impulse to shut his eyes.

Her little squeeze had shot straight to his groin like a blast from a taser. God, he was too tired for this. He'd tossed and turned on the couch for hours.

'Of course we are,' he agreed heartily as he picked up the thread of the conversation. He covered Tess's hand with his own. 'I really just didn't want to disturb you, that's all.'

Jean's fretting eased as she patted their joined hands. 'You're such a sweet boy, darling, but, trust me, sleeping on the couch can be the beginning of a slippery slope. Look at Aunty Lynne, she and Joe sleep in different bedrooms now because of his snoring and they can barely stand the sight of each other. That all started at the couch, you know.'

Fletch glanced at Tess, his sexual frustration tempered by his feelings of helplessness. Did he tell his mother that both Lynne, his father's sister, and her husband Joe had died in the last few years?

Tess saw the inadequacy in his gaze and squeezed his thigh again. This could not be easy for him. 'Well, Fletch doesn't snore,' she said, diverting the conversation, 'so I think we'll be fine.' She gave Jean a wry smile. 'Now, how about a mug of nice warm milk?'

'Good idea,' Fletch said, leaping at the opportunity to escape the steady torture of her hand.

He reached for his trousers, desperate for some more cover. Tess's foot anchored one leg to the floor and she stood to release it. But then her bare thighs were at eye level. And even though they were thinner than he remembered—ballerina thin—and skinny wasn't something that had ever really appealed to him, his hard-on didn't seem to care, especially given how a quick flick of his eyes upwards also put her knickers squarely in his line of vision.

He looked down and hurriedly stuffed his feet into the legs of his trousers. He rose quickly, not looking at her, dragging them up his legs and over his hips in one fluid moment, zipping the fly as he took his first stride away.

'I'll make them. Sit down,' he threw over his shoulder as he headed towards the kitchen. And sanity.

Tess felt a blush creep up her cheeks and was grateful for the low light as she sank down next to Jean. She wished she hadn't caught his heated gaze on her thighs or that brief glimpse of the bulge being contained by his underwear—but she had.

He was aroused?

Mugs clattered in the background and Jean chatted away beside her, oblivious to Tess's internal conflict as she grappled with the incident. Had her touch, her completely artificial touch, on his leg done that?

It had been too long surely? Too much had happened between them. Too much angst. Too much sorrow.

Yes, Fletch had always been a very virile man and their sex life had always been firmly in the mind-blowing category. Nothing had seemed to dent it. Not shift work, pregnancy or living with a newborn.

Until Ryan's death anyway.

And then it had all changed. She just…couldn't. She'd barely been able to eat or string a sentence together for so long. Anything beyond that, anything requiring any kind of emotional energy or physical effort, had been too much.

And Fletcher had been understanding and patient.

But in the end it had defeated him.

Or at least she'd thought so. Until now. Seeing the evidence of his arousal had been startling. Was that just a normal male reaction to the proximity of a semi-clad woman or could he still really desire her after all these years?

It was a shocking concept.

A dangerous one.

The microwave dinged behind her and Tess dragged her thoughts away from her ex-husband's libido. It certainly wasn't something she was going to analyse. Now or at any other time.

'Okay, three warm milks coming up,' Fletch announced, placing the beverages on the coffee table.

Tess pushed everything aside as she picked up her mug and pulled her recalcitrant thoughts firmly back to Jean.

After leaving his mother with assurances that he would be returning to the marital bed, Fletch did indeed head to his room. Tess had volunteered to settle Jean back to sleep and he needed a shower.

He hadn't had one earlier as he hadn't wanted to disturb her. Sure, he could have had one in the main bathroom but all his stuff, his toiletries and clothes, were in his bedroom so he'd put it off till morning. But after the events of the night, after his involuntary reaction to her, he was prescribing himself a cold shower.

*A quick, cold shower.*

In and out before Tess even knew he was there. His mother often took quite some time to settle once she'd been wandering—the darkness exacerbating her dementia—so he should be well and truly clear before Tess came back.

Not that he wanted to be thinking about his ex-wife as he shed his clothes and stepped into the shower. Or what had happened at her tentative touch. Things started to stir again and he turned the cold spray on full bore, sucking in a breath as the icy spray pelted his flesh.

He dunked his head beneath the shower head, squeezing his eyes shut. He absolutely didn't need this.

*Whatever the hell this was.*

Some latent attraction? A vestige of what they'd once shared? Those endless hours in each other's arms, making love like the world was about to end, like their skin was brushed with crack cocaine and they *just couldn't get enough.*

Fletch shook his head against images that usually only visited him in his dreams. It was dangerous ground.

He turned so the spray drummed hard down his back, hoping it would scour the memories from his pores. Praying they'd sluice off his skin and disappear for ever down the drain hole.

But the drumming in his head mocked even louder.

*Tess. Tess. Tess.*

Tess sat with Jean for a while after she'd fallen asleep, surprised that her ex-mother-in-law had gone down as easily as she had. Surprised but relieved. Many a night she'd spent with an Alzheimer's patient trying to calm them so they'd sleep and it was rarely an easy task.

Tess was so tired when she entered the bedroom she almost missed the sound of the shower. She blinked as she stared at the closed en suite door.

*Fletch?*

She didn't move for a moment as a sense of déjà vu swept through her. Walking into their bedroom, the shower running.

Of course, once upon a time she'd have pushed open the door—not that Fletch would have bothered with shutting it—stripped off her clothes and joined him.

Which wasn't an option now.

But what the hell was? This *was* his room.

*She was the intruder.*

She clutched at her abdomen to allay the funny tightness building there. Her fingers hit warm flesh and she looked down absently at her clothes, or lack of them. She remembered how her bare thighs had burned beneath his gaze earlier. How his body had responded…

Her legs sparked into action. She could at least get into her pyjamas. She opened her carry-on case, which was all she'd thought she'd need for her whistle-stop foray back to Australia, and located the over-sized man's T-shirt she wore to bed. She'd got into the habit of wearing Fletch's T-shirts to bed during their marriage and, out of comfort, had continued the practice.

Not that they belonged to him any longer. Or any other man, for that matter. Her men's shirts these days came to her courtesy of the men's department at a store.

With the shower still obviously running, she whisked off the T-shirt she had on and threw the other one over her head. It came to mid-thigh and she felt infinitely more covered even if it was too broad across the chest, causing it to constantly fall off her shoulder and the V-neck to hang too low on her bra-enhanced cleavage.

She scrambled into the bed—Fletcher's bed—getting under the covers this time, and waited for him, her eyes firmly trained on the en suite door. It didn't matter how tired she was, that her eyes felt like they'd been rolled in shell grit, that the room seemed to tilt precariously every now and then.

Or that something had happened before that had the potential to be a real problem between them.

They needed to talk. About Jean.

Sitting with her before, Tess had come to a decision. A crazy one for sure, but the right one nonetheless. She and Fletch needed to have a conversation—no matter how difficult the subject matter. And the sooner they had it, the sooner she could get to sleep.

*All providing she actually could sleep if he agreed to what she had to say.*

The door opened suddenly and she took a deep, steadying breath.

Fletch's breath hissed out as he spied Tess sitting up in his bed, looking exhausted but grimly determined and somehow sexy as hell with her huge amber eyes and one shoulder bare except for a narrow bra strap.

'Oh, God, sorry, I thought you'd still be in with Mum...'

Tess didn't drop her gaze to take in her fill of his

bare chest or the long length of his legs not covered by the boxer shorts. But she was uncomfortably aware of them in her peripheral vision.

'It's okay,' she said softly. 'Jean went straight off to sleep. She was exhausted.'

The tension coiling the muscles in Fletch's neck as tight as piano wire eased a little. Already the decision to ask Tess to stay seemed to have paid off. 'Thank you. You're great with her.'

*His mother had never settled so quickly for him.*

Unfortunately it wasn't enough to fully dissipate the tightness in his neck. And after his reaction to her earlier, he doubted it ever would. Not while they were living under the same roof.

Still, keeping focused on the reason why she was there—his mother—and keeping as much distance as was possible inside the confines of his apartment, Fletch figured he could just about survive it.

Tess pulled the shirt sleeve up onto her shoulder. *That helped.*

It promptly slid off again. *Oh, boy...*

'So...' He hesitated. He didn't know why. 'Goodnight, then...see you in the morning.'

He turned to go but her soft 'Fletcher' pulled him up short. He turned back and quirked an eyebrow. 'Yes?'

'I think you should sleep in here with me.'

Fletch could have sworn he actually heard the synapses in his brain misfire. Certainly for quite a few moments he was struck completely dumb.

*Well, this sure blew the distance ploy out of the water.*

Tess watched as a range of emotions flitted across her ex-husband's face. Did he think she'd suggest something so out there if she didn't think it was absolutely necessary?

'We can't have a repeat of tonight, Fletch.'

Fletch shrugged. There'd been so many disrupted nights like this since he and his mother had moved into the apartment two weeks before, it seemed normal to him now. Still, the sentiment weighed heavily in his mind.

'She's not going to remember what happened in the morning.'

Tess raised her legs beneath the covers, tenting them as she propped her chin on her knees. 'I know. But do you want her to go through the same distressing anxiety every time she wanders in the middle of the night and finds you on the couch?'

Fletch knew the short answer was no. Of course he didn't. And Tess's solution was, obviously, a quick, simple fix. But nothing had been simple between them for a long time.

They were bereaved, aggrieved and divorced.

That was a whole lot of baggage to take with them to a bed they hadn't shared in nine years.

'If you're not on the couch,' she continued, 'there's no reason for any distress.'

Tess projected a calm, measured professionalism, like she was talking to a relative of a patient, but on the inside the mere thought of what she was suggesting was making her quake. She hadn't seen him in nine years and now she was proposing they share the same bed.

Maybe she'd wake up in the morning and it would have all been a bad dream.

*She was used to that.*

Fletch hastily diverted his gaze from the bed, mentally sizing up the room. 'I suppose I could sleep on the floor...'

Tess could barely hear him over the thudding of her heart, like a drum in her ears. She knew he was trying to do the right thing but did he really have to look at the bed like it was a viper's nest?

Did he really think *she* wanted to share the thing with *him*?

'Don't be ridiculous, Fletch,' she dismissed impatiently. 'You can't sleep on the floor for two months.'

Fletch lifted his gaze to meet hers. 'So...to be clear. You're suggesting that I sleep in the bed. With you?'

Not a suggestion he'd ever imagined he'd hear coming from her mouth ever again. The tension in his shoulders headed south to grab a stranglehold on his gut.

Tess heard the note of incredulity in his voice and shrugged. 'Will it really be *that* difficult to sleep with me again?'

Fletch swallowed hard, the knowledge of his recent monster erection colouring his reasoning. 'No.' He gave a self-deprecating smile. 'That's what I'm worried about.'

Tess couldn't help but be amused at the absurdity of it all and the rather sceptical look on Fletch's face. He'd always been so decisive, so take-charge, it was a novelty to see him so completely flummoxed.

Her mouth kicked up at one side briefly before returning to a determined line. 'We're not teenagers, Fletch. I'm not proposing reconciliation. We're just two adults making the best out of a less-than-satisfactory situation. I'm sure we can control ourselves.'

Fletch heroically refrained from mentioning that controlling herself when they were in bed together had never been a forte of hers.

Or of his.

Not until after Ryan's death anyway. Her control then had been savage. She'd stopped needing him, stopped wanting him, overnight.

But he'd still needed her. So very, very much. More than that—he'd needed her to need him back.

Fletch stood at the end of the bed, still hesitating as a decade of distance yawned between them. 'I could put a roll or something down the middle of the bed,' he suggested.

Tess surprised herself with her laugh. 'How very Victorian.'

He laughed back. 'I thought a fan of Georgette Heyer would appreciate it.'

Their smiles lit the room briefly then slowly faded. Tess sighed. 'It's almost three in the morning and I'm jet-lagged to hell and back, Fletch. I'm too tired for this conversation. Just get into bed.'

He nodded, coming to a decision. She was right. It *was* half past stupid hour. And they *were* adults. 'Okay. Let me just check everything's locked up one more time.'

Fletch went through his usual pre-bed door-checking routine. It was a particular nightmare of his that his mother would manage to find her way onto the balcony during one of her many night-time walkies and plunge to her death.

Still he lingered over it, his heart pounding loud enough to wake the whole building. Certainly loud enough to wake his mother.

He was about to sleep with his ex-wife. With Tess. And even though it wasn't sexual, he felt like a virgin again, like he was sleeping with a woman for the first time.

Satisfied everything was locked up tight and unable to put it off any longer, Fletch made his way to his bedroom, quickly checking on his mother as he turned appropriately neutral opening sentences over and over in his head.

*Something to break the ice.*

Decrease the awkwardness that she surely must feel as keenly as him. Something like *What's the weather like in Devonshire at the moment?* Or *How about those English cricketers?*

Fletch stopped in the hallway just shy of his door and allowed an internal groan free rein.

*How lame!*

But anything was better than *Take all your clothes off and let me make love to you.*

Because a few lousy hours back in her company and the imperative to be with her, to peel off her clothes and bury himself inside her, was raging in his blood like a fever. It was a bad time to discover she was a habit that he'd never managed to shake.

*It had been ten years and he wanted her as much now as he ever had.*

Guilt, hot and fierce, rose in him and he squeezed his eyes shut to dispel the images of their intertwined bodies.

*He didn't deserve her.*

*He had proved himself unworthy.*

He took a deep, steadying breath, shaking off the tug of dark memories and guilt, and stepped into the bedroom. But whatever pithy comment had been on the tip of his tongue died before even a syllable was spoken and he sagged against the jamb as a knot of tension released like the strings of a marionette.

*Tess was asleep.*

Sound asleep if her soft snore was any indication.

She lay on her side, knees tucked up, sheet anchored beneath her arms. The bedside lamps threw shadows that darkened the hollows of her cheeks and the smudges beneath her eyes. Even in slumber she looked like she carried the weight of the world on her shoulders.

He watched her for a long time, keeping his distance. Knowing he'd do anything to erase her burden. Wishing that he could go back to this day ten years ago and fix the damn lock, take away her migraine, remove the bucket, stop the overnight deluge, make the ambulance come faster.

Feeling again the rage and the helplessness. His complete impotency that when it had counted most, he hadn't been able to protect his family.

He squeezed his eyes shut, pushing his thumb and

forefingers hard into the lids, blocking the images. God, he was tired. So very tired.

He needed perspective.

*He needed sleep.*

He pushed away from the jamb and drew level with the bed. Slowly he eased himself onto it, being careful not to disturb her, sticking close to the edge and lying as stiff as a centuries-old mummy.

After a moment he slowly turned his head to look at her. Or her back anyway. Once upon a time he would have reached out and stroked his hand down the notches of her spine, drawn her in closer. Instead he turned away and reached for the lamp switch, extinguishing both with one action, plunging the room into darkness.

She stirred and he held his breath. She muttered in her sleep, rolled over, settled again. She was closer now. And facing him. He could feel her breath fanning his shoulder and as his eyes adjusted to the darkness he could make out the outline of her mouth.

*Great.*

Fletch rolled his head back until he was staring at the ceiling. There weren't that many more hours left in the night. But he had a feeling he was going to see every one of them.

He did finally fall into an exhausted sleep just as dawn was spreading its first blush across a fading night sky. After lying tense and unmoving for a couple of hours, listening to her breathe, his body finally succumbed to its baser dictates and slowly relaxed into the folds of slumber.

Unfortunately, thanks to those baser dictates, it didn't last long. They didn't seem to mind that he'd had less than four hours' sleep all night. All they cared about was that it was morning, something warm, soft and female was snuggled into him, his hand was full of a smooth, clad buttock and a certain part of his anatomy was wide awake.

Fletch's eyes flew open as every muscle contracted in painful unison. His heart pounded in his chest as, for a brief moment, total disorientation reigned.

Then Tess moved a little, readjusting her head against the ball of his shoulder, murmuring something nonsensical, her lips grazing his skin, her hand skating close, too close, to his painfully tight erection.

And he was suddenly one hundred per cent orientated.

His first instinct was to leap out of the bed like the mattress had caught fire. He doubted Tess would appreciate that they didn't have control of their bodily functions while under the influence of sleep and he had no desire to have her accuse him of taking advantage of the situation.

He'd realised yesterday just how hard this was going to be, but with her draped all over him, this was a whole other level of difficult. Too many mornings like this and he might just forget the reason she was there. Forget that this was fake and they were only pretending for his mother's sake.

He had to be careful they didn't cross a line—even in their sleep—because emotionally he didn't think she was up to it.

And he knew for sure he wasn't.

But right at this moment she was hard to resist. Her head was tucked into his shoulder, her breath was warm on his bare pec and she was all soft and supple against him. And his nostrils were full of her—passionfruit, honey and something else distinctly feminine.

He drew in a deep steady breath, sucking her deep into his lungs, savouring her.

Tess had always smelled so good.

So he didn't move. Not yet. He would—soon.

But not yet.

Tess woke slowly through myriad layers of a heavy sleep surrounded by a feeling of heat and solidness, a powerful malaise infecting her bones. She chased the last vestiges of a dream she couldn't quite remember across the fading edges of her sleep like a child would chase the tail of an escaped balloon as it rose in the sky.

She murmured a protest—her dreams were so rarely good and she fought against the sticky fingers that were trying to drag her away from the tail, back into the world of the conscious.

A hand curving around her bottom was comforting and she wriggled into it, bending her knee higher, revelling in the hairy bulk of a leg under it. Her lips brushed against firm, warm skin and an earthy aroma, very male, tickled her nostrils.

*Hmm.* Fletch had always smelled so good.

Beneath her hand, a solid slab of flat muscle undulated and tensed as if it was agitated. She smoothed it absently, stroking it lightly. Her fingers brushed something hard, something familiar and it twitched against her hand.

She frowned. *Something very familiar.*

The last strand of sleep fell with a loud clang like a metal shackle.

*Fletch?*

Her hand froze. The breath hitched in her lungs. Her eyes opened with a start. She was instantly awake, instantly aware of her situation.

She pushed away from Fletch abruptly, scrambling back to her side of the bed like an epileptic crab until her back hit the bedhead and she yanked the sheet up to her chin.

'What the hell?' she demanded, glaring at him.

Fletch glared back as he too boosted himself up against the bedhead. Okay, he was guilty of not separating from her earlier but no way was she going to make him the big bad wolf when she was the one draped against him with her fingerprints all over his belly.

'It's the morning,' he said defensively. 'It happens.'

*Particularly if a woman is rubbing herself against me like a great big tabby cat.*

Tess fought the urge to blush as she remembered how many times his biological wake-up call had led to a little morning glory. He looked so virile with his tousled hair, his big bare chest and his frown but, still, she couldn't believe she'd been…pawing at him. She dropped her gaze.

Fletch wasn't satisfied. 'You were the one touching me,' he reminded her downcast head for good measure.

Tess nodded, mortified at her behaviour. He was right.

*They were divorced, for crying out loud!*

'Yes.' She looked up at him. 'I'm so sorry, I was… dreaming and… God! Sorry.'

Fletch sighed at her obvious embarrassment. He should have known this was going to happen, that their bodies would naturally gravitate towards each other. That they'd subconsciously seek affection.

He rubbed a hand through his hair. 'No…I'm sorry. It's just… I don't know, Tess. It was probably inevitable. Our bodies were just reverting to type, I guess… in sleep…'

She knew what he was saying was most likely correct but it had still been a shock. She'd known last night when she'd felt the heat of his gaze on her thighs that they were on shaky ground. The fact that he didn't look any happier about it than she helped.

She grimaced. 'Maybe we're going to need that roll between us in the bed after all.'

Fletch was momentarily taken aback by her glum observation. Then he chuckled, tension slowly oozing from his muscles. 'Maybe we just need to realise that we can't control what we do when we're asleep and not get ourselves in a tizz about it when we wake up.'

Tess look affronted, crossing her arms. 'I did not get in a tizz.'

Fletch chuckled again as he threw back the sheet and swung his legs to the floor. 'Oh, you were in a tizz all right.'

'You don't have to leave, Fletch,' she said as he stood

and the mattress shifted a little beneath her. It was *his* bed, for crying out loud. 'I promise no more tizzies in future.'

He looked down at her. 'Are you sure? Because if there's one thing I've learned over the years it's that morning hard-ons are part and parcel of being a man. Are you okay with that or should I buy myself a sleeping bag?'

Tess swallowed. She hadn't had a single sexual urge in a decade. She doubted her libido, weird dreams aside, would be a problem. But he was giving her a choice. Which would be a lot easier to make if it hadn't felt so good being pressed against him just now.

She thought she'd suppressed those feelings a long time ago.

Obviously not.

Still, she couldn't let him sleep on the floor in a sleeping bag when there was enough room for both of them in the bed. She swallowed. 'I'm okay with it.' They just needed to be careful, that's all. 'As long as you keep them on your side of the bed.'

Fletch nodded. *Fair enough.* 'I'll check on Mum.'

Tess watched him go. Watched the strong lines of his bare back as he disappeared out the door. She shook her head to clear it. To try and grasp the rapid events that had led to her being back in her ex's bed.

Yesterday morning her life had been on track. It hadn't been rock-'n'-roll exciting but she liked it that way. Today she'd been sucked back into her baggage-laden past. Not a place she would ever have volunteered to visit.

But she'd told Fletch she'd do it for Jean and she'd meant it. And if that meant she had to be on her guard, even in her sleep, well, she guessed she could hack it for two months.

Determined to divert her thoughts, she sank down into the bed, thinking about her mother-in-law, already planning a schedule and thinking of ways things could be made a little easier.

'Still out to it,' Fletch announced as he re-entered the room a minute or so later. 'She usually sleeps late the morning after a disturbed night.'

Tess nodded. 'I've just been thinking about that,' she mused, surprised to feel the urge to check out his naked chest. 'I may have something that could help.'

'Oh?'

'What does the lease say about pets?'

# CHAPTER FIVE

AFTER the embarrassment of their early-morning start, the day flew by. Tess took advantage of Fletch's flexible working hours and went out as soon as the shops opened. Nothing to do with needing some breathing space—*not at all*—and everything to do with needing some clothes.

She spent a couple of hours bargain hunting to extend her meagre wardrobe and did a bit of a grocery shop. Jean had always liked to cook and there was no reason why she still couldn't do so with Tess around to 'help'.

So she brought some basics that were needed for the meal plan she and Fletch had worked out whilst trying to make awkward conversation over breakfast and extras for daily baking, which had always been a particular favourite of Jean's. In fact, Jean had been a champion cake-icer in her day so Tess made sure she included those ingredients in the trolley. Hopefully this skill could be nurtured and retained for as long as possible.

So much about Alzheimer's was focused on what the sufferer couldn't do, couldn't remember, instead of making the most of what they could.

She did not think about Fletch and their early-
morning predicament. Or at least every time she did
she stopped herself. Denial she was good at.

*Denial she'd perfected.*

And having to pretend they were happily married
was something well worth denying.

When Tess got home Fletch went into St Rita's for a
few hours to meet with the ethics committee over the
parameters of his study. It wasn't his favourite part of
the research process but a very necessary evil that not
only protected trial subjects but also himself and the
hospital from any potential liability.

When he was done he accompanied Tess and his
mother to get the pet Tess assured him would help with
Jean's anxiety. He was still sceptical as they entered
the animal shelter and were greeted by a cacophony of
barking but when Jean's face lit up he had to concede
it might have merit.

Jean looked at them. 'What are we doing here?'

'We're getting a kitten,' Fletch said patiently for the
tenth time in the last thirty minutes.

Jean beamed at him. 'Really?' She clapped her hands
together. 'Can I go and look?'

Tess laughed at Jean's childlike relish, feeling vindicated. It had been a hard sell talking Fletch into fla-
grantly disregarding the lease agreement but she'd seen
with her own eyes how much difference a pet could
make in the life of someone suffering from dementia
and had refused to be easily deterred.

When presented with the evidence, of which she
could quote both anecdotal and scientific verbatim,

Fletch had reluctantly agreed. She would have liked to push for a dog but common sense and apartment living took precedence and she'd suggested a house-trained cat.

'Of course. Go ahead.' Tess grinned. 'We'll just have a quick chat to the attendant and be along in a moment.'

When Tess and Fletch spotted Jean ten minutes later she was crouched down in front of a cage, talking animatedly to the animal inside. 'Oh, look, darling.' Jean waved at her son impatiently to move faster. 'It's Tabby.'

Tess quickened her steps, smiling at Jean's eagerness. It seemed Jean had already chosen her kitten and named it!

'Thank goodness you found her,' Jean told the shelter attendant following closely behind Tess. 'I didn't realise she'd gone missing. Trish would be worried sick if she knew her beloved Tabby dog had wandered away.'

Tess frowned. *Dog?* They drew level with the cage and looked down at a chunky, white-whiskered, ancient golden Labrador.

'You obviously haven't starved while you've been away, have you, girl?' Jean tutted. She poked her bony fingers through the cage wire to stroke the dog's ear. The dog whined appreciatively and angled its head for Jean to reach the sweet spot.

'Tabby?' Tess murmured to Fletch.

'Childhood dog of Trish's. She thought she was getting a cat and already had the name picked out,' he said quietly.

Tess pressed her lips together to suppress a smile, not game to say a word.

'Yes,' he said testily. 'The irony is not lost on me.'

'Come on, then, girl.' Jean gave the yellow-grey head one last scratch and stood. 'Let's get you home.'

Fletch looked askance at the dog. Putting aside that he lived in a nineteenth-floor apartment, the Lab looked like it was going to expire any moment either from old age or a triglyceride-induced heart attack. Maybe both.

He shook his head and muttered, 'Great,' as he sent Tess a *fix this* glare.

A bubble of laughter surged into her chest and Tess bit the side of her cheek to prevent its escape. It felt good to have the spectre of their living arrangements temporarily removed from the forefront of her brain by something so frivolous. 'Er, Jean,' Tess said, gently cupping Jean's elbow and leading her towards the next cage. 'We're here for a kitten, remember? Let's have a look around a bit more first, hey?'

*And hopefully forget all about the dog.*

Jean dug her feet in and looked at her reproachfully. 'Tessa! We can't leave Tabby here. Trish would be heart-broken. She belongs at home.'

Tess flicked a glance at the dog, which looked at her steadily with those big brown eyes, then at Fletch. He shook his head very firmly from side to side. 'We agreed on a cat,' he murmured in a low voice. Like a rumble of thunder.

Tess rolled her eyes. 'Okay, sure,' she soothed, turning back to Jean. 'We can take her home but how about looking at some cats as well? Look,' she said, pointing to a nearby cage containing a very playful kitten pouncing on a squeaky toy. 'Isn't that little fella cute?'

Jean turned to her son. 'Fletcher,' she admonished, wringing her hands, her voice high and worried. 'It's Tabby. We can't just leave her here!' She sank to the ground in front of the obese, elderly Labrador's cage and rocked slightly on her haunches. 'It's okay, Tabby, I'll get you out of here.'

Tess shrugged at him as Fletch rubbed a hand through his hair. His frustration wafted towards her in almost tangible waves.

'Maybe I can help?' the attendant, a middle-aged woman, intervened. 'I know you had your hearts set on a cat but you came here looking for a companion for your mother who suffers from dementia, right?'

Fletch nodded and she continued.

'Then you really can't go past old Queenie here. She was brought in two days ago after her owner of fourteen years, an elderly lady, died in hospital. Queenie had lain next to her owner, who had taken a fall and broken her hip, all night and into the next day. The lady said that Queenie had refused to leave her side until the community nurse arrived. She'd be a perfect companion for your mother.'

Tess felt goose-bumps prick her skin at the touching story. She watched Jean's agitated movements settle as she stroked Tabby/Queenie's head and murmured to her. What else did they need to make up their minds?

'How did she come to be here?' Tess asked.

'The lady's son brought her in. He travels a lot and doesn't have the time required to care for an arthritic, deaf dog.'

'Deaf?' Fletch shook his head. *Of course*. Queenie was a walking disaster zone.

'Yes.' The attendant smiled. 'She's old and fat. She has arthritic hips and is deaf. She's no pretty young thing, that's for sure. But that just makes her even more ideal for your mum. She's used to being a companion to an elderly lady. She's not young and spritely requiring someone young and spritely to keep up with her. She's content to sit and just be. And she's loyal to a fault.' The woman folded her arms across her chest. 'You won't regret it. Mark my words.'

Tess nodded heartily in agreement, also folding her arms. She turned beseeching eyes on Fletch. He gave her an exasperated look. 'I live on the nineteenth floor.'

'She's fully toilet trained,' the attendant jumped in.

'And exercise is good for Alzheimer sufferers,' Tess added. 'We can go for a few walks a day so Queenie can do her business. It'll be a good routine for Jean as well.'

Fletch looked down at the dog who looked up at him, flopped her head to the side, thumped her tail twice and whined at him, leading him to suspect that she probably wasn't all that deaf.

But three women, four if he counted Queenie, were looking at him like he was lower than a snake's belly, and he knew when he was outgunned.

'Okay, Mum.' He sighed, looking down at her. 'Let's get Qu—Tabby home.' He helped Tess get his mother to her feet and met her sparkling amber gaze above Jean's snowy head. She grinned at him and he growled, 'Smarty pants,' at her.

But as they filled out the paperwork and he watched

his mother sitting in the waiting area, stroking a contented-looking Tabby, he couldn't help but smile. Because despite what his lease said, he could already see how the dog had a calming effect on his mother.

And that was most definitely worth it.

It was midnight when Fletch headed to bed. He'd been working on study paperwork—or at least that was what he'd been telling himself. He hadn't exactly been very productive. Tess had been out on her feet early this evening and he'd ordered her to bed at seven.

It had been hard to think about anything else since. Other than her, *Tess*, in his bed.

And how they'd ended up this morning.

*And how they might end up tomorrow morning.*

But she'd been asleep for a good five hours now. She should be completely immersed in the land of nod. God knew, he was so tired he could barely see straight.

He looked in on his mother as he passed her room and lingered in the doorway for a moment. She was curled on her side, her snowy hair visible in the moonlight streaming through her window. Her hand rested on Tabby's dozing head. Just then the dog shifted, looked behind her straight at him and again Fletch wondered just how deaf their deaf dog really was.

She gave a quiet whine and Fletch said in a low voice, 'It's okay, Tabby, it's just me. Good girl. You come and let me know if Jean gets out of bed, okay?'

Tabby thumped her tail twice and whined again in what Fletch could only assume, what he hoped, was agreement then laid her head back on the bed. He smiled to himself and continued down the hallway to his bedroom.

Tess was sitting up in bed, reading his detective novel, when he entered. 'Oh…sorry,' he said. 'I thought you were asleep.'

She looked up from the book. 'I was, but you know how jet-lag is. I woke an hour ago like I'd been asleep for a week and I checked on Jean and I tried to go back to sleep but I couldn't so…I thought I'd read.'

'Yeah,' he murmured, trying not to look at her bare shoulder. 'Jet-lag can be a real pain like that.'

Tess nodded. 'It's awful.' Every year it took two weeks to recover from her three-day jaunt to the other side of the world.

Fletch stood for a few more moments as the silence grew between them. 'Anyway, I just came to have a shower and then get back to it.' He resigned himself to another night of little sleep—there was no way he could crawl into bed with her while she was still awake. It was too…happy families.

*And they hadn't been that in a very long time.*

She nodded. 'Sure.' And dropped her eyes back to the page she was reading.

Tess was aware of him disappearing into the en suite in her peripheral vision and breathed a sigh of relief when he was gone.

*It was going to be a long couple of months.*

She steadfastly ignored the sound of the shower as she read the same page three times. It was bound to be awkward for a while. Especially being back in bed together. It wasn't easy pushing the memories away as she always did when he was right there beside her, a very painful reminder.

And not just the memories of Ryan, but of them.

Especially after this morning.

But she'd committed to help with Jean. And it wasn't for ever—it would get easier.


Fletch made sure he had a shirt on as well as his boxers before stepping back into the bedroom. Tess, still reading, looked up from the book. He stayed in the doorframe, leaning his shoulder against the jamb, and smiled at her. 'Since when do you read detective novels?'

Tess shrugged. 'It was that or one of those very scintillating medical journals on your desk.'

Fletch chuckled. 'They may have been more conducive to sleep.'

She smiled. 'Actually, I personally find articles on the latest mitochondrial studies and or DNA sequencing real page-turners.'

Fletch threw his head back and gave a deep belly laugh and for a moment Tess couldn't breathe. How long had it been since she'd heard that sexy laugh?

Ten years? Since just before Ryan had died?

The long tanned column of his throat, sprinkled with dark whiskers, drew her gaze. Her nipples tightened as an image of her rising from the bed, crossing the room and kissing it took her by surprise.

*What the hell?*

She blinked rapidly to dispel it.

'Mum seems very settled tonight with Tabby curled up beside her.'

His calm observation dragged her out of a quagmire of confusion. She nodded absently whilst she sorted through appropriate responses.

'I think we're onto a winner there,' she said as her faculties returned. 'Tabby's stuck really close to Jean. It was great to see them sitting on the couch earlier, watching television together, Tabby's head resting on Jean's knee.'

Fletch nodded. 'It was a little confusing for Trish, though, when Mum rang her to tell her we'd found Tabby and she really needed to take better care of her dog.'

They laughed together this time. Listening to the one-sided telephone call had been comical. Tess was just pleased that Trish had caught on fast and knew enough to go along with her mother's false reality.

'Sorry,' she apologised after her laughter had died away. 'It's awful to laugh at something like this.'

Fletch shrugged. What could they do? This thing was happening to them whether they liked it or not. There was a long row to hoe and they needed some relief from the grim reality of it all.

*He knew that better than anyone.*

'Gotta laugh or you cry, right?' he said philosophically.

Tess didn't respond. What could she say? She'd made a decision when she'd moved to England to lock her grief away and try and get on with things. And it had worked for her. But there wasn't a whole lot of laughter in her life.

'Anyway, I hope it's a sign of things to come,' Fletch continued. 'Mum being this settled.'

Tess shook herself out of her reverie. 'I'm sure it will be. Studies show there is much less nocturnal wandering where pets are present. And even if the person does wander, the theory is that the pet will wake also and either stay with the person or raise the alarm.'

Fletch snorted. 'Except we got ourselves a deaf dog.'

Tess smiled. 'Dogs sense these things intuitively. I think Tabby's already bonded with your mother. I think she already knows, somehow, that Jean needs looking after.'

Fetch didn't answer and Tess wondered if his thoughts had turned to another dog in another time, as hers had.

Memories of Patch, the little Jack Russell terrier that Ryan had been given for his first birthday, arose unbidden. How he'd tried to alert them to what was happening to Ryan that dreadful day.

How he'd tried to save Ryan.

It still hurt to think about her son's faithful companion, about that day, and how she'd blamed Patch for so long for not doing enough. Not barking earlier. Not trying hard enough. But Ryan had adored his puppy dog and suddenly she needed to know what had happened to him.

'Did you take Patch to Canada with you?' she asked into the silence.

Fletch shook his head. 'Trish took him for me. He died from a snake bite a few years ago.'

'Oh.' Tess's guilt at how she'd shunned Patch flared

to life again. But the little dog had just been one more painful reminder she hadn't been able to bear to look at.

Fletch watched a series of emotions chase shadows across her face. 'He did his best, Tess,' he murmured gently. 'The bucket was wedged into the corner of the sandpit and weighted in the bottom with sand. It was heavy and he was a little dog.'

Fletch remembered it as if it was yesterday. Patch's incessant barking, something different about the tone of it waking him even before he'd heard Tess's frantic 'Fletch!'. Tearing out of the house just behind her into the back yard as a blur of brown and white hurled itself at the bucket over and over, toppling it as they reached him, disgorging water and sand and a pale, blue-lipped Ryan.

Tess shut her eyes, shutting down the images of her shaking Ryan, of the rag-doll feel of him against her chest. 'I know.' She nodded. 'I know.'

Fletch wanted to go to her. But, like at the cemetery for the last nine years, he held himself back. She didn't look any more open to his comfort now than she had all those years ago and he'd been rejected too many times to travel down that road again. So he gripped the jamb and waited for her to regain her composure.

She opened her eyes and grimaced at him. 'Sorry.'

Fletch shook his head. 'Don't be. This is hard for both of us but…thank you. Thank you so much for doing this for me. I know it's not easy being here with us again, reminding you of things you don't want to be reminded of.'

He'd hated it that Tess had shut him out in that year

after Ryan's death. She'd decided the only way to cope had been avoidance and it hadn't mattered that he'd wanted to talk about it.

Had needed to talk about it.

To talk about Ryan.

She hadn't been able to even bear having his name mentioned so he'd stopped trying and internalised everything and they'd grown further and further apart.

So he knew that being here, being confronted by him every day, had to be challenging for her. He just hadn't realised how challenging it was going to be for him as well.

'It's fine, Fletch.'

Dredging up the past was something she'd avoided at all costs and even a small foray into it had left her suddenly weary again. She shut the book. 'Think I might try and get back to sleep again.'

Fletch nodded as she climbed back into her shell. 'Sure.' He pushed off the doorjamb. 'I've got some paperwork to get back to. I'll be in later.'

*Just like old times.*

Fletch waited another couple of hours and got into bed when she was asleep and that was pretty much the pattern for the following couple of weeks.

They went to bed at separate times, Tess first, he crawling in with her at some time after midnight, turning his back to her lest he do something crazy and reach for her because lying with her again, night after night, had been much harder than he'd ever suspected it would be.

Sure, there'd been other women since their divorce. Not many, but a few. They'd been brief episodes, a handful of dates, a slaking of a thirst more than anything, where he'd given in to the dictates of his body but had kept his heart well and truly out of the equation.

But he couldn't do that with Tess.

Lying in bed with her was a painful reminder of how good it had been between them back at a time where they'd been emotionally free to love each other. And in that strange twilight zone between sleep and waking it was easy to believe that nothing had changed between them.

His heart certainly thought so. After years of keeping it heavily guarded, it refused to buy into the happy-families façade. In those sleeping hours, when he had no conscious control, it knew her.

Knew Tess on a primal level.

*Recognised the woman beside him as his mate.*

It was only the slow dawning as he became more conscious that things got back under control. As each new day loomed ahead he remembered his place on the page. Days of her constant companionship, of smiling and laughing and pretending that things were fine. Of playing happy families.

No respite from her or the fears and failures of the past. No escape for his poor confused heart.

No escape from the fact that things weren't fine.

The embarrassing mornings didn't help. No matter how scrupulously they maintained distance as they drifted off to sleep, by morning their bodies had subconsciously sought the warmth and comfort neither of them would ask for consciously.

Fletch often woke spooned around her, an erection pressing into the soft cheeks of her bottom. Or on his stomach, one arm flung out, his hand spread possessively on her belly. Or on his side, snuggled up to her, his leg bent at the knee pinning her to the bed.

And then there were the times when he woke and she was spooning him. Or had *her* hand on his belly. Or *her* leg entwined in his.

The only way to cope with their intimate postures had been to get up before her. Untangle himself and get out of the bedroom under the guise of taking Tabby outside for her morning toilet.

*Do not stop. Do not look back.*

And pretend it hadn't happened.

It certainly hadn't made for easy days despite outward appearances. The trepidation with which he greeted each day was tempered by Tess's academy-award-winning performance as chief organiser, but was there, nonetheless.

He knew it was difficult for her too yet she soldiered on, planning an activity every day to keep his mother, whose night-time wandering had settled dramatically, stimulated. Some days they cooked. Some days they rented classic movies that Jean knew well or visited some of Jean's old friends. Other times they went out to a museum or lunch in the city at a teahouse that had been around for a century.

His mother particularly enjoyed the morning and afternoon walks they took for Tabby's sake. Whether it was just Jean and Tess or he and his mother or the three of them, Jean chatted away happily as they trod the riverside boardwalk.

He knew his mother loved it when they were all together but frankly he preferred it when it was just the two of them. It felt forced with Tess there. Like they were trying too hard to be something that they weren't, that they hadn't been in a long time, that they could never be again, no matter how much their bodies betrayed them in their sleep.

And it felt...dishonest. Even if it was for a good cause.

And he knew she felt it too.

At the beginning of the third week there was a knock on the door as Fletch stacked the dishwasher after lunch. He'd not long got back from the hospital where the first patient in their study, a twenty-six-year-old motorbike accident victim, had been enrolled. 'I'll get it,' he said, waving off Tess who had put her sandwich down and risen from the table.

It was Trish. She was leaning against the door, looking huge and glowing at thirty weeks. Doug stood behind her, holding an excitable Christopher. Fletch's heart contracted at the sight of his nephew, at the features so familiar to him.

Trish kissed her brother's cheek. 'Okay,' she said, advancing into the apartment, 'I'm going stir crazy at home. The doc said I could have a little foray and your apartment was the only place that Doug would agree to take me to. Before you ask, all I've done is sit in a car and walk from my house to the car and from the car to your apartment.'

Fletch's lips twitched as Doug rolled his eyes. 'Okay, then.'

'Unc, unc, unc,' Christopher chanted, squirming in his father's arms, leaning forward and reaching out for Fletch. Just as Ryan had done when he'd come home from being at work for long hours. It was only natural for Fletch to take him and to plant a kiss on the baby-soft cheek.

'I'd kill for a cup of tea, which, by the way,' Trish said, smiling at him sweetly, 'you have to make because I'm not allowed to do anything.'

Fletch laughed. 'Well, come on in, then, and I'll make you one.'

Christopher still in tow, he entered the open lounge area, laughing at something Doug had said. It wasn't until he'd made it to the kitchen and heard an audible gasp that he realised the fuller implications.

He turned. Tess was frozen at the sink, her hands in sudsy water, staring at him. Or more correctly at Christopher.

He took a step towards her. 'Tessa.'

Tess held up her hands to stop him, suds sliding off them into the sink. The ache in her chest, the one that was always there, just smothered under years of push-ing all the pain away, intensified.

The little boy in her ex-husband's arms smiled at her. A green-eyed little boy with blond hair that stuck up in the middle from his double cowlick.

A buzzing in her ears became so loud that for a moment she thought she was going to faint.

*Ryan?*

# CHAPTER SIX

FLETCH handed Christopher back to his father. 'Tessa,' he said again, stepping towards her.

She backed up, her hip sliding along the bench. 'It's fine,' she said quickly, shaking her head. She didn't want him to touch her, to comfort her.

She just needed a moment.

There'd been other children in the last nine years. Of course there had been. Granted, they weren't common at the nursing home. But residents' grandchildren would come to visit and she'd coped. Smiled and agreed they were the most beautiful babies in the whole entire world and got on with her job.

But they were on the other side of the globe—not here.

Not in Fletch's arms.

Not looking like a carbon copy of Ryan.

She watched as the three adults looked at her, frozen in their positions, lost for words, waiting for her next move, not daring to even breathe in case she cracked into a thousand pieces. Only Christopher seemed oblivious, bouncing up and down in Doug's arms, making truck noises with his little bow lips.

Just as Ryan had done.

*God, she was going to be sick.*

'Excuse me for a moment, please,' she gasped as she whirled away from them and hurried to the main bathroom.

She lost her lunch and probably her breakfast too as she heaved into the toilet. A knock sounded on the door. 'Go away,' she yelled, knowing it would be Fletch.

Tears pricked at her eyes and she pressed her lids shut tight, beating them back. She'd cried her yearly allocation of tears at the cemetery a few weeks ago.

They were the boundaries she'd set herself and they'd worked for her.

And if she started now she might never stop.

After a few minutes Tess pulled herself up to sit on the closed lid, psyching herself up to go back out there. She had to do it, she knew that, but her cheeks warmed at the very thought. She'd completely and utterly embarrassed herself. Trish and Doug were guests in Fletch's home, not to mention family, and she'd made them feel uncomfortable.

And then, of course, there was Christopher...

Tess stood and looked at herself in the vanity mirror. She looked even whiter than her usual English pallor.

*She looked like she'd seen a ghost.*

She grimaced at the irony then turned on the tap, brushing her teeth and scrubbing vigorously at her face with cool water to put some colour back into her cheeks.

She dried off then inspected her face again. Marginally better.

'Go!' she ordered her reflection.

Thankfully her feet obeyed and Tess found herself walking out to join everyone, the thrum of her heartbeat in her ears. They had all joined Jean in the lounge area and were laughing at Christopher, who was patting Tabby.

Fletch, who wasn't really tuned in to the conversation, rose immediately when Tess came into his peripheral vision.

'You okay?' he asked anxiously.

Tess nodded as she drew closer. 'I'm sorry,' she apologised to Trish and Doug, whose attention was now also firmly on her. Thankfully, Jean was preoccupied with her grandson and Tabby. 'It was just a bit of a shock.'

Trish nodded. 'It's okay,' she assured gently. 'It really is quite freaky how similar they are.'

'No.' Tess shook her head. 'It's not okay. It was rude and I'm sorry.'

'Well, let's just agree to disagree on that one.' Fletch's sister grinned. 'Are you going to join us?' she asked.

Tess wanted to say no. To plead a headache or busy herself in the kitchen. But she'd already been unforgivably rude.

'It's fine if you don't want to,' Trish murmured.

'Don't be silly, Trish,' Jean said as her wandering attention came to rest on the byplay. She frowned at her daughter.

'Of course Tess wants to join us.' She patted the empty lounge next to her. 'Come and sit here, darling.

Trish has brought one of the centre's little cherubs over for a visit.'

She squeezed Christopher's cheek and he squealed in delight then she looked at her daughter reproachfully. 'Trish, you know how much Tess adores children, why wouldn't she want to join us?'

Nobody said anything for a moment as Tess realised that Jean didn't have a clue that Christopher was her grandchild. Tess saw the flash of grief in Trish's eyes and noticed Doug's hand slide onto his wife's shoulder and squeeze.

'Of course I'll join you.' Tess smiled at Jean brightly.

Jean smiled back. 'Come and meet…oh, dear.' She turned to her daughter. 'What did you say his name was, Trish?'

Trish gave her mother a wan smile. 'Christopher, Mum.'

'Oh, what a gorgeous name.' Jean clapped her hands a few times. 'Maybe you can call this one…' she tapped Trish's belly '…Christopher if it's a boy? Tess?' She turned back to Tess. 'Did you know Trish was pregnant? You girls are so secretive these days!'

There was no need for a reply as Christopher's giggle distracted them all. Tabby was sniffing the toddler and her whiskers were buzzing the little boy's neck. He looked at his mother excitedly and said, 'Doggy!'

Trish laughed. 'Yes. Tabby. Can you say Tabby?'

Christopher gave another dribbly smile. 'Yabby, yabby, yabby!'

Everyone laughed then. Even Tess. Even though her heart ached just looking at Fletch's nephew.

After half an hour that stretched interminably Doug stood and announced it was time for a yawning Trish to go back to bed. Trish protested but Doug was firm. After a noisy round of goodbyes Jean and Fletch saw the trio to the door.

Tess watched them go, a lump rising in her throat as Christopher, who was grinning at her from over Doug's shoulder, waved madly at her. She'd spent the time they were there scrupulously not looking at him, not touching him, but there was just something about a happy, waving toddler that had her automatically waving back, even if she couldn't raise a corresponding smile.

Ryan had been such a friendly, easygoing little boy too.

It wasn't until she heard the door click closed that Tess finally relaxed.

Fletch crawled into bed just before midnight. It had been an eventful day. He'd tried to engage Tess in some conversation over his sister's unannounced visit but she'd insisted she was fine and didn't want to talk about it.

It was a touch too déjà vu for him but he'd learned ten years ago that Tess was hard to sway when her mind was made up. He lifted the sheet carefully and slowly lowered himself onto the mattress. He'd fallen into the habit of immediately turning his back on her but tonight, try as he may, he just couldn't. He propped himself up on his elbow and watched her for a while.

Her breathing was deep and steady but even in her sleep tonight her eyebrows seemed to be knitted in a frown. He wished he'd had the desire to confront her today about her avoidance issues. To say the things that needed to be said. That should have been said a decade ago.

But this wasn't a do-over of their marriage. This was her doing him a favour for a couple of months. He couldn't change what had happened back then in the aftermath of Ryan's death. The way grief had pushed them apart. And ultimately what he'd done when he'd been at emotional rock bottom.

There were so many things that had come between them. One heaping on top of the other until neither of them had been able to see the other any more.

And that wasn't going to be fixed by any enforced intimacy.

Fletch fell back against the pillows as a familiar rush of disgust enveloped him, his actions that September night still haunting him.

But that too couldn't be changed.

He'd known it the second it had been done. And wishing it was different didn't make it so.

So he did what he'd done every night since she'd been back in his bed, what he'd done for so many nights after Ryan had died and she'd started shutting him out.

He rolled away from her and shut his eyes.

Tess woke to a wet feeling on her hand. Her eyes flew open as if they'd been zapped by a bolt of electricity. She backed up, accidentally nudging a prone Fletch as Tabby's dear old face filled her entire vision and the low, urgent whine went straight to a place deep and dark inside her.

Her heart beating like a runaway train, Tess's thoughts were incoherent for a moment or two.

It was Fletch who said, 'What is it, Tabby? Is Jean okay?' as he climbed out of bed.

Tess followed on autopilot. To Jean's room. The bed was empty. The bathroom—also empty. Then quickly out to the lounge. His laptop occupied the coffee table but there was no Jean. Around the dividing wall into the kitchen, where Jean was muttering to herself as she paced up and down.

Fletcher felt a rush of relief like a slug of tequila swamp him. 'Mum?'

Jean's hair was wild, like that of a mad scientist, as she looked at both of them with crazy eyes. 'Where's Ryan?' she demanded, her voice high with distress, her tone urgent. 'Tess? Where's Ryan? I thought I could hear him crying and I've searched the entire house but he's nowhere.' She put a hand to her mouth and her eyes grew large. 'What if he's been kidnapped?'

Whatever Tess had been expecting, it hadn't been this. She felt as if Jean had punched her in the stomach and she grabbed for the bench top to steady herself. Fletch had assured her that Jean didn't remember Ryan.

Just as she hadn't remembered poor little Christopher.

Tess didn't know what to say. Not after today. Not with Christopher's sweet little face such a poignant reminder of her own little boy. She could barely breathe, let alone form a coherent response.

'He's at Trish's,' Fletch said. 'Having a sleepover.'

Tess flinched as his hand came to rest on her shoulder, just as Doug's had done today with Trish.

'Trish wanted to give us a night off,' he embellished.

Jean seemed to sag as her agitation settled almost immediately. Tabby licked her hand and the transformation was complete. 'Well, why didn't you say so?' she accused mildly. 'I was worried half to death.'

Fletch flicked a glance at Tess. She still hadn't moved. Her distress wasn't as palpable as his mother's had been but he could tell she was rocked to the core. He wanted to go to her but his mother's needs were more immediate.

And a lot easier to fathom!

Jean patted her chest where the lacy yoke of her nightie met bare neck whilst she absently stroked Tabby with her other hand. 'That is so like Trish, though, isn't it?' She shook her head. 'I wish those two would stop wasting time and get pregnant. They'll make such great parents.'

Fletch nodded, his pulse settling. 'Would you like a warm milk, Mum?'

Jean gave him an indulgent smile, the missing Ryan already forgotten. 'That would be lovely, dear. Tess?'

Tess blinked. She could see Jean's lips moving but she couldn't hear any of the words. There was a pain in her chest, right in the centre of her heart, that was expanding rapidly and she could barely breathe.

'Tess?'

Fletch's deep grumbly voice pierced her inertia. She looked at him. What did he want? What had he said?

'Milk?' he prompted in response to her blank look.

Tess shook her head as the pain became a pressure

that built relentlessly. Pushing against her rib cage, clogging her throat, pressing against the backs of her eyes.

She couldn't stay here. And drink milk. She couldn't pretend that her mother-in-law's state tonight hadn't affected her. It may have sprung from Jean's confused condition but to her anything to do with Ryan was absolutely crystal clear.

And sometimes still so very real.

No matter how much she tried to ignore it.

'Tess?' Fletch prompted again, laying his palm over hers.

She pulled away. 'No.' She shook her head. 'Thanks,' she added. 'I think I'm just going to go back to bed. It's late…'

Fletch nodded. 'Of course.' He searched her face, her amber eyes looking huge in her thin, haunted face. 'I'll be in later,' he murmured.

But he doubted she'd heard him as he spoke the words to her retreating back.

Tess lay in the dark, staring at the ceiling, while her body waged a war between sleep and grief. She wanted to sleep. She wanted to be able to shut her eyes and let a black tide wash her away into the embrace of a deep, dreamless slumber. And she wanted to be there before Fletch came back to bed.

But memories of Ryan—memories she'd spent a decade suppressing—refused to be quelled and swept her along on another black tide. A rough-and-tumble ride that left her feeling bruised and battered.

The way his hair had smelled. His delighted little

giggle. His fat pudgy fingers that had wound into her hair as he'd sucked his thumb. His father's silver-green eyes that had lit with mischief or wonder. The way every single discovery had been met with complete awe. The way he'd looked up at her as he'd fed at her breast, with such unconditional love and trust.

Trust that she had destroyed completely as she'd slept that morning ten years ago while her son had drowned.

'Tess?' Fletch approached the bed tentatively half an hour later. His mother was settled back in bed with Tabby, blissfully unaware of the emotional carnage she'd left in her wake. 'Tess?' he said again.

The room was dark and her back was to the door but he knew she was awake. He could sense her turmoil as if it had flashed out at him like a lighthouse beacon.

'I'm sorry, Tess. She hasn't mentioned Ryan in well over a year. It was probably having Christopher here today that triggered latent memories.'

He climbed into bed beside her, sitting up with his back against the headboard. Her shoulder was bare and his fingers itched to touch it. To loan her some comfort.

To seek some comfort.

But he couldn't bear her to flinch at his touch again. 'Tess?'

Tess, her eyes squeezed tight, contemplated continuing to ignore him but it was patently obvious he hadn't bought into her act. She opened her eyes on a huffed-out breath. She rolled onto her back. 'It's fine, Fletch. Go to sleep.'

He looked down at her, her amber gaze glimmering with unshed tears and tightly reined emotions. 'I can't.'

Her eyes, accustomed to the dark, watched him for a moment or two. He looked like someone had knocked the stuffing out of him and she realised that Jean's outburst hadn't been easy for him either. Both the distressing state of her and the subject matter.

She pushed herself up to sit beside him, ensuring there was a decent distance between them, and they sat contemplating the darkness around them for a few moments.

'I'm sorry,' Tess murmured. 'It was… I got a bit of a shock when Jean said… I wasn't expecting it.'

Fletch nodded. 'I know.'

They fell quiet again. 'I miss him,' he said eventually.

Tess squeezed her eyes shut again as the pressure spiked behind her eyeballs. 'Don't, Fletch.'

'He loved her, though, didn't he, my mum? Do you remember how he used to call her Ninny?' He laughed. 'And she used to call him Rinny?'

Tess drew her knees up and shook her head. She didn't want to be sucked back into those days. When their lives had been perfect and nothing had been able to touch them. The pressure became unbearable. 'Fletch.'

Fletch heard the note of warning in her voice underpinned by a tautness that could have strung piano wire. He shoved a hand through his hair. 'Damn it, Tessa, I'm so sick of not talking about him…of not having anyone to talk about him to. Surely after ten years we can reminisce without it being so…fraught?'

His voice may have been low and husky but to Tess

it sounded like a clanging gong in the silence, and the dam holding back her grief started to crack.

Fletch turned to implore her. He just wanted to remember his son for a few minutes with the one person who had loved him with the same intensity and devotion.

Couldn't she give him that at least?

He noticed her hands trembling first against her drawn-up thighs. Then her shoulders shaking. Then a low noise, like a wounded animal. 'Tessa?'

Tess shut her eyes on a sob that broke free from her throat. A tear squeezed out. Then another.

Fletch felt as if a giant hand had grabbed a big loop of his intestine and twisted—hard. Why hadn't he just kept his big trap shut? 'Tess?'

She couldn't respond. Couldn't talk. Daren't open her mouth for fear all her locked-in grief would come spewing out and she'd never survive the fallout.

He turned on his side, reaching out a hand, touching her shoulder, waiting for the flinch, determined this time to push through it and comfort her. But there was only more sobbing.

Not great honking sobs either. Pitiful, muted ones.

Apportioned. Rationed. Kept strictly under control. But he knew what they'd cost her.

When she'd announced two months after Ryan's death there'd be no tears, she'd been true to her word.

Still, he hadn't meant to upset her. He'd just needed... *What?* What had he needed?

Connection.

'I'm sorry,' he murmured, scooting closer. 'God, Tess don't…please.'

He pushed his hands into her hair and swiped at her tears with his thumbs. 'Shh, it's okay, honey, don't.'

Even though he knew if anyone needed to cry it was Tess, her pathetic mewing was so heart-wrenching he couldn't bear it. He leaned in and kissed her forehead. Kissed her eyelids. His lips mingled with her tears. 'Shh,' he crooned as he tasted both their salt and their anguish.

His palms moved down to cradle her face as he followed the tracks of her tears, sipping at them as he went. Down the slopes of her prominent cheekbones. Into the dip of the hollows beneath. Past her nose. To the corner of her mouth.

'Shh,' he murmured against her lips. 'Shh.'

And then the soft butterfly presses became something else. Something different.

Something more.

Tess felt her wretchedness ease as something altogether took over. Something unusual yet familiar. Hesitant yet insistent.

*Something separate from her grief.*

And she grabbed on for dear life.

Her mouth opened beneath his and the harsh suck of his breath echoed around them. Her tongue reached out tentatively, seeking his, and she felt his deep groan reach right down inside her to places she'd long since forgotten existed.

Places that were coming to life with a roar, not a whimper. Heating and liquefying and pulsating.

Fletch's hand slid from her jaw to the back of her head, angling it so he could deepen the kiss. Tess obliged, letting him in a little more, sighing against his mouth. He slid his hand to her back, gathering her closer, their chests touching, their hips aligned, their legs brushing.

She wound her arms around his neck, the motion squashing her breasts against his chest, and Fletch could feel their softness and the twin points of her aroused nipples that told him more than her sigh ever could.

His head spun, his pulse tripped. Her lips tasted sweet and every time he drew in a breath the aroma of Tess, imprinted on his DNA, filled up his senses.

It was intoxicating. She was intoxicating. And it had been *so damn long*.

He didn't know what was going on but right now he couldn't have cared less. All he knew was that he needed this, needed her, with a gnawing, aching desperation.

Tess could feel her body igniting. From the sealed heat of their mouths, liquid warmth oozed like quicksilver into her marrow. Into every muscle and sinew. Into every cell. Pushing forth into areas that had been shut down for a decade. Where she'd felt cold and bleak for a decade.

She felt Fletch's hand at her breast and she moaned into his mouth, arching her back, pushing herself harder into his palm, her hips moving more intimately against his. She felt the thickness of his arousal and rocked herself into it. The guttural sound he made at the back of his throat fuelled the flames licking through her blood and the urgent hand he clamped against her bottom, where cheek met thigh, pressed her closer. She had no idea what she was doing. All she knew was it felt good. And in the storm of sensations she'd found a new way to reach the oblivion she craved.

Respite from thoughts of Ryan that had been hammering at her skull ever since Jean's clueless ramblings.

Suddenly she wasn't a grieving mother or a failed wife. She was a woman. And she felt whole again.

*Whole.*

The word was like a glacial hand on her neck and Tess froze in his arms. Since when had she needed a man to feel whole?

*Especially this man, whom she'd loved too much and knew too well?*

She'd moved to the other side of the world to get away from him, to get the emotional distance she'd needed just to survive. And she hadn't so much as looked at a man in a decade. Yet one touch from Fletch and she was practically climbing on top of him?

Undoing all the hard work. Knocking down all the emotional barriers she'd erected to survive in a world that had been turned upside down.

*What was she doing?*

She couldn't need Fletch to feel whole again. She just couldn't. She had a life to go back to. A life that worked.

A life without him.

*She wasn't here for this. She didn't want this.*

*She didn't need it.*

Fletch realised suddenly that Tess had stopped responding. He drew back, his heart racing, his breath ragged. 'Tess?'

She could see desire turning his silvery-green eyes all smoky. Her chest rose and fell in the same agitated rhythm as his. She pushed against him. 'Let me go.'

Fletch blinked. *Huh?*

She pushed harder. 'I can't do this. Let me go,' she said, more frantic this time.

Fletch felt like the bed had been yanked out from under him as she wrenched away. 'Tess. No.' He grabbed for her but she'd removed herself from the arc of his reach.

She shook her head as she scrambled to the farthest point of the bed from him, her back against the headboard again. She yanked her oversized shirt down over her drawn-up knees until only the tips of her toes were visible.

As a physical deterrent it was fairly flimsy but symbolically it screamed *Keep out* very effectively. She hunched into it. 'I'm sorry,' she whispered. 'I can't.'

Fletch fell back against the mattress, suppressing a roar of frustration. His pulse hammered, his breath rasped, his erection strained.

'It's fine,' he said after a few moments, staring at the ceiling.

Even though it wasn't. Even though déjà vu was pressing him into the mattress with the weight of a hundred bitter memories. Reaching out for her on too many occasions and being rebuffed. Desperate to hold her, to reaffirm their love, all met with stony resistance.

And whilst she may not have flinched away this time,

her sudden change of mind was just as gutting. Because for the first time in a decade she'd needed him.

He'd never been surer of anything.

*She'd needed him.*

'I don't know what happened,' Tess said.

Fletch's obvious wretchedness added guilt to the mix of her ricocheting emotions. The need to explain herself took her by surprise.

Fletch shut his eyes. 'It's fine,' he dismissed again.

But it wasn't. She didn't want him to think she was playing games. 'I haven't… I don't… It just…took me away. Before I knew it, nothing else existed.'

Fletch shoved a hand through his hair as her meaning sank in and he felt cold all over. So she *had* needed him.

As a distraction.

A sudden surge of anger boiled away the ice.

*She'd used him.*

Tess realised what she'd said as he rolled out of bed. 'Wait, Fletch…I didn't mean… It's not like that…'

Fletch looked across the rumpled bed at her, anger simmering in his veins. 'Yes, it is, Tess,' he said quietly, his jaw locked tight, keeping rigid control of his response. 'It's exactly like that.'

And before he could say something he regretted, he did what he'd always done, turned away and walked out of the room.

# CHAPTER SEVEN

TESS lay awake long after Fletch had left, staring into the darkness. He didn't come back to bed and she knew in her bones he wouldn't. She fell asleep as dawn was breaking across a velvet sky and didn't wake until the sun was high.

Even then she couldn't move. She just lay on her side and watched a vapour trail leave a white streak across the slice of sky she could see through the bedroom's large windows, her thoughts full of Fletch.

And their kiss.

It was time to admit to herself that living in such close quarters with him had loosened the lid on feelings she'd thought long suppressed.

*She was attracted to Fletch.*

It was simply undeniable. It had been there from the first moment she'd spotted him at the cemetery. Fletch had improved with age and there was a sexiness to his maturity that pulled at her in places entirely different from those the first time around.

And to someone who hadn't felt attraction or desire in such a long time, *who'd actually shunned it*, it wasn't an easy admission.

It was made worse by the answering flicker she'd seen in him. From the moment he'd looked at her bare thighs that first night to the way she'd caught him looking at her in unguarded moments, it was obvious he felt it too.

It had been wrong of her, stupid actually, to think they could just pick up where they'd left off—two human beings going through the motions, shells of what they'd once been—with this attraction raging between them.

But she hadn't meant to use him.

It had just been so good to forget for a while after Jean's unintended stirring-up of their past.

Her stomach muscles tightened as the kiss played in her head again and for a fleeting moment Tess regretted pushing him away last night. Maybe she should have just got lost in him, like she used to. Let him and the magic she knew their bodies could make obliterate everything.

The time between going to bed and falling asleep was always the hardest—last night particularly—and he could have helped with that.

But she just…couldn't.

She'd known she was getting herself into dangerous emotional waters, a torrent she'd barely survived the last time, and she just hadn't been able to let go.

Her life was too regimented for that.

She'd tried to live her life simply and on a level emotional plane ever since they'd separated. She'd moved far away and started anew. She lived modestly, kept friendships light, actively discouraged men. She worked and she slept and in between times she kept herself busy in her garden or doing online research for the local historical society.

She didn't even have a pet.

Jumping head first into a sexual liaison with Fletch as a way to keep the memories at bay during her stint in his apartment was a huge leap and one that was pure folly. Pretending they were happily married for Jean's sake was enough of a lie without throwing sex into the mix.

Because even she knew with their history and this latent attraction, it could never be that simple.

And she didn't want to need Fletch again like she once had. Ten years of separation had afforded her a true sense of self. She didn't need anybody these days and that was fine and dandy as far as she was concerned.

Because when she was done here she *was* going back to England, back to her perfectly fine life in a small Devonshire village where everyone knew her name and no one knew her pain.

*Just the way she liked it.*

But first she had to get through the next weeks and to do that she had to get out of bed and go and talk to Fletch.

Fletch squinted against the harsh morning sunshine reflecting off the river as he stood at the railing of his deck. He and his mother had just come back from taking Tabby for a walk along the river path he could see snaking down below.

He took a long swallow of the ice-cold berry smoothie they'd whipped up together on their return. Tess had stocked the freezer with frozen berries, quoting something about their antioxidant properties being good for Jean's memory retention.

He was pretty sure it wouldn't stand up to any rigorous scientific testing but the nutritional value of berries was well documented and blended with ice and a little cream they went down very well on a hot morning.

He yawned as his lack of sleep caught up with him. His neck ached from hunching over the laptop at the coffee table, pretending to work, while his brain had turned the incident with Tess over and over until he'd thought he was going to pass out from the spinning.

He'd been angry with Tess when he'd walked out on her last night. And it hadn't been from some thwarted sexual fulfilment. Or the fact that she had been using him to forget for a while.

*Well, not entirely anyway.*

It was her rejection of his closeness, her continual refusal to let him in, to talk to him, that had steam blowing out of his ears.

It was déjà vu.

By the time his mother had woken at seven he had been angry with himself. For a start, he'd been foolish to believe he could just share a bed with Tess and not want to get her naked. Despite their history he was still dangerously attracted to her and he'd known that from the first night when she'd put her hand on his thigh.

Secondly, he was angry because he should have never given up on her.

On them.

He should have insisted on counselling instead of the gently-gently approach he'd taken. Demanded she come with him. Picked her up and carried her there if necessary.

Maybe they'd still be together.

He should have said no when she'd asked for the divorce.

But things had been so dark and bleak for so long and he'd just done something utterly and completely unconscionable. Sure, there had been a thousand excuses and justifications but he hadn't believed any of them then and the passage of time hadn't made them any more palatable.

It had been too hard to look at her, and impossible to look at himself.

And she'd given him the perfect out.

Walking away had been the only option. Because telling her hadn't been.

Just as starting something with her while she was here wasn't an option either. Not with so much unsaid between them.

Fletch drained his glass and moved inside, his eyes instantly grateful. His mother was washing up at the sink and she smiled at him as he placed his glass into the soapy water and picked up a tea towel.

'Tess on an early today?' she asked.

Fletch shook his head as he'd done the last six times she'd asked. 'She's on a day off. She's having a lie-in.'

It had been hard for him, watching his mother's memory slowly regress. Worse for Trish who had done more of the hands-on caring over the last couple of years. That she'd remembered Ryan last night had been completely unexpected. And if she'd been in her right mind Fletch knew his mother would have been mortified by what she'd said.

He wished he knew what was going on inside her head. He wished he knew so he could fix it. But there were just some things that couldn't be fixed.

*He knew that better than most.*

He turned to put the glasses away in the cupboards behind him and he smiled at the little sticker that had a picture of a tumbler and had *glasses* written in neat black print. Thanks to Tess, nearly every single surface in his apartment bore labels—cupboards, light switches, electrical appliances. Her handiwork was everywhere.

*She* was everywhere.

In a short space of time she'd made such a huge difference—cupboards and drawers had symbols on them, labels above power points reminded Jean to turn the power off when she was finished with it. Tess had added to the book that Trish had instigated containing basic but important information like name, age, address, appointments, etc. A map and directions back to home had been included and Tess wrote in it each day what they were going to do so it had become a communication tool as well.

She'd bought Jean a journal and encouraged her to write down her thoughts and ideas, to use the book each day as a way to keep her mind exercised. She'd even made an appointment for Fletch at the family lawyer to review and update the legal and financial documents that he and Trish and Jean had put into place five years ago when his mother had first been diagnosed with Alzheimer's.

And then, of course, there was the dog.

There was no doubt about it—Tess had made herself indispensable. And his mother was more settled, more content than he'd seen her in a long time.

But her presence was a double-edged sword.

It reminded him of what he'd had. What had happened.

And how badly he'd screwed up.

Tess took some deep, cleansing breaths as she walked down the hallway to the lounge area. She could hear the clinking of dishes and Fletch and Jean chatting as she grew nearer, and it felt so domestic she wondered if she hadn't been caught in some kind of bizarre time warp.

The urge to pack up her things and return to her isolation on the other side of the world grew with each footstep closer. But she'd told Fletch she'd stay until after Trish's baby was born and she wouldn't go back on her word.

Fletch looked up as Tess appeared in the kitchen. She was wearing above-the-knee denim cut-offs and a tank top. Her hair was damp and spiky, her feet were bare and she wore no make-up.

She looked utterly gorgeous. A soothing sight for tired eyes. A decade ago he would have teased her about sleeping in. Hell, a decade ago he would have been right in bed beside her.

But their kiss from last night stood large between

them and he gave her a polite smile instead. 'Morning,' he murmured. She gave a wan nod in reply.

'Tess, don't you have an early today?' Jean asked as she squeezed out the dishcloth.

Tess shook her head. 'Not today.'

Fletch watched as she stood there looking awkward. 'Berry smoothie?' he asked.

She nodded. 'I can get it.'

Fletch was already halfway to the fridge. 'It's fine,' he dismissed. 'Why don't you go out to the deck and I'll bring it out to you?'

Tess acquiesced. She figured it was best to get the inevitable out of the way and try and move forward from the awkwardness of last night.

Bright sunshine enveloped her as she stepped outside and headed straight for the railing. She shut her eyes and turned her pale face to the source of the heat, revelling in it as if she were an unfurling flower. The hit of UV was so intoxicating she didn't hear Fletch approach a few moments later.

Fletch was engrossed by the image before him. Tess on his deck, her face raised to the sun in silent supplication. He wanted to stroke the ice-cold glass down her bare arm, drop a kiss against her nape. What had happened last night had changed things between them and despite her rejection of him, he still wanted to touch her.

'Here,' he murmured, holding out the glass to her from a safe distance.

Tess opened her eyes reluctantly. She'd forgotten how good it felt to be deep-down-in-your-bones warm.

'Thank you,' she said, taking the offering but avoiding his gaze.

Fletch took up position beside her but not too close. He leaned heavily against the rail, waiting for her to take a couple of sips before he said what he'd come out to say. 'I owe you an apology over last night.'

Tess shook her head, her gaze fixed on the river below. 'It's okay, Fletch.'

'No, it's not. I was rude.'

She shrugged. 'You were right.'

Fletch glanced at her sharply. He hadn't expected her to say that.

'I *was* using you,' she said, her eyes fixed on the wide expanse of the water below. 'Not intentionally… but deep down…'

Fletch looked at her for a long moment before glancing at the view below. Her candour vindicated him but it didn't make him feel any better. 'I'm sorry things got so out of hand, Tess. I wouldn't blame you if you wanted to turn tail and run.'

Tess looked up for the first time. 'I told you I'd stay until after Trish has the baby and I will.'

He glanced at her again and their gazes meshed. 'Thank you.'

Tess nodded. He looked so serious. So different from the smoky-eyed lover of last night.

'I was thinking…' he said. 'Mum seems settled now with Tabby for company. Maybe I should go back to the couch?'

Tess regarded him for a moment then looked away.

It was a sensible suggestion, given what had happened, but this thing wasn't about them. It was about Jean.

'She's still wandering, Fletch.'

'Not very often.'

'Yes, but you know how upset she became that night when she thought you and I were going to get divorced. I don't know about you, but I don't want her to have to go through that again—it's not good for her or her blood pressure. Actually…' Tess thought back to her own response to the distressing incident. 'It's not good for any of us.'

Fletch nodded. He knew what she was saying was right.

But…

'It would make things easier for us,' he pointed out.

Or him anyway. Sharing a bed with her had been hard enough without last night's little session playing like an erotic movie on slow-mo through his head.

And now he'd tasted her again? And realised he was as hot for her as he ever was? He wasn't sure he was capable of waking tangled up in her and not letting his natural urges take over.

Tess looked at him. 'It's not about us, Fletch.'

Fletch met her calm amber gaze. She was right, of course. But he wasn't so sure he could compartmentalise it as easily as she had.

She'd always been the expert in that department.

A few nights later Tess was woken again in the wee hours. Fortunately this time it was Fletch's pager and not his mother.

It had been a long time since she'd been woken by a pager. When they'd been married it had been a regular occurrence that had barely caused her to stir but all these years later it was disorientating for a moment.

'What's that noise?' Tess murmured as she groped through layers of sleep. The soft pillow beneath her head was warm and pliant and she snuggled into it farther.

Fletch was instantly awake. Tess's head was on his shoulder, her body curled into his, her hand on his belly dangerously close to a piece of his anatomy that had obviously been up for a while. 'Shh, it's okay,' he murmured. 'It's just my pager. Go back to sleep.'

He gently eased away from her as he reached for his pager, dislodging her hand and her head and her thigh crossed over his at the knee. He wished it was as easy to remove the lingering aroma of her hair in his nostrils and the warm imprint of her body against his. He pushed a button on the device and read the back-lit screen.

Displaced, Tess roused further. She frowned. 'You have a pager?'

'I'm on call for the study,' he explained quietly as he swung his legs over the side of the bed and his feet hit the floor. 'They need me to consent an admission. There's no one on that can do it.'

Only certain medical and nursing staff that'd done in-service on the study had been cleared to give consent. A large percentage of the staff across the two units had been trained up to ensure there was always someone on shift who could do it but occasionally it worked out that some shifts just weren't covered.

Tess yawned, her heavy eyes refusing to open. 'What time is it?' she asked as she tried to snuggle into her actual pillow, finding it nowhere near as comfortable.

'Two-thirty,' Fletch whispered as he stood. 'Go to sleep.'

No answer was forthcoming and he turned to look at her. She had taken his advice. The urge to lean over and drop a goodbye kiss on her mouth surprised him with its intensity. It was certainly what he would have done had they still been married.

But they weren't.

Twenty minutes later Fletch was walking into the PICU at St Rita's. He'd pulled on some jeans, thrown on a T-shirt, stuffed his feet into a pair of joggers and finger-combed his hair. He'd quickly brushed his teeth and ignored the fact that he needed a shave.

Time was of the essence where head injuries were concerned.

Every female staff member on the unit practically swooned as he entered. Any distraction from weariness was welcome at three a.m. and Fletch's particular brand of scruffy chic especially so.

'What have we got?' he asked Dr Joella Seaton, the registrar covering the night shift.

'Kyle Drayson. Eighteen-month-old immersion retrieved from Toowoomba area.'

She handed Fletch the chart and continued, unaware that Fletch had stopped listening.

'Incident occurred at a local swimming hole where the family were camping at just after midnight. He'd woken and wandered away from the camp site. Local ambulance arrived within twenty minutes of call. After an extended down time they got a rhythm. He was medivaced out. He's not quite three hours post-injury.'

Joella stopped talking and waited for Fletch to say something. He blinked when he realised they were standing outside room two and he hadn't been aware they'd been walking.

Of course. *Room two.*

'Dr King?'

Fletch looked blankly at Joella. What had she said? 'I'm sorry, Joella, go on.'

'Mum came in the chopper with him. She's obviously very distressed. She's currently with the on-call social worker.'

Fletch nodded as his demons prowled in front of the closed double doors. A glass window allowed him to see some of the activity as nurses scurried about, trying to stabilise the patient.

An eighteen-month-old patient. Who had nearly drowned.

Not a forty-year-old motorcyclist who'd been going too fast around a bend. Or a nineteen-year-old skateboarder who hadn't wanted to look uncool in a helmet. Or a sixty-year-old golfer who'd been smacked in the head with a flying ball.

A boy. A little boy.

And he had to go into the room. He had to go in and stand at the end of bed two and look at little Kyle who had nearly drowned. Just as he'd done with Ryan ten years ago.

As a doctor this time, not a father.

For a moment he doubted he could. Not this room. Not another eighteen-month-old boy.

His pulse roared in his ears. His gut felt as if it had tied itself into the mother of all knots. Right now he would have paid Joella every cent he owned not to.

But he believed in this study. He believed in thera-peutic hypothermia for acute brain injury. Had seen over and over how neuro-protective decreasing a pa-tient's body temperature could be. How it could reduce the harmful effects of ischemia by reducing the rate of cellular metabolism and therefore the body's need for oxygen. How it stabilised cell membranes. How it mod-erated intracranial pressure.

He believed he could give Kyle and kids like him— *kids like Ryan*—a better neurological outcome with a simple non-invasive therapy.

And to do that, he had to do his job.

He had to walk into room two and be a doctor.

Tess was getting back into bed from her dash to the loo when Fletch entered the bedroom a couple of hours after he'd left. She glanced at the clock. Four-thirty. There was a moment of awkwardness as their eyes briefly met but his gaze slipped quickly away and he barely acknowledged her before he headed for the bathroom.

'Did you get your consent?' she asked his back as it disappeared. She pulled the sheet up as the light went on in the bathroom. He didn't answer. In fact, she wasn't even sure he'd heard her.

'Yes.'

Tess turned her head towards the bathroom and for a brief moment caught his backlit haggard face before he snapped the light off.

She stifled a gasp. He looked like he'd aged ten years in a couple of hours.

Drawn, pinched, tense.

*Old.*

He looked like he had that day with Ryan.

She sat up. 'Are you okay?'

Fletch sank down on his side of the bed, his back to her. He shut his eyes for a moment, rubbed a hand through his hair. Kyle Drayson's face, his blond hair and green eyes so like Ryan's, seemed to be tattooed on the insides of his eyelids. He opened them, lifted the sheet and slipped under it.

'I'm fine,' he said, conscious of her face peering down at him.

Tess may have spent nine years apart from Fletch but she still knew him well enough to know that he wasn't fine. Knew that whatever he'd gone to see at work hadn't been pretty. She'd worked in ICU. She remembered too well those times when it was even too much for seasoned veterans.

And she'd been on the other side of the bed too. So had Fletch. Except he was still there, at the coal face.

*How did he do it?*

'Was it bad?'

Fletch sighed. 'I'm fine,' he repeated.

His voice was telling her to leave it alone but his utter wretchedness provoked her to push. 'Was it the kids or the adults?'

'The PICU.'

His terse reply put an itch up her spine. 'Do you… want to talk about it?'

Fletch shut his eyes. He wanted to do anything but. He wanted to be able to get in a time machine and erase the last few hours. He wanted to go back and stop Kyle from leaving his tent. Or further still. Stop Ryan from leaving the lounge room via a door Tess had been nagging him to fix.

'It might help,' she murmured, looking down into his tense face, his forehead scrunched, his lips flattened.

He snorted, his eyes flying open. 'Oh, and you would know that how?'

*How many times had he begged her to talk to him?*

Tess blinked at the flash of venom reflecting like a great orb in his silvery-green gaze. He was right. Psychological advice coming from her was hypocritical in the extreme. But something was very obviously wrong.

And she couldn't bear to see him so troubled.

She'd been blind to his torment a decade ago but she could see it with absolute clarity now.

'Forget it,' he said, flicking the covers back and vaulting upright. He swung his legs over the edge of the bed.

Tess frowned at the expanse of his back. 'Fletch?' She reached out a tentative hand and touched his shoulder. He flinched and her hand fell away. The rejection stung.

Fletch buried his face in his hands for a few moments, the spike of rage dissipating as fast as it had arrived. His hands dropped into his lap and his shoulders sagged. 'I'm sorry.'

Tess watched him for a moment, feeling utterly impotent in the face of his turmoil. She wished she had some words for him but she was at a loss.

'It was a little boy. Blond hair. Green eyes. Eighteen months old. An immersion. They'd put him in room two.'

The words fell like stones—like huge boulders, actually—into the silence. If Tess thought she'd been lost for words before, she was practically rendered mute now.

There were no words.

So she did the only thing she could think of. The only thing that felt right. She reached for his shoulder again. This time he didn't flinch. This time he covered her hand with one of his own.

She moved closer then. Parted her legs so his back fitted into her front, his bottom pressed into the place where her thighs joined, her legs bracketing his. She pressed her cheek against his T-shirt just below his shoulder blade. It smelled of detergent and sunshine and man.

She felt and heard the steady thump of his heartbeat. Found comfort in its slow, assured pulse.

She wasn't sure how long they sat there. All she knew was that when she whispered, 'Come on,' to him, he let her pull him back, let her draw him down until his head was resting on her chest, his ear over her own heartbeat, her arm around his shoulders.

'What's his name?' she asked after a while.

'Kyle.'

Tess ran the name around in her head for a moment. 'Did they give consent? His parents? For your study?'

Fletch nodded. 'The mother did.'

And because neither of them wanted to talk about Kyle or Ryan, she stroked his hair and asked him about the medicine. The medicine was safe. It was clinical. Unemotional. Free of baggage.

'Was he part of the treatment group or the control?'

'Treatment,' Fletch confirmed. 'They had the cooling blanket beneath him and were actively cooling him when I left.'

'What's the goal, temperature-wise?'

'We only want to induce moderate hypothermia for forty-eight hours.'

Tess shivered at the thought. She knew that freezing water would currently be running through the latex underblanket and that Kyle's skin would be icy to touch in a matter of hours. He would be oblivious, kept in an induced coma, but still the thought gave her chills and she was grateful for the heat of Fletch and his big arm encircling her waist.

'That's different from your earlier studies,' she murmured.

He turned his head to look up at her. 'You've read my studies?'

Tess allowed a ghost of a smile to touch her lips. 'I've read all your published stuff.'

Fletch was speechless for a moment. A hundred things to say crowded to his lips but he dismissed them all. He'd often wondered if she'd ever thought of him.

It was good to know she had.

Tess let him talk. Listened to the rumble of his voice as he told her about his earlier studies. About his experiences in Canada with cold-water immersions having better neurological outcomes than those he'd seen in Australia. How because of Ryan he'd developed a special interest in the subject, which had fast developed into an obsession.

And somehow hearing her son's name when they were both wrapped up together, keeping their demons at bay, didn't seem so gut-wrenching.

The irony of it all wasn't lost on her. Not even at five in the morning after another disrupted night.

Why had it taken her ten years to comfort him?

This was what he'd needed, what he'd asked for so many times in so many ways, and she'd denied him because she just hadn't been capable.

When he'd needed her most, she'd pushed him away.

She should have been there for him more.

She'd failed Fletch as well as Ryan.

# CHAPTER EIGHT

Two weeks later Tess was in the middle of a lesson in making royal icing flowers when the phone rang. She reached across to the nearby wall where it was hanging and plucked it off the cradle, all without taking her eyes off the deft precision of Jean's wrinkled fingers as they created sweet perfection.

Tabby lay at their feet, ready for any morsel that inadvertently landed on the floor, and Tess absently stroked the dog's back with her foot as she said, 'Tess speaking.'

Jean held up a perfectly formed miniature rose for her approval and Tess grinned and silently applauded.

'Oh...hi, it's Trish. How are you?'

Tess heard the disappointment in her ex-sister-in-law's voice. She'd spoken to Trish a few times on the phone since the day they'd turned up with Christopher, just a quick hello and goodbye as she'd handed the phone to Jean or Fletch. But she knew that Trish rang religiously every day to speak to her mother.

'You want to talk to Jean?'

'No. I was hoping to speak to Fletch, actually. Is he there?'

Tess shook her head, even though Trish couldn't see her. 'He's at the hospital at the moment.'

'Oh…do you know when he'll be home?'

There was more than disappointment in Trish's voice. There was something else. Worry?

'Not till about five. They've had quite a few study enrolments the last couple of weeks so he's got a bit to catch up on.'

'Right. Damn it.'

'Is there something wrong, Trish?'

'I was hoping he could watch Christopher for me for a couple of hours. I have an appointment for my thirty-two-week scan. Normally I'd take Christopher but he's unwell at the moment. Doctor says it's a virus, but he's totally miserable so I don't want to drag him from pillar to post. And I can't leave a sick child with any of my friends—they all have kids. It's fine, Doug will just have to stay home and look after him instead of coming to the scan with me.'

Tess remembered how Fletch had been there at all her scans. How he'd revelled in the experience as much as she had. How it had bonded them even closer when they'd been able to share the images of their unborn son together, watch his little heart beat, his perfect little limbs kicking away like crazy.

'What about Doug's mother?' Tess asked.

'She's up north, visiting relatives.'

And they both knew Jean wasn't capable. 'Could you reschedule?'

'They've already squeezed me in on a cancellation. My obstetrician is always booked to the eyeballs.'

Tess felt an encroaching dread as she contemplated the right thing to do. Back in the old days she wouldn't have hesitated to offer her services. But the mere thought of looking after Christopher terrified her.

'Doug won't mind,' Trish assured her. 'He's pretty easygoing.'

Tess hated the awkwardness between them now. That Trish wasn't even asking her. That she was obviously trying to reassure her. Once upon a time Trish would have just asked, secure in the knowledge that Tess would say yes.

She shut her eyes, knowing she couldn't let Doug miss out on this experience when she was perfectly capable of looking after a small child. 'I...I can do it.'

Her voice quavered, her heart pounded, but she'd offered.

Silence greeted her from the other end. Then, 'Oh, Tess... It's fine, you don't have to do that...'

Tess shook her head. 'Doug shouldn't miss out on this, Trish.' More silence. 'Of course I'd understand if you preferred I didn't.'

There was silence on the other end again for a long time and Tess wondered if Trish had hung up. *God, Trish really didn't want her looking after Christopher.* And as much as she didn't want to do it either, it hurt.

'Look, it doesn't matter,' Tess said, gripping the phone hard. 'It was just a thought. Forget it. I know my track record's not...'

She couldn't finish. She couldn't say that the last little boy she'd been left in charge of had drowned.

'What? Oh, Tess, no! I'm sorry, I was just thinking. Christopher doesn't really know you, that's all. It's not about… I didn't mean to…'

Trish fell silent and Tess heard a long, deep sigh.

'I don't blame you, Tess…for what happened to Ryan.' Trish's voice was husky with sincerity. 'No one has ever blamed you. Not Mum. Not me or Doug. And certainly not Fletch.'

'I know.'

And she did know. But what Trish and Jean and Fletch didn't realise was that no matter what they thought, no matter how much time passed, she would *always* blame herself.

'I would very much appreciate it if you could watch Christopher for me, Tess. It would be a big help.'

Tess felt a thunk in her chest and had the insane urge to take the offer back. But it was out there now and Trish's voice was suddenly unburdened of the worry and disappointment that had been present at the beginning of the conversation.

And it meant something that Trish had faith in her.

'What time's the appointment?' she asked.

'In an hour. Do you mind me asking if you and Mum could come here? He's asleep now and I'm pretty sure he's going to be out to it for the afternoon—I'd rather not disturb him. Tell you what, why don't I take Mum with us to the scan? That way it'll be just you and Christopher and Mum will get to see her grandchild.

Not that she'll remember.' The husky note had crept back into Trish's voice.

'I'm so sorry, Trish. It's hard to watch, isn't it?'

'The worst,' Trish agreed. 'She was such a great grandmother, wasn't she? It's awful that my kids are never going to know that. They'll only know the shell she's going to become.'

Tess thought back to how wonderful the older woman had been with Ryan. How the two of them had been practically inseparable. How he'd hung on her every word and Jean had declared him the most loveable child on the planet.

*No bias, of course.*

'But you'll keep the real her alive for them, Trish. You and Fletch. You'll tell them all about the wonderful, smart, kind, funny person she was and how very, very much she loves them. That person's always going to live inside you.'

'I know,' Trish murmured. 'Sorry. It just gets to me on some days more than others. I blame the hormones.'

Trish laughed and Tess joined in. It wasn't very jolly laughter but it broke the maudlin conversation.

'We'll be half an hour,' Tess said.

'Perfect.'

Tess hung up the phone and looked at Jean and the small pile of white sugar flowers on the bench top. 'Let's go and visit Trish,' she said.

'Oh, yes,' Jean said, her eyes sparkling. 'Yes, please.'

Tess was nervous as she and Jean walked up the stairs of Trish and Doug's massive, beautifully renovated Old

Queenslander. Not even the warm welcome of the big, wide wraparound verandas helped to quell the low-level nausea that had afflicted her ever since she'd bundled Jean into the car.

But they were here now and then Trish was opening the front door and ushering them inside. She followed them down the hallway past rooms that Tess assumed to be bedrooms running off either side and into a large lounge with soaring ceilings. A dining room and kitchen spilled off the edges in a very open-plan arrangement.

'Wow. This is beautiful,' Tess commented as the warm honey of the polished floorboards and the rich tapestry of Middle-Eastern rugs attracted her attention.

Trish smiled. 'Thanks. It's been a labour of love.'

Tess remembered the cottage that she and Fletch had been renovating together and understood the pride and accomplishment on Trish's face.

'So, Christopher is asleep on the lounge. I've just given him something for the fever.' Trish half turned and indicated the little sleeping figure on the lounge chair behind her.

Tess looked over but kept her distance. Christopher was wearing just a nappy and lying on a sheet that had been tucked into the lounge cushions. A ceiling fan directly overhead blew a cool breeze downwards, ruffling white-blond hair with two little cowlicks.

Trish padded towards her son and gently stroked his forehead. She grimaced at the fine red rash sprinkling his torso. 'The doctor assures me the rash is a post-viral thing.'

Tess nodded absently. He looked so still. An image

of Ryan in PICU popped into her head—so still and pale—and for a second Tess wasn't sure she could do it.

Then Trish turned to her and smiled. 'Thanks so much for doing this, Tess.' Her hand stroked her belly. 'It means so much to Doug and me.'

Tess smiled and assured her it was fine.

She handed Tess a piece of paper. 'Mobile numbers. Mine and Doug's. Just, you know…if you need to know where the pickles are or something.' She smiled at Tess then crossed into the kitchen. 'He can have a drink of water and a cup of milk if he wakes up and if he's hungry I've made up a couple of different things to tempt him in the fridge too—he's been off his food.'

Trish opened the fridge and indicated the stacked tower of plastic containers that looked like they could feed a small nation.

'Thanks. I'll try him if he wakes.'

Doug, who had entered the kitchen, rolled his eyes at Tess. 'Is she showing you the food she prepared for the masses?'

The knot of nervous tension eased slightly at Doug's teasing and Tess even laughed.

'We have to go, darling,' he reminded his wife, his arm slipping around Trish's non-existent waist.

Trish looked over at her son and Tess could tell that leaving him when he was sick was a real wrench for her. She remembered how that felt.

'Okay, let's go,' Trish murmured. 'Mum?'

Jean had found a little jug and was watering Trish's indoor plants. 'Yes, dear?'

'Let's go,' she said.

Jean smiled at her daughter. Then she frowned. 'Where are we going?'

'To the hospital. For the scan.' Trish patted her big round belly.

'Oh, yes,' Jean said. 'Splendid. We can drop Tess at work for her shift while we're at it.'

Tess smiled at Jean. 'I've got a day off today so I'm going to stay and look after Christopher.'

Jean looked down at her sleeping grandson. She frowned and looked up at Tess, perplexed. 'What a sweet boy,' she said vaguely.

Trish sighed. 'C'mon, Mum,' she murmured, laying a gentle hand beneath her mother's elbow and ushering her along. She smiled at Tess. 'See you in a couple of hours.'

Tess nodded, then the door closed behind them and then it was just her.

And Christopher.

Tess sat on the edge of the couch opposite Christopher. She felt awkward at first, desperately looking around the room at anything and everything other than him. Art on the walls. A DVD collection. Some bookshelves.

A set of open French doors led out onto a massive deck. Tess could see a tangle of wild, lush greenery from this vantage point and suddenly wished she was out there, digging in Trish's garden, not in here, looking after her most treasured possession.

But she daren't leave him. He looked so still and pale.

She sat back and pulled a book out of her handbag,

determined to distract herself with Fletch's crime novel, which she still hadn't managed to finish.

Or would try to, at least.

But inevitably her gaze was drawn to the sleeping cherub. His little bow mouth, so like Ryan's, clutched at her heart. She dropped her gaze to focus on his chest, watching for the barely perceptible rise and fall, felt the hot spurt of panic as an occasional respiratory pause delayed the onset of the next breath.

Tess shook herself as she realised she was counting Christopher's breaths.

She returned her attention to the book with renewed vigour and for twenty minutes, apart from the odd sneak peek, she managed it. The story finally pulled her in and the only sounds breaking the silence were the fan whirring overhead, magpies warbling in the back yard and the rustle of paper as she turned a page.

Then Christopher stirred. Then he woke and sat up. He took one look at Tess and his bottom lip dropped, his forehead wrinkled.

'Mumma, Mumma,' he called, looking around wildly for Trish.

Tess's heart banged noisily against her ribs as she stood to comfort the child who, for all intents and purposes, was her nephew. 'It's okay, Christopher,' she crooned, approaching him slowly as he started to cry. 'Mummy and Daddy will be home very soon.'

She sat down beside him and he cried louder.

'I know, honey, I know. You're not feeling well, you just want your mummy.' She put her arm tentatively around his skinny little shoulders. They were warm beneath her cool palm. 'She'll be here really soon.'

Then Christopher really lost it. He screwed his face up, which went as red as the rash covering his body, and howled for all he was worth. Within seconds his eyes were streaming and his nose was running and he'd shrugged her hand away.

The poor little guy looked utterly miserable.

She suddenly understood Trish's earlier reticence as the crying child made her feel completely inadequate. Christopher didn't know her. So how could she console him properly? Mild panic set in at the thought that he might cry for the entire time Trish and Doug were away.

*No. Think, Tess.*

*Think!*

She'd been a paediatric nurse, for crying out loud. And a mother!

Yes. What would she have done if this had been Ryan? The problem was she'd fought so hard not to think about her son over the years it was as if all that basic maternal intuition had also been suppressed.

*Come on, Tess, think!*

Distraction.

Yes, distraction.

'Would you like a drink, sweetie?' she asked over the din.

Christopher showed no sign that he'd even heard the question so Tess hurried to the kitchen and retrieved the two plastic sippy cups from the fridge. She sat back down again and offered them to Christopher.

He pushed them both away. 'Are you sure?' Tess asked, offering them again.

Christopher looked at them, then at her, then back at them as his crying died down. He looked at her with red eyes and pointed to the milk. Tess smiled at him and handed it over. He took it on a shuddery indrawn breath and drank half the cup without pause.

'Good boy,' Tess murmured. 'More?'

Christopher went again, slower this time, his huge green eyes never leaving her face. When he'd finished he thrust the cup back at her.

'Are you hungry? Would you like something to eat?'

Christopher shook his head then pointed to the stack of books sitting on the nearby coffee table.

Tess smothered a smile. Christopher obviously knew what he wanted. Ryan had been like that too.

Fletch had called it stubborn. She'd called it decisive.

'You want me to read to you?' He nodded and she picked up the first book. 'This one?' she asked. He shook his head. He shook it four times before one met with his approval. 'You like cars?' she asked as she opened the book.

'Car, car,' Christopher said, nodding his head.

So Tess read it to him. On the first read-through he sat upright beside her, his little legs out in front of him, his ankles just dangling over the edge of the couch cushion. The next time he leaned in closer so his side was jammed against hers. By the third read he'd climbed into her lap.

Tess froze as he snuggled down, making himself at home. She hadn't held a child in a decade and it felt so bitter-sweet. Looking down on his blond head, she had a feeling of déjà vu, like holding Ryan all over again.

She pressed her nose to his hair, feeling the fine down that stuck up at the crown tickle her nose as she inhaled deeply. The sweet little-boy smell lodged in her throat and when he turned his face up to look at her, unshed tears shone in her eyes.

'Car,' he prompted, one little pudgy finger pointing at the words.

Tess bit down on her lip. 'Car,' she murmured, swallowing hard against all the emotion and memories.

Eventually Christopher allowed her to read some other books but after about half an hour he started to feel very warm against her and started to grizzle. Tess felt his forehead.

'Gosh,' she murmured, 'you're burning up.'

She laid him on the lounge and reached for the tympanic thermometer that was also sitting on the coffee table. Christopher lay docilely as she inserted it into his ear canal and waited for it to beep. She read the display and was shocked to see his fever had spiked rapidly—no wonder he was lethargic and looking miserable again.

Trish had said she'd just given him something for the fever before she'd left so that was out as an option to bring the temperature down. Maybe a tepid sponge would help and also be soothing for Christopher.

'It's okay, sweetie. Tess is going to get you something nice and cool. Won't be a moment.'

Tess looked over her shoulder as she scurried towards the kitchen. Christopher lay quietly on the cushion, his gaze tracking her movements. In less than a minute she'd found a glass bowl in a cupboard and filled it with lukewarm water. Under the sink she'd located an unopened packet of dishcloths.

Christopher hadn't moved as she hurried towards him but he was staring now, his gaze not fixed any more. He looked out of it and an itch prickled at the bottom of her spine. She was two paces from him when he let out a little cry and his limbs stiffened.

Tess gasped and dropped the bowl, water spreading over the floorboards, soaking into the rug, as Christopher went into a full-blown seizure.

Tess lunged for the lounge. 'Christopher? Christopher!' she shouted as she threw herself down next to him.

His little body twitched and jerked and her brain came to a complete standstill as terror rendered her utterly useless.

'Christopher,' she whimpered again, not even game to touch him.

*Oh, God, oh, God, oh, God!*
*Don't die, don't die, don't die.*

She watched in horror, completely paralysed. She couldn't think what to do. She didn't know how to make him stop.

Some latent part of her brain was screaming at her and it finally made itself heard.

*Ambulance.*

Tess picked up her phone that she'd put on the coffee table earlier and with useless, trembling fingers somehow managed to dial three zeros. A voice she could barely hear over the roar of her pulse in her head asked her if she wanted police, fire or ambulance, and she knew she was yelling but she just couldn't stop. 'Ambulance, ambulance, ambulance.'

She tried not to think about another time, another call she'd made to triple zero. She'd been an incoherent mess then too.

Another voice came on seconds later. 'I need an ambulance now!' she told the voice frantically. 'My nephew is having a seizure.'

The soothing female voice asked her name and the address. For an awful moment Tess couldn't even remember the number of Trish's house—she just knew which one it was in the street as it had been so long since she'd needed to know. But in a blinding flash she remembered.

'Number sixteen,' she panted. 'Please, please, hurry, you must hurry. He's still fitting.'

The voice told her a car had already been dispatched with lights and sirens but it didn't reassure her. Tess looked down at Christopher, whose stiff, jerky movements continued unabated. How long had it been? Too long. It felt like for ever.

His lips lost their pinkness and Tess wailed into the phone, 'His lips are turning blue.'

'Okay, here's what I want you to do...'

Somehow Tess managed to follow the instructions from the emergency call-taker. Quite how, she wasn't sure. Her fingers were shaking, the roar in her head made it almost impossible to hear and she wanted to throw up. But putting Christopher on the floor and turn-

ing him on his side improved his colour even if it didn't
stop the seizure.

*All stuff that Tess knew but was too panicked to do
herself.*

'Why isn't it stopping?' she demanded of the woman
who had assured Tess repeatedly that she would stay
on the phone with her until the ambulance arrived. 'It
should be stopped by now.'

As if speaking it had made it so, the jerking reduced to twitching and then stopped altogether. 'It's
stopped,' Tess announced victoriously into the phone.
'It's stopped.'

'Okay, that's good,' the calm voice continued in her
ear. 'Keep him on his side. He'll be very sleepy for a
while. The ambulance is about a minute out.'

Suddenly Tess heard a siren. 'I can hear it!' Her insides practically went to water at the relief that coursed
through her system.

'Okay, I'm going to go now. Go and open the door
for the paramedics.'

Tess nodded. 'Thank you,' she gasped. 'Thank you
so much.' The connection had been momentary but in
those awful minutes the stranger's voice had been a
lifeline.

Tess pushed the 'end' button then hurried to the front
door to greet the paramedics coming in through the
front gate.

'This way,' she said. 'The seizure's just stopped.'

The paramedics greeted her as they crossed to a
limp-looking Christopher lying on his side on the beau-

tiful Turkish carpet that Tess had admired when she'd first arrived.

It seemed like an age ago now.

They knelt beside him, one in a puddle of water, and Tess apologised profusely. He smiled at her. 'It's okay, it'll dry,' he assured her.

They were hooking Christopher up to a monitor and trying to rouse him when he cried out again, his little limbs stiffening for the second time. 'He's going again,' the female paramedic said.

Tess clamped a hand over her mouth to muffle her wail as she looked on in abject terror. The paramedic kneeling in the water spoke into his radio. 'This is one five three. About to administer midazolam. ETA on the ICP.'

Tess couldn't watch. She just couldn't watch. She needed...she needed Fletch. And, oh, God, she had to tell Trish!

How was she going to tell Trish?

Fletch would tell her. Fletch would know what to do.

She grabbed for her phone as the paramedics worked on Christopher. She turned her back, walked out to the front veranda. She couldn't look. She just couldn't. And he was in better hands with them than he had been with her.

She'd been utterly useless.

She dialled Fletch's number, her hands shaking so hard she had to try three times before she was success-ful. It went to voice mail. 'Fletch, it's Tess. You need to ring me urgently. Urgently!'

If she'd been in her right mind she wouldn't have left

such an alarming message. Or the five more that followed. But she wasn't.

Another ambulance pulled up and a single paramedic raced into the house. Tess heard them say that Christopher had stopped breathing. That they were going to have to intubate.

A terrible foreboding settled over her. Déjà vu. Ryan all over again.

*God! Where was Fletch?*

She dialled his number again. 'Fletch! Damn it, ring me!'

She walked back in the house. Christopher had stopped seizing but they had a mask over his face and were puffing air into his lungs. The female paramedic was inserting an IV. The newcomer paramedic looked up at her standing by the door.

'He's stopped breathing. It's probably the drug we used to stop him fitting. It happens sometimes. We're going to put a tube into his lungs to help him breathe.'

Tess nodded. She knew all this, had seen it a hundred times. But this was Ryan.

No. No, wait. She blinked. *Christopher.* It was Christopher.

'Just hurry,' she urged, standing by the door her hands curled into fists. 'Hurry!'

Tess couldn't look away now. She sank to the floor and watched while they put a tube down Christopher's throat, exactly like they'd done with Ryan. Her heart was banging so loudly her whole body seemed to bob to its rhythm. She could hear the blip, blip, blip of Christopher's heart rate on the monitor and almost collapsed on the floor when the intensive care paramedic announced, 'I'm in. Let's get this tube secured so we can scoop and go.'

In five minutes they had Christopher on a trolley and were heading out the door. 'We're taking him to St Rita's. Do you want to come with us in the ambulance?' the female paramedic asked.

Tess wanted to shake her head. Christopher was in safe hands and she wanted to run away. Go straight to the airport and get a ticket back to the UK. Her head felt like it was about to explode. Her heart was being ripped to shreds in her chest.

But she couldn't leave him. He looked small and pale and fragile dwarfed by all the medical equipment and she couldn't leave him alone. She nodded and followed them in a daze. She didn't take her bag or even shut the front door.

Tess sat in the front seat as the ambulance sped away from the kerb, lights and siren on. The intensive care paramedic and the female paramedic—they'd told her their names but she couldn't remember them—were in the back, tending to Christopher.

Her phone rang and the sudden noise was so startling she stared at it for a moment, trying to remember what it was. Fletch's name was flashing on the screen as Tess looked at it and suddenly she realised what she was holding and relief washed through her like a raging tsunami. She pushed the answer button in a rush.

'Fletch?'

'What's wrong?' he asked, his voice frantic after

eight missed calls from Tess with increasingly alarming messages. 'Is it Mum?'

It took a moment for Tess to figure out why Fletch would think something was up with Jean. But, of course, he hadn't known of her plans to look after his nephew. 'No. It's Christopher.'

'Christopher?'

'It's a long story,' she said, suddenly so strung out from an excess of adrenaline she just wanted to curl up in a foetal position somewhere and rock.

'Is that a siren?' Fletch demanded.

Tess ignored him. 'I've been looking after him for a couple of hours while Trish went for her scan. He had a…a convulsion. They gave him midaz… He stopped breathing. They…they t-tubed him, Fletch. We're in an ambulance on our way to St Rita's.'

She swallowed hard as a lump of emotion bigger than the iceberg that sank the Titanic lodged in her throat. 'I'm scared, Fletch.'

Fletch gripped the phone, trying to assimilate what Tess was telling him. She sounded close to hysteria and he shut his eyes, knowing that whatever had happened today Tess wasn't emotionally equipped to deal with it.

'It's going to be okay, Tess,' he assured her, even though he had absolutely no idea what the hell was going on. 'I'm coming downstairs,' he said, already abandoning the computer work he'd been doing and striding out of the unit. 'I'll be waiting for you when you pull in.'

Tess could feel the tight control she'd been keeping

in place slowly unravel as Fletch's calm, soothing voice spoke assurances into her ear.

'Promise?' she demanded. 'Promise you'll be there?'

'I promise.' He paused for a moment. 'Are you okay, Tess?'

Tess shook her head. She was about as far from okay as was physically possible. 'No. But as long as you're there, I will be.' She was surprised to realise just how true that was.

'I'll be there.'

Tess had never heard three more beautiful words in her life.

# CHAPTER NINE

FLETCH drummed his fingers impatiently against his thigh as he stood in the ambulance bay, listening to the urgent wail of a siren draw closer and closer.

*It couldn't get here soon enough.*

His gut churned as worry about Tess's state of mind warred with his fear for Christopher.

What exactly had happened?

He'd left for work a few hours ago and Tess and Jean had been planning on doing some baking, and now he was standing outside the emergency department, waiting for his intubated nephew to arrive in the back of an ambulance with a frantic Tess in tow.

He should have known things had been going too well lately. His mother was content, the study was running smoothly and things with he and Tess were finally...easy.

It was a subtle difference, probably not noticeable to anyone else especially as, from the outside, he doubted anyone would have even noticed that things *hadn't been* easy.

It was just a feeling between them.

Ever since she'd comforted him that night, things had changed between them. The awkwardness that had been there since she'd come back to live with him, which had been exacerbated by the kiss and which they'd ploughed through every day to keep things as normal as possible for Jean, had dissipated.

In all the small ways it felt just like they were married again. Finding mango ice cream in the freezer, putting toothpaste on her toothbrush when he brushed his teeth just like he used to do, a shared memory making them smile.

Even going to bed at night, which had been fraught with anxiety for him, had changed. He didn't wait now for her to be asleep before he came in or get up before she woke. They just got into bed together and went to sleep. Sometimes they talked a bit about their day or discussed Jean, other times they read companionably or she read while he worked on his laptop, but the apprehension was gone.

Or at least it had been.

The siren almost upon him, a portent of doom if ever he'd heard one, was a sign that the dynamic had shifted again. And whatever ground they'd gained was about to be lost.

*Maybe for ever.*

The siren was killed as the ambulance screamed into the bay. A paramedic jumped from the vehicle and hurried to the back doors, a doctor and a nurse from Emergency joining him there. Fletch headed straight for the front passenger door and opened it. A pale-faced Tess looked down at him with a dazed expression.

'Tess!'

Relief stormed his system. He'd been half-crazy, listening to those increasingly desperate messages. He'd expected her to be a hysterical mess, like she'd been that day with Ryan. Seeing her dry-eyed and relatively calm was a miracle.

It shouldn't be—this was classic Tess after all. Stoic. Controlled. Keeping it all together.

But what she'd just been through would have shaken anyone. Especially someone who'd already been through something this terrible before.

'Are you okay?' he asked as he held out his hand to help her down.

'I don't know what happened,' she said, shaking her head at him as her feet touched the ground. 'He just started fitting.'

Her frightened, confused face grabbed at his gut and an overwhelming urge to protect her coursed through him. He swept her into arms and kissed the top of her head. 'It's fine. He's going to be fine.'

Tess sagged against him, absorbing the heat and the solidity of him. Remembering how good it always felt, how right. 'I didn't know what I was supposed to do, Fletch. I was useless.'

Fletch pulled away slightly, grasping her upper arms, and put his face close to hers so he could make sure she understood what he was about to say. 'You called the ambulance, didn't you?' She nodded, and he acknowledged it with a brisk nod of his own. 'That's what you were supposed to do.'

Tess bit her lip. *She would not cry.* She wouldn't.

'I was so scared it was like…it was like Ryan. All I could see was Ryan lying there. Ryan's blond hair. Ryan's blue lips.'

Fletch pulled her in close again as those images, never far away, rolled through his mind. He'd give anything at this moment to have erased what she'd just been through. No one should have to go through something so shocking twice.

'I'm sorry you had to go through that, Tess. I'm so sorry. But you did good. Trish couldn't have left Ryan in safer hands.'

Tess pulled away from him on a gasp. 'Oh, God, Fletch. Trish! I haven't… I couldn't call her. She doesn't know yet.'

Fletch nodded, already dreading that conversation. 'It's okay, I'll call her. Let's go inside and find out what's happening then I'll call her, okay?'

'Okay.'

She followed him in on autopilot. Into the resus bay where staff swarmed around Christopher, loading him with anti-epileptic drugs and putting in another IV. It looked like chaos but Tess knew that everyone there had a job and that their teamwork would get Christopher through.

Still, she found it hard to breathe. Resus looked the same as it had ten years ago when they'd brought Ryan here, and she couldn't stand it. Flashbacks flared in her head as a doctor fired questions at her just like they had with Ryan.

*Yes, a virus. No, she didn't know how long he'd been unwell for. No, she didn't know if he'd ever had a febrile*

*convulsion before. Fletch thought not. Yes, his temp
had spiked. No, she didn't know how long he'd had the
rash for or how many wet nappies he'd had that day.*

They went on and on until there was a roaring so
loud in her ears she could barely hear them. She turned
to Fletch, who was talking to a colleague, and tugged
on his sleeve. 'I can't stay here,' she said. 'I can't…do
this. Get me…get me out of here.'

Fletch saw the shadows in her eyes and the tautness
around her mouth. 'Come on,' he said, putting his arm
around her.

He led her outside. 'Margie, can I use your office?'
he asked a middle-aged matronly woman in a nurse's
uniform striding by.

Margie narrowed her eyes for a moment but Tess
could only assume she must have looked close to a nervous breakdown because the woman didn't hesitate.
'First on the left at the end of the corridor,' she said
briskly.

Fletch made a beeline for the office and had Tess en-
sconced in a chair in twenty seconds flat. He crouched
in front of her. 'The consultant thinks it's just fever re-
lated and that Christopher decided not to breathe properly after the midaz dose. They're going to wait for him
to wake up and then pull the tube.' He placed a hand
on her knee and gave it a squeeze. 'He's going to be
fine, Tess.'

She nodded. She'd heard the consultant telling Fletch
as much. It was just taking a little while to work through
the soup that her brain had become.

Fletch frowned. He'd thought she'd be over the moon at the news. 'Tess?'

'Yes.' She nodded. 'I know. That's great.' She smiled at him. 'Really great. It's just a lot to…absorb, you know?'

Yes, he did know. And she was in shock, which probably made it that much harder. 'I'm going to call Trish. Will you be all right in here?'

Tess nodded vigorously. 'Of course. Go, call your sister.' She consulted her watch. 'They must be on their way home by now.'

He was back in ten minutes and Tess looked at him expectantly. 'How is she?'

He shoved his fingers through his hair. 'Pretty frantic. They've just got out of the scan. They're coming straight here. They're only five minutes away.'

Five minutes but Tess knew it would feel like an age to Trish. She knew intimately how her sister-in-law would be feeling. The lead in her belly, the tightness in her chest, the rampant fear knotting every muscle.

The if-onlys.

*If only I'd been there. If only I'd cancelled the scan today. If only I'd taken him to the hospital for a second opinion.*

Fletch sat beside her and Tess looked at him. 'What are you doing?' she asked.

'I'll wait with you until they get here,' he said.

Tess shook her head. 'No.' She pushed his arm, urging him to get up. 'You can't leave him in there by himself, Fletch.'

'He's surrounded by people, Tess.'

Fletch knew his nephew was in good hands but he didn't have a clue what was going on in Tess's head. He could do nothing for Christopher now—he was being taken care of by experts.

But he could be here for Tess.

She shook her head vigorously. 'Not by people who love him. He's so small, Fletch. He looks so tiny and fragile surrounded by all that…stuff.' She pushed at his arm again. 'You have to be there with him. Don't let him be alone.'

Fletch didn't dare argue. She was breathing hard and there were two bright red spots high on her spare cheekbones. She hadn't wanted to leave Ryan alone either. Not even after he'd been declared dead. She'd sat for ages and just held his hand.

'Okay, Tess,' he said quietly as he stood. 'It's okay, I will. I'll be with him until Trish arrives. Apparently they have Mum…' In all the drama Fletch had temporarily forgotten about his mother. 'So I'll bring her back here to be with you if you don't mind?'

Tess nodded. 'Of course. Just go,' she urged again.

Tess checked her watch every minute for the next fifteen as the four walls pushed in on her. She read the posters for hand washing and a couple of anti-violence ones designed to warn emergency department patients that violence against staff would not be tolerated.

A wall-mounted bookshelf was crammed with thick, heavy textbooks. Some had fallen over and others were leaning drunkenly against each other. The desk was controlled chaos with a lot of paper and a computer displaying a screensaver.

A cork board behind the door had postcards and work photos tacked to it. Smiling nurses and doctors snapped in the middle of their jobs or temporarily acting the fool for the lens.

It looked like a happy work place. Where people liked each other and got along.

But how anybody could deal with the kind of things that came through those doors, things like Christopher—and Ryan—and stay as normal as the snaps suggested was beyond Tess.

They all deserved medals.

*Or to have their heads read.*

Fletch appeared in the doorway with a worried-looking Jean and a red-eyed Trish. 'Here's Tess,' he said to his mother, injecting a light note into his tone.

'Oh, Tess, there you are.' Jean's voice was light with relief. 'I don't know why we're at the hospital, do you?'

Tess smiled reassuringly at her then looked over Fletch's shoulder to a devastated Trish. She looked like she was close to collapse and it was only Fletch's arm around her waist that was holding her up.

'It's okay, Jean,' Tess said, focusing back on her mother-in-law. 'I'm going to take you home. I think Tabby needs to be walked.'

'Oh, goodness, yes!'

'Just have a seat here for a sec,' Tess said, helping Jean into the chair, 'And we'll be on our way in a jiffy.'

Jean sat down with minimum fuss, which left Tess facing Trish. It was like looking in a mirror. 'How's he doing?' she asked.

'Oh, Tess,' Trish wailed, her face crumpling as she pulled Tess into her arms and gave her a fierce squeeze. 'He looks so small.'

Tess stared over Trish's shoulder at Fletch as his sister purged her emotions. 'I'm sorry,' Tess murmured, hugging her tight. 'I'm so sorry.'

'No,' Trish said, pulling back and wiping at her tears with the backs of her hands. 'This is not your fault, Tess. It was a febrile convulsion. I need to thank you. Thank you for being there. I would have been completely useless.'

Tess shook her head. 'I just called the ambulance.'

Trish nodded. 'Exactly.' She pulled a tissue out of her pocket and blew her nose. 'I know this can't have been easy for you today, Tess. Looking after Christopher was a huge step for you and then to have this happen... it must have bought up a lot of stuff with Ryan that I know you don't like to think about.'

Tess froze at the mention of her son. She'd been trying so hard not to think of him during this whole ordeal but the very essence of him was building inside her, demanding to be let out, and she just couldn't let it.

'It's fine,' she dismissed quickly.

She didn't want to get into this. Not now. Not ever.

Trish shook her head. 'I don't think I could survive if something happened to Christopher. I don't know how you've managed, Tess.'

Tess looked over Trish's shoulder at a grim-looking Fletch. 'Some would say I haven't managed very well at all.'

'Then they don't know what it's like, do they?'

Tess glanced back at her sister-in-law. 'No, they don't.'

Trish sniffled and wiped her nose with the tissue again. 'I have to go…I have to get back to Christopher. Doug's not very good in hospitals. They're transferring Christopher to the PICU where they're hoping they'll be able to take the tube out in a couple of hours.'

Tess nodded. 'Best place for him. Give him a kiss for me.'

'Do you want to… Do you want to come and see him?'

Tess recoiled from the suggestion. Circumstances had dictated that she be part of this nightmare scenario but now it was over, she just wanted to put it away in the same place she put her Ryan stuff.

Deep down and out of reach.

Besides, Jean was getting restless, pacing around the small office and anxiously asking every ten seconds when they could leave.

'Ah, no. I'm going to get Jean home. I think the stress of this environment is increasing her anxiety level and you guys just need to be able to think about Christopher today.'

Trish nodded. 'Take our car,' she said as she reached into her handbag for her set of keys. 'It's parked in the two-minute emergency parking and needs shifting any-way, and it's not like we're going anywhere soon.'

'Thanks,' Tess said, taking the keys.

'I'll follow shortly,' Fletch said.

Tess shook her head. 'No, Fletch, you need to stay with Trish—she needs you now. So does Doug.'

It was such a cowardly thing to set him up for. She couldn't bear to do it herself so she was putting it on him when she knew it had to be just as difficult for Fletch to go into the PICU—as a relative, not a doctor—and sit with his sister while she watched a machine breathe for her little boy.

A little boy that looked remarkably like his own little boy.

It was cowardly to ask him to have to relive the whole nightmare of Ryan again while she fled to the safety of home.

But Trish and Doug shouldn't go through it by themselves either, not when they had someone with a wealth of ICU experience in the family. Not when they'd been such a tower of strength to her and Fletch a decade before.

Trish needed her brother now.

And, yes, she probably needed Tess now too, but Tess had given all she could.

'I'd like you to stay, Fletch,' Trish whispered. 'I'm sorry, I know that's asking a lot.'

Fletch smiled at his sister. 'Of course.' He squeezed her shoulder. 'Whatever you need.'

'Are we going yet?' Jean asked again.

Tess nodded briskly. 'Yes, we're going right now. Come on, let's be off.'

She gave Trish a quick hug, mouthed 'Thank you' to Fletch and then ushered Jean out the door and didn't look back.

'I'm sorry, Fletch,' Trish said as they watched the two women disappear around the corner. 'Will she be okay?'

Fletch grimaced. 'I don't know, Trish. I don't know how much longer she can go on like this, just keeping it all bottled up, keeping it all inside.'

Trish squeezed his hand. 'You still love her, don't you?'

He looked down at his little sister as her words seemed to make sense of the jumble of emotions that had been tangoing inside him since Tess had been back in his life. 'I don't think I ever stopped.'

And the guilt he felt at what he had done all those years ago magnified tenfold.

Tess kept busy when she got back to the apartment.

Busy, busy, busy.

They walked Tabby, baked a double batch of muffins—one for Trish and Doug—and then cooked a huge lasagne for tea, half of which could also go to Trish. They cleaned up the kitchen and watched Jean's television game shows. They took Tabby down again for one last toilet stop before bedtime.

Normally Tess loved the river at this hour of the late afternoon as the shadows turned it an inky velvet and she and Jean and Fletch too, if he was home, would watch it for a long time, chatting about the different boats, and Jean would usually tell a story from her childhood.

But Tess didn't want to indulge in anything that didn't involve brisk activity. The events of the day had stirred up too many memories and if she stood still for too long they might just take over.

When they returned to the apartment Fletch still

wasn't home. Tess felt a spike of worry and pushed it away.

*It would be fine. Christopher would be fine.*

They ate the lasagne without him, Jean doing him up a plate and covering it with cling film just as she always used to when she'd come to stay with them and he was on shift. Then she washed up.

'Oh look, *Vertigo* is on,' Jean said, pointing to the television as she dried her hands on a tea towel. 'Jimmy Stewart is magnificent in it, don't you think?'

Tess marvelled over the complexities of the human memory and the bizarre progression of a disease like Alzheimer's. Earlier Jean hadn't known what a whisk was but she could remember a film that was over fifty years old.

'Shall we watch it?' Tess asked.

Fletch still hadn't returned by the time the movie faded to black and Jean declared she was off to bed. Tess watched as she and Tabby headed for the bedroom.

Then there was just her, a quiet apartment and the relentless pulse inside her of things she didn't want to think about.

She texted Fletch. *Everything okay?*

He texted back. *Extubated twenty minutes ago. Will be home soon.*

Tess didn't know if she was relieved that he would be coming home soon or not. It was good to know that Christopher had been successfully extubated but it had been a momentous day and she was pretty sure Fletch was going to be physically and mentally exhausted.

She remembered how shattered he'd been that night

after being woken to do the study consent on the immersion. How much worse would he be after hours in the very PICU where his son had died, watching as a machine pumped air into a carbon copy of him?

She took a shower and tried not to think about it. She hummed out loud to keep the images of Christopher and Ryan at bay as they rose and blurred in her head unbidden. She scrubbed at her body vigorously with the towel afterwards, rubbed at her hair so hard the sound of it temporarily obliterated everything else from her head.

Then she heard 'Tess?' and her heart contracted with the force of a sonic boom then tripped along at a crazy clip.

*Fletch.*

'In here,' she called out. 'Just a sec.'

She looked around the bathroom for something to wear. With Fletch not home yet, she hadn't thought to bring her pyjamas in with her. There were two options—the towel she was using or the T-shirt he'd been wearing to bed, which he'd hung on the towel rack that morning and had left there.

She shied away from the whole idea of the towel. A towel said *I'm naked under here*. A T-shirt said *I'm dressed*.

So she quickly threw it over her head and was immediately surrounded by the very essence of Fletch. That strange mix of aftershave and deodorant and pheromones that all combined to make a wild, heady aroma. She inhaled deeply and her nipples tightened against the fabric, rubbing erotically on the inside where his own naked skin had imprinted.

*Dear God! Get a grip.*

She'd worn his shirts a hundred times in the past and with what they'd been through today her nipples and his pheromones shouldn't even be registering.

*She was just stalling.*

And she doubted he'd even notice.

'Hi,' she said as she stepped out of the bathroom, flicking the light out and leaving just her bedside lamp to illuminate the room. He was sitting on his side of the bed, taking his shoes off, his back to her.

'Hi,' he said, turning to look at her. She was in his shirt and a rush of emotion filled his chest. He wanted to lose himself in her so badly at the moment he had to turn away from her lest she see it and run screaming out of the apartment.

'You're wearing my shirt,' he said, for something to say other than *I love you*.

Tess grimaced. *So much for him not noticing.* 'Yes. Sorry. It was…at hand.'

'Don't apologise,' he said. 'My shirts always looked better on you.'

Tess walked around the bed, approaching his side tentatively. She stopped when she was standing in front of him an arm's length away. 'Are you okay?' she asked his downcast head.

He lifted his head and pierced her with his wattle-green eyes. 'What do you think?' he demanded, his voice low.

Tess looked at him. His salt-and-pepper three-day growth looked more salt suddenly, his eyes bloodshot and the lines on his forehead and around his mouth

deeper. His tie was pulled askew, his top button undone and it looked like he'd worn a track in his hair
from constant finger ploughing.

'I'm sorry,' she whispered. 'I just couldn't…I
couldn't stay.'

Fletch reached out a hand and squeezed her forearm, dropping it again straight away. 'I know. You did
enough today…it's fine.'

'Is he okay?'

Fletch nodded. 'Grizzly but curled up in Trish's lap
in a recliner by the bed when I left.'

Tess visibly sagged at the news—she hadn't realised
she'd been holding herself so upright. She knew from
her past PICU experience that it would happen that way
but the whole drama had been too close to home and
deep down she'd been preparing herself for disaster.

'Oh…thank God,' she murmured, clutching a hand
to her breast.

Fletch rubbed a hand through his hair and then
scratched at his chin. It rasped like sandpaper in the
still of the night. 'He's just so much like…Ryan, you
know?' he said, marvelling at how Tess had managed
to keep it together at Trish's today when it must have
been the most horrendous experience for her.

'I just kept seeing him…Ryan. Looking at
Christopher's chest rise and fall and thinking it was
Ryan.'

Tess saw the moisture in his eyes and felt a corresponding moisture in hers. The tears she'd been trying to keep at bay all day—no, all decade—burned for
release. But still she wouldn't let them. She'd already

shed more than her allotted amount since coming to stay with Fletch.

And the tears threatening were world-is-nigh tears and she knew once she'd shed them there was no way back. That part of Ryan would go with them and as much as she tried not to think about him, she wanted to know he'd be there if and when she was ready.

'It was awful,' he murmured.

'I know,' she said, remembering how hard it had been to separate Ryan and Christopher in her own head. 'I know.'

And it seemed like the most natural thing in the world to take a step closer. To step right into the circle of his arms and enfold him in hers.

Fletch shut his eyes as she fitted against him. She cradled his head against the soft part where neck met shoulder, and he inhaled the scent of her. Her shampoo and her perfume and the strange heady mix of his shirt on her skin. He drew her close and just absorbed her.

He felt the kiss at his temple first. It was so light he didn't even realise for a moment. But his mouth must have because his lips were nuzzling her neck and then her fingers were in his hair and his hand was sliding down her back and she moaned in his ear as his hand skimmed her bare skin where buttock met thigh.

He pulled back, one hand clamped on the back of her leg, the other firmly on her opposite hip. His heart banged against his ribs as desire ran thick and undiluted to every nerve in his body.

'Tess?'

Tess read his question loud and clear and knew the

answer even before he'd asked it. She could already feel the taint of the day sliding away with her inhibitions. The memories of Christopher and Ryan and ambulances and hospitals fading with every fan of his breath on her neck.

She couldn't remember a time when she'd needed him more.

# CHAPTER TEN

'MAKE love to me,' she whispered.

Fletch drew in a shuddery breath at her request. That he could do—loving her had always been easy.

Loving her had never gone away.

He tilted his head, his gaze zeroing in on her mouth. The flesh of her thigh was hot and pliant beneath his palm and he squeezed. A tiny, almost imperceptible gurgle at the back of her throat went straight to his groin and his breath stuttered out between them.

He opened his palm and traced the inside of her thigh with his fingertips. He watched as she shivered and her eyes widened before fluttering closed. His fingers traced higher, over the sweet curve of a naked buttock, into the dip that formed the small of her back, across to the bony prominence of her hip.

Tess sucked in a breath. 'Fletch,' she murmured, opening her eyes.

Their gazes meshed as his fingers trailed upwards. The curve of her waist, the bumps of her spine, the fan of her ribs. Each slow, lazy stroke ruching his shirt ever northward.

Tess bit her lip as cool air caressed bare, heated flesh from her waist down. It pricked at her skin, leaving thousands of goose-bumps and two erect nipples in its wake.

'Lift your arms,' he whispered against her mouth.

She clutched his shoulder at his husky command. Long-forgotten muscles clenched deep inside. Then she did his bidding, slowly raising her arms above her head, her gaze never leaving his.

Fletch swallowed at the directness in her gaze and her complete compliance with his command. His palms skimmed up her sides, hooking his T-shirt as they went, past the swell of her breasts, up over her shoulders and finally over her head.

His breath hissed out as she stood between his legs totally naked.

He dropped his gaze to look at her. She was different now. Thinner, less round, her breasts smaller, her bones more prominent. But there was still a slight curve to her hips and her waist still dipped and her breasts were still dominated by large areolas that had deepened to mocha during her pregnancy and were as fascinating tonight as they'd always been. He swallowed, just anticipating taking them into his mouth.

He dropped a kiss at the hollow at the base of her throat and whispered, 'Tess,' against her neck, his erection straining painfully against the confines of his trousers. 'My Tess.'

Tess shut her eyes as his lips moved along a collar bone and his palms stroked up and down her back, urging her closer.

She *was* his Tess. Had *always* been his Tess.

He turned his head and made for the other collar bone and she whimpered as his hot tongue lapped at her skin like she was dusted with honey. Fletch pulled back, already breathing too hard as the aroma of her swirled around him in an intoxicating haze.

A trail of glistening skin shone in the lamplight where he'd laved her collar bones but her mouth, so tantalisingly close, looked parched in comparison. He claimed it then, biting back on a groan as she instantly granted him the entry he craved. His tongue plunged inside then flicked over her lips, desperate to also make them moist with his possession.

His hands slid down to her smooth bare bottom, pulling her pelvis into the cradle of his. One hand moved lower, stroking down the backs of her thighs, the other moved higher, seeking the fulfilment only a round female breast could offer.

Years ago one of her breasts would have spilled out of his palm but now it fit perfectly, the hard nub in the middle scraping erotically against the dead centre. He squeezed it and she whimpered. He flicked his thumb over the tightly ruched nipple and she cried out, breaking their lip lock.

'Fletch,' she moaned.

Fletch felt her fingers plough into his hair as he kissed down her neck, homing in on his target. His mouth salivated at the feast that awaited. His hand at the back of her thigh moved up swiftly to her other breast and by the time his mouth had closed over her nipple his fingers had claimed the other.

Tess gasped, her knees buckling slightly. She felt his arm tighten around her waist as she clasped his head to her chest. Partly to stay upright, partly because she *did not want him to stop*. The heat and the pull of his mouth as he paid homage to her breasts was turning everything liquid.

Her head spun as he continued to use his mouth and tongue on nipples so aroused she wanted to throw her head back and howl her pleasure. She dropped a hand to his shoulder to steady herself, her palm instantly lamenting the feel of thick starched fabric instead of hot male skin.

She opened her eyes, suddenly aware that whilst she was buck naked, he was still fully clothed.

*That wouldn't do. It wouldn't do at all.*

She groped for his buttons, her eyes rolling back as he switched attention from one nipple to the other, taking it from cool and puckered to hot and hard in a second as he sucked it deep into his throat.

Her fingers fumbled and somehow found his loosened tie despite the havoc he was creating. She only just managed to strip it out from his collar as his teeth grazed the sensitive tip in his mouth and she lost all coherent thought for a beat or two.

Determined to plough on whatever the provocation, Tess straddled his lap and started in on his buttons, pleased to hear a guttural groan escape his mouth as she rocked herself into him. He released the nipple he was torturing, placing his forehead against her chest and breathing hard as he grabbed her hips and held here there.

She smiled then slowly pushed at his shoulders until he was lying back on the mattress and she had him at her total mercy. His eyes, smoky with desire, glittered up at her as she rotated her pelvis again and he swore under his breath, his fingers gripping her hips hard.

She marvelled that ten years of abstinence hadn't dulled her sexual instincts. But, then, it had always been instinctive with Fletch. There'd been guys before him but they'd always been such hard work. With Fletch it had been easy.

So very, very easy.

Still, she'd have thought she'd be nervous about having sex again after such a long dry stretch. Or that she might even have forgotten how. But towering over Fletch's reclined form, she knew that her body knew what to do.

And she knew it was going to be better than ever.

Tess leaned forward slightly, her gaze locking with his as she reached for his first button. It popped easily and she lowered her mouth to where it had been and pressed a kiss there. She repeated the process with each button until they were all undone and his shirt had fallen open.

Fletch let out his breath on a hiss as she sat up to admire her handiwork and her breasts bobbed enticingly. Once upon a time her long hair would have flowed down her front and covered them and he liked it that they were free to his gaze. He reached up and traced a finger from her collar bone to the tip of a rapidly hardening nipple and repeated it on the other side.

She arched her back and thrust her hips forward a

little, and he curled up to claim her mouth because he doubted she had a clue how provocative she looked, straddling him stark naked, her breasts thrust out, while he was practically still fully clothed. She whimpered against his mouth, opening to the insistent thrust of his tongue and the bruising crush of his lips as he ground his pelvis into hers.

Tess could barely breathe as the onslaught of Fletch's out-of-control kiss sucked away all her oxygen. She desperately dragged in air through her nostrils as she rode the wild bucking of his hips.

'Tess,' he groaned against her mouth.

Tess could feel the hard length of him rubbing against the centre of her splayed thighs and she wanted more. She wanted him naked and inside her. She didn't want the barrier of two layers of fabric and a metal zipper. She wanted him thick and hard and proud the way she remembered him in dreams she couldn't always quell. She wanted to feel him in her hand. She wanted to relish every inch of him as he entered her and took her to a place far, far away from this world where they just didn't do things like this.

She broke away from his mouth, pushing him back again, more urgently this time. She looked down at his erection clearly outlined beneath the taut pull of fabric. She reached for it, walked her fingers up it, walked them back down.

'Tess.'

The growl was deep and low, stroking deep and low inside her as he looked at her from beneath half-shuttered eyelids.

She heeded his warning, quickly unbuckling his belt, popping the button and peeling back his zip. The opening of metal teeth was loud in a room where the only other noise was the rasp of breath.

One glimpse of the long hard length of him and she was pushing aside the flaps of his fly and grasping him still encased in his underwear. Her insides clenched and she rocked against him, a completely involuntary movement.

Fletch shut his eyes on a groan as she rubbed herself against his thigh while she stroked his thickness and then impatiently broke through the last barrier to put her hand around him, skin on skin. He cried out as the muscles in his groin and belly and deep inside his buttocks shuddered.

He vaulted up again, his hands sliding to her breasts, his mouth slamming into hers, their tongues thrusting as their hips rocked to a rhythm pounding simultaneously through both of their bloodstreams and she milked the length of him.

Fletch couldn't bear it a moment longer. It had been so long and he'd dreamed of them coming together again too many lonely nights to count. He grasped her thighs and tumbled her to the side, rolling on top of her in one easy movement.

'I need you,' he muttered against her neck.

'I'm yours,' she whispered straight into his ear.

Fletch felt everything stutter to a halt. He shut his eyes as the familiarity of the words slugged him right between the eyes. He felt her mouth at his neck and her hand pushing beneath the loosened waistband of his trousers, sliding beneath his jocks to grasp his buttocks, but everything inside him had turned cold.

The words played in his head over and over. A different place. A different time.

*A different woman.*

He saying, *I need you*. She saying, *I'm yours*.

It was like a blast of arctic air in his face. *He couldn't do it.* He couldn't go ahead with it. Because he knew with a certainty that came from deep in his bones that he loved Tess and he wanted more than this, more than one night.

He wanted every night.

He wanted his wife back.

But there were things that had to be said first.

It took a moment or two for Tess to realise that Fletch wasn't responding when she pressed her mouth to his. She pulled back. 'Fletch?'

Fletch looked down at her, a frown knitting her brows together. 'I'm sorry…' He dropped his head on her chest, giving himself a moment to take stock. 'I can't do this…' he said.

His voice was muffled but Tess could sense his withdrawal in every muscle of his body.

*No, no, no.* She mewed her disappointment as Fletch pushed himself away from her. *She needed this, damn it!*

Fletch's hands trembled as he gripped the side of the mattress, keeping his back to her. He tucked himself away with difficulty, pulling up the zip over his bulge, feeling instantly uncomfortable. His fingers shook as he did up a couple of buttons to cover his chest. He bent down and retrieved her shirt, *his shirt*, from the floor, dropping it behind him without looking.

The shirt landed on her belly, cold against her heated flesh, and Tess just stared at it for a moment. Her blood was still thrumming thick and sludgy through every cell in her body, rendering her completely useless.

'There's something you need to know,' he said, staring out at the darkness beyond his floor-to-ceiling windows.

Tess blinked at his back as a sense of foreboding pushed the sticky remnants of desire violently aside. She scrambled upright, throwing the shirt over her head, then wriggled off the bed to stand in front of him. 'Whatever it is, I don't want to know,' she said.

Because it didn't take a genius to figure out this was something to do with Ryan. She didn't want to talk about Ryan. Surely he knew that by now? She didn't want to think about him or reminisce about him. She didn't even want to say his name.

*Didn't he realise how much it hurt to even say his name?*

Fletch almost gave up. But that was what he'd always done with her because her grief and her guilt had been so great he'd tried to make everything else easy for her. He'd let her avoid and deny and shut things out because she'd asked him to and he'd been at a loss as to how to help her.

*Well, not any more.*

He wanted something real with her. Warts and all. It meant making some hard decisions but he was finally going to fight for her instead of letting her slip away again. 'I need to talk about this.'

Tess crossed her arms. 'Damn it, Fletch, why do you think we're on your bed, making out like teenagers? Especially after today? So we don't have to talk.'

He shook his head. 'I don't believe you, Tess. You want more than that.'

'No,' she denied.

Fletch felt a wellspring of frustration and anger bubble up inside him at her stonewalling. 'Well, if all you wanted was for me to *screw* you then why did you ask me to make love to you?'

Tess blinked at his profanity. 'I guess because asking you to *screw* me was just a little too crass,' she hissed.

'Well, at least I would have known where I stood,' he snapped.

'Oh, come on, Fletch. You can't tell me you weren't trying to forget about today just a little bit too.'

Fletch snorted. He stood and stalked passed her, stopping in front of the windows, his reflection staring grimly back at him. *God, he looked like hell.*

He turned his back on it. 'I was doing what you asked me to do, Tess. I was *making love* to you.'

They stared at each other for long moments, their chests rising and falling rapidly, this time in anger.

Fletch ran a hand through his hair. 'It's not about Ryan,' he said. 'Not directly anyway.'

Because they both knew that everything in their lives since Ryan had always stemmed from Ryan.

'Don't, Fletch. Please, don't.'

He heard the plea in her voice and knew it would be

so easy not to tell her. To take the coward's way out. He'd decided nine years ago to keep it to himself—why not just stick to it?

Because their relationship nine years ago had been a train wreck and he couldn't go there again.

He wanted to be with her, he wanted to make love to her.

But he couldn't make love to her with this on his conscience.

*It's why he'd walked away all those years ago without a fight.*

They had a lot of work to do with their relationship. A lot of honesty and dealing with their unresolved grief and unspoken feelings around Ryan. There was going to be a lot of soul-searching and it demanded total honesty.

*And that had to start now.*

Fletch knew it was the only way they could build a relationship that could survive and thrive the second time around. And if he had to drag her kicking and screaming along with him, he would.

Because he knew deep down that she still loved him too.

*And this time he was fighting for that love.*

'I'll give you fair warning. I'm not just going to let you disappear out of my life again, Tess.'

Tess blinked at his audacity. 'You don't get a say, Fletch. I'm leaving here and going back to England as soon as Trish is home from hospital.'

Fletch ignored her. He'd move heaven and earth to keep her with him and with several weeks left before Trish was due, he had time on his side.

*There would be no more playing it her way.*

'Before we can go forward, there's something you need to know first.'

Tess glared at him. 'There is no forward, Fletch.'

He ignored her. 'There was a woman…'

The four words free-fell into the space between them and seem to stay suspended, hovering there for an age.

When they finally landed Tess felt each one slam like a bullet straight through her heart.

Fletch had…cheated on her? 'Do you mean you—?'

'Yes,' he said, cutting her off because he couldn't bear to hear her utter his transgression aloud.

Tess stared at him. She'd known on some level just how messed up she was and that she'd been closed off and shut down and it was not fair to Fletch, but she'd never have thought in a million years he would find someone else.

*Her faith in his fidelity had always been rock solid.*

Fletch's stomach clenched at the look of shock on her face. She was looking at him like she had that day after the ambulance had whisked Ryan away. He wanted to reach out to her but knew her well enough to know that it wasn't the right time.

'It was at the intensive care conference I went to the weekend before we split up,' he continued, his hands shaking, his voice husky. 'She was in the bar late on the Saturday night. I couldn't sleep. She smiled at me, we talked for a while…' He shook his head. 'It was just the once… Hell, I don't even know her name. I left her room straight away afterwards, but…' he shook his head '…I couldn't believe I'd done it. Knew I'd never forgive myself. Knew that we were over…that I'd signed our marital death warrant. So when I came home on Sunday night and you asked me for a divorce, I agreed.'

Tess remembered that weekend. Remembered the overwhelming sense of relief as he'd left, knowing she didn't have to look at him for forty-eight hours. The sudden realisation that their marriage was over. That they'd drifted too far apart.

She remembered him coming home from the conference that Sunday evening. *How could she not?* Asking for a divorce had been her first act of courage in a year.

She also remembered his lack of fight. Remembered being surprised by it even as she'd rejoiced in his capitulation.

But she hadn't demanded to know why, had just accepted it at face value, knowing she could move on in her own way, in her own time. No more listening to him talk about Ryan and what had happened, ad nauseam. No more analysis of every single detail. No more requests for her to go to counselling.

It had been a green light to deal with things her way and she'd embraced the end of her marriage as a way to begin again—far away from everything that hurt so much.

And things had been just fine—until now.

Now she had to face the fact that her husband had picked up some woman in a hotel bar while she'd been at home grieving for their son.

'Why are you telling me this?' she asked him, shaking her head as the knowledge hurt much, much more than she expected. 'Why didn't you just keep it to yourself?'

'I can't, Tess. I love you and I want you back. And this is something that's been eating at me, would continue to eat at me. It would erode any chance we had for the future.'

'So you get to feel better and unburdened and I get to feel like shit?' She lunged forward and pushed him hard in the chest. 'Gee, Fletch, thanks a lot!' She glared at him wild-eyed. 'I don't even get an orgasm to take the sting out of it!'

Fletch took a step back as his body absorbed her shove. 'I'm sorry. I'm so sorry, Tess. But would you rather we'd had sex and then I told you?'

Tess looked at him, flabbergasted. 'I'd rather you hadn't done it in the first place, you lousy, cheating bastard!' she hissed, conscious of Jean sleeping down the hall. 'Then, yes, I'd have preferred you'd kept it to yourself.'

Fletch snorted. 'Do you know most wives would have demanded to know why I did it, not why I told?'

'Well, I guess you already knew I'm not like most wives!'

He shook his head. 'You're not even curious?'

'I'm assuming that one year without sex was your personal limit and seeing as you weren't getting it from me, you got it where you could.'

Fletch's hands curled into fists as he almost roared out loud at the unfairness of her assessment. *She didn't have a clue.* Not a single clue. He turned away from her, planting his fists up high on the windows, hanging his head, fighting for control.

'Hell, Tess,' he said after a long moment or two. 'It wasn't about the sex.'

Tess turned so she was looking at his back. 'So it was love?' she scoffed, her voice ripe with sarcasm.

He waited until his temper was truly in check before he turned around again. He placed his hands behind his back and lounged against the glass, trapping them there.

'It wasn't about sex or love, Tess, it was about affection. She looked at me like I was a man,' he said in a low voice. 'An interesting man. An attractive, interesting man with interesting things to say. Not as a grieving father. Or an inadequate husband. She didn't look at me like I'd let her down. Like I'd failed her. Like I'd killed her child.'

Tess gasped, wrapping her arms around her body to fend off his shocking words. 'I didn't do that, Fletch.'

'She didn't flinch when I touched her, Tess,' he continued ignoring her protestation. 'She looked at me, *at me*, Tess. Not at what I *hadn't* done but what I could do.'

He shifted, bringing his arms up to cross his chest. 'It's not an excuse for my behaviour. I was weak and it was wrong and I've regretted it every day since. And I'm sorry that you'd rather not know about it, but I want to start anew with you, Tess. We've spent all this time avoiding the hard stuff—second time round it has to be warts and all.'

Tess couldn't even begin to assess the revelations that had just occurred. Knowing that Fletch had indulged in a one-night stand was mind-blowing. Hearing his reasons had been shocking.

Confessing that he wanted her back was just way too much altogether.

*It was too much. It was all too much.*

She was trembling but she wasn't sure if it was from anger or shock.

She dropped her arms. 'I'm sorry too, Fletch,' she murmured, then turned away from him and headed for the walk-in wardrobe.

'What are you doing?' he asked as he watched her disappear inside.

Tess grabbed the overnight bag that she'd arrived with just over a month ago. 'I'm packing,' she said.

Fletch frowned. He pushed off the glass and strode briskly to the large open cupboard space. She was emptying the drawers he'd cleaned out for her. Grabbing her few paltry belongings off hangers.

He folded his arms. 'I thought you were staying until Trish had the baby.'

Tess steeled herself against the guilt of her broken promise. Fletch's family was not her family.

Not now. Not for a long time.

'Nope. Not any more.'

Fletch heard the finality in her voice and realised she was serious. 'Tess, don't,' he said, shoving his hands in his pockets. 'This is crazy. What about Mum? You promised you'd stay.'

Tess hardened her heart. 'That was before your little revelation tonight.'

She zipped up the bag with a vicious flick of her

wrist, dragging it past him and throwing it on the bed. She went into the bathroom, clothes in hand, and threw them on. As usual she didn't bother with any make-up and she refused to look in the mirror as she gathered her paltry toiletry supplies.

She felt like she was about to shatter into a thousand pieces and she didn't want to see what that looked like. She'd made a habit of avoiding mirrors this last ten years—tonight would not be a good time to start. Her heart was pounding and her ears were ringing when she strode out two minutes later.

'Where are you going?' he demanded. 'It's the middle of the night.'

'To the airport,' she said, more calmly than she felt.

She knew she had to go now. If she waited until the morning, when both Jean and Tabby were looking at her with their big eyes, she'd knew she'd cave in.

*Much easier to look into the eyes of an adulterer and walk away.*

Fletch wondered if he hadn't maybe tipped her over the edge. She looked so calm and yet was acting so crazy. 'You haven't even got a flight booked,' he reasoned.

'I have a credit card.' She shrugged, picking up her watch from the bedside table and slipping it on. 'I'll get on the first airline with a flight out to London.' She shoved her feet into her shoes by the bed and grabbed her bag.

'Tess.' He put a stilling hand on her arm. 'Please, don't go. Don't run like you always do. Stay and help me work it out.'

Tess looked down at his hand. 'Don't touch me,' she warned. 'Don't you ever touch me again.'

And then she turned on her heel and marched away and she didn't look back and she didn't stop until she got to the safety of her car, where she locked all the doors and burst into tears.

# CHAPTER ELEVEN

Six weeks later Tess was just about cried out—talk about the straw that broke the camel's back!

She'd cried big, fat, silent tears for twenty-four hours solid on her plane trip home. The air hostesses had been so concerned about her that three of them had surrounded her outside the loos about four hours into the flight and asked her what was wrong.

'My husband cheated on me,' she'd told them, because it had been easier than the whole truth and it had hurt too much to keep it inside any longer.

Before she'd known it and in a startling display of female solidarity, she'd been whisked into business class for a little more privacy. Silent tears had rolled down her face as she'd thanked them.

She'd cried louder tears in her car, hurtling down the motorway towards Devon. She'd cried herself to sleep, she cried when she woke up and she cried at work. Hell, she'd even cried at the supermarket yesterday when a baby sitting in a trolley had smiled a dribbly smile at her.

She doubted she'd ever cried this much in her life. Not even in those first two months after Ryan had died.

Even sitting here right now snuggled in her pink polar fleece dressing gown in front of her fire on a chilly November night cradling a photo of Ryan in her lap, she could feel the tears pricking at her eyes again.

She shut them. 'Please, no,' she whispered. 'No more.'

The phone rang and her eyes flew open. The muscles in her neck tensed as they'd formed the habit of doing every time it rang since she'd returned home. Her answering machine was full of messages from Fletch, who had taken to ringing several times a day for the first couple of weeks.

Wanting to talk. Wanting her to understand. Wanting her to come back.

The last time had been two weeks ago when he'd rung to tell her that Trish had given birth to a bouncing baby girl and he was an uncle again. Her heart had swelled with joy and happiness for Trish. She'd been standing right beside the phone, listening to the message as he'd left it, and she'd almost picked it up that time to share the occasion with him.

But she'd gone to bed and cried instead.

The answering machine clicked in and the tension oozed from her muscles as old Dulcie Frobisher, the secretary of the historical society, informed her she was sending Peter around with some jam she'd made because she knew how much Tess enjoyed it.

Tess rolled her eyes at the message, knowing that Dulcie also thought that her great-nephew, who after years of frustrating bachelorhood had finally come out of the closet three months ago, just needed the love of a good woman and that Tess, being practically the only single woman in town in his age bracket, filled that criterion.

Tess was used to well-intentioned villagers trying to fix her up with their sons, grandsons, nephews and widowed neighbours.

She looked down at her wedding ring, which seemed to mock her in the firelight. It may have been a force field to keep men at bay but she'd always believed in what it had represented.

Love, commitment, fidelity.

A knock interrupted her thoughts and she gave an inward groan. Dulcie must have nagged the poor man into action immediately because she just didn't get visitors at eight o'clock at night. She grimaced as she stood, mentally preparing herself for the encounter. She flipped on the outside light as she pulled open the door.

'Hi, Tess,' Pete said apologetically, holding out three jars of jam.

'Hi, Pete, thanks. Dulcie just called.' She took the jars from him. 'Do you want to come in?' she asked, hoping sincerely that he didn't.

He shook his head. 'No, I'd better get back. I have some pots firing.'

But he seemed reluctant to leave so she asked, 'How are things?'

'About the same.' He sighed.

'You know, you really need to go and live in London for a while, Pete,' she said gently. 'Gay men are pretty thin on the ground in this neck of the woods.'

He nodded glumly. 'I know. But I can't leave Dulcie.

Or the art gallery. And I'm sure I'm way too country bumpkin for the big smoke.'

Tess put her hand on his arm. 'You're a nice man, Pete, and very nice-looking to boot. You're smart and articulate and arty. Any man would be lucky to have you.'

Pete gave a half-laugh. 'You're good for my ego, Tess,' he said as he leaned in to kiss her on the cheek and sweep her into a hug.

It felt good to relax in a man's arms with no expectations and she hung on for a little longer than she normally would until a sudden harsh cough behind them had them both leaping apart guiltily.

*It was Fletch.*

Standing on her garden path, his strong, beautiful jaw clenched tight, his hands jammed in the pockets of a warm, heavy coat.

He looked from Pete to Tess then back to Pete again. 'Hello, Tess.'

Tess blinked. 'Fletcher?'

Fletch threw a steely glare towards Peter. 'Yes.'

'What are you doing here?' she asked dazedly.

'We need to talk,' he said tersely, his gaze not leaving the other man.

Peter took one look at the magnificent, tight-lipped guy staring him down and concluded that if this was a London man, then he truly did need to get there pronto. 'Is everything okay?' he asked Tess, dragging his eyes away from the stranger. 'Do you want me to stay?'

Tess could see Fletch bristling and came out of her daze, stepping in before things got any more tense. She introduced the two men—Fletch as her ex-husband and

Peter as a jam-bearing friend—and assured a rather disappointed Peter she'd be fine.

She saw Fletch through Peter's eyes and sympathised. He cut a dashing figure in his heavy wool coat, which only seemed to emphasise the power of his chest, the breadth of his shoulders. The alcove light caught the streaks of grey at his temples that had been tousled to salon perfection by the brisk November breeze. The three-day growth looked shaggy and touchable. He looked tired. But solid and warm and sexy.

Very, very sexy.

'Tell Dulcie I'll ring her tomorrow,' Tess said as Peter turned to go.

Fletch watched the man retreat down the path and out the gate, giving Tess a wave as he turned left down the street. Even though he was obviously gay, Fletch felt a spike of jealousy. He didn't want *any* man's hands around her unless they were his!

He turned back and looked at her, capturing her gaze. She looked so good in her pink polar fleece he wanted to sweep her up in his arms and bury his face in it. But it was freezing out here and there were things to say.

'Can I come in?'

This was not the way that Tess had expected her day would finish up. She didn't usually hug gay men on her doorstep or have her ex-husband turn up out of the blue.

But, then, not a lot had been normal lately.

'Sure,' she said, standing aside.

He brushed past her, ducking his head to fit under her low cottage doorway, and every cell in her body went onto high alert. He shrugged out of his coat to reveal charcoal slacks and a round-necked, fine-knit sweater in navy blue, which clung to every muscle in his chest, and those same recalcitrant cells went into overdrive.

But the full lights inside accentuated rather than softened the lines around his eyes and mouth and he looked every day of his forty years.

'You look awful,' she said.

'Thank you.' He grimaced as the cosy atmosphere wrapped him in a big warm hug even if her observation hadn't. 'Don't suppose you have proper coffee? I've just got off possibly the longest transpacific flight in living human memory with a grizzly baby behind me and a man who sounded like he had whooping cough in front of me.'

Tess smiled despite her state of confusion. 'Sure,' she said again, and headed for the kitchen. She made them both a cup while Fletch watched her with brooding silvery-green eyes.

She passed him a steaming mug and led him over to the lounge area where a three-seater couch and a coffee table stood a safe distance away from the glowing fireplace.

She sat at one end and he at the other. 'How's Trish and the baby?' she asked, because it was easier to start with the inane stuff.

Fletch took a reviving sip of coffee, shutting his eyes as the caffeine buzzed into his system. 'Great. She went into labour at thirty-six weeks but the obstetrician was happy with that.'

He fished around in his trouser pocket and pulled out

his phone. He touched the screen a few times and pulled up the pictures of baby Katrina and handed it to Tess.

Tess swiped her finger across the screen, smiling at the pics of Trish and Doug and their daughter. One of Christopher holding his sister very carefully scrolled up and Tess felt her heart contract.

'You can tell they're brother and sister,' she murmured as Katrina's two cowlicks became more evident next to her brother's. 'Christopher looks no worse for wear,' she mused, examining his sweet little face for signs of long-term damage.

Tess had learned from one of Fletch's many phone messages that Christopher had been discharged from hospital two days after his seizure and that nothing had turned up on any of the investigations the hospital had run.

'Oh, yeah.' Fletch smiled. 'Back to normal.'

The next one that scrolled up was of Fletch holding his little niece. He was smiling but she knew him well enough to see that it didn't reach his eyes.

He'd always wanted a daughter.

Then it was Jean's turn. She looked fit and happy but Tess could tell from her eyes that she didn't feel any kind of connection with the little bundle in her arms. Not like the hundreds of pictures they'd had of Jean holding Ryan as a newborn, where her love and pride and awe had shone from her eyes like a beacon.

'How's your mum?' Tess asked, touching Jean's cheek with her finger.

'She's okay, I guess. Not as settled as when you were there, although Tabby has helped enormously.'

Tess could tell that Fletch was trying to keep the accusation out of his voice. 'I'm sorry,' she said, looking up at him, 'for leaving you in the lurch.'

Fletch shrugged. He couldn't really blame her. 'I managed.' It had been a huge juggling act but somehow he'd got through the last six weeks. 'She went back with Trish yesterday. Or…' he looked at his watch '…the day before…whatever the time is now.'

Tess gave a half-smile. Jet-lag and time zones always left her at sixes and sevens. She handed him back his phone and they sat and watched the fire without saying anything for a minute.

'I'm sorry too,' Fletch said. 'For a lot of things, but especially for not coming sooner. I wanted to follow you… I would have followed you but…'

Tess nodded. She'd flown to the other side of the world because running away was what she did best but part of it was also about knowing he was stuck at home with Jean and couldn't follow.

But he was here now.

He'd come after her this time.

Last time she'd asked him to leave her alone and he had. This time he'd come anyway.

Fletch put his mug down on the coffee table, feeling the boost of the caffeine bolster his nerve. He'd made a vow that he wouldn't come back to Australia until Tess was with him, and the time to make his pitch was now.

He noticed a face-down photo frame near where he placed his mug and he picked it up and turned it over. A close-up of Ryan stared back at him, his green eyes sparkling. Not even a party hat at a jaunty angle was able to disguise how his blond hair stuck up on top from that impossible double cowlick.

He'd taken the picture at Ryan's first birthday party.

He looked at Tess, surprised—she'd taken all the photos of Ryan down two months after he'd died, declaring she just couldn't look at them any more.

*It had been as if he'd never existed.*

'Reminiscing?'

She nodded. 'I've been looking at that picture for six weeks. It doesn't hurt to look at it any more.'

'That's good,' he said tentatively, encouraged that Tess finally seemed to be facing things instead of locking them all away.

Had their argument the night she'd left been the catalyst?

Tess looked into the depths of her milky coffee. 'You never blamed me,' she murmured. Then she looked at him. 'Not once.'

Fletch frowned then scooted to the middle cushion, folding one leg under him till he was turned side on in the lounge. He placed a hand on her arm. 'It wasn't your fault, Tess.'

She shook her head as tears welled in her eyes and rolled down her cheeks. 'I fell asleep, Fletch. I was supposed to be watching him and I fell asleep.'

Fletch had finished a run of five night duties and had been sleeping in the bedroom. Normally Tess would have had Ryan outside to keep him quiet for Fletch or even taken him out, but it had rained quite heavily overnight and had still been drizzling that morning. And she'd felt too ill herself to go anywhere. So she'd set him up with a DVD on low and his building blocks on the lounge-room floor. At some stage she'd drifted off sitting upright in the lounge chair as she'd watched over him.

'Tess, you'd been up all night with him, teething. You'd had only marginally more sleep than me for the three previous nights and you had a really bad migraine that you'd taken something for. You were exhausted.'

Fletch had offered to stay up with Ryan for a few hours while Tess had got some sleep but she had assured him she'd be fine and he *had* been very grateful. He'd been so tired he hadn't been able to see straight.

Normally in that kind of situation they would have had Jean come and look after Ryan but she'd been going off to the coast for the day so they'd decided they'd tag-team and manage between the two of them.

'He was shut in the lounge room with you,' Fletch continued. 'You had no reason not to think he was safe. If *I'd* fixed the dicky latch on the door you'd been nagging me to do for a week, he wouldn't have been able to get out.'

Tess shook her head, wiping at the tears. 'I should have turned the bucket over the day before. Put it away like I always did.'

Tess had been playing with Ryan the afternoon before in the sand pit. She'd pulled the deep bucket out of the shed because Ryan had loved to fill it with sand. But because his clumsy toddling kept knocking it over and he was becoming frustrated, she'd dug it into the sand a bit and wedged it into the angle of wooden framework to stabilise it.

And then the phone had rung and they'd raced to answer it so it wouldn't wake Fletch but it had and they'd all had some family time together before Fletch had gone off to work again and she'd forgotten all about the bucket in the sand pit.

'Tess, you weren't to know it was going to pour down with rain that night. It was an accident, Tess, a freak accident. A freak set of circumstances. Don't you see we can go back and forth for ever like this? You shouldn't have fallen asleep. I should have fixed the door. We should have put the bucket away. I should have done a better resus job.'

He cupped her cheek and swiped at a tear with his thumb. 'At some stage we've got to forgive ourselves.'

Tess raised her hand to cover his. 'He died, Fletcher. Our little boy died.' She looked into his eyes. 'I keep wishing I could go back to that day and change just one thing, you know?' she implored him. 'I'd stay awake. Because then none of that other stuff matters—if I had been watching him, everything else would be moot.'

Fletch couldn't bear the pain in her amber eyes. He would have given anything to take it from her. But he knew that by finally talking about it she was taking the first steps towards expunging it herself. Steps towards living a full life again instead of the half-life she'd allowed herself tucked away in the middle of nowhere.

He pulled her towards him and wrapped her up tight. 'The door,' he said against her temple. 'I should have fixed that door when you first complained about it.'

Tess heard her own anguish echoed in his words and when the sob rose in her chest she didn't try to stop it.

She let it out. And the low wail that followed it. The gut-wrenching wail that cut like razors on its way out but instead of leaving her bloodied it left her feeling infinitely lighter.

Fletch held her while she sobbed. It was the first time apart from at the hospital and the funeral that she'd let him hold her while she'd cried. His own tears mingled with hers as they finally grieved for their son together.

Tess didn't know how long she cried for or even where the tears had come from, considering how much she'd already cried these past six weeks. But she did know that she felt better for it and that it had felt right to share her tears with Fletch.

She eventually lifted her head from his shoulder. She was surprised to see his eyes also rimmed with red.

She smiled at him as she gently fluttered her fingers over his eyelids. 'I'm sorry,' she murmured.

He shook his head, his eyes closed. 'Don't be.'

She traced the slopes of his cheekbones down to the corners of his mouth. 'Why didn't you tell me about… the other woman? Back then? Was I that fragile?'

Fletch opened his eyes. 'Yes, you were. But mostly…' he shrugged '…I was just ashamed and sick to my stomach over my actions. I could barely face you. I certainly didn't feel like I deserved you after what I'd done. When you gave me the chance to end it I grabbed it with both hands. It seemed like a better alternative than having to confess.'

Tess traced his bottom lip with her thumb. 'I guess that couldn't have been an easy thing to tell.'

Fletch felt the stroke of her thumb right down to his

groin. 'You don't seem so mad about it any more,' he said tentatively.

Tess nodded realising he was right. 'I've done a lot of soul-searching since coming home. I wasn't easy to live with, Fletch. You tried so hard…every day…you were so patient with me. But I was so caught up in my denial stage, avoiding even the slightest mention of Ryan, that I forgot you were grieving too. That you needed someone to lean on as well. I don't blame you for finding a little solace somewhere else for a few hours.'

She dropped her hand into her lap. 'Don't get me wrong, it hurts…but I need to own my part in that.'

Fletch picked up her hand from her lap and pressed a kiss to the back of it. 'I'm sorry. I'm so sorry. I didn't just stop loving you because you were done with me, Tess, but we went to bed each night and there was this great divide between us that I just couldn't breach, no matter how I tried.'

Tess nodded, swallowing a lump that had risen to her throat. She'd been so inside herself she hadn't realised just how much he'd been suffering too.

'But I want us back together, Tess.' He raised her chin so they were looking into each other's eyes. 'I think you still love me and I don't want to live any more of my life without you in it.'

Tess nodded. He was right. She did still love him. She didn't need a clanging of gongs or a light bulb over her head to know it. It hummed quietly in every cell, as it always had. She just hadn't been listening.

And the truth was their marriage hadn't ended because they'd fallen out of love—it had ended because they'd given up on that love when everything else had got too hard.

'I do, Fletch. I do love you.' She sniffed and wiped at yet another tear. 'But do you really think we deserve a second shot when we screwed it up so badly the first time? Do you think we can truly be happy?'

Fletch cradled her face, pushing his long fingers into her hair. 'Yes, Tess, yes. Everyone deserves a second chance. I'm not pretending that the road ahead is going to be all roses and sunshine. We need counselling, Tess, both together and separately. We have a decade's worth of guilt and grief that needs to be talked about and I imagine that's going to be pretty harrowing at times. I know you've never wanted to talk about this before but we can't go on like that again. We have to do it differently this time round.'

Tess could see the love and determination mingling in his silvery-green gaze. 'I don't want to walk around with this stuff inside me any more, Fletch. I'm so tired of carrying it around.'

Fletch leaned in and brushed his mouth against hers. Finally he felt that everything was going to be all right.

Tess pulled back from his kiss, a swell of emotion blooming in her chest. He looked warm and solid and calm and she needed him more than ever. 'I love you,' she murmured.

Fletch smiled. 'Then the rest will come,' he whispered, claiming her mouth once again.

And for the first time in a decade Tess looked forward to the future.

\* \* \* \* \*

*Give a 12 month subscription to a friend today!*

## Call Customer Services
### 0844 844 1358*

## or visit
### millsandboon.co.uk/subscriptions

# MILLS & BOON®

## Why shop at millsandboon.co.uk?

Each year, thousands of romance readers find their perfect read at millsandboon.co.uk. That's because we're passionate about bringing you the very best romantic fiction. Here are some of the advantages of shopping at www.millsandboon.co.uk:

* **Get new books first**—you'll be able to buy your favourite books one month before they hit the shops

* **Get exclusive discounts**—you'll also be able to buy our specially created monthly collections, with up to 50% off the RRP

* **Find your favourite authors**—latest news, interviews  and new releases for all your favourite authors and series on our website, plus ideas for what to try next

* **Join in**—once you've bought your favourite books, don't forget to register with us to rate, review and join in the discussions

Visit **www.millsandboon.co.uk**
for all this and more today!

# The World of
# MILLS & BOON®

## HISTORICAL

*Awaken the romance of the past*
6 new stories every month

## MEDICAL ROMANCE

*The ultimate in romantic medical drama*
6 new stories every month

## MODERN™

*Power, passion and irresistible temptation*
8 new stories every month

## By Request

*Relive the romance with the best of the best*
12 stories every month

---

**Have you tried eBooks?**

With eBook exclusive series and titles from just **£1.99**,
there's even more reason to try our eBooks today

**Visit www.millsandboon.co.uk/eBooks**
for more details

---